BROTHERS IN ARMS

The air was full of clouds of powder smoke. Over the din of the booming gunfire, the screams of dying men and horses could always be heard.

James emptied both of his Paterson Colts and downed seven men with ten shots. Nearby, Jonathan used his rifle to parry the thrust of a bayonet, then crushed the unbalanced Mexican's skull with a quick stroke of his own weapon.

Andrew fought like a man possessed. An officer on horseback swooped toward him, saber upraised, but Andrew acted first, thrusting up with his bayonet and letting the force of the officer's charge drive the blade all the way through the man's body . . .

This book also contains a special preview of Giles Tippette's exciting new western novel, *Cherokee*.

Berkley Books by Tom Early

The SONS OF TEXAS Series

SONS OF TEXAS

Book Six

THE DEFIANT

— TOM EARLY —

BERKLEY BOOKS, NEW YORK

SONS OF TEXAS: THE DEFIANT

A Berkley Book / published by arrangement with
the author

PRINTING HISTORY
Berkley edition / June 1993

ISBN: 0-425-13706-6

A BERKLEY BOOK ® TM 757,375
Berkley Books are published by The Berkley Publishing Group,
200 Madison Avenue, New York, New York 10016.
The name "BERKLEY" and the "B" logo
are trademarks belonging to Berkley Publishing Corporation.

PRINTED IN THE UNITED STATES OF AMERICA

10 9 8 7 6 5 4 3 2 1

PART I

THE WILD MUSTANGS TEXAS, SPRING 1842

☆ Chapter ☆

1

As he stepped out of the dogtrot between the two sturdily built log cabins, Mordecai Lewis raised a hand to shade his eyes from the bright April sunlight. Tall and dark, with the lean hips and broad shoulders of a natural rider, Mordecai was practically the spitting image of his late father Michael, who had been an early settler of this land called Texas. Now, as his keen gaze swept out over the plains that rolled along beside the Colorado River, he announced, "Here they come."

A couple of hundred yards away, a wagon had just topped a small rise and was coming toward the cluster of cabins making up the compound that had come to be called the Lewis Fort. On the seat of the wagon were a man and a woman, and a horse was tied on at the back of the vehicle, trailing behind. The man handling the reins of the mule team must have spotted Mordecai, because he lifted an arm and waved his hand, a greeting that Mordecai returned.

A young man a few years shy of Mordecai's age came out of one of the cabins to join him. Mordecai's second cousin Edward, who carried the same Lewis stamp as all the other members of the family, grinned and shook his head. "How'd you know they were almost here?" he asked Mordecai. "There's no way you could've heard the wagon that far off."

Mordecai shrugged. "Instinct, I reckon. Or else I inherited a little second sight from my mama."

The woman in question emerged from the cabin that served as the kitchen, her face flushed from the heat of the stove. Marie

3

Lewis, with her combined French and Spanish heritage, was still quite attractive in middle age. Her dark hair was only lightly touched with gray and silver, and the lines on her face gave her character rather than detracting from her beauty. She had weathered years of hardship here on the Texas frontier and had endured the loss of a husband and a child and the near-loss of another child. She had, however, emerged from the storms stronger than before, the kind of pioneer woman needed to help settle a wild land.

Still, Marie was not above worrying, and she put a hand on her son's arm now. "You are sure about this, Mordecai?" she asked.

Mordecai nodded without hesitation. "The men who've been down there say there's more mustangs along the Nueces than anybody could ever catch," he told his mother, repeating part of the discussion they'd had several times before. "And if we can lay our hands on that white stallion . . . well, five hundred dollars is nigh onto a fortune. With that much money, we wouldn't have to worry about a bad year and losing a crop now and then."

For a long moment Marie was silent, then she said quietly, "I know this, but I cannot help but remember the things your father told me . . ."

Mordecai slipped an arm around his mother's shoulders. He understood how she felt. His grandfather—his namesake—old Mordecai Lewis had been killed on a mustanging trip into Texas, back in the days when the land had belonged to Spain. Mordecai had heard his father, Michael, tell the story about how Spanish soldiers had murdered just about everybody in that mustanging party, leaving Michael himself for dead. Those had been dark and bloody times, all right.

But they were in the past, Mordecai thought. Texas was a republic now, and although there was still plenty of danger from Indians who went raiding every now and then, it wasn't like the old days. He wanted to tell Marie that he and Edward and Manuel would be just fine, but he knew he'd be wasting his breath. No matter what he said, his mother wouldn't rest easy until they were all safely back home.

The wagon rolled into the yard in front of the main double cabin and came to a stop. "Mama!" cried the young woman on the seat, and she looked as if she wanted to throw herself down from the wagon and into Marie's arms. As it was, she waited for the darkly handsome young man beside her to hop down and come around the wagon to give her a hand.

Once Angeline's feet were on the ground, though, she hurried over to Marie, and mother and daughter embraced tightly.

His little sister had grown up, sure enough, thought Mordecai. With her long black hair and the olive-tinted skin she had inherited from Marie, she was a real beauty. And she wasn't Angeline Lewis anymore; she was Angeline Zaragosa, the wife of Mordecai's good friend Manuel Zaragosa. In fact, Manuel was a friend to the whole family, just as his father Elizandro had been a good friend to the Lewises back when he was alive. Michael had never quite gotten over the resentment he felt toward brown-skinned folks, a natural resentment considering that Mexican soldiers under the command of a Spanish officer had murdered his father right before his eyes and tried to kill him, too, but the Lewises and the Zaragosas were living proof that people could get along no matter what their race. As Manuel came over to him, Mordecai grabbed his hand and pumped it furiously.

"Good to see you," Mordecai said as he slapped Manuel on the back. "You ready to go catch some mustangs?"

"*Sí*," Manuel replied with a nod. His face had a long scar on it, a souvenir of the hatred some people felt because he had dared to love a white girl, but he was still a handsome young man.

"Come on into the dogtrot and set a spell," Mordecai told him. "I've got some news you haven't heard about yet."

Manuel looked puzzled, but he shook hands with Edward and then followed Mordecai into the shade of the dogtrot. All three young men sat down on caneback chairs while Marie and Angeline went into the kitchen.

"How is your father?" Manuel asked Edward out of politeness.

"Doin' all right," Edward replied. "Him and Mama'll be over here later. The whole family's givin' us a big send-off." The young man couldn't seem to stop grinning as he spoke. The prospect of going off on an adventure like this with Mordecai and Manuel had Edward about as excited as he'd ever been.

"How about you and Angeline?" asked Mordecai. "How're the two of you doing?"

The grin that stretched across Manuel's face matched and maybe even exceeded Edward's. "I am going to be a father," he said.

Mordecai and Edward just stared at him for a second, then Mordecai let out a whoop and leaned over to slap him on the shoulder again. "You mean I'm going to be an uncle? Well, all right!"

"I can always use another little cousin," Edward put in.

Manuel leaned back in his chair and nodded in satisfaction. "That is one reason I did not want to leave Angeline at the ranch. At such a time, a woman needs to be near her mother if it is possible."

"That's right," Mordecai agreed. His voice dropped a little as he hesitated, then asked, "Is Angeline . . . well, is she happy about it, too?"

Manuel's expression became more solemn. "I believe so. There are still times when she seems to remember too much. She becomes quiet, and then I cannot tell . . . I do not know . . . but I believe she is happy."

Mordecai nodded and didn't say anything. Angeline had been through a lot in her relatively short life of seventeen years. First, she had endured long weeks of captivity by a band of hostile Comanches, then again by a pair of Mexican traders who had found her when she escaped from the Indians. She had been lucky in a way, however. There had been plenty of women who had been captured by savages, then shunned by so-called civilized folks when they were either rescued or ransomed, as if it were somehow their own fault they had been raped by their captors. But Angeline had had a strong, loving family to welcome her back, and Manuel had been there for her, too. Still, the ordeal had left its scars.

Added to that was the horrible experience of witnessing James Lewis's wife, Libby, giving birth to a stillborn baby and then dying herself, so Mordecai could understand if maybe his sister might not be too thrilled about being pregnant. For Angeline's sake, he hoped everything turned out all right.

"So," Manuel said into the awkward silence, "tell me this news of yours."

Mordecai brightened considerably. He leaned forward again, resting his elbows on his thighs and lacing his fingers together. "Have you heard about the white stallion?" he asked his brother-in-law.

"White stallion?" repeated Manuel, frowning. "I have heard stories of a magnificent white horse that runs like the wind and cannot be caught, but that is all they are—stories."

Mordecai shook his head. "Nope, it's the truth," he insisted. "Enough folks have seen him now for me to believe it. He's like no other horse in the whole Republic and he's got a herd of mares that are almost as good as him. It's true, Manuel."

Still sounding skeptical, Manuel replied, "If you say so, Mordecai."

"Well," Mordecai added, "some doctor fella up in Austin believes in the white stallion, too. Believes enough to have put up a five hundred dollar reward for anybody who captures him."

Manuel's interest perked up and he sat forward, mirroring Mordecai's pose. "Five hundred dollars?" he repeated in a low voice.

"That's right," Mordecai said with a nod.

Letting out a low whistle, Manuel leaned back again. "When you wrote and suggested this mustanging trip, I thought it was a good idea and a way to make some money," he said. "But I never dreamed of so much! Five hundred dollars, just for bringing back the white stallion?"

"The white stallion you don't believe in," Mordecai said with a grin.

Manuel waved his hands back and forth. "Never mind what I said. For that much *dinero*, I will believe!"

The sound of hoofbeats and the creak of wagon wheels caught the attention of the young men before the discussion could go on, and the three of them left their chairs and stepped out of the dogtrot again. A couple of wagons were approaching from the southeast. One of them carried Frank and Hope Lewis, Edward's parents, along with his brother David, who at eighteen was two years younger than Edward and resented mightily not being included in the trip to South Texas to catch mustangs. Frank had declared that having one son at a time go off adventuring was enough, however. David would have to stay home and help with the work on the family farm during the upcoming spring and summer.

On the seat of the other wagon were Andrew Lewis, the eldest of Mordecai's three uncles, and his wife Petra, who bore a decided resemblance to Marie even though the two women were not related except by marriage. Behind them in the wagon bed rode their children, seventeen-year-old Ben and thirteen-year-old Rose. Andrew was living on his own farm full-time now, having retired from politics and left the Republic's capital of Austin. Mordecai knew from listening to Andrew talk that his uncle regarded the venture into politics as something of a mistake. Lewises were meant to be close to the land, Andrew had been known to say, and there were too many damn buildings in Austin shutting off a man's view of the hills and plains. Petra was glad to have him back, too.

Mordecai shook hands with Andrew and Frank and resisted the impulse to tousle Ben's hair as if he were still a little boy. That would just make his cousin fighting mad, and Mordecai knew it. Ben shared David's gloom about being left behind enough without having his nose rubbed in it. Petra, Hope, and Rose joined Marie and Angeline in the cabin while Andrew, Ben, Frank, and David strolled into the shade of the dogtrot with Mordecai, Edward, and Manuel.

"Good to see you again, Manuel," Andrew said. He had never felt any of the same lack of warmth toward Mexicans that his brother Michael had. "How's Angeline?"

Manuel glanced at Mordecai and Edward. "Perhaps I should let her tell you," he said.

"Oh, ho!" Frank said with a smile. "Do I sense an impending announcement of some sort?"

"Perhaps," admitted Manuel.

Andrew put a hand on his shoulder. "Well, we'll save the official congratulations for later, I reckon, but you know how we all feel, Manuel."

"Thank you," Manuel said sincerely. Mordecai knew that Manuel had felt some of the same hostility toward whites that Michael had felt toward Mexicans, but he hoped Manuel knew by now that he had been fully accepted into the Lewis family.

"Where's Annie and Sly?" Frank asked. "They're coming, aren't they?"

"Them and the girls," Mordecai replied. "At least they said they were, so I reckon they'll be here."

"What about James and Jonathan? Heard anything from them?"

Mordecai shook his head. "I sent word to the minuteman post and said for them to stop by today if they could, but you know how it is. No telling where they might be. I reckon Sam Houston can disband the Rangers if he wants to, but he can't stop men like James and Jonathan from ranging."

There were solemn nods from the circle of men. President Sam Houston's disbandment of the Rangers was a bone of contention in the Republic. Some folks said that the battle of Plum Creek the year before had broken the back of the Comanches' power and that the savages were no longer a threat to civilized Texas. Others thought that saying "civilized" and "Texas" in the same sentence was stretching things a mite too far and that the Comanches were just lying back in the weeds for a while, waiting for the right time to make life hell for the settlers again.

Mordecai tended toward that latter view himself, but there was nothing he or anybody else could do about it except stay as ready for trouble as possible. The Rangers were officially gone except for a small force of scouts under the command of Captain Jack Hays, but quite a few of the men who had been part of the organization had formed their own volunteer groups to protect the frontier until Houston came to his senses. Some of the bunches called themselves minutemen, after the old patriots back in Revolutionary days. James and Jonathan Lewis, half brothers and the other two of Mordecai's uncles, had formed one such group with its headquarters a few miles up the Colorado.

Nobody wanted to talk too much about politics, since Andrew's dealings in Austin had caused a rift in the family for a while, so instead the men discussed how it was turning out mighty warm for April.

"Crops are going to be early this year," said Frank.

"If we don't get a late freeze that kills everything," Andrew pointed out. "I get a little nervous when I see the fruit trees starting to blossom this early. There'll be one last norther coming along, and it'll be a son of a bitch. I've never seen it fail yet."

"Well, I'd rather be optimistic," Frank countered, "and besides the almanac says to plant early this year."

"A man can go hungry if he gets to believing too much in the almanac and not enough in what his own head tells him—"

Marie came out of the kitchen and said to her brother-in-law, "You and Frank can settle this later, Andrew. Right now I need some strong backs to carry the tables out so we can get the food on them. Mordecai . . ."

Mordecai looked at Edward, David, Ben, and Manuel. "I think she's talking about us, fellas."

"Isn't there something about weak minds that goes with that business about strong backs?" asked Edward.

Frank slapped his son on the back. "Then she's definitely talking about you boys," he laughed.

Mordecai's aunt Annie and her husband Sly Shipman, along with their children, arrived while the young men were carrying a couple of tables from the cabins and placing them in the dogtrot so that they could be loaded down with the platters of food Marie had spent the morning and part of the night before preparing. Mordecai had gone hunting the previous day and brought in not only a fine deer, but a wild turkey as well. So, in addition to venison steaks, there was plenty of roasted turkey on hand, along with seemingly enough beans, corn bread, and buttermilk for the whole Republic of Texas.

"Quite a spread, Marie," Sly complimented the mistress of the house. A slender man with lean, keen-eyed features, Sly had made his living for years as a smuggler, moving goods back and forth across the Sabine River, which formed the border with Louisiana in the southeastern part of the republic. Now that Texas had gained its independence, smuggling was no longer a profitable profession, so Sly had settled down with Annie Lewis, claiming a good-sized section of land near the rest of the family. He suffered from an occasional attack of restlessness, but overall he had become a pretty good husband, father, and farmer, from what Mordecai could gather.

Sly went on, "I know you're not overly fond of the menfolk venturing off like Mordecai, Edward, and Manuel are about to do, but if not for that we wouldn't have as many of these get-togethers."

Marie nodded and said, "You are right. But I would trade all of these 'get-togethers' for the knowledge that my family will continue to be safe and healthy."

Annie overheard Marie's comment and put an arm around her shoulders. "You don't have to worry, Marie," she said. "Mordecai is Michael all over again."

"Yes," Marie replied dryly. "That is exactly why I am concerned."

Mordecai was close enough to hear the comment, and he felt a mixture of pride and annoyance. He was proud of the fact that he reminded folks of his father. Michael Lewis had had his shortcomings, true enough—he had always been quick to leave his family whenever a new adventure beckoned—but he had also been a brave, strong man, the kind without which Texas would still be a virtual wilderness, a sparsely inhabited backwater province of Mexico. At the same time, Mordecai knew it was time he was thought of as his own man, not just as Michael Lewis's boy. He'd had some adventures of his own, and he could handle a Paterson Colt about as well as anybody he knew except for his Uncle James.

"We about ready to eat?" Frank called over from the other table.

"Yes, I think so," Marie said. She looked over at Mordecai. "You will ask the blessing." There was no room for argument in her tone, so Mordecai didn't waste any breath objecting.

Besides, even though Andrew was sort of the head of the family now, here on this piece of ground Mordecai was the man of the household, and so he felt another surge of pride as everybody got quiet, even Annie's two little ones, and he began saying, "Lord, we thank You for the blessings You've bestowed on us and for the bounty of the land You've shared with us. Thank You for this meal we're about to eat, and watch over us—"

The rapid pounding of approaching hoofbeats made Mordecai stop in mid-prayer and look up sharply.

Two horsemen were riding along the river, and while they weren't wasting any time, a closer look told Mordecai they weren't traveling at the hell-for-leather pace that bespoke immediate trouble. Everyone else turned to look, too, and a second later Ben called out, "It's Uncle James and Uncle Jonathan!"

Both men rode into the yard a few moments later, their buckskin pants and homespun shirts covered with trail dust, as were their tanned features. James Lewis wore a short poncho over his shirt, and his broad-brimmed, flat-crowned hat dangled on the back of his neck, held on by its chin strap. A pair of Colts were belted around his waist. A few years earlier he had arrived in Texas from Tennessee with a carefree attitude, but tragedy had hardened him so that his face usually took on a grim cast. Despite that, he was a good man and had been a good Ranger until that fighting force had been broken up.

Jonathan bore the same stamp as the other male Lewises, but his resemblance to his brothers was tempered by the fact that his father was Benjamin Lewis, old Mordecai's brother. Mordecai's widow Patience had married Benjamin after Mordecai's death in Spanish Texas, so Jonathan was both brother and cousin to Andrew, James, Annie and the other siblings still back in Tennessee. He had come along rather late in life for Benjamin and Patience, so that although he was the current Mordecai's uncle, the two young men were about the same age and might as well have been brothers themselves, from the look of them. Mordecai tried not to think overmuch on the matter, because it made his head hurt if he dwelled on it for too long.

Both James and Jonathan looked weary, and after they had swung down their saddles and shook hands all around, James explained, "We just got back from picking up some supplies over at Bastrop. The men at the post said Mordecai sent word for us to ride over.'' James looked around. ''I thought there might be trouble, but I see now it's just a reunion.''

''Edward and Manuel and I are headed for the Nueces,'' Mordecai told him. ''We're going mustanging. I told you a while back we were thinking about it.''

James nodded. ''I remember. You boys mind your hair while you're down there.''

Marie stepped up to him and put a hand on his arm. With a frown, she said, ''There's something else, isn't there? I can tell you're upset about something.''

James glanced over at Jonathan, then said, ''The message from Mordecai wasn't the only one waiting for us at the post. There's been word of Indian trouble west of here, over toward the San Marcos River. Jonathan and I thought we'd take a *paseo* over there and look around a mite.''

''You know for sure there's been a raid?'' Andrew asked quickly.

James shook his head, and Jonathan said, ''You know how it is, Andrew. Somebody told somebody else that they'd talked to somebody who'd seen some Indians. Probably doesn't amount to much of anything.''

''It could, though,'' James said grimly. ''The Comanches have been sitting out there since—'' He broke off sharply with a glance at Angeline, who met his eyes squarely. All of them know what James was talking about. The Comanches had not made any hostile moves in the area since the raid in which Angeline had been captured. After a moment, James went on, ''They've been sitting out there just waiting. Could be they're ready to make a move again. I intend to find out.''

''Best be careful you don't run into a big bunch,'' cautioned Frank.

''I intend to be,'' James said.

Mordecai didn't feel much like finishing his prayer now. The news James and Jonathan had brought cast a pall over the celebration, and it raised some doubts in Mordecai's mind. He wasn't worried about conditions down on the Nueces. That was basically out of the Comanches' usual stomping grounds, and Mordecai was sure he and Edward and Manuel would be safe enough. But he asked himself if he wanted to go off and leave his mother and Angeline here at the compound if there was about to be a fresh round of Indian trouble.

He was still pondering that as everyone sat down and began to eat. Marie took the chair next to Mordecai, and she said in a low voice to her son, "I know what you are thinking. There is no need to worry about Angeline and me, Mordecai. We will be fine. Andrew and Frank and Sly are nearby, and the Rangers . . . I mean the minutemen . . . will not let the Indians get close without plenty of warning."

Mordecai's thick dark brows drew down in a frown. "You're telling me to go ahead with the mustanging?"

"Yes," Marie said. "That is what I am telling you."

"Well, then, I don't understand you at all," Mordecai said, shaking his head. "Wasn't but two hours ago you were asking me if I was sure it was a good idea and all and you tried to talk me out of going."

She smiled at him, and there was more than a hint of sadness in her smile. "I will worry about you and Manuel and Edward, it is true. But I would not have you stay because of that worry. Many times I watched your father when he wanted to go but stayed because of his concern for his family. Your father was a good man, Mordecai, who always wanted to do the right thing for the people he loved. But he also had to do the right thing for *him*, and when he did not, something inside him began to die each time, like a flame flickering out in the night." She leaned closer to him and urged him in a whisper, "Go. But always remember to come back."

"I will, Mama," Mordecai promised. "I will."

☆ Chapter ☆

2

When the meal was over, Mordecai hugged his mother and his sister, picked up his female cousins and bid them farewell, and shook hands with all the men. Edward did the same, trying to look brave and excited but obviously feeling a little nervous now that the time to set out had actually arrived. Manuel's good-byes were the most poignant because he was leaving a wife behind, and a pregnant one at that. He took Angeline in his arms and kissed her for a long time, heedless of anyone who might be watching. Angeline clutched her husband with a hint of desperation and whispered something in his ear, something to which Manuel nodded emphatically.

Then it was time to go, and there was no point in delaying any longer.

James watched the three young men mount up, Manuel putting a saddle on the horse he had brought along tied behind the wagon. Their mounts were fine animals, with plenty of sand and speed, but James uttered a silent prayer that they would not need the horses to carry them out of trouble. Both Mordecai and Edward were leading packhorses, too, although to a large extent the would-be mustangers expected to live off the land as much as possible.

James's memory went back to the times when, as a child, he had watched first his father, and then later his brother Michael ride away from the farm in Tennessee, bound for God knew where and whatever adventure they would find there. To a young boy, they had been tall, godlike figures, and the fact that one time old

Mordecai had never come back and Michael had returned pale and weak from his ordeal, seemingly from the grave itself, had done little to dampen James's enthusiasm for what they were doing. Texas had been a magic word in those days, a name that summoned up the thrill of the unknown.

Well, James thought, he knew Texas these days, knew it to be a rich, beautiful country . . . but also a harsh, unforgiving, ruthless land that could kill you in the blink of an eye. Either that, or it would grind you down over the years with troubles.

Still, this was his home, and he was damned if he was going to sit by and watch everything his family and other pioneer families had worked for be destroyed by marauding savages.

Mordecai, Edward, and Manuel weren't even out of sight yet when James strode over to Jonathan and asked, "You ready to ride?"

Jonathan frowned in surprise. "So soon? I thought we might visit awhile first."

"We've visited all we need to," James told him. "I want to see if there's any truth to that rumor we heard."

"All right," Jonathan said with a shrug.

The farewells were quick, just like James wanted them. Within a few minutes, he and Jonathan were heading for the crossing where they could swim their horses across the Colorado and then point the animals west, toward the region where Indians had reportedly been seen. As he rode, James's eyes were already out of habit scanning the horizon for smoke, usually the first visible sign of trouble out here, although they probably would not reach the San Marcos River until sometime the next day.

One thing about Texas. You never could tell where you might run into trouble, James thought. Sometimes it was right in your own backyard.

"James seemed a mite upset," Andrew said to Frank as they smoked their pipes and sat beside Marie's cabin after James and Jonathan had ridden off. Sly was taking a walk, having said something about working off that big meal. David and Ben had wandered down to the river, not surprising considering that they had as much Lewis blood in them as any of the others. Rose was keeping an eye on Annie's two little ones, while Marie, Angeline, Annie, Petra, and Hope were inside the cabin, doing whatever it was that females did at such moments. Talking about how

Angeline was in the family way, most likely, thought Andrew. He didn't know and wasn't sure he wanted to.

"James is usually a mite upset these days," Frank replied, tilting his chair back so that it leaned against the log wall of the cabin. "I don't think he ever quite got over Libby dying like that. And the baby, too, of course."

Andrew shook his head. "A real tragedy, right enough. But a man's got to put such things behind him and move on. Otherwise all that pain and sadness . . . well, it's liable to just eat him up inside."

"At least James has got something to occupy his time. He never was much of a farmer, but he was one hell of a Ranger, from what I've heard. And he's doing the same thing now, even if him and the men like him aren't called Rangers anymore."

"You know Jack Hays?" asked Andrew.

"Can't say as I've ever met him," Frank replied with a shake of his head.

"James wants to ride with him again, with the only troop of Rangers that's still operating. But they're down around San Antonio most of the time, and James wants to stay up here, too, so he can keep an eye on all of our places. It's hard on him, I reckon."

"Well, he's got Jonathan with him. Maybe between the two of them, they won't get into too much trouble."

"Who won't get into too much trouble?" Petra asked as she stepped out the nearby door of the cabin in time to hear Frank's final comment. She was drying her hands on a piece of cloth, and Andrew figured the women had been washing up the dishes from dinner.

"James and Jonathan," he said in reply to her question, then reached up and caught her wrist. Before she could say anything else, he pulled her down into his lap.

"Andrew Lewis!" she said, half-scolding and half-laughing. "You are an absolutely shameless man."

"So I've been told."

"Oh? And who besides me has told you this thing?"

"I disremember," Andrew said with a sly grin. "But it must have been somebody."

"Well, you let me up before Marie and the others come out here and you completely scandalize me."

"Shoot, can't a man even have his wife sit on his lap anymore without getting in some sort of trouble?"

"Another time," Petra said, a promise in her dark eyes that made Andrew's insides feel all hot and tight and good, even after all the years they had been together.

As she stood up, Petra went on, "Besides, we should be starting home soon. I want to stop by the Barnstable farm on the way."

"Luther Barnstable's place?" Andrew asked with a frown. "What in the world for?"

"I've heard that Ophelia hasn't been feeling well lately, and I want to stop and see if there is anything I can do to lend her a hand."

Andrew wanted to tell her that Ophelia Barnstable could manage perfectly well by herself, but he knew he would be wasting his breath. Any time somebody in the area got down for any reason, Petra was the first one there offering to cook or clean house or take care of the children or do whatever needed doing. It was just part of her nature to be helpful, Andrew supposed and, as such, one of the things that made him love her, so he couldn't very well say no.

"All right," he told his wife. "We'll stop by the Barnstable place."

James and Jonathan didn't see any Indians the rest of that day. They camped on Plum Creek, not far from the site of the battle the year before that had sent the Comanches fleeing back into West Texas. The night passed peacefully, and early the next morning, after a quick, cold breakfast, they were on the trail again.

The terrain in this part of the Republic was a mixture of rolling prairie, flat bottomland along the creeks and rivers, and thickly wooded hills. As they headed west, the hills became more prominent, and both men were careful not to let themselves be caught against the horizon. If there really were Indians around, it would be wise not to let them know somebody was on their trail.

"Pretty country," Jonathan commented along toward mid-morning. "But then I haven't seen much of Texas that wasn't pretty."

"I have," James grunted. "Comancheria. Nothing out there but rocks and sage and mesquite trees, and a bunch of gullies for those red savages to hide in."

"Yeah, well, I guess that's right enough. But even West Texas has got a certain kind of beauty to it, don't you think?"

James just looked at him with a frown, obviously unable to

comprehend what he was saying, and Jonathan shook his head. "Never mind."

"Let's keep our eyes open," James said.

This part of the country was sparsely settled. Austin was about thirty miles to the north, and San Antonio de Bexar was around fifty miles to the southwest. So they were right in the middle of nowhere, as Jonathan phrased it that afternoon, and they pressed on without seeing hide nor hair of anybody—white or red.

"Aren't there any farms or ranches over here?" he asked.

"A few," James replied. "Last time I was in Austin, I heard talk that there's some folks who want to move in a whole colony in these parts, probably from some foreign country. Don't know that anything'll ever come of it, though. A big settlement would sure be tempting to the Panetekas."

"That's the band of Comanch' that got run off from hereabouts, isn't it?"

"One of 'em," James said. "But I reckon they'll be back sooner or later. Sooner, if what we heard has any truth to it."

They rode on, reaching the San Marcos River not long after. As they stopped to water their horses, Jonathan swung down from his saddle, stepped upstream a few feet, and bent to fill his hat with water. He lifted it to his mouth, drank deeply, and then splashed the rest of the water over his head. As he shook his head, sending a cascade of droplets flying from his face and hair, he said, "Lord, that's good! A lot better'n that muddy Colorado River water around home."

James nodded. "The San Marcos rises in the hills just west of here and flows into the Guadalupe down southeast a ways. I've heard tell there's a few families living along it, so we ought to run across a cabin before too much longer."

"Maybe find a place to spend the night?" asked Jonathan. "I don't mind sleeping under the stars so much as long as the weather's warm, but I reckon a home-cooked meal'd beat jerky and those biscuits you make."

James grinned a little. "We'll see what we can find," he promised.

When the horses had drunk their fill and both men had refilled their canteens, they rode northwest along the river. A tall bluff rose ahead of them, and James realized it was what the Mexicans called the Balcones, for obvious reasons. It looked a little like a balcony, sticking up and out like that. From the top of it, a man could look back east and see a long way, almost clear to Louisiana.

But as he was looking at the escarpment, he saw a sudden puff of black smoke rising before it.

James reined in his horse and put out a hand, his fingers closing hard on Jonathan's arm. "Look yonder," he said sharply, pointing with his other hand.

Jonathan brought his mount to a stop, too, and peered into the distance where James was indicating. At first it was difficult to see because there was a pretty good spring breeze blowing and, as the smoke rose above the level of the Balcones, the wind caught it, shredded it, and blew it away. But now there was no mistaking it, because it was coming up in dark billows.

"That's a cabin on fire," Jonathan said tautly.

"Damn right. Come on!" James heeled his horse into a fast trot even as he spoke. Jonathan was right behind him.

As they rode, they slipped the long-barreled Colts from their holsters and checked the loads. The .36 caliber revolvers, with five shots per cylinder, were already changing the face of the frontier. Several times small groups of frontiersman had been surrounded by Comanches, only to blast their way out of the ring of overconfident Indians by using their Colts. The Comanches, who were pretty much limited to single-shot weapons, had already grown to hate and fear the big revolvers. James Lewis carried two of them on his hips and two more in holsters attached to his saddle, giving him twenty shots before he had to reload. He also had a Colt's Model 1839 smoothbore revolving carbine snugged in a saddleboot under his right leg. That provided him with six more shots. With odds like that on his side, James would charge right into hell.

Which, considering the thick smoke rising into the sky ahead of them, might be exactly what they were doing.

The brothers topped a small rise and looked down on what should have been a pretty picture. The tree-lined river ran through a large open valley ringed by hills. It was good land, perfect for farming or ranching; James could tell that at a glance.

Someone else had thought so, too, because close by the river was a large double log cabin with the usual dogtrot between the buildings, and off to one side was a corral and an impressive-looking barn. Before today, this had obviously been a prosperous spread.

But now both the cabin and the barn were burning, sending thick clouds of black smoke into the sky, and that pretty much ruined the beauty of the scene. That and the huddled shapes lying motionless on the ground near the blazing buildings.

With an angry shout, James kicked his horse into a gallop. The rangy buckskin responded, pounding down the hill at a run. The wind of his passage tugged James's hat off his head, and it fell behind his neck, held on by the rawhide chin strap. Jonathan settled for guiding his racing horse with one hand while he held his hat with the other.

James's eyes scanned the landscape around the ranch and saw nothing moving. He spotted a few cows lying on their sides, shot down just like their owners and as motionless as the men near the cabin. There had probably been some horses in the corral, James thought, but the Comanches would have taken any horses with them when they left.

As he reached the level valley, James pulled his horse back to a lope. There was no need to hurry, he knew now. He had hoped that someone might have survived the raid, but the Comanches would not have left anyone alive behind them.

He held out a hand to slow down Jonathan. "Take it easy," James warned his half brother. "I think the Indians are gone, but we don't want to ride right into them if they're not."

"Amen to that," muttered Jonathan. He pulled his horse back to a more reasonable gait and rode alongside James with one hand on the butt of his gun.

Even though the river was close by, there was no point in trying to fight the fires. The blazes were too well-established and would have to burn until the cabin and the barn were consumed. If they could find some buckets, though, James thought, it would be a good idea to wet down the ground around the buildings, just to make sure the fires didn't spread.

He gestured to the right and told Jonathan, "Swing over that way and take a look around. I'll go the other way."

Jonathan nodded curtly and veered his horse away from James's mount. James rode around the other side of the cabin and the barn, going between them and the river. As far as he could see, the valley was deserted. Pausing beside the stream, he looked down at the muddy bank and saw the tracks of unshod horses, quite a few of them, moving into the water and then disappearing. The Comanches had left this way, crossing the river and probably heading southwest.

"Nothing," Jonathan called as he rode all the way around the homestead and rejoined James.

James pointed at the muddy tracks. "They've already ridden out, but probably not very long ago. No more than fifteen or twenty minutes."

"Are we going after them?"

His eyes still on the jumble of tracks, James grimaced. "There's at least a dozen of them," he said, "maybe more. Not good odds."

"Damn it!" Jonathan exploded, his normally good-natured face going dark with anger. "This isn't the first burned-out place we've seen, James. You remember what happened last time. We didn't go after that bunch, either, and Angeline wound up getting carried off."

James's jaw tightened. "We don't know the same band was responsible for taking Angeline as burned out those other folks. But it doesn't really matter. Foolish is foolish, and chasing after a bunch of Comanch' and getting ourselves killed won't do anybody any good, least of all the other settlers around here who have to be warned that the Indians have started raiding again. That make sense to you, Jonathan?"

For a moment the two men traded glares, then Jonathan sighed and nodded. "Reckon it does," he said. "But knowing you're right doesn't make it any easier." He summoned up a faint smile. "You're going to have to quit thinking so straight, James, if you want to hang on to that reputation you've got as a hothead."

"I'll be hotheaded when the time's right," grunted James. "Right now, we've got some buryin' to do."

Jonathan's face grew solemn again as he turned his horse and followed James back to the blazing cabin. The heat was too intense to get close, but James was able to dart up and hook the handle of an overturned bucket near one wall. The bucket had started to scorch a little, but it hadn't caught fire yet. He and Jonathan took turns dipping it in the stream and wetting down the ground around the cabins and barn. It was a tedious chore, but with a lot of the grass still dead from the winter just past, the flames could spread easily. James stomped out a couple of smaller fires started by drifting embers.

The roof of the barn collapsed, sending up a huge column of smoke and ashes. A few minutes later, the roof of the cabin went as well. James nodded in grim satisfaction. "The fires ought to burn themselves out now. Reckon there's no reason to postpone the other chores any longer."

He had known as soon as he rode up that the three men lying on the ground were dead. Nobody could have bled as much as they had and still be alive. Two of them had been riddled by gunshots, while the other one had been literally hacked to pieces with knives and tomahawks. All three had been scalped. Debris that had been dragged out from inside the cabin was scattered around the bodies. The raiders had taken anything that struck their fancy from the cabin before setting it on fire. James saw the remains of demolished furniture, and a good-sized trunk had been chopped open, its contents strewn all over the ground. Mostly they were clothes: pants and brightly colored shirts. With a grim shake of his head, he even spotted a beaver top hat among the leavings.

"Look at this," Jonathan said, bending over and picking something up from the ground. He held it out so that James could see it. It was a necklace, a cheap little trinket that could have been picked up for a few cents down in Galveston. But it sparkled in the sunlight, and the sight of it etched the lines in James's face even deeper.

"There's some dresses amongst these leavings, too," he said.

"Oh, Lordy," breathed Jonathan. "That means there was a woman here. You reckon the Indians took her with 'em?"

"Either that—" James nodded toward the cabin, where the fire was now burning down at last. "—or we'll find her in there. For her sake, I don't know which one to hope for."

There were short-handled spades in the gear on their pack animals. James and Jonathan used them to dig graves for the three men. It was a grisly task getting the bodies into the ground, and by the time they were finished, Jonathan was pale and haggard. James felt a little sick himself. He had buried victims of Indian raids before, but it was something a man never got used to.

When the graves all had mounds of freshly turned dirt atop them, James looked at the ruins of the cabin and barn and said, "Those ashes might be cool enough by now for us to poke around a little."

"James . . . what if the woman's not in there? If they took her with them, we've got to go after them, don't we? No matter how many of them there are?"

James considered for a moment, then nodded. After what Angeline had gone through, there was no way he could condemn another woman to that sort of hellish ordeal without at least trying to rescue her. But at the same time, someone had to deliver the news of this attack, so he said, "I'll go after them. You'll have to ride back downriver and start spreading the word."

He knew from the look of surprise on Jonathan's face that he was in for an argument. Jonathan said, "Wait just a minute! You can't go after a dozen Comanches by yourself. You'll lose your hair for sure."

"Well, it's my hair to risk," James replied. "And a lot more people will be in danger if we don't let them know the raiding has started again."

Stubbornly, Jonathan began to shake his head.

James turned on his heel and stalked toward the burned-out cabin. There was no use wasting his breath arguing until they had taken a look around. He still had the spade in his hand, and he used it to move aside pieces of debris as he stepped over what was left of the cabin wall. Small clouds of ashes puffed up around his high-topped black boots as he walked carefully into the ruins.

He paused a moment later. "Damn," he said softly and fervently.

"What is it?" Jonathan called from behind him.

"We won't have to go after those Comanches after all," James said, his features set in bleak, hard lines. "I found the lady."

It looked like the woman's skull had been crushed by a blow from a tomahawk. James supposed she had fought back so much when the Indians tried to drag her out of the cabin that the savages had gotten tired of struggling with her and just killed her outright. He hated to think it, but she was probably better off this way, dying a quick death rather than suffering the torments that would have awaited her in a Comanche camp. The best she could have hoped for there would have been a short, miserable life as a slave.

As Jonathan started toward him, James turned and took his half brother's arm, pulling him away from the woman's burned, mutilated corpse. "Get started digging another grave," James said. "I reckon this woman was probably married to one of those men, but we don't have any way of knowing which one. We'll just have to lay her to rest beside all three of them and hope we get it right."

Jonathan nodded.

"I'll finish looking around," James continued, his thoughts on the horrible possibility that there might have been children on this ranch, too.

But he found no other bodies anywhere in the burned-out ruins, and there were no toys or children's clothes in the things strewn around on the ranch. Another stroke of grim luck, he thought.

When they had finally done all they could for the victims of the raid, James took off his hat and muttered a brief prayer. He was no good at such things and wished that Andrew was here. Andrew had always been better at talking, whether it was to God or to other folks. But he and Jonathan were the only ones around, so James sent the departed souls on their way the best he could.

Then the brothers saddled up and James said, ''We'll ride a ways together, but then I want you to swing north to Austin while I head back home. Tell Sam Houston the Comanches have started raiding again and that he was a damn fool for doing away with the Rangers.''

''You want me to tell that to Sam Houston?'' Jonathan asked. ''You want me to tell the President of the Republic that he's a damn fool?''

''Reckon it wouldn't be the first time he'd heard somebody say that,'' James replied coolly. ''But you're probably right. Spread the word about what happened here, any way you can.''

Jonathan nodded. ''I'll do it.''

''And I'll tell the folks around home to get ready. Trouble's on the way again, no doubt about it.

They heeled their horses into motion and rode away from the burned-out ranch, two tall, grim-faced men who were carrying the news every Texan hated to hear.

But as he rode away, a frown creased James's face. Something about what he had seen today stuck in the back of his mind, in a dim corner where he couldn't quite get at it. Whatever it was, it was wrong somehow, and he wished he could figure it out. The thought was slippery as a catfish, though, and kept eluding his grasp. Finally he gave it up.

Whatever it was, it couldn't be as important as the fact that the Comanches were on the warpath again.

☆ **Chapter** ☆

3

Andrew Lewis hauled back on the mule team's reins and brought his wagon to a stop in front of Luther Barnstable's cabin. The place was starting to look run down. The roof needed patching, and the garden off to one side was full of weeds. The soil between the rows was cracked and dry, too, and Andrew could tell that it hadn't been worked in a week or more.

"I won't be long," Petra said as she got down from the seat beside him. She reached into the wagon bed and lifted out a pot of beans she had cooked the day before, her lips thinning with the effort of lifting its weight.

"I'll get that for you," Andrew said quickly as he hopped down from the seat.

Petra swung around and started toward the cabin door, still carrying the beans. "No, that's all right, Andrew, I have them. I just want to see how Ophelia is doing and give these beans to Luther."

Andrew watched, hands on hips, as his wife reached the door of the cabin and went on inside. There was an old hound lying in the dirt beside the door. It had bayed at them the first time they stopped at the Barnstable place, but by now it was used to seeing them, Andrew supposed. The dog barely opened its eyes to look at them and didn't even lift its long-eared head, let alone bark.

This was the third day in a row he and Petra had visited Luther and Ophelia Barnstable's farm, a half-mile downriver and on the opposite side of the Colorado from Andrew's homestead. Petra had made him stay outside on each visit, saying that he wouldn't want to embarrass Ophelia by seeing her while she was so sick. Andrew hadn't protested too much. He wasn't overly fond of the Barnstables to start with. Luther was a Cracker from Georgia who was slow to do anything except what he had to do. Andrew didn't hold being poor against folks; he and his family had seen bad times, both here in Texas and back in Tennessee. But a man ought to at least try to improve his situation, Andrew thought, instead of trusting to luck and the kindness of his neighbors.

Petra wouldn't put up with any such talk, however, and Andrew knew it, so he kept his thoughts to himself. To Petra, it didn't matter who you were or where you were from or what you did with your life. If you needed a helping hand, she was there to extend it. And, Andrew supposed, that was the way it should be. Maybe he ought to take a lesson or two from his own wife, he told himself.

There was a hoe leaning against the wall of the cabin. Andrew walked over, picked it up, and headed for the garden. The least he could do while he was waiting for Petra was to work that garden soil for Luther.

Andrew's frown grew deeper as he chopped at the dry ground, raking back the cracked upper layer and respreading it so that the soil would hold moisture better. He didn't much care for the way Petra had looked today, sort of washed-out and flushed at the same time. When she thought he wasn't looking, he had seen an expression of utter weariness on her face. She was pushing herself too hard, he thought. It was a plenty big enough job for her to take care of Ben and Rose. She didn't need to be taking on extra responsibilities . . . like Ophelia Barnstable.

The sun was hot, and Andrew felt beads of sweat popping out on his forehead as he hoed the garden. Where the hell was Luther? This was Luther's garden, and it ought to be his job to take care of it. Andrew's mouth tightened grimly.

"Andrew! Oh, God, come quick, Andrew!"

The shout came from the cabin, and Andrew's head jerked up in response to it. It wasn't Petra standing there calling to him so frantically, but Luther Barnstable instead. Luther wore pants and suspenders over a pair of red longjohns. His round face sported several days' worth of beard stubble, and the fringe of hair around his bald skull was wildly askew. He looked scared, downright scared.

Andrew dropped the hoe and ran toward the cabin. His heart was pounding wildly in his chest, but it wasn't from the work he had been doing. Something bad must have happened to shake up Luther like that.

And if something had happened to Ophelia, why wasn't it Petra outside calling him?

Luther caught Andrew's arm as Andrew ran up to him. "Oh, Lordy, I don't know what happened," he babbled. "She was just standin' there leanin' over Ophelia and washin' her face, then she give this little moan and keeled over!"

Andrew jerked his arm loose from Luther's ham-fingered grasp. "Petra?" he asked. "You're talking about Petra?"

"Your missus has been so good to us, I never meant for this to happen . . ."

There was no point in talking to Luther. He was too shaken to make much sense. Andrew tore past him and ran into the cabin, his eyes darting back and forth as he searched for Petra. Damn, he must be getting old! His eyes were having trouble adjusting to the dimness of the cabin's interior.

There! There she was, slumped on the puncheon floor next to the bed where Ophelia Barnstable lay. Ophelia was weakly moving her head back and forth and moaning quietly in her delirium, but Petra was so still, so goddamned *still* . . . !

Andrew rushed to his wife and knelt beside her, gathering her up in his arms as he said urgently, "Petra! Petra, dear God!"

She was alive. She moaned faintly, and he could feel her heart beating erratically as he crushed her against him. He leaned back slightly and touched her face, and her cheek was searing hot where he laid his fingers on it. She was burning up with fever. Her eyelids fluttered a little as she tried to open her eyes, but the effort was too much for her in her weakened state.

"Luther!" Andrew shouted. "Luther, get in here, damn it!"

Looking frightened and ready to bolt, Luther appeared in the open doorway. "Y—yeah, Andrew?" he said. "What is it?"

"Get me a bucket of water. Now!"

Luther disappeared, and Andrew hoped fervently that the man would come back and not just keep going when he reached the river. Holding Petra's head gently in his lap, Andrew stroked her feverish forehead and said soothingly, "It'll be all right. You just hang on, Petra, and everything'll be fine."

He glanced at Ophelia Barnstable. Whatever sickness had laid her low had now struck Petra, too. That was one of the things Andrew had always worried about. No matter what was wrong with somebody, Petra always rushed in to help take care of them, without sparing a thought for her own health. For years, she had been lucky, but now it seemed her luck had run out.

But she would be all right, Andrew told himself. There was an amazing amount of strength in that slender frame; he knew that from experience. After all, she had once nursed him back to health when he could just as easily have died, but through sheer strength of will she had not permitted that to happen. She was a fighter—always had been and always would be.

"Luther, where the hell's that water?" he muttered aloud.

A couple of minutes later, Luther came through the door, water sloshing out of the bucket he carried. He brought it over to Andrew and set it down on the floor. "Here you go, Andrew," he said. "What do you want me to do now?"

"Have you got some clean pieces of cloth?"

Luther looked so befuddled by the question that Andrew didn't wait for him to work out an answer. Instead he reached down to the bottom hem of Petra's underskirt and tore off a couple of pieces of the fabric. Dipping one of them in the bucket, he got it thoroughly wet and then began swabbing Petra's face with it.

Without looking up, he snapped to Luther, "Get some quilts and make a pallet in the bed of my wagon. Make it as comfortable as you can, hear?"

"Sure, Andrew. I'll sure do it." Luther swallowed hard and got to work, pulling some quilts out of a trunk and hurrying out of the cabin. While he was gone, Andrew kept washing Petra's face with the wet rags. She was so hot that the coolness of the water quickly vanished, and he had to dip the cloths in the bucket frequently. It was the only thing he could think to do for her, though.

When Luther came back in, the farmer said, "Got the wagon fixed up just like you told me to, Andrew. You goin' to take your missus home?"

Andrew didn't bother answering such an obvious question. He wet both of the rags again and laid them over Petra's face, then got his arms under her shoulders and legs and stood up, grunting with the effort. She had always been slender, but unconscious like this she was dead weight, and he wasn't as young as he had once been. Steadying himself, he started toward the door, turning sideways so that he could carry Petra through the opening. "Bring the bucket," he told Luther.

Carefully, gently, he placed Petra on the folded quilts in the wagonbed, her head toward the front so that he could turn around the seat and still reach her. He took the bucket from Luther and put it on the seat beside him. He wanted to keep wetting down the rags and wiping her face with them even while he was driving back to their place on the other side of the river. It would be awkward handling the team that way, but he knew it was important to keep Petra as cool as possible.

When he had hurriedly climbed to the seat, he paused long enough to tell Luther, "You saw what I was doing with Petra. Get another bucket of water and do the same with your wife. Keep her from getting any hotter, damn it, or the fever will take her, sure as hell. Can you do it?"

"I . . . I'll try," Luther stammered.

"Trying's not good enough, damn you! My wife risked her own life to help Ophelia, and by God you're going to pull her through or I'll know the reason why! Now get in there, Luther, and do what I told you." Andrew drew in a deep, ragged breath. "And may God help us all."

With that, he slapped the lines down on the backs of the mules and shouted to them, and the wagon jolted into motion as the team strained against its harness.

The journey back to his own homestead—relatively short though it might have been—was a seemingly endless nightmare to Andrew Lewis. He guided the mules one-handed, half-turned on the seat so that he could reach back and swab Petra's face with one of the wet rags. From time to time she moaned loud enough for him to hear over the clopping hooves of the mule team, and the sound tore at his insides.

Finally he came in sight of his cabin, where Ben and Rose had been left earlier in the day. Ben was plowing and Rose was sitting beside the cabin, working a butter churn. Both of them saw their father coming, pushing the mule team harder than he normally would have, and they must have sensed that something was wrong. They abandoned their chores and came running to meet the wagon.

"Get back!" Andrew cried, waving an arm at them to stop them before they got too close. "Don't come over here!"

"What is it, Pa?" Ben asked as he slowed to a stop, a confused and worried frown on his young face.

"Where's Mama?" put in Rose, sounding even more worried than her brother.

Andrew told them, "She's in the back of the wagon. Now just

don't come any closer, you two, because she's real sick and I don't want you getting whatever it is she's got. Understand?''

"Mama!" Rose took a step forward, then stopped again at Andrew's stern look.

Ben had gone pale, but he swallowed hard and asked, "What can we do to help, Pa?"

"Get that big red horse of yours, Ben, and fetch your Aunt Marie. Just tell her that your mama's real sick and I need a hand if she can spare it.''

Ben nodded, then turned and hurried toward the barn where his horse was. Rose stood there, one hand tightly clutching the other, and asked, "What about me, Pa? What can I do?"

"Make sure there's plenty of water on hand," Andrew told her. "I don't want you coming in the cabin once I've taken your mama in there, though. Just leave the buckets outside the door."

"All right," Rose said, her voice quivering a little with fear. There was nothing more frightening for a child, Andrew supposed, than for a parent to be bad sick like this. But he couldn't worry too much about Rose and Ben right now; Petra had to be his main concern.

As Rose moved well aside, Andrew drove the wagon up to the cabin. As he was taking Petra out of the vehicle, Ben flashed past on his horse, the big bay little more than a streak of red as it stretched its legs into a gallop. Ben rode bareback, clinging to the horse like a burr—or an Indian. The boy was a good rider, Andrew told himself, and he would fetch help in no time.

Andrew got Petra into her own bed, throwing back the covers and leaving them back. Some folks said it was best to make a fever burn itself out by heaping covers on the sick person, but Andrew had never agreed with that idea. He had heard of too many people dying after treatment like that. Keep them as cool as possible, that was the thing to do. He hurried back outside and got the bucket of water he had brought from the Barnstable place. It was almost empty now, but Rose was already coming back from the river with two more buckets full of fresh water, straining under their weight.

While Rose waited anxiously outside, Andrew washed Petra's face and hands and feet. He thought she seemed a little cooler now, but he knew that might be just wishful thinking. He wished she would wake up enough to look at him and recognize him, maybe even speak to him. It would have meant a lot to him to hear her voice right about now, telling him that everything was going to be all right.

After a while he heard the sound of hoofbeats outside, followed by the creaking of wagon wheels, then Marie's voice called out to the team as she brought them to a stop. A moment later she appeared in the doorway and said, "Andrew? Dear Lord, what has happened, Andrew?"

"Petra's been going over to the Barnstable farm the last three days," Andrew said tautly, "nursing Ophelia Barnstable. The fever's got Ophelia, and now it's got Petra, too. She looked like she felt bad this morning, and then she collapsed over at Luther's a little while ago. I've been keeping her face wet as best I can, hoping that'll cool her off."

"You have done the right thing," Marie said as she took a step into the cabin.

"Wait!" Andrew said. "You don't have to come in here if you don't want to, Marie. Whatever this stuff is, it's catching, that's for sure. If you don't want to risk getting it yourself, I'll understand."

"Don't be absurd," Marie said, sweeping into the cabin. She came straight to the bed, took the wet cloth from Andrew's hand, and began wiping Petra's face. "When one member of this family is in trouble, the others do everything they can to help. That is the way it has always been and, God willing, it will remain so."

Andrew stood up, stretching tired muscles as he did so. The tension that had gripped him as soon as he saw Petra sprawled on the floor of the Barnstable cabin had taken its toll on him. He managed to smile faintly and squeezed Marie's shoulder as she knelt at Petra's bedside. "Thanks, Marie. I knew I could count on you. You didn't bring Angeline with you, did you?"

Marie shook her head. "That would have endangered the baby, too, and that I would not do. I left her at the compound and sent Ben on to pass the word of Petra's illness to Annie and Sly, then to Frank and Hope. They will look out for Angeline."

"Good thinking," Andrew muttered. He walked slowly back and forth across the plank floor of the cabin's big single room. "I worried right from the start about Petra trying to take care of everybody. Look where it's got her now."

"We are Texans," Marie said simply without looking up. "We help our friends and neighbors."

Andrew felt a surge of shame. She had summed it up, all right. Not everybody was as generous as Petra and Marie, but by and large folks looked out for one another out here on the frontier. The odds against survival in this rugged land were already high enough without having to go it completely alone.

When he walked over to the bed a few minutes later, he saw that Petra didn't seem quite as flushed, and she had stopped moaning. She was resting quietly now, and if Andrew hadn't known better, he might have thought she was just sleeping. But Marie kept a cool rag on her forehead and continued washing her face with another wet cloth.

Andrew heard hoofbeats outside and looked up. "Reckon that'll be Ben," he said. "I'd better go outside and tell him and Rose that their ma looks a little better now. They must be pretty scared."

Marie nodded. "That is a good idea."

Andrew walked over to the door and stepped out into the dogtrot just as the rider drew rein in front of the cabin. It wasn't his son Ben who swung down lithely, though, and the horse wasn't the big bay on which Ben had ridden away. A barrel-chested buckskin stood there, blowing after a long hard ride, and it was Andrew's brother James who turned a grim face toward him. James was still covered with trail dust and looked even more haggard than he had a few days earlier when he and Jonathan had stopped by at Marie's to say farewell to Mordecai, Edward, and Manuel.

"Uncle James," Rose said, coming into her uncle's arms for a quick hug. Even under the circumstances, she was glad to see James, Andrew figured, and that was good. But he wished he knew what James was looking so bleak about, and there was only one way to find out.

Before Andrew could say anything, Rose went on, "I'm so glad you came, Uncle James. I knew you would once you heard Mama was sick."

James glanced sharply at Andrew. "Petra's sick?"

Andrew nodded and said, "The fever's got her. She picked it up tending to Luther Barnstable's wife. Marie's inside with her now."

"I didn't know. I'm sorry," James murmured. "How's she doing?"

"We're doing all we can for her," Andrew said with a shake of his head. "Reckon it's too soon to tell." He glanced at his daughter. "But don't you worry, Rose. Your mama was always a fighter. She saw a lot of hard times when she was younger, and she came through all of them just fine."

"But that wasn't like this," Rose said, a catch in her voice. "It wasn't like she was sick and might . . . might die."

Andrew gripped the girl's shoulders. "Listen to me. Your mother is *not* going to die. She's going to be all right, Rose."

But Rose pulled away from him, turned, and ran sobbing toward the barn. Andrew took a couple of steps after her, then stopped short. What could he do, what could he tell her? He was every bit as scared as she was, maybe more so. Fine lot of good he could do for her right now.

James said quietly, "Best let her go. I may not have any young'uns of my own, but I know sometimes you've got to let 'em work things out by themselves. Reckon Rose is pretty frightened right now."

"I know I am," Andrew said with a sigh. "What brings you here, James, if you hadn't heard about Petra? When you rode up, you looked like you were upset about something."

"Comanches."

The single word was enough to make Andrew's eyes narrow and his hands clench into fists. "You found Indian sign?" he asked.

"More than that," James said, lifting a hand to massage his temples as if he could rub away the memories as well as the ache in his head. "Jonathan and I ran across a burned-out ranch over on the San Marcos. We got there about a quarter-hour after at least a dozen Comanches raided the place. They killed four people, three men and a woman. Reckon you know it wasn't a very pretty sight."

Andrew shook his head. "It wouldn't be. I hope you and Jonathan had enough sense not to go after that bunch of savages by yourself. You must've, or you likely wouldn't be here now."

"No, we rode back to spread the word. I sent Jonathan on up to Austin to warn folks there and let Houston know about it, while I came on here. Wish I'd come at a better time." James put a hand on Andrew's shoulder. "Anything I can do to help?"

"Can't think of a thing, but thanks for offering. You . . . you'd better keep spreading the word about that Indian raid. Folks need to know things could get bad again."

James considered for a second and then nodded. "Yeah, I reckon you're right. But I'll be back, Andrew. In the meantime, you'd best make sure all your guns are cleaned and loaded, just in case those Comanch' get real daring and come this far again."

"I'll do that," Andrew nodded. The chore might help take his mind off Petra's illness, he thought as he watched his brother swing back up in the saddle.

James pulled his horse's head around and lifted a hand in farewell, then heeled the animal into a fast lope that carried him away from the homestead. Andrew let out a long sigh. Illness and savages and hot summers and cold winters and hard ground and every manner of biting and stinging animal and insect under the sun. . . . Why did anybody ever get the idea that Texas was a fit place for a man or beast to live, he wondered.

Yet once they were here, damn few people left of their own accord, he admitted. There was something about the place . . .

But right now he would have traded the whole damn Republic for the health of his wife.

The next couple of days were the longest and hardest of Andrew's life. There was work to be done around the farm, but he ignored it. He made sure his guns were ready, as James suggested. Other than that he spent most of his time either sitting in the dogtrot or beside Petra's bed, keeping the cool cloths on her face. Annie came to spell both him and Marie, and the three of them kept up a round-the-clock vigil. Petra's fever stayed high, and she couldn't seem to take any nourishment. They tried to feed her, even though she was only semiconscious, but whatever they gave her came right back up.

She was wasting away right before his eyes, and there wasn't a damn thing he could do about it.

Sly Shipman rode to Austin in an attempt to fetch a doctor, but when he came back alone he told Andrew that there was a virtual epidemic of this fever, whatever it was. Lots of folks in town were down with it, and Sly had been unable to find a doctor willing to come back down the Colorado with him. Short of kidnapping one of them at gunpoint—which, knowing Sly, Andrew figured had been a consideration—there was nothing else he could have done. But more than one physician had given Sly the same advice to carry back home with him: keep Petra as cool and comfortable as possible and pray for all they were worth.

Andrew tried. He wished old Reverend Fairweather was still around. The man might have been a scoundrel and a charlatan, but he could also be a comfort at times.

Andrew watched Marie and Annie very closely for any sign that they might be coming down with the illness themselves. As for himself, he was exhausted from worry and lack of sleep, naturally enough, but that was all. He could tell that so far the pestilence hadn't touched him. Annie and Marie still seemed to be all right, too.

Sometime in the middle of the second night, while Andrew was dozing in a rocking chair on the other side of the room, Marie touched him on the shoulder. He came fully awake with a start, dread welling up in him. "What is it?" he asked raggedly. "Is Petra . . . ?"

"She is awake," Marie said, brushing back a strand of dark hair that had fallen over her eyes. "She wants to speak to you."

Andrew rushed across the room and knelt at the bedside. He expected the worst, but when he caught up one of Petra's limp hands, it was cool instead of hot. Andrew cried out in surprise. He touched his wife's face and it was cool, too. Petra's hair was sodden with sweat. She smiled feebly at him and whispered, "I have been very sick, haven't I, Andrew? I'm sorry to have put you through this."

At first Andrew tried to blink back his tears and then he let them flow freely. "Don't you worry about that. Are . . . are you feeling better?"

Petra was able to nod. "Marie says the fever has broken. Now I am just so very, very tired." Slowly, she lifted her hand and touched his cheek. "But I did not want to sleep until I had seen you and spoken to you, Andrew. My dear Andrew . . . I love you so."

"And I love you," he told her, folding her hand in both of his. "You just rest now, and maybe in the morning you'll feel like eating something."

Petra smiled and nodded, and her eyes slipped closed.

Andrew let himself sag to the floor, keeping his grip on her hand as he did so. He listened to her deep, regular breathing and closed his eyes to utter a silent prayer of thanks.

A few minutes later, Marie came over to him and said quietly, "You should sleep now yourself. I'll be here with her if she needs anything."

Carefully, Andrew placed Petra's hand on the bed beside her and stood up. He put the balls of his hands against his eyes and rubbed hard. "You're right. But I'll be there in the chair if you need me."

"Sleep," Marie told him with a smile.

Andrew crossed the room and sank down in the rocker. It felt a lot more comfortable now, almost as comfortable as a feather bed. As soon as he closed his eyes, he felt sleep stealing over him, and this time it carried him away into a dark, dreamless place where the nightmares were finally over.

In the morning, Petra was dead.

When Annie woke him, Andrew saw Marie slumped at the foot of Petra's bed, weeping, and he knew what had happened. He burst up out of his chair, choking back a scream, and flung himself across the room to drop to his knees beside his wife's bed. Petra's face was as white and cold and lifeless as stone, and there was no holding back the horrible cry of anguish that tore itself from Andrew's throat.

The fight had been too much for her, had drained too much of her strength. Along toward morning, Marie told him later, the life had just gone out of Petra in a long, shuddery breath that was awesome in its finality. She had hung on long enough to see him again, to talk to him and tell him that she loved him, and that had been her last act of defiance against the fate that was struggling so hard to claim her.

Now it was over, and when he stopped crying, Andrew was numb. He barely knew what was going on around him as people bustled here and there, getting ready for the funeral. He was aware that Frank led him out of the cabin and then later helped him get into his best clothes. More people showed up, coming in wagons and on horseback, the women all looking sorrowful, the men solemn and watchful at the same time, because nobody had forgotten about the renewed threat of Indian trouble. The men were all carrying rifles, and some had pistol belts strapped around their waists.

Jonathan got back from Austin in time to help James dig the grave on a small hill overlooking the river, and this was even worse than the graves they had dug over beside the San Marcos. The woman going into this one was a woman they had both known and loved, a woman who had been everything a pioneer lady had to be—strong, compassionate, courageous. Petra Lewis would be missed by everyone who had known her.

But most of all, she would be missed by Andrew, and as he struggled to maintain his composure during the funeral, he wished that he could just lie down and die, too. There was no point in going on without Petra, no point at all.

Then, beside him, his daughter leaned against him and shook with sobs, and Andrew slipped his arm around Rose's shoulder and hung on tightly. At this moment, there was little comfort in him, but what he had he would share with Rose and with Ben, who was crying silently on Andrew's other side. Andrew put a hand on his son's shoulder and squeezed.

He had been wrong. He had two very good reasons to live. More than that, because there were other Lewises, too. All of the Texas branch of the family were here except Mordecai and Edward, and there had been no way to get word to them in time for them to attend the funeral. They were long miles away, somewhere down in South Texas along the Nueces River, going after mustangs. Andrew couldn't hold their absence against them.

There were plenty of other friends here, too. The Lewises were well liked for the most part. Even the Barnstables were there, Luther and Ophelia both. Ophelia's fever had broken too, after Luther followed Andrew's example and kept his wife as cool as he could for long days and nights. But Ophelia had been strong enough to recover, and although a part of Andrew wanted to hate her for that, he couldn't.

Petra wouldn't have wanted it that way, he told himself.

There was no preacher, but Frank read from the Scriptures and talked about what a good woman Petra had been, and everybody murmured, ''Amen.'' Then it was over, and Frank led Andrew, Ben, and Rose away while James and Jonathan and some of the other men tended to the rest of it.

Andrew was tired, and he wanted to sleep. There would be plenty of work to be done on the morrow. Fields needed plowing and crops needed planting. Petra had never been one to lay about, nor to allow anyone else to do so, not when there were chores that needed doing.

''Best damn farm in Texas,'' Andrew muttered to himself. That's what this place was going to be before he was through with it. He would throw himself into the work until he was too worn out to think, let alone to remember or to feel the pain that memories would bring. That was all that was left to him.

And he hoped that Petra, wherever she was, would understand.

☆ Chapter ☆

4

Mordecai reined in and let the dust cloud stirred up by his horse's hooves settle before removing his hat and wiping the sweat from his forehead with his sleeve. Beside him, Edward and Manuel looked equally hot, tired, and discouraged. It was late May, and summer had already arrived with a vengeance here in the Nueces country. The three young men had been mustanging for a month, and they had damn little to show for it. Their base camp was back upriver a ways, near the spot where the Nueces and the Frio flowed together. They had cut down quite a few mesquites and used the scrubby trees to build a corral, fully expecting to quickly fill the enclosure with the mustangs they caught.

There were less than half a dozen mustangs inside the corral at the moment—if Mordecai and his companions were lucky. More than once, they'd run some mares into the corral only to have a stallion come along later while they were gone and break down the fence to free the captured horses. They had spent almost as much time repairing the corral, Mordecai thought bitterly, as they had chasing down mustangs.

''What now?'' he asked as the three young men sat dispiritedly beside the deceptively placid river. In times of heavy rain, the Nueces could become a raging torrent cutting across the chaparral-covered flatlands.

Edward leaned forward in the saddle to ease his sore muscles. ''We haven't seen any wild horses in two days, and the last ones we did see, we couldn't catch. I'm starting to think coming down here was a bad idea, fellas."

"There are horses here," insisted Manuel. "But they are like spirits, able to vanish into the chaparral whenever anyone comes too close. To catch them, we must begin to *think* like them."

Mordecai shook his head. All this talk of spirits and thinking like horses was too much for him. The mustangs were real enough for their hooves to raise dust when they ran, and he wasn't sure they even thought much or acted on anything other than instinct. But he didn't say as much to Manuel, who was as good a brother-in-law as anybody could want.

"The choice is simple," Mordecai declared. "We either keep looking, or we give up and go home. And I'm not much on quitting."

"Nor am I," Manuel said. "I think we should continue searching."

Edward nodded grudgingly. "Reckon I do, too. I'd pure-dee hate to come home with our tails draggin' between our legs and only a handful of horses to show for all our trouble."

"Who knows?" Manuel said with a grin. "Perhaps we will yet capture that white stallion."

Mordecai didn't say anything. It was strange how life worked out, he thought. At first, Manuel had been the one who scoffed at the idea of the mysterious white stallion, but lately he had been talking about it quite a bit. It was more than the idea of the five hundred dollar reward that appealed to Manuel, too. He seemed almost obsessed with the legend. Probably that romantic Spanish blood in him, Mordecai mused with a half smile.

"Let's get riding," he said, nudging his horse into a walk.

The land along this part of the Nueces was pretty much unchanging in its appearance. It was prairie with very little roll to it, huge open sections of short, hardy grasses marked off by areas of chaparral, mesquite, and gnarled oak trees that spread out broadly while not growing very tall. The chaparral was thorny and would cut both man and horse to ribbons if given the chance, but somehow the wild mustangs were able to negotiate most of it, vanishing into razor-sharp strongholds where pursuers dared not follow. The landscape was pretty much the same all the way to the Gulf of Mexico, Mordecai had been told. The Nueces was supposed to empty into a pretty bay there, and he wouldn't mind seeing it someday. His uncle James had told him about the Gulf, about how its blue-green waters seemed to extend into forever, and that sounded like something Mordecai ought to see. It would have to wait for another time, though.

As the three young men rode on, Edward suddenly reined in and flung an arm up. "Look over there!" he called out excitedly, pointing across the river to the south.

Mordecai's eyes narrowed as he saw the column of dust rising in the air. "Got to be a lot of horses to stir up that much dust," he muttered.

"*Sí*," Manuel agreed, excitement coloring his own voice. "*Muchos caballos.*"

"Do we go after 'em?" asked Edward.

"Damn right," Mordecai said. He turned his horse toward the river and heeled it into motion. "Come on."

As they splashed through the shallow river and climbed onto the opposite bank, a disturbing thought went through Mordecai's head. There could be other explanations for that dust cloud. It was undoubtedly being raised by the hooves of many horses, but those horses might not be mustangs. Maybe they were being ridden by Indians or, even more likely in this part of the country, by a Mexican army patrol that had ventured across the Rio Grande. The Mexican government had never really accepted the outcome of the revolution that had freed Texas from its rule, and there were still skirmishes along the border from time to time as Mexico tried to reestablish its influence over the Republic.

Of course, they were a long way from the border here, but you could never be sure what the Mexican soldiers would do. It might be possible to run into a contingent of cavalry, even this far north.

"Let's take it easy," Mordecai warned, sensing the eagerness in his companions. "We don't want to ride into any kind of surprise."

Knowing what he meant, Manuel and Edward matched the stride of their horses to his, and the three of them rode ahead cautiously.

Soon they could see the horses at the base of the dust cloud, and as the dark, roiling mass resolved itself into individual shapes, Mordecai could tell that the beasts were riderless. Those were mustangs, all right, a good-sized bunch of them.

"Come on," Mordecai said excitedly. "Let's see if we can cut 'em off!"

He urged his horse forward and the animal responded, breaking into a gallop across the plains carpeted with buffalo grass. Manuel and Edward were right behind him as they all three raced toward the herd of mustangs at an angle. It would be difficult to get a lasso on any of the horses with them running that way, but Mordecai hoped they could turn the herd and get them started running in a circle. They would tire themselves out that way, and then would be the time to slip in and dab a loop on the likeliest members of the band.

Suddenly, Mordecai became aware of something else. A smaller plume of dust was spiraling into the sky just behind and to the side of the mustangs. As he and the others drew closer, Mordecai saw that this dust was being raised by two riders who were already stalking the wild horses. Mordecai bit back a curse. It seemed that someone else had first claim on this bunch of mustangs, by right of proximity if nothing else. The two horsemen were a lot closer than Mordecai, Edward, and Manuel. They would certainly get first crack at the mustangs.

"Blast it!" Edward burst out, and Mordecai guessed he had seen the strangers, too. "Who in blazes is that?"

"Rivals of ours," Manuel called over to him. None of them had slowed their horses, and now it was becoming easier to pick out details about the other horsemen. One of them was small and looked even smaller because of the big black horse he rode. The animal seemed to be eating up the ground as it ran, stretching out its long legs to draw even with and then pass most of the frantically fleeing mustangs. The other rider, on a sturdy chestnut, lagged behind a little. Both of them wore the broad-brimmed, high-crowned sombreros of Mexican *vaqueros*, as well as thick oxhide *chaparejos* to protect their legs if they had to venture into the thorny brush.

And the smaller one, the one out in front on the big black, rode like the wind, Mordecai thought admiringly as he finally slowed his horse to a walk and watched the other mustangers at work.

He could tell which of the wild horses the mustangers had settled on to catch first. A fine-looking sorrel stallion ran near the front of the herd. Perhaps the sorrel was not the leader of the band yet, but he no doubt would be within another year or two—if he got the chance. The way the rider on the black was closing in on him, however, it was obvious the sorrel was to be the target of the first capture attempt.

Manuel and Edward had come to the same conclusion. Manuel said with a frown, "He should have his rope out by now. He will not have time to form the loop for a cast if he does not hurry."

"Look at him!" Edward exclaimed. "Shoot, he's riding right next to that sorrel!"

Mordecai was just as puzzled as his two companions as he watched the rider maneuvering the big black closer and closer to the sorrel. The mustanger was one hell of a horseman, that much was clear, but even so he couldn't be thinking of trying. . . . No, Mordecai told himself as the thought crossed his mind. That was ridiculous.

But then, right before his eyes, the diminutive figure on the back of the speeding black gathered himself and launched out of the saddle, flying through the air mere feet above the thundering hooves that would pound him to a bloody mess if he misjudged his leap. An instant later, almost before the gasp of surprise reached Mordecai's throat, the mustanger landed on the back of the sorrel. For a split second, he slipped and threatened to plunge off the sorrel on the other side, but then his legs clamped down and the fingers of one hand tangled in the sorrel's flying mane to hold on for dear life. With the other hand, the mustanger whipped what appeared to be a short length of hair rope from around his slender waist.

Mordecai's mouth dropped open in amazement at the deftness and dexterity with which the mustanger fashioned a crude hackamore out of the rope while hanging on to the sorrel with his knees. The mustanger leaned far forward and slipped the hackamore over the sorrel's nose, and that was the last Mordecai saw of them as the sorrel and the rest of the mustangs disappeared over a small rise. The dust cloud enveloped them as they vanished.

"Did you see that?" Mordecai asked a moment later when he could talk again. "I never saw anything like it!"

"Nor did I," agreed Manuel. "And I have seen *vaqueros* do some amazing things on horseback."

Edward said, "Here comes the other one."

That simple statement of fact got the attention of Mordecai and Manuel in a hurry. They looked over to see the second mustanger trotting his horse toward them. He was leading the big black by the reins, which he had caught up after the first mustanger's daring leap. Mordecai rested his right hand on his thigh where it would be handy to the Colt on his hip. Manuel and Edward did likewise. The second mustanger didn't appear to be hostile, but out here it generally paid a man to be suspicious of a stranger's motives until he found out for sure otherwise.

As the man rode nearer, they could tell that he was Mexican, as his clothing indicated. He was also fairly young, probably around Mordecai's age. He wasn't wearing a gun as far as Mordecai could tell, but the butt of a rifle was visible sticking up from a saddle boot. When he was still some twenty feet away from Mordecai, Edward, and Manuel, he brought his horses to a stop and held up a hand in greeting. ''*Buenos días*,'' he called.

Mordecai and Edward both spoke Spanish fairly well, but they left it up to Manuel to return the greeting, which he did. Then Manuel said, still in Spanish, ''Your friend is quite a rider. That was a trick the likes of which I have never seen.''

The mustanger laughed, nodded, and simply said, ''*Sí*.'' Then he switched to English and went on, ''This is true. Most people catch the mustangs with a lasso, instead of flying onto their backs like a bird.''

Mordecai couldn't restrain his curiosity any longer. He said, ''How in blazes is that little fella going to stop that runaway sorrel? The way those mustangs were stampeding, I don't think they're going to stop until they get to the Gulf of Mexico!''

The young Mexican laughed again and replied, ''The sorrel will be back soon, and not only that, it will be under control. You have my word on that, and the word of Amadeo Sigala is sacred, *señor*.''

''That's your name, Amadeo Sigala?''

''*Sí*.''

''Glad to meet you,'' Mordecai said. ''I'm Mordecai Lewis, from up on the Colorado. This is my cousin Edward and my brother-in-law, Manuel Zaragosa.''

Amadeo Sigala nodded to each of them in turn, then lifted his arm to point toward the horizon where the herd of mustangs had disappeared. ''As I was saying . . .''

Mordecai, Edward, and Manuel turned to look, and to their astonishment they saw the sorrel coming toward them at an easy lope, the small mustanger on its back guiding it deftly with the hair rope. ''How the hell . . . ?'' Mordecai muttered.

''Once again, if I had not seen this thing with my own eyes, I would not believe it,'' Manuel added. Edward just let out a low whistle of surprise and admiration.

The sorrel's now-docile manner was not the final surprise in store for them, however. As the small mustanger drew nearer, he reached up, pulled off the wide-brimmed sombrero, and shook his head. Thick waves of midnight black hair cascaded down around honey-skinned features.

"She's a girl!" Edward said in amazement.

Amadeo Sigala's grin widened as he said, "*Señores*, allow me to introduce my sister Felipa."

Mordecai, Edward, and Manuel all had the habit of politeness ingrained in them, and they touched the brims of their hats, despite their shock, as they nodded to the young woman, who could not have been more than eighteen years old. Mordecai got over his tongue-tied state enough to say, "It's an honor to meet you, ma'am."

Evidently, Felipa Sigala had little patience for pleasantries. She nodded curtly to them, then took the halter her brother handed to her and slipped it over the sorrel's head. "Here," she said, handing Amadeo the reins. She slipped down from the back of the captured mustang, her movements lithe and graceful. "Take him back to the camp. Papa will be waiting to begin work with him."

"*Sí*," Amadeo nodded, showing no offense at his sister's peremptory tone.

"Wait just a minute!" Mordecai burst out.

Amadeo had been ready to swing the horses around, and Felipa was about to swing up onto the black horse's Mexican saddle with its high cantle and broad-based, flat-topped horn. Both of them tensed as they looked over at Mordecai, who sat on his horse with one hand extended toward them.

"Yes, *señor*?" Amadeo asked. "You have further business with us?"

"Well . . ." Mordecai hesitated, having a hard time putting into words why he had stopped them from leaving and going back to their own base camp. He wasn't sure himself what had motivated his exclamation. But he went on, "We're mustangers too, and I thought . . . well, maybe we could go back to your camp with you and pass the time of day some more, meet the rest of the folks in your bunch. It's sort of lonely down here in this Nueces country."

Amadeo relaxed slightly at his explanation, but Felipa folded her arms across her chest and glared at him with outright suspicion. She said, "If you think to steal the mustangs we have captured, I should warn you. We are a large and well-armed band, and we will not hesitate to kill any foolish *gringo* horse thieves!"

Mordecai just gaped at her while Amadeo scolded, "Felipa! These men have given us no reason to doubt their honor. Have you forgotten how Papa feels about the hospitality of the range?"

"Papa is a good man," she shot back at him, "and like all good men he is sometimes too trusting for his own good."

Manuel edged his horse forward slightly and said, "*Señorita*, my family has lived here in Texas for many, many years. My father Elizandro Zaragosa was an honored soldier and then a successful rancher near San Antonio. My family owns that ranch still. As for my friends here, the Lewises are one of the most respected families in all of Texas, since the time of the empresario Stephen Austin. My late father-in-law was one of the first Anglo settlers, and his brother served as a representative to the Congress of the Republic. What I am telling you, *señorita*, is that we have neither the need nor the desire to steal anything from you and your companions."

Felipa flushed slightly with anger. She jammed her sombrero down on her raven hair and turned back to her horse. "Come with us if you will," she flung over her shoulder. "But if you try anything I will not hesitate to shoot you down myself."

Amadeo looked at them and gave a miniscule shrug, as if to say that he was used to his sister's harsh temper and that there was nothing he could do about it. But he said, "We would be pleased to have you share our camp tonight."

Mordecai nodded. "Thanks. We've got some beans and a little salt pork for the pot. Shot one of those wild hogs a couple of days ago. He's a little stringy but not bad eating."

"Thank you, *señor*. Your contribution will be welcome, as will you yourselves."

Mordecai, Edward, and Manuel fell in alongside Amadeo as they began riding east. Felipa pushed out ahead a little and did not look back at the others. She rode with her back stiff and straight, and Mordecai had seen enough of her outstanding horsemanship earlier to know that such a stance could not be normal for her. If she hadn't been mad, she would have been riding easy in the saddle.

The captured sorrel wasn't as cooperative with Amadeo as it had been with Felipa. It pulled and tugged on the reins and came along only reluctantly. Edward looked back at the sorrel's capering and commented, "If you'd put a rope on that critter and a heavy bit in his mouth and jerk him around a mite, he'd soon get the idea who's boss."

Amadeo shook his head. "If I took a horse back to my father with a bleeding mouth, I would have reason to greatly regret it," he said. "He has taught us to be gentle with animals. That is why we capture them the way we do, rather than roping them."

Mordecai had never heard of such a thing. Mustangs were wild creatures, and as far as he had ever known, treating them roughly was the only way to make them accept the domination of a human. He said, "How can you be gentle with a mustang and still break it?"

Amadeo just smiled at him. "If you stay with us for a time, you shall see for yourself, *amigo*."

He obviously wasn't going to say anything else on the subject, so Mordecai let it drop. He contented himself with watching Felipa ride ahead of them. With her hair tucked up under the hat as it had been earlier, it was easy to understand why they had taken her for a boy. She was slender, and the *chaparejos* and short leather jacket she wore effectively disguised whatever womanly curves she might possess. Mordecai felt his face grow a little hot with embarrassment just from thinking about such things as womanly curves, and he tore his eyes away from the way her pants hugged her rear end as she rode. Looking too closely at somebody's sister was a good way to get some hot-blooded Mexican gunning for you, and he liked Amadeo Sigala and didn't want any trouble with him.

The small group rode for several miles before coming in sight of three tents set up in a grove of oaks near the river. Beyond the tents was a pole corral that looked considerably sturdier than the one Mordecai, Edward, and Manuel had thrown together. Mordecai told himself to take a close look at the corral while they were here, so that maybe he could get some idea of how to improve their own.

It was what was inside the corral that was really impressive, however. At least two dozen mustangs were penned up there, and they began to mill around as the newly captured sorrel called out plaintively to them. As far as Mordecai could see, they were all excellent horses, clean-limbed and strong. Obviously the Sigalas went to some trouble to capture only the best of the numerous herds roaming through the Nueces country.

A man was leaning on the corral fence watching the horses, but as the riders approached he turned and strode out to meet them. While he was doing that, a woman and a girl emerged from one of the tents. Mordecai thought at first that the woman tensed as she looked at them, but then she relaxed when she saw that Amadeo and Felipa were with them. The man and the woman and the child were the only people in sight, and Mordecai had the feeling that this party of mustangers wasn't as large as Felipa had wanted them to believe.

As they reined in, the man walked up to the sorrel, patted it on the flank, and nodded approvingly at Amadeo. He spoke in rapid Spanish, so fast that Mordecai couldn't keep up with all of it. He could tell that the man was complimenting Amadeo on the mustang, though. Amadeo smiled, nodded, and said, "It was Felipa who caught him, just like the others."

"Then I will thank your sister, too," the man said in English. He looked around, but Felipa had already dismounted quickly and vanished into one of the tents. He turned his attention back to the others and asked Amadeo, "And who are your friends?"

"Some other mustangers Felipa and I met while chasing down the band the sorrel was running with," Amadeo explained. "This is Mordecai Lewis, his cousin Edward Lewis, and Manuel Zaragosa." He looked at the three of them and went on, "And this is my father, Ernesto Sigala."

"Welcome to our camp, gentlemen," Ernesto said as he gestured for them to dismount. "Visitors are always welcome at the *casa* of Sigala and, for the moment, these humble tents are our *casa.*"

He shook hands with each of them in turn. Mordecai put his age at around forty, still young enough to be vital, but old enough for his skin to have taken on the qualities of tanned, well-worn leather. His eyes were dark and full of animation over a prominent nose and a thick mustache. He was short in stature, and although the years had thickened his waist somewhat, he was still slender enough to make it clear where Felipa got her petite build.

Ernesto led the visitors over to the woman and the little girl, whom he introduced as his wife Isabel and his younger daughter Anita. Isabel was taller and heavier than her husband, and while she lacked Ernesto's effusive manner, she welcomed the guests politely, especially Manuel, and Mordecai ducked his head to hide a grin as he thought that Manuel had better make it clear that he was already married, otherwise that mama was obviously going to consider him as a potential husband for one of her daughters. For her part, little Anita, who was around twelve years old, seemed quite taken with all of them. Mordecai could understand that; it was probably lonely for a child out here on these chaparral-covered plains.

Felipa reappeared from the tent where she had vanished. She

had taken off her jacket and chaparejos, revealing a bright red silk shirt and a pair of tight black pants, the seat of which Mordecai had already noticed. Again he blushed as that thought came to mind. He resolved to keep his eyes elsewhere instead of on Felipa and the red shirt that revealed she did indeed have some womanly curves, even though they were on the modest side.

"How was the sorrel?" Ernesto asked as she came up to the rest of them.

"Full of spirit, just as you like them, Papa," she answered. "Amadeo can tell you how he fought."

"*Sí*," Amadeo said with a nod.

"*Señor* Sigala," Edward put in, "I hope you don't mind me asking, but where'd your daughter learn to jump from horse to horse like that?"

Ernesto chuckled. "I taught her, just as I learned from my father. For generations now, Sigalas have been working with horses. We have learned how to treat them with gentleness and respect, so that they will be gentle and respect us in turn. For many years I captured mustangs in the manner which you witnessed today, young man, but now these bones are too old and brittle." He slapped his thigh with another chuckle. "And my son took after his mother and grew too tall and sturdy for such things. So now my daughters carry on, while Amadeo and I tend to the rest of the work."

Mordecai smiled down at Anita and asked, "You don't jump from horse to horse, do you?"

"Not yet," the little girl replied. "But Papa is teaching me, and soon I will know how, just like Felipa. Felipa can do anything."

Mordecai recognized the sound of hero worship when he heard it, even when the object of the emotion was an older sister. He turned his smile toward Felipa and said, "I'll just bet she can."

If he was hoping the compliment would thaw her out a little, he was doomed to be disappointed. Felipa was civil but no more, and she virtually ignored the visitors as Ernesto showed them around the camp. Mustanging was a family business for the Sigalas, and all the members of the family were on hand. With Felipa to catch the horses, Ernesto to gentle them, Isabel and Anita to cook and keep the camp in order, and Amadeo to tend to everything else, they were pretty much self-sufficient for long periods at a time, sometimes staying out the entire summer as they captured the best of the mustangs roaming the area. Then the animals were driven up to San Antonio and sold for a good price, good enough to see the Sigalas through the winter and the spring until it was time to go mustanging again.

It sounded like a pretty good arrangement to Mordecai, and he said so that night as the entire group gathered around the Sigalas' campfire and shared the stew, beans, and tortillas that had been prepared by Isabel and Anita. "We haven't had much luck," he went on. "We've got about half a dozen mustangs penned up northwest of here. . . . That is, if they haven't busted out and run off since we left 'em there."

Ernesto shrugged. "You are young yet. This is your first time mustanging, you said?"

"That's right."

"You will learn. I have been searching for the wild horses in this country for many years, as I told you. It takes time to know how to see the mustangs when you think there are none there to be seen."

Manuel leaned forward, a half-eaten tortilla full of beans rolled up in his hand. "*Señor* Sigala, in your travels have you ever seen anything of a white stallion?"

Ernesto smiled, his teeth glittering against his dark-hued features in the firelight. "Ah, the white stallion!" he said. "So his fame has spread all the way to the Colorado River."

"There's a man in Austin who's offering five hundred dollars for him," Mordecai said.

"And the three of you think to earn this reward?" Felipa asked, her tone making it clear she thought that was highly unlikely.

Mordecai grinned a little sheepishly. "I won't lie to you," he said. "The idea crossed our minds. But we really came just to catch as many mustangs as we can and take them back up to Austin. The white stallion would just be something extra."

"Then perhaps you will the ones to finally capture him, my young friends," Ernesto said. "And to answer your question, *Señor* Zaragosa—yes, I have seen the white stallion of which you speak. But from a distance only, mind you. He has always been too wily to let me get near him."

"Then he *does* exist!" Manuel exclaimed. "It is not just a legend."

"No, not a legend . . . at least not a false one. The white stallion lives, and he is even more magnificent than the stories that are told about him. I have never seen a bigger, faster, smarter horse."

Felipa made a face and said, "You speak of him as if he is

something more than a mustang, Papa. Like he is some sort of spirit that can be seen but never touched.''

"No. He is a horse," Ernesto said emphatically. "He can be touched, and he can be caught by the right man—or woman.''

"Then I will catch him," Felipa declared as she lifted a cup of coffee to her lips.

With a smile, Ernesto said, "We will see. I hope you are right, my daughter. We could use that five hundred dollars.''

Mordecai, Edward, and Manuel joined in the laughter of Ernesto and Amadeo, but Felipa just sat there with her lips tightly compressed. She had a lot of anger in her, Mordecai thought, and he couldn't help but wonder why. Seemed to him like she had a good family and a good way of life here, even though the work was hard.

Ernesto insisted that the three visitors spend the night, and they were glad to do so. Mordecai, Edward, and Manuel spread their bedrolls under the oak trees and slept well. The next morning they watched as Ernesto began working with the sorrel Felipa had captured the day before, which Amadeo had roped and led into a smaller pen. Ernesto approached the horse slowly, talking all the time in a soft, soothing voice. The mustang trembled and snorted but stood still as Ernesto eased a rope hackamore over its nose. Then, with a lithe movement that belied his age, the little Mexican vaulted easily onto the mustang's back. That prompted the horse to buck and rear, but Ernesto immediately slipped off its back and started talking again until the sorrel once more grew calm. Then he mounted again, and this time the sorrel stood for a second or two under the man's weight before starting its antics. Ernesto slid down, calmed the horse once more with his voice, and the whole process was repeated over and over.

"Sometimes it takes days before the horses will do more than allow my father to sit on them," Amadeo explained as he stood beside the fence with Mordecai, Edward, and Manuel. "With other horses he is able to ride them in less than a day.''

"Felipa rode that sorrel yesterday, right after she caught it," Edward pointed out.

"Yes, but then he had been running a long way and was tired. Since then he has had the night to rest and grow angry with us for having the audacity to pen him up.''

Mordecai nodded. "I can see how this would be a good way to work the horses, if you've got the touch for it and the time to do it right. You can gentle them down without breaking their spirit.''

"Exactly. My father says a horse without spirit may be fit for plowing, but it is not fit for riding."

The guests spent the morning watching in admiration as both Ernesto and Felipa worked with the horses in the corral. Then, after another savory meal prepared by Isabel and Anita, Mordecai said to Ernesto, "You've made us very welcome, *Señor* Sigala, but I reckon it's time we were moving on. We've got some horses of our own to catch."

"And what will you do with them once you have them?" Ernesto asked, looking at Mordecai intently.

"Well . . . maybe we'll give your way a try. Not the jumping from horse to horse—we'd likely break our necks doing that, so I reckon we'll have to settle for lassoing them—but afterwards, we'll see how your method works."

Ernesto nodded. "I am pleased." He shook hands with all of them, as did Amadeo, then Ernesto added, "And as for that white stallion of which we spoke last night . . . I would look for him south of here, if I were searching for him."

"You know for a fact he's down that way?" Edward asked excitedly.

Ernesto gave an eloquent shrug. "No man can know these things for certain without the evidence of his own eyes—and sometimes even those lie. But for what it is worth . . . I would ride south."

"Then that's what we'll do," Mordecai told him. "*Gracias, Señor* Sigala. Thank you for everything."

"You are welcome in my camp any time, young *amigo*," Ernesto said with a broad grin, then lifted a hand to wave farewell as Mordecai, Edward, and Manuel swung up into their saddles. Anita stood holding her mother's hand nearby, but she waved enthusiastically with her other hand.

Mordecai glanced around the camp. Felipa had gone off somewhere after the meal and had not come back. Mordecai wished she was here so that they could say good-bye to her. Maybe she hadn't been overly friendly during their visit, but he still wanted to see her again.

He couldn't very well wait around for her, though, not without making it look like he was . . . well . . . interested in her, and he didn't want to offend her mama and papa by doing that. They would ride on now, but there was nothing stopping them from coming back this way when they returned to their own base camp in a few days. Maybe by then Felipa would be in a better mood.

"Let's ride, boys," Mordecai said, and as they turned their horses and left the camp, Amadeo called after them, "*Vaya con Dios!*"

Mordecai half turned in the saddle to wave again, and then he saw her, sitting on that big black horse under the trees at the edge of the camp. She was watching them ride away, and her hand started to come up. Then the gesture stopped short, and abruptly she whirled the black and rode around the corral, out of sight.

Well, she had almost waved good-bye to him, Mordecai thought. Give her time. Give her time . . .

☆ **Chapter** ☆

5

"There!" James said, his features and his voice equally grim as he pointed toward the horizon. "That's too much smoke for a cook fire."

Jonathan nodded in agreement as he reined in his horse. Behind the brothers, half a dozen other men also brought their horses to a stop. They wore the same sort of rough range clothes as James and Jonathan, and they were as heavily armed with Paterson Colts, single-shot carbines, and a few of the Colt's revolving rifles. Former Rangers like the Lewis brothers, they were now fellow volunteers in the effort to protect the frontier from the depredations of the Comanches.

James had reined his buckskin to a halt at the crest of a thickly wooded bluff. From this point, he and his companions looked out over the valley formed by a creek that meandered its way south toward the Guadalupe. The San Marcos, where James and Jonathan had found the first evidence of the Comanches' resumption of raiding, was off to the north a good ways.

It was early June, and a hot, sticky haze had settled down over the land. James took off his hat and wiped sweat from the band as he stared with narrowed eyes at the column of smoke rising into the sky some four or five miles away on the other side of the valley.

"That's too far off for us to help those folks," Jonathan said quietly. He added, "If that *is* a cabin burning."

"That's what it is, all right," James declared. "The Comanches

53

have burned out every ranch they've raided so far this summer. They're not going to change now.''

In the six weeks or so since James and Jonathan had found the grisly leavings of the first raid, the Comanches had struck four more times, hitting isolated homesteads scattered across this part of the Republic between Austin and San Antonio on the edge of the rugged, hilly country rising just to the west. Once the Texas volunteers had only heard about the raid from a rider they met. Twice they had found burned-out ruins and fresh graves where neighbors had already buried the slaughtered inhabitants of the ranches. And once they had come upon an atrocity only an hour or so old, with the mutilated bodies of four men lying near the heap of ashes that had recently been a cabin. That time the volunteers had tried to follow the trial of the raiders, but it had petered out in an area of rocky ground and thick underbrush.

James figured the Comanches were running back to the hills after each raid. They might even have a stronghold of sorts back up there in one of those twisting, brush-choked canyons. It would be hell rooting them out of a place like that. He and the men with him would have a better chance if they could catch the raiders out in the open . . . like on the broad plateau on the other side of the valley.

''Come on,'' James called as he sent his buckskin sliding and leaping down the face of the bluff in front of him. ''We're going to catch up to those bastards this time!''

As the men followed him, a few of them let out exuberant whoops. They were glad to finally have a chance to deal out some justice to the savages who had been terrorizing the frontier.

James couldn't bring himself to be happy about the impending conflict. In fact, he hadn't been happy about much of anything since the deaths of Libby and the baby. But he felt a grim satisfaction now that he and the other men might actually have a chance to do some good. Of course, stopping this Comanche war party did not insure that another band of warriors wouldn't ride down out of Comancheria and start the bloody cycle all over again. But at least they could make certain that this particular bunch would never again spill the blood of Texans.

And if he was to fall during the battle . . . well, there were worse things than dying in a good cause, James thought.

James and Jonathan led the men down the bluff into the valley. Their path wound between groves of trees and across open meadows. James kept his eyes open for any sign of an ambush, but he didn't think the Comanches would have come in this direction. After all the other raids, they had immediately headed west, and he was sure that was what they had done this time, too.

A short while later, the volunteers splashed across the shallow, cottonwood-lined creek in the center of the valley, muddying the clear water as the hooves of the horses stirred up the sandy bottom. The Texans charged up the far bank, barely slowing as they threaded their way through the trees. Time was of the essence now, because with each passing second, the Comanches got farther away from the site of their latest atrocity.

Ten minutes after crossing the creek, the Texans pounded up to what had become an all too familiar sight: a ranch house and barn set ablaze, the flames already dying down because the roofs of the buildings had collapsed. The corral poles had been toppled over, the dogs, cattle, chickens, and hogs had been shot, and the horses were gone, stolen by the marauders. The toll in human life was the worst yet, James saw, harsh lines etching themselves deeper into his tanned face as he saw the sprawled bodies. A man, a woman, two boys in their late teens, two girls a little younger, and a boy and a girl around eight or ten. James reined in, rested his hands on his saddle horn, and turned his eyes away from the grisly scene. A couple of the men were retching; all of them had seen violence before, but this was one of the worst instances that they had ever witnessed. James glanced over at Jonathan and saw that his half brother was as white as milk.

Jonathan swallowed hard and said, "Reckon we'd better break out the shovels, huh?"

James shook his head. "We can't bury these folks. Not now, anyway."

"Not bury 'em?" repeated one of the other men in surprise. "You can't mean we're just goin' to leave 'em to rot, Lewis."

"I didn't say that," James grated. "But we can't take the time right now to lay them to rest. I want 'em to have a decent Christian burial as much as the rest of you, but right now we've got to get after those Comanch'."

Jonathan nodded. "You're right. They're gaining ground on us right now while we're sitting here arguing about it, aren't they?"

"Damn right," another man agreed. "We got to be ridin', otherwise them Honey-Eaters are goin' to get away from us."

James heeled his horse into motion again and began riding around the burned-out ranch, his gaze fastened intently on the ground as he searched for the trail. A few minutes later he found the tracks of unshod horses headed west, just as he had supposed. Waving for his companions to follow him, he put his horse into a gallop toward the plateau rising on the far side of the valley.

The trail was fairly easy to follow. It appeared that the raiders had made little, if any, effort to conceal their tracks, and that also followed the pattern of the other attacks. The Comanches rode hell-for-leather for a while, putting as much distance as possible between themselves and their victims, then turned wily and started pulling tricks to throw off any possible pursuers. James wanted to catch them while they were still running, otherwise he and the other men stood a good chance of losing the trail.

The Texans' horses were not fresh, though, and it was impossible to coax any more speed out of them than they were already making. James just had to hope that the Comanches' mounts weren't any more rested.

As the ground began to slope upward toward the plateau, the Texans hit a thick stand of timber, and finding their way through it took valuable time. James's jaw tightened with impatience at the delay. Finally they emerged from the trees and faced a long, fairly open stretch of ground that slanted up for several hundred yards. Although James didn't like to use his spurs on the buckskin, he roweled the horse into a gallop.

Jonathan surged up beside him and grabbed his arm. "Hold it!" the younger man called. "You run these horses up this slope, they'll lose whatever they've got left. We'd better take it easy and save that last burst of speed for later."

What Jonathan was saying made sense, James admitted grudgingly. His impatience to get after the Comanches had almost betrayed him. He pulled his horse back to a walk and nodded his thanks to his half brother. "That's good thinking," he said.

Jonathan grinned at him. "I had a good teacher."

They proceeded slowly up the rise, then when they finally reached the crest and could look out over the broad plateau that stretched for miles to the west, James said, "We won't waste any time, but we can't push the horses too hard, either. We'll ride for fifteen minutes, then walk five."

"Hell, that won't catch up to no Comanch'," complained one of the others.

"It'll keep us on their trail," James shot back. "I've heard tell that's the way they keep their horses going for so long, by walking part of the time. We'll give it a try, too. When we catch sight of them, that'll be the time to make a run at them."

"What if we lose their tracks before then?" asked someone else.

"We won't," James declared emphatically.

He just wished he felt as confident as he sounded.

As it turned out, James was right. He wasn't the tracker that, say, old Abe Goldthwaite was, but his eyes were sharp enough to follow the signs left by the Comanches' flight. The volunteers stopped only when it was too dark to keep trailing their quarry, the sun having set a half hour earlier. But the moon would be rising in a little while, James knew, and it might give enough light to allow them to continue following the trail.

If they could do that, James thought, it would give them an edge and let them close the gap between them and the Comanches, because the Indians had undoubtedly halted for the night, thinking themselves safe from pursuit in this vast wilderness.

"No fire," James warned the men rather unnecessarily; all of them knew how far flames could be seen at night out here on the prairie. "We'll eat a cold supper and rest a little while, then get after them again when the moon comes up."

"How far you intend to chase these here savages, Lewis?" asked the man who had done most of the complaining during the day. His name was Gilliam, and while he was a former Ranger like the others and as good a man as any in a fight, he was known to be short-tempered and surly most of the time. This evening was no exception, as he went on, "We're already way the hell out and gone from civilization."

"Can't catch a Comanche in the middle of town," James pointed out, "especially not since the Council House Fight."

"Well, I don't much like this," Gilliam said. "You been givin' orders like you're some sort o' big muckety-muck. Hell, we ain't even Rangers no more. We're all volunteers, all equal."

James felt himself tensing and tightened the reins on his own anger. Slapping down Gilliam wouldn't do any good. They needed to be devoting their energies to their common enemy, the Comanches.

"Look, Gilliam," he said quietly, "I'm not trying to take over. If you don't like what we're doing, you're welcome to head back home. I won't stop you."

In the thick darkness, it was practically impossible to see Gilliam's face, but his voice had a worried whine in it as he said, "By my lonesome, you mean?"

James shrugged. ''Anybody who wants to go back is welcome to. I don't reckon you'll have much company, though.''

Gilliam turned to the other men and said, ''Fellas?''

Stony silence was the only thing that answered him. Nearly all of these men had lost friends or relatives to Indian raids. They were not just about to turn back now.

''Well, hell,'' Gilliam muttered. ''If you feel that way about it, I reckon I'll stick around and fight them redskins with you.''

James clapped a hand on his shoulder. ''Thanks. I figured you'd feel that way once you thought about it.''

Jonathan sidled up to him a few minutes later and said quietly, ''Maybe you should've been the politician in the family instead of ol' Andrew.''

With a quick shake of his head, James said, ''No thanks. I can generally talk sense to an honest man, even if he is stubborn and wrongheaded most of the time. I don't reckon politicians would pay any attention to me, though.''

The men gnawed jerky and corn bread that had gotten almost as hard as a rock, washing down the unappealing mixture with water from their canteens. Then, as the moon slid over the horizon and began to climb in the eastern sky, they mounted up again and started off once more on the trail of the raiders. They traveled more slowly now that James had to find the tracks in the silvery illumination washing down over the Texas prairie from the three-quarter moon.

Several times during the night, James had to get off his horse and kneel on the ground as he searched for the trail. On each occasion, he located it again when he had thought it was lost, but a fine sweat had popped out on his forehead that had nothing to do with the muggy warmth of the night. One of these times, he thought, the trail was really going to be gone, and then they would have no choice but to turn around and go home, having once again failed in their quest to find the savage marauders.

But as the moon lowered in the west and the eastern sky began to take on a gray tinge that heralded the oncoming dawn, James crouched beside another set of tracks and reached down to let his fingers gently brush the indentation in the earth. Feeling excitement start to hammer through him, he looked up and said softly, ''Take a look at this, Jonathan.''

''A look at what?'' Jonathan asked as he climbed down from his horse. ''I can barely see those tracks, James, and I'm not sure how you can.''

"Touch the edges of them," James told him.

Jonathan knelt and did as James had requested. His breath hissed between his teeth, and after a moment he said, "The edges are still packed pretty tight, and so's the dirt in the prints themselves. How far ahead of us do you think they are?"

"An hour," James replied grimly. "Maybe."

The other men heard the exchange, and one of them asked excitedly, "What do we do now?"

James straightened and swung up into his saddle, motioning to Jonathan to do likewise. "We'll ride on a little ways," James said, "but it'll soon be too dark to see anything for a while. We'll have to stop then, until there's a little more daylight. Then we'll keep following the trail. With any luck, we'll come up on those Comanches before they're wide awake."

It was a chance, a good chance at last, James thought as he waved the men forward. The Comanches were cunning fighters and probably the most dangerous enemies James had ever faced, but they thought of themselves as lords of these plains and sometimes got overconfident, especially where white men were concerned. To a Comanche, the very idea that a white man could be just as good a tracker, fighter, or horseman was ludicrous.

This was one time their overconfidence was going to be fatal, James hoped.

Shortly after that, the moon set and utter darkness closed in, just as James had expected. The lightening of the eastern sky earlier had been only a false dawn, and the Texans waited impatiently, standing beside their horses and holding the reins, until the red-hued real thing began to come along. When it was barely light enough for them to see again, James ordered the men into their saddles and said in a soft voice, "We'll have to be quiet from here on out. Sound can travel a long way out here."

There was a faint stirring of the air as the men set out on the trail again. The movement was hardly enough to be called a breeze, and it was by no stretch of the imagination cool, but even the faintest relief from the sticky heat of the night was welcome. James took off his hat and rode holding it beside the saddle horn, letting the whisper of air play over his face.

Another hot one was on the way, he thought, but with any luck, the fighting would be over before the sun had risen very far into the sky. One way or another. . . .

Twenty minutes later, he held up a hand to stop the other men. Something else had just drifted to him along with that sluggish breeze from the west, and what he smelled made him frown and lean forward in the saddle. Turning to Jonathan, he said in a voice that was little more than a whisper, "Do you smell that?"

Jonathan inhaled deeply, and in the growing light of dawn, James could see a matching frown appear on his brother's face. "That isn't . . ." Jonathan began. "It can't be . . . That isn't *coffee* I smell, is it?"

"That's what I think it is," James said.

"Well, then," Jonathan said, "those must be white men ahead of us. I never heard of Comanches drinking coffee."

There was a faint murmur from the other men, and several of them started to relax and exchange nervous laughs at the news that they had accidentally been following a band of white men. Gilliam said, "Their trail must've crossed the one them Comanch' left, and we got confused."

James whipped around abruptly in the saddle and hissed, "Shut up!" His mind was spinning crazily, trying to make some sense of this. He *knew* he hadn't gotten mixed up about which tracks he had been following all night. The trail they were on now was the same one that had begun at that burned-out ranch. And the tracks were the marks of unshod Indian ponies; he was equally certain of that. Maybe some of the Comanches *had* taken to drinking coffee. That would explain the smell that was becoming stronger as the wind freshened a little.

But suddenly his mind was going back, sifting through old memories until he reached the day he and Jonathan had found the scene of the first raid. The scene was still vivid, burned into his brain by the horror of it. He could see the piece of cheap but pretty jewelry Jonathan had found, and the brightly colored shirts strewn around the place, and the beaver top hat some settler had brought with him from back east . . .

"Son of a bitch," James breathed, the awful implications sinking in on his stunned brain.

"What is it?" Jonathan asked, reaching out to put a hand on James's arm.

James shook free of him and said, "We're going on, slow and easy and quiet. I don't want those bastards to know we're coming."

"I don't understand," Jonathan said. "If they're white men—"

Between gritted teeth, James said, "The fact they're white doesn't mean they haven't been raiding those ranches. Think about it, Jonathan! If you wanted to steal a bunch of horses and loot some homesteads, what better way to do it than to make it look like the Comanches are responsible?''

"But . . . but that's crazy!'' The other men muttered agreement with Jonathan's protest.

James gripped his brother's arm tightly. "Think back. Would a Comanche brave have left that necklace you found? What about those shirts and that top hat? You know how they like to take their victims' clothes and parade around in them! I knew something was wrong when I saw that, but I never could figure out what it was until now. Comanches would have taken those things—but they'd be just worthless junk to white men.''

"Oh, my God,'' Jonathan said, horror and amazement on his face. "You're right.''

James said, "Doesn't matter if they're red renegades or white. They're still a bunch of murdering savages, and I mean to see justice done. Come on if you're going with me.'' He put his horse into a careful walk, heading toward the source of the coffee smell that had finally enabled him to figure out the cold-blooded scheme.

One by one, led by Jonathan, the other men fell in line behind him.

Ten minutes later, James crawled forward on his belly and cautiously eased aside some of the undergrowth through which he had been making his tortuous way. He was in one of those brush-choked gullies so common to this part of the country and, just as he had thought earlier, the raiders did have a hideout here. He could see them some thirty yards ahead of him where the gully widened out and became a flat-bottomed wash. They were gathered around a small camp fire that would not have been visible more than a hundred yards away. The smell from the coffeepot bubbling at the edge of the flames had traveled quite a bit farther than that, however, and that was what had given them away.

They were white, all right, fifteen men who all looked rough as a cob in the growing light. Some of them wore the clothes of the farmers they had once no doubt been, while others were dressed in buckskins. All of them were well armed. A rope corral had been strung up farther down the wash to hold the Indian ponies that grazed there. Where the raiders had gotten hold of ponies like that, James didn't know, but the question wasn't really important. What mattered was that the men talking, laughing, and passing a bottle of whiskey back and forth to spike their morning coffee had casually slaughtered a couple of dozen innocent Texans, all in the name of greed.

James felt himself trembling, and it was all he could do not to burst up out of the brush and empty his Colt at them as he shouted out his rage. That would just get him killed in a hurry, though, and he couldn't hope to down more than a couple of them in the process. The odds against him and his companions were already bad enough. He had to hang on and control himself.

He started backtracking the way he had come, working his way along the sandy bottom of the gully until he was well out of sight of the camp. Then he stood up and made his way in a crouch back to the spot where Jonathan and the others were waiting. When he got there, they crowded around him asking anxious questions, and he quickly told them what his scouting trip had uncovered.

"How are we going to take 'em?" Jonathan asked.

"The horses are the key," James said. "Two men will sneak around on the far side of that rope corral and stampede the ponies back through the camp. The rest of us will be up on the rim, and we'll open fire while the bastards are scattered and confused."

"They won't have much of a chance," someone muttered.

"More'n they deserve," James replied sharply. "Don't forget how many innocent folks they've killed."

"You're right, James," Jonathan said. "Who's going after the horses?"

Without hesitation, James said, "You and Gilliam."

He halfway expected Gilliam to complain about the assignment out of habit, but the man just nodded grimly. The time for a little good-natured bitching and moaning was over, and they all knew it.

Jonathan and Gilliam slipped away from the group first after checking their guns. In one way, their job might be safer, because they would have the horses between them and the renegades most of the time. But once the stampede was over, the two of them would be down there on the floor of the wash with their enemies, while the other volunteers would at least have the advantage of high ground.

James warned, "No more talking," then led his men toward the camp. He and Jonathan had already decided how the attack would proceed. Jonathan and Gilliam would give the others about five minutes to get into position, then start firing their guns to stampede the horses. If James and his men weren't where they were supposed to be, Jonathan and Gilliam would be left pretty much high and dry and in deep trouble. But James didn't anticipate any problems reaching the gully in time to start the attack in concert with the stampede.

He was right about that, but he didn't anticipate what actually happened. He and the other volunteers climbed quickly onto the slope that rose above the rim of the wash, then angled their way down toward the camp, using the thick brush on the hillside for cover. He hoped none of the horses caught the scent of strange men and started raising a ruckus, at least not until it was too late to do anything about it. But as he came to a stop behind a small outcrop of rock and slipped his gun from its holster, he heard a yell of alarm from down below.

"Hey! There's somebody over there on the other side of the horses!"

Damn! Jonathan and Gilliam had been spotted. James pushed out from behind the rocks as a gun blasted down in the wash. More shots thundered through the dawn, and James heard Jonathan's voice shouting at the horses. The Indian ponies surged forward against the rope corral, just as James had planned, and the flimsy enclosure was no match for the strength of the frenzied animals. They burst though it and pounded down the wash toward the camp. Renegades howled curses and leaped to get out of the way.

James pulled back the hammer of the Paterson Colt, lined his sights on one of the scurrying killers, and lifted his thumb. The Colt boomed and bucked against his palm, and through the sudden haze of smoke that had erupted from the barrel, he saw his target spin around from the impact of the .36 caliber ball. Before the man even hit the ground, James had shifted his aim and fired again.

All along the rim of the gully, James and his five companions poured lead down on the renegades. Jonathan and Gilliam charged forward through the remains of the corral and added their fire. The raiders were not going to go down easily, though. Some of them were already fighting back, and James heard the familiar whine of shots ricocheting off the rocks around him.

A ball tugged at his sleeve, and another just missed the side of his thigh. He fired the fifth and final shot from his right-hand gun, then traded it for the one on his left hip and slid down the side of the gully, his boots thudding solidly against the bottom as he landed. One of the renegades loomed up right in front of him, and James shot the man in the throat, the blast practically separating his head from his body at this close range. James leaped over the twitching corpse and then twisted to avoid a man who lunged at him swinging a tomahawk. White or not, the raiders had armed themselves with some Indian weapons, too, so that they could leave convincing injuries behind on the bodies of their victims. James lashed out and slammed the barrel of his gun against the skull of the man with the tomahawk, feeling a satisfying crunch as the skull gave way.

The other volunteers were leaping down into the gully now, carrying the fight to their enemies. James heard Gilliam shouting about something, and then the man ran up to him out of the cloud of dust and powder smoke that filled the air. Gilliam started to say something, but he staggered back a step as an arrow thudded into his chest.

James spun around and saw the man a few yards away fumbling to get another arrow from a rawhide quiver and fit it to his bow. The killer was a lot more awkward and slower than a Comanche would have been in the same situation, and James had plenty of time to shoot him before he could loose another shaft.

There were just three shots left now in his gun, so he picked his targets carefully. He led a man running across the gully and then squeezed the trigger, and the man flipped backward like he had just smashed into an invisible wall. Then James heard Jonathan bellowing, "Hold your fire! They're all done for! Hold your fire!"

James gulped down a deep breath of air laced with acrid gunsmoke. His pulse was hammering in his head, and he slowly became aware of an ache in his left arm. He looked down and saw that his sleeve was bloody. Sometime during the fighting a ball had creased him, and in his runaway rage he hadn't even noticed the wound.

He turned and knelt beside Gilliam, but it was too late to do anything for him. His eyes were staring sightlessly up at the sky, and he would never complain about anything again.

James stood up and sighed, then turned around to see if anyone else in his party had been killed.

As it turned out, Gilliam was the only fatality, although several other men were wounded, mostly just creased like James. One man had a broken arm, though, where a ball had shattered the bone. Jonathan patched him up as best he could and, with luck, the man would make it back home without losing the arm, although it would probably never be much good to him again.

Farther up in the hills, where the gully turned into a canyon, they found a sturdier corral where several dozen horses were being kept. These were not Indian ponies, but rather the horses that had been stolen from the ranches hit by the renegades. As some of the other volunteers rounded up the animals and drove them out of the corral, Jonathan asked James, "What do you reckon they were going to do with them?"

"Trade them with the Comanches, maybe," James said with a shrug. "Either that or push them down to San Antone or Galveston and sell them there. They'd've wound up clearing a nice profit."

"But they were *white*," Jonathan protested. "They were just like us. How could they have killed all those folks, just to steal some horses? I could understand it if they'd been Indians, like we thought, but this . . ." Jonathan shook his head. "This just doesn't make any sense."

James flexed his left arm, which was tightly wrapped with bandages. "They weren't like us," he said. "They were cold-blooded bastards, a hell of a lot more evil than the Comanches. I reckon the Indians at least think they're fighting for what's theirs by right, whether we agree with 'em or not. But these gents . . ." James gestured at the bodies which still lay sprawled where they had fallen. "They're just vultures. And I'm afraid we'll see a lot more of 'em just like these as time goes on."

Jonathan grimaced. "I hope not. Bad enough we've got to fight the Comanches without worrying about white men, too."

"Well, we'll see what happens. Right now, let's go home."

They buried Gilliam's body and said some words over him. Then, driving the recovered horses in front of them, the Texans headed east, away from the gully and toward the fringes of what passed for civilization out here.

They left the bodies of the renegades behind them for the carrion birds, which circled lazily in the sky and then began to dip lower and lower as the survivors rode away.

Mordecai leaned far forward in the saddle, swinging the rawhide reata over his head as he urged more speed out of his own horse and closed in on the mustang he had picked out from the herd. It was a long-legged dun, somewhat similar to the rangy line-back mount that Mordecai rode. Using his spurs judiciously, Mordecai sent his horse galloping up alongside the wild mare and held his breath as he made his cast.

The loop in the reata snapped open as it sailed through the air and fell unerringly over the head of the speeding mustang. Mordecai felt a surge of relief that his throw had been true. He whipped a dally around the horn, making sure his thumb was clear before he pressed down on the stirrups with his feet and hauled back on the reins. Nothing could yank a man's thumb off quicker than getting it caught between the dally and the horn when the weight of the captured mustang hit the rope.

Mordecai had perfected his technique during the time he and his companions had been down here mustanging, and his horse knew what was expected of it, too. Bracing its legs, the horse slid to a stop. The mustang raced on for another second or two, and then it reached the end of the reata. With a twang that could be heard even over the thundering hooves of the other mustangs, the rawhide rope went taut, and the mustang at the other end of it suddenly pinwheeled through the air to come to a crashing halt.

Mordecai slipped from the saddle to the ground and ran toward the mustang, leaving his horse behind him to keep the tension on the rope. Being careful to avoid the wild horse's flailing hooves and nipping teeth, Mordecai fastened a blindfold around the animal's eyes. The shock of being jerked off its feet, plus the sudden darkness that enveloped it, had the horse too confused and weary to keep fighting. Snorting angrily, it lay still except for a trembling that ran though its limbs.

On the other side of the herd, Edward and Manuel were supposed to be doing the same thing as Mordecai had just done, but he couldn't see them because of all the dust in the air. Each of the young men had picked out one of the mustangs to center in on, however, and then the chase had begun.

As if their visit to the Sigalas' camp had been a good omen, their luck had changed almost immediately. Late that afternoon, they had run into a good-sized bunch of mustangs and had captured six of them, equaling the number they had left upriver at their base camp. The next day had seen them dab a loop on four more, then had come the best day of all—ten mustangs caught, giving them a total of twenty, which was about all the three of them could handle easily. The pickings had been too good down here to turn and head north again, though, especially since they hadn't spotted the white stallion yet.

So they had agreed to stay another day, and this morning had scared up yet another band of wild horses, the finest yet. Now, as the herd moved on and the dust began to blow away, Mordecai saw that Edward and Manuel had both been successful in their efforts. They were riding toward him, each of them leading a recalcitrant mustang behind their saddle horses. The rawhide reatas with which they had caught the mustangs had been replaced by grass ropes woven from maguey fibers. Reatas were more durable, but they would break under a great enough strain; ropes made from the tough fibers of the maguey plant would hold up to almost anything. Mustangers generally used the reatas for catching the wild horses and grass ropes for leading them once they were caught.

Mordecai took care of that now, fetching the grass rope from his saddle and slipping it over the mustang's head before releasing the reata. Then he unfastened the blindfold and stepped back quickly as the mustang scrambled to its feet. Its wild-eyed gaze jerked around, then it lunged away from him, intent on running. Mordecai's saddle horse was still standing with its legs braced, however, and once again the mustang flipped and crashed to the ground as the slack in the rope ran out.

Mordecai stayed well back and let the mustang get to its feet again. Then he went to his horse and stepped up into the saddle. As he rode to meet Edward and Manuel, the rope tightened on the mustang's throat, and it had no choice but to go along with him.

"An excellent catch," Manuel called out, gesturing at the mustang Mordecai had captured.

"So's yours," Mordecai said. "This was a good bunch. I hope we can get some more of them after they tire out." The three young men swung their horses side by side and headed back toward their temporary camp. Mordecai went on, "Did either of you ever get a look at the leader of that herd?"

Manuel shook his head, and Edward said, "Nope. Why? Was he something special, Mordecai?"

With a slight frown, Mordecai replied, "I didn't see him, either. They all took off running so fast when we came up on them, I never worked my way far enough forward to spot the leader. He's got himself quite a bunch of mares, though."

Manuel looked over at him. "You are thinking that such a fine herd must have an equally fine leader?"

"The thought crossed my mind," admitted Mordecai.

"Like, perhaps, the white stallion?"

Mordecai grinned. "I haven't given up on finding him. I reckon he's around here some—"

With a sudden flurry of hoofbeats, a white streak flew up out of a small gully the three young men were riding past. Mordecai broke off his sentence and let out a startled yell. The huge white horse rammed into his dun, and he felt himself falling as his mount staggered and went out from under him.

"Look out!" Manuel cried.

Mordecai hit the ground hard, his hat flying off and the breath puffing from his lungs. He rolled over a couple of times, gasping, and then came up on his hands and knees in time to see the fearsome apparition looming over him. Hooves that looked razor sharp lashed out at his head. He yelped in alarm and dove to one side, barely avoiding the slashing hooves.

"Get out of there, Mordecai!" Edward screamed at him.

Mordecai scrambled to his feet as the white stallion lunged at him again. He darted away from the big mustang's attack. The stallion was between him and his own horse, which was just now regaining its feet. Mordecai turned and sprinted toward Manuel's horse. Manuel held down a hand to help him, urging him on.

Clasping his brother-in-law's outstretched hand, Mordecai swung up behind Manuel. As he did so, the stallion thundered past again, making Manuel's horse shy frantically away from it. Mordecai and Manuel stayed on the horse, but only barely.

Edward spurred his mount toward the stallion, shouting and swinging his coiled reata. It was a brave move, meant to draw the stallion's fury away from Mordecai and Manuel, but it was also dangerous. "Look out, Edward!" Mordecai called to him. "He's too fast!"

Indeed, the stallion had whirled around and was meeting Edward's charge with one of his own. Edward hauled back on the reins and jerked his mount aside just in time to avoid the collision. As the stallion raced past, he leaned his head down and got the grass rope in his teeth. It parted under the strength of those massive jaws, and the mare Edward had caught was suddenly free.

"Watch it!" Edward shouted. "He's coming back around!"

There was so much dust in the air now it was hard to see. The stallion darted here and there, a blur of white as it fought to free the other two mustangs. Mordecai's horse was still loose, and it was only a matter of moments for the stallion to bite through that rope and free the dun Mordecai had captured earlier. Then the stallion turned its attention toward Manuel.

"I'll stop him," Manuel said angrily as he slipped his carbine from its sheath. Mordecai leaned past him and caught the barrel of the weapon.

"No!" Mordecai said. "You can't do that. He deserves better than to be shot down. Besides, he's worth five hundred dollars!"

Manuel nodded, looking shocked at himself for even thinking such a thing. He said to Mordecai, "Use my reata! I'll try to get close enough!"

Suddenly, the stallion looped behind them, and with a groan Mordecai saw the third rope part under the teeth of the huge animal. Their whole morning's work was now gone. But if they could catch the white stallion, that would make everything all right again. He shook out a loop in the reata as Manuel spurred his horse toward the stallion.

"Now!" Manuel cried.

Mordecai let fly with the reata, and it was as good a cast as he'd ever made. The loop settled cleanly and firmly over the stallion's neck. The stallion didn't even seem to notice it. With his goal—the freedom of the three mares—achieved, all he wanted to do now was get out of here.

"He's taking off fast!" Mordecai warned. "Get that thing dallied!"

Manuel took a turn around the horn with the reata, then reined in his horse and called for it to stand. The horse obeyed, and Mordecai was glad it was carrying double now. They would need all the weight they could get on their side if they were going to stop the white stallion.

The stallion was galloping full-out as it reached the end of the reata's slack. There was an incredible tug on the reata as it went tight, and Manuel's horse lurched forward a step or two. Then with a sound like the crack of a whip, the reata parted. What was left of it snapped back and coiled around the prancing feet of Manuel's horse like a hissing snake.

The white stallion kept going, trailing two or three feet of reata from its neck, never slowing down as it followed in the wake of the mares it had just rescued.

"Damn!" Mordecai uttered the heartfelt curse as he slipped down from behind Manuel's saddle. The stallion was going so fast it was already just about out of sight. "We had him!"

"No, my friend," Manuel said, shaking his head ruefully. "For an instant there, *he* had *us*. And then he threw us back, like a man would a fish that is too small."

Edward rode up beside them, his face full of sweat, dust, and excitement, and he waved toward the vanishing stallion. "Aren't we going after him?"

For a long moment, neither Mordecai nor Manuel said anything, then Mordecai began slowly shaking his head. "You saw him," he said. "You think a thing like that belongs in Austin, all his pride and spirit gone, just some play-pretty for that doctor fella to show off?"

"That would never happen," Manuel said. "Such a horse would never be tamed. Before he would allow such a fate to befall him, he would simply lie down and die. This I know."

"So we're letting him go, with those mares he stole from us?" Edward demanded.

"He didn't steal 'em," Mordecai said, "just set 'em free again." He bent over, picked up his hat, and slapped it against his leg to get some of the dust off of it. "And as far as I'm concerned, now that I've seen him, I don't want to catch him anymore. He's meant to be roaming free out here."

"That gal Felipa would go after him if she was here," Edward said.

"Maybe she would," Mordecai said with a shrug. "But don't be so sure about that." He went over to his horse, coiled what was left of his grass rope and put it away. "I guess we got too greedy, and it almost did us in. Maybe we'd better take the mustangs we've got and start back north again, pick up those others we left behind. Twenty-six is a good-sized herd."

"*Sí*," Manuel agreed. "I think I have seen enough of this country now."

Edward just stared at both of them for a moment, then shook his head in disbelief. "I'll swan, I don't know what's come over you fellas. We came down here to catch mustangs, and now you two act like that white stallion's got you spooked. Hell, he's just a horse!"

Mordecai remembered how big and fast and smart the stallion had been, how he had come damn close to losing his life to the big white brute, and he said dryly, "Yep, he's just a horse. But I'm going home anyway."

With that, he put his horse into a walk, and Manuel followed silently, his face solemn.

After a few seconds, so did Edward.

By late afternoon, Edward seemed to have gotten over his anger at Mordecai and Manuel for calling an end to the horse-hunting expedition. At least he acted like he was in a much better mood, talking about how the folks back home wouldn't believe them when they told the story of how the white stallion had stolen back the mares. Mordecai and Manuel let him go on, the two of them riding in silence for the most part.

The mustangs they had left in camp that morning were still safely behind the poles of the corral. Mordecai had been half afraid that the white stallion would circle around and free those horses, too, just to get revenge on the three humans for having the temerity to put a rope on him. But evidently nothing had been disturbed at the camp. Come morning, they would start north again.

One of the most important things a man could learn out here on the frontier was when not to push his luck, Mordecai thought. And he and Manuel both agreed that time had come.

The night passed quietly, and the three men were up early the next morning, getting ready to move on. There had been no time to even start the process of gentling the captive mustangs, but when the horses were roped together, they could be pushed along in a group. The feel of the rope and the unfamiliarity of the situation kept them from bolting. Mordecai, Manuel, and Edward spread out, two on the flanks and one in the rear of the herd, alternating positions so that nobody had to breathe trail dust for too long at a time. They covered quite a bit of ground during the morning, then stopped for a short lunch and to let the horses rest and graze.

"Are we going to stop at the Sigalas' place again?" Edward asked as they sat under the shade of a scrubby live oak. There was a sly grin on his face as he looked at Mordecai.

"We'll see," Mordecai answered, trying not to scowl as he felt his features coloring again. Damn, he wished his reaction to the thought of seeing Felipa again wasn't so obvious! Both Edward and Manuel seemed to know everything that was going through his head right about now.

"I would like to visit them again," Manuel said. "*Señora* Sigala is a very good cook."

"That ain't why Mordecai wants to stop," Edward gibed.

"Why don't you mind your own business?" Mordecai said. "Like watering those horses."

"Sure, cousin," Edward said, grinning as he got to his feet.

Mordecai was glad when they got started again. And he made sure that Edward was riding behind the herd again, just as he had been when they stopped. Maybe an extra dose of trail dust would make Edward think twice about making fun of his elders, Mordecai told himself, then grinned sheepishly at the thought. Edward had only been funning, after all, and Mordecai would take a double turn later, to make up for sticking the youngster back there again.

After another couple of hours under the hot, unforgiving sky, Mordecai was wishing they'd stayed back there in the shade and waited for evening to push on. He took off his hat, wiped the sweat from his face, then looked up ahead of them. Some dust caught his eye, and he frowned as he settled his hat on his head again. With the brim to shade his eyes, he could make out what he was seeing even more clearly. Somebody was driving another big bunch of horses toward them.

Manuel had seen the telltale signs, too, and he galloped over to Mordecai's position. "Can you tell who that is?" he asked. "Perhaps old Ernesto and his family are moving south."

Mordecai wished he had a spyglass; then he could tell for sure who the men driving the mustangs before them were. He squinted, peering through the dust and heat haze, and said, "I don't think it's the Sigalas. There's too many of them. Look, there must be seven or eight men.''

He was right, and the other herd was close enough now for Manuel to see that as well. With an uneasy tone in his voice, Manuel said, ''Perhaps we should move aside and let those men bring their horses through here. I do not want to meet them head on.''

''Neither do I,'' Mordecai said. He waved to Edward to start their mustangs veering toward the west. It would be a good idea to get some distance between the two herds of wild horses before they passed.

When they had angled to the west a few hundred yards, Mordecai, Manuel, and Edward turned the horses north again. The men driving the other bunch must have seen their dust by now, just as Mordecai and Manuel had seen the cloud kicked up by the hooves of the southbound herd. The larger group drove straight on, though. They seemed to be in a greater hurry than Mordecai and his companions. As the herds passed each other with some two hundred yards of prairie between them, Mordecai paused and turned in his saddle for a good look at the other men. He couldn't tell much about them at this distance, but they were Mexicans, he was sure of that. Their swarthy faces and broad-brimmed, high-crowned sombreros were proof enough of that.

Manuel was closer to them, and when they had passed, he rode over to Mordecai and said, ''I did not like the looks of those *hombres*. They rode like men accustomed to pursuit.''

''Like they might be outlaws, you mean.''

''That is right. And something else I noticed . . .'' Manuel hesitated, as if he was not sure whether he should go on or keep silent.

''Well, spit it out,'' Mordecai said impatiently.

''I could not tell for sure . . . because of the dust and the distance, you understand . . . but in that bunch of horses they were driving, I thought I saw a pretty sorrel—and a big black gelding.''

Mordecai blinked in surprise. ''Like the one Felipa was riding?'' he asked.

''Yes. I cannot be sure it was the same horse, or that the sorrel was the one we saw her leap upon . . . but it could have been.''

Edward had brought their own mustangs to a halt and trotted his horse over to listen to the conversation. He got there in time to hear what Manuel was saying, and he asked, ''But why would the

Sigalas get rid of Felipa's horse? Looked like a mighty fine one to me.''

"It was," Mordecai said grimly. "And I don't reckon they'd give it up of their own accord."

"You think those men were horse thieves?" asked Manuel.

"I don't know, but I'll be glad when we get back to Ernesto's camp, so we can see whether or not everything's all right."

"I'm sure it will be," Edward said in an obvious effort to be optimistic.

Manuel rubbed his jaw in thought, then said, "If those men were thieves, they may covet our horses, too."

Mordecai nodded. "I intend to sleep mighty light tonight. They could be planning to leave those mustangs with one or two men, then the rest of them double back and jump us. I reckon if they thought they could gun us down without much trouble, they'd like to get their hands on these mustangs."

"If they try, they will have an unpleasant surprise waiting for them," Manuel vowed.

The three of them were the ones who were in for a surprise, however. It showed up about an hour later as they hurried on, Mordecai setting a quicker pace now that he was anxious to reach the spot where the Sigala family had been camped. He pulled back abruptly on the reins as he spotted a single rider coming toward them.

"Who the hell's that?" he called to Manuel, lifting an arm to point.

The figure on horseback was moving rather erratically, but there was something familiar about it to Mordecai. Suddenly, with a jolt like he had just been hit by lightning, he knew where he had seen that rider before.

It was Felipa.

And as he watched in horror, she abruptly sagged to the side, slipped from the back of the horse, and fell to the ground.

"*Felipa!*" Mordecai cried as he spurred his horse into a run. Faintly, he heard the hoofbeats of Manuel's mount as his brother-in-law followed him, but he paid no attention to that. All of his thoughts were focused on the small, still form lying motionless on the ground ahead of him.

Mordecai hauled his horse to a stop and was out of the saddle and running over to Felipa even before the dust started to settle. As he dropped to a knee beside her, he desperately searched her face for signs of life. She was lying on her left side, with that arm trapped awkwardly beneath her. The right side of her face had a large smear of dried blood on it. Gingerly, and with as much fear as if he had been about to pet a rattlesnake, Mordecai reached out and touched her head just above the hairline, where the bloodstain seemed to originate. He found a raised welt a couple of inches long, the top of which was covered with crusted blood. Felipa had a bullet crease there on the side of her head, but such wounds were rarely fatal. In fact, when he touched it, she let out a low moan and shifted a little on the sand without opening her eyes.

"How is she?" Manuel asked as he leaned over Felipa from the other side. Mordecai hadn't even noticed him riding up, so intent was he on the injured girl.

"I think she'll be all right," he said. He looked her over, feeling no embarrassment now in his scrutiny of her body. There was no time to worry about such things. What mattered was that as far as he could determine, she didn't have any other wounds.

Edward rode up, leading the scrubby mustang which Felipa had been riding. He called out to Mordecai and Manuel, asking how Felipa was. Mordecai ignored the question for the moment and got his arms under her body, one arm at the knees, one at the shoulders. He straightened, shaking his head when Manuel started to reach out and help. "I've got her," he said.

She seemed light, too light, like part of her wasn't there anymore. The thought scared Mordecai, and his heart was pounding heavily from more than the effort of carrying her as he went over to his horse. With Manuel's help, he got mounted and put Felipa on the horse in front of him, holding her on with one arm firmly around her waist.

"Let's find a good place to camp," Mordecai said, his tone making it clear that he wasn't going to put up with any arguments.

Edward added the mustang Felipa had been riding bareback to their own herd, then he and Manuel got the wild horses moving again while Mordecai rode on in front. Fifteen minutes later, they found a good-sized clearing in a veritable forest of mesquite trees, none of which were more than six feet tall. The mesquites would offer some shade from the late afternoon sun, however, and there was even a water hole in the clearing, a little basin in the rock where a tiny spring bubbled out. Mordecai waited until Manuel caught up to give him a hand, and between the two of them they got Felipa stretched out in the shade, her head pillowed on a rolled-up blanket.

While Manuel went to help Edward with the horses, Mordecai

got a tin cup from his saddlebags and filled it with cool, clear water at the spring. He knelt beside the unconscious girl and forced some of the water between her lips, which he noticed were dry and cracked, as if she had been out in the hot sun for a long time with nothing to drink. She sputtered and choked, but she swallowed some of the water. Mordecai wet his fingers with what was left in the tin cup and wiped her face, leaving streaks in the dust until he got most of it cleaned away.

Felipa's eyelids were fluttering now, and after a moment she opened them to stare up at him. For a second, there was no comprehension or recognition in her gaze, just fear. Her eyes widened, and she took a great, gasping breath, coming up off the ground a little. Then she settled back, blinked a couple of times, and said in a hoarse, rasping voice, "M—Mordecai Lewis?"

"That's right," Mordecai told her, trying to keep his own voice quiet and reassuring. "You're all right, Felipa. We'll take good care of you until we get you back to your folks."

It was the wrong thing to say, and Mordecai knew it as soon as the words were out of his mouth. Felipa wouldn't have been out here by herself if she had any family to take care of her. Her face twisted, and she rolled onto her side and hunched up a little, as if she had the world's worst bellyache. It was the pain of memory, Mordecai figured, and a moment later she confirmed the guess by saying, "My parents are dead. My brother and my sister are dead, too. I am the only one left, and those *cabrones* would have killed me, too, had they not thought I was already dead."

Her voice got colder and calmer as she spoke, as if she was forcing all the hurt down somewhere deep inside her. She rolled back to face him again, and he struggled for words to say to her. He'd never been much good at comforting anybody, but he was going to damn sure try under the circumstances.

"I'm sure sorry, Felipa," he began. "We saw some men driving horses south this afternoon, but we never figured . . . well, Manuel wondered, but we didn't know . . ." He was just making things worse, he thought, by fumbling around this way. He swallowed and concluded, "Well, I'm sorry, mighty sorry, that's all."

Felipa managed to nod weakly. "I thank you for your concern," she said, "but I must be riding again. Those men are getting farther away, even as we speak." She started to sit up.

Mordecai would have stopped her, but he didn't have to. Her eyes rolled up in her head, and she fell back. Mordecai lunged forward and caught her before her head could hit the ground. He lowered her carefully again, then heaved a sigh.

He wasn't sure exactly what had happened, but it was a foregone conclusion from what he'd learned so far that the men he and Manuel and Edward had seen earlier had stolen the Sigalas' horse herd, killing everybody except Felipa in the process. And now Felipa was doing exactly what he would have expected from her under those circumstances.

She was riding for revenge.

"We had no warning," Felipa said grimly as she sipped from a cup of coffee, which the three young men had only in short supply but which Mordecai had deemed necessary tonight. Manuel and Edward had not argued the matter.

Felipa went on, "They struck early this morning, before the sun, riding into our camp and yelling and shooting. Amadeo and my father ran out to try to fight them, and both of them were shot down. They had no chance. Nor did my mother when she came out of the tent and tried to reach my father's gun. Two of them fired at her. One of them hit her—and the other shot hit Anita as the two of us ran out of our tent. I saw her fall, and then something struck me in the head. That is all I knew until I woke up and found my family slaughtered and our horses stolen."

Mordecai felt cold, despite the fact that the night was hot and humid. The story Felipa had just told was appalling in its viciousness. It was hard to believe even horse thieves would stoop so low as to murder a defenseless woman and child.

"Did they . . . while you were unconscious, did they—?"

"Molest me?" Felipa shook her head, which Mordecai had carefully cleansed of the dried blood from the crease. "I am sure they thought I was dead. I was shot in the head and bleeding badly, after all. Of course, with men like that such a thing might not have made a difference . . . but no, I was spared that indignity." Her voice broke a little. "All they took from me was my family."

Mordecai closed his eyes for a moment and fought back the rage that was howling like a wolf inside him. He had to stay calm and keep his wits about him. Trouble was close by; he sensed it. The only way to live through the night would be to keep a cool head.

"And when you came to and saw what they had done, you came after them?" he asked.

"What else was I to do? That mustang you saw me on had been

left behind as being of no account, which was almost true. But he served to carry me to you.''

"And we'll be ready when those gents pay us a visit,'' Mordecai promised. "You can count on that.''

The two of them sat alone by the camp fire, easy targets and Mordecai knew it. Twenty yards away, at the edge of the clearing, the mustangs moved uneasily in a rope corral. Manuel and Edward were nowhere to be seen, but Mordecai knew they were out there in the darkness. They had made their preparations as well as they could in a short amount of time, getting ready for the visitors they were sure would come tonight.

Felipa wore Manuel's sombrero, and her long hair was tucked up underneath it. A few yards away, a blanket-rolled shape could have been a man sleeping, instead of the trail gear it really was. To anybody who had seen them earlier, it would look like all three of them were here around the camp fire, settled down for a peaceful night and not expecting trouble at all.

Mordecai and Felipa had made supper on jerky, corn dodgers, and a small mess of refried beans Mordecai had been saving. Now they drank coffee and waited, and Felipa had told the story of what had happened to her family in a low voice that wouldn't carry much farther than the opposite side of the campfire where Mordecai sat.

Tension had him drawn tight, although he tried not to show it. He was certain that the men they had seen earlier, the men who had murdered the rest of the Sigala family and stolen their horses, would return in an attempt to kill and steal again. If that conclusion was wrong, then Edward and Manuel would spend an uncomfortable night, and an even more uncomfortable choice would be waiting for them in the morning. Would they continue north—or would they turn south and go after the killers? One thing was certain: Felipa could not continue on her quest alone. And Mordecai was pretty sure she wouldn't be willing to give it up. If he'd been in her place, he wouldn't have wanted to turn and ride the other way, either.

He was leaning forward, reaching for the coffeepot, when the branches of the thickly growing mesquites rattled together behind him.

Mordecai didn't wait for more warning than that. He dove forward, dropping his empty tin cup and reaching for the gun on his hip. He palmed it out as he cleared the camp fire, then landed on his left side and rolled over. His thump looped over the Colt's hammer, so that the act of bringing the gun up cocked it. Somebody let go at him from the mesquite. He saw the muzzle flash, heard the dull boom of black powder, and lifted his own thumb. The Colt roared.

Felipa had gone the other way, just as they'd planned. He hadn't wanted her in on this, would have preferred it if she'd been out of the camp and had left either Manuel or Edward with him. But she had insisted on being part of the bait, and Mordecai was already learning that she was a hard person to argue with. Right now, as she snatched up the Colt's revolving rifle that had been lying hidden under a blanket at her feet and started blazing away with it, Mordecai was glad she was on his side.

More guns opened up from the mesquite, but off to the side, rifles cracked as Edward and Manuel took a hand in the fracas. Mordecai had been careful not to stare into the flames of the camp fire, so his eyes adjusted quickly and let him pick up the muzzle flashes. He aimed at them, fired again and then again. Somebody yelled, and with a great crackling of brush, a man burst out of the mesquite. Blood streamed from his nose and mouth and his chest was sodden with the stuff, but he was still on his feet and still had a pistol in each hand. Mordecai came up on his knees, gritted his teeth, and shot the man in the head, putting him down in a hurry before he could fire either of those hoglegs he was waving around.

Mordecai heard the pounding of hoofbeats, another couple of shots, and then another scream. After that it got quiet in a hurry, and he motioned for Felipa to hold her fire. A few seconds later, somebody moved in the brush, and Mordecai's thumb was taut on the hammer of his gun until Manuel called out, "Do not shoot! It is only Edward and me." The young Mexican stepped out of the mesquite, his face grim and his rifle clutched tightly in his hands. He looked at Mordecai and Felipa and said, "They are all dead."

"You sure?" Mordecai asked.

"Six of them counting this one," Manuel replied as he nodded toward the man who had fallen beside the camp fire. "And they had only six horses. Edward is trying to catch them now, so that they do not go back to where they came from."

Mordecai stood up and holstered his gun. "We figured they'd leave two men with the mustangs they stole earlier, so that'd make for six of 'em, all right."

"Edward and I will tend to the other two," Manuel said. "We can take the herd and push it ahead of us. The ones left behind will think their *compadres* are returning with their ill-gotten booty.'' A savage smile stole across his lean, dark face. ''They will have quite a surprise. Just like those fools when they tripped over the rawhide thongs we strung between the mesquite trees. That was a good idea, Mordecai. We had enough warning to be able to deal with them.''

''Just barely,'' Mordecai muttered, thinking of all the lead that had gone flying around the clearing a few minutes earlier. He and Felipa had been damned lucky to come through the fight unhurt. But luck was on the winning side of every battle out here on the frontier.

Edward came back with the horses that had been ridden by the dead men, and then he and Manuel got the mustangs moving and headed off into the darkness. They'd talked it over among the four of them, and there was no way they were going to let any of the horse thieves escape with the Sigala mustangs. Old Ernesto and Isabel and Amadeo and little Anita had died for those horses, and the Texans were damned if they were going to let any of the killers escape unpunished.

''Should you not go with them?'' Felipa asked as she sat down shakily beside the fire. That head wound had taken a lot out of her, and Mordecai figured she had been functioning on sheer grit tonight.

''They'll do fine,'' Mordecai said, hoping he was right. Manuel could handle himself in just about any fight, and Edward was growing up quick. And this time the odds would be even.

Mordecai took a torch into the brush and double-checked the dead men, just to make sure none of them had any life left in them. They were all dead, just as Manuel had said. Mordecai hadn't ever seen an uglier bunch, and he couldn't bring himself to feel any pity for them, not that he tried very hard to do so. In fact, whenever he thought about little Anita Sigala, he was damned glad they'd run into some hot lead. He propped the torch in the dirt and got down to the grisly business of digging out the rifle and pistol balls that had killed the horse thieves. A little melting and molding, and the misshapen lumps of lead would be transformed back into fresh bullets.

A little later, he heard a flurry of shots in the far-off distance, and when he returned to Felipa's side, her face was pale and drawn. Mordecai took a deep breath and said, ''Now I reckon we wait and see who comes back.''

PART II

THE WHITE FLAG
TEXAS, AUTUMN
1842

☆ Chapter ☆
7

The summer of 1842 was hot, as that season in Texas usually is, but Andrew Lewis barely felt the heat as he worked in the fields on his farm. He put in row after row of beans, corn, squash, peppers, black-eyed peas, onions, and greens. When one field was full, he plowed up another, and when he had planted all that one man could plant, he took his hoe and spent long hours each day working the soil between the rows. Rainfall in this part of the republic was usually adequate for growing, but there was never a surplus of moisture. The land had to have a helping hand in holding on to what rain there was. And when the weather stayed too dry for too long, Andrew filled a couple of dozen buckets from the Colorado River, loaded them in the back of his wagon, and took the water to the fields that way. It was backbreaking, time-consuming labor.

Which was exactly what he wanted these days.

As long as he was working hard enough, his gaze didn't stray to the hillside where Petra was laid to rest. So he kept pushing himself, and his already lean body became more slender still, until it was practically all bone and wiry muscle. His hair was almost totally gray, and there were deep lines etched at the corners of his eyes and mouth. He looked considerably older than he really was.

Ben and Rose worried about him. "You can take it a mite easier, Pa," Ben often said when Andrew was working at something. "I'll handle that for you."

"No thanks, son," Andrew just grunted, and he kept on hoeing or patching the roof or whatever other chore was occupying his mind at the moment. He knew the children thought he was working too hard, but they didn't understand. They had grieved for their mother, and grieved mightily, but by now they had been able to put that behind them and get on with their lives.

Andrew would never be able to stop grieving. The hurt would never go away. He was convinced of that, and all he could do was try to dull the pain with hard work.

As a result, the Lewis family had more produce than they could possibly eat that summer. As it came time to pick the crops, Andrew would load up the wagon and take a mess of vegetables to Marie, Annie, and Frank. At each stop, his relatives tried to get him to come in and sit a spell, to put his feet up and smoke and talk. But Andrew was having none of it. There were things to do, he always said, things to do.

And yet, through his pain, he was beginning to see things again. He saw his niece Angeline growing more beautiful each day as her body swelled with the new life growing within her. He saw how Frank and Hope were as happy with each other as ever, and he didn't feel the pangs of jealousy he might have experienced once at such a sight. He had to smile a little at David's continued grousing because he hadn't been allowed to go off mustanging with his older brother. And Andrew saw how Annie had flourished in her marriage to Sly Shipman, and he knew that was a good thing, too.

Maybe there was a little hope, he allowed himself to think. Maybe one day some of the pain would go away and he would be human again. Until then, he had his work to occupy his days, and he labored so hard that the nights passed in exhausted, dreamless slumber.

There had been no sign of Mordecai, Edward, and Manuel, nor any word from them. That wasn't unusual, Sly assured the rest of the family when they met at Marie's for Sunday dinner. "That Nueces country is so thick with mustangs those boys could spend the whole entire summer catching 'em, and there'd still be more horses they never even got a look at," Sly said. "I reckon they'll come back in when the weather starts to cool off some."

The only real excitement of the summer came when Sly broke his leg in August by falling out of a wagon while he was loading up some supplies in Bastrop. It was a hell of a way for a man like him to get hurt, considering that he had fought through the revolution against Mexico and had operated for years as a smuggler along the Texas-Louisiana border, which was a risky occupation at best. The doctor said it was a clean break and should heal up nicely, and splinted the leg and wrapped it tightly in bandages. Then Sly had been propped up in the back of the wagon and driven home by Annie. He seethed all the way, unaccustomed to being even partially incapacitated.

Andrew volunteered to help keep up Sly and Annie's place while Sly recuperated from his injury, since their two girls were too young to do much work around a farm. The extra work was a blessing for Andrew, who had his own place producing so efficiently and spectacularly that there weren't quite enough chores to keep him busy anymore. While Andrew tended to the fields, Sly sat in the shade of the dogtrot with his leg propped up in front of him on another chair, his face set in a glare most of the time. Annie had to keep a close eye on him to make sure he didn't get up and stump around too much on the crutch he had carved out of a tree limb.

"I swear, Sly Shipman, you're about the worst patient I've ever seen," she scolded him one day when she caught him heading toward the henhouse to gather eggs. "That's one of the few chores the girls can handle, and you're trying to take it away from them!"

"Sorry," he muttered as he sank back into his chair. "I'm not used to sittin' this long at a time, though, and I'll *never* get used to havin' another man do my work for me."

Other than that, summer passed peacefully for the Lewises, and August turned into September. James and Jonathan rode in from an extended scout along the Guadalupe River, where Indians had been reported. Unlike the raids by the white renegades, this time there was some truth to the rumor, James explained as he and Jonathan sat down for a meal with the rest of the family at Marie's house.

"It was just a little bunch, four or five Comanch'," he said. "They didn't have any guns, just bows and arrows and lances. They raided a farm over on the Guadalupe."

"And stole some chickens," Jonathan added with a grin.

"We ran 'em to ground, and they surrendered without a fight."

"Did you shoot 'em?" David asked eagerly.

James shook his head. "I don't cotton much to shootin' defenseless folks, even Comanches," he said. "We took their horses and told 'em to walk back to their people. They had a chance that way. Never thought I'd see the day when a Comanch' was brought so low as to steal a chicken. Reckon they'll never live down what happened to 'em."

"You should have killed them," Angeline said quietly.

James looked at his niece and sighed. Everyone at the table remembered all too well the ordeal she had suffered at the hands of the Comanches. "Well, honey, I thought about it. I truly did. But it seems like there's got to come a time when the hatin' and the killin' stops."

"Maybe," Angeline said dubiously.

Marie slipped an arm around her daughter's shoulder. "Your Uncle James is right," she said. "The only thing killing usually brings . . . is more killing."

Angeline pushed back her chair and walked quickly out of the room, stepping outside into the dogtrot. James looked miserably down at his plate, wishing he had never brought up the subject of the Comanches. But everyone had wanted to know what he and Jonathan and the other volunteers had found over there on the Guadalupe, and he hadn't seen what it could hurt to answer their questions.

Well, now he knew.

"Sorry, Marie," he muttered without looking up. "Didn't mean to get a lot of bad old memories stirred up again."

"Do not concern yourself, James," she assured him. "Angeline is unhappy most of the time now, regardless of what is going on around her."

"Must be hard," Annie said, "having a baby on the way and her husband not around, not knowing when—or if—he's ever going to be back." She shot a glance at Sly. "I know I never liked it when Sly was off roaming around."

Marie's smile was bittersweet as she said, "I remember how it was with Michael. He roamed more than any of you other men. But that was the only way he could be truly happy."

Andrew commented, "Give a Lewis man a gun to put over his shoulder and some woods to wander around in, and he'd be happier'n a hog in slop. That's what people used to say about us in Tennessee, especially about our pa. I reckon there's a lot of truth to it. My feet have been getting a little itchy lately."

They all looked at him in surprise, and after a second Frank said, "You, Andrew? We all figured you'd got that out of your system. You never had that same wandering urge as Michael and old Mordecai."

"Not as strong, maybe," Andrew said, "but it was there, just the same." He shook his head wryly and added, "Reckon I'll stay at home, though. Things have settled down so much, there's not much place to go anymore."

Angeline stepped back into the cabin and said with an edge of worry in her voice, "Somebody's coming. They act like they're in a hurry, too."

The people around the table exchanged glances, and the men got up and went out into the dogtrot. Several rifles were propped against the wall of the cabin, and callused, experienced hands took them up. Even Sly came out, leaning on his crutch as his other hand rested on the butt of the pistol holstered at his hip. His busted leg had still not healed properly, most likely because he wouldn't stay off of it long enough, Annie claimed.

As the Lewis men looked down the road, they saw two riders approaching and, as Angeline had said, they weren't wasting any time. They were pushing their horses pretty hard, and the animals were winded as their riders brought them to a halt in the yard in front of the double cabin.

James recognized the visitors as Ben Harvey and Jordan Chesney, two of the men who rode with him and Jonathan in the minutemen. He lifted a hand in greeting and called, "Howdy, Ben, Jordan. What're you boys doing here?"

"Spreadin' the word," replied Ben Harvey. "Howdy, Andrew, Frank, Sly, young David, and Ben."

"Enough time for howdyin' later," Jordan Chesney snapped. "Ain't you folks heard about the Meskins?"

Andrew shook his head. "They're not up to mischief again, are they?" The previous spring, an army had marched up from Mexico, reaching as far as San Antonio. It had caused all sorts of havoc, but no real damage, before turning around and hotfooting it back to the border before the Texans could mount any sort of real response. It had been thought at the time that the short-lived invasion had been just a feeler to see if a full-scale attack could conceivably take back what Mexico had lost in the revolution six years earlier.

But other than a minor skirmish or two along the Rio Grande, nothing of the sort had happened since then—until now.

"San Antonio's in Meskin hands again," Chesney said grimly. "Fourteen hunnerd troops under that French gen'ral of Santy Anna's have done took over."

"General Woll?" James snapped, remembering the French mercenary from the days before the revolution.

"That's the feller," Harvey said. "Marched right in like they owned the place. But here's the good news—we're gettin' together a force o' fightin' men to go down there and take Bexar back. Cap'n Jack'll be headin' things up again." Harvey threw his head back and let out a whoop. "Th' Rangers are back, boys!"

"Damn well about time," Jonathan exclaimed. "Let me get my horse and I'll ride with you." He turned to James. "What about you, brother?"

James had to think about it for only a moment. "I'll go," he said with a curt nod.

"I thought you said the killin' had to stop sooner or later," Frank pointed out.

"I don't like it," James said, facing his cousin squarely, "but this is defendin' our homeland. A man can't turn his back on that, no matter how much he wishes folks would just get along."

Andrew said, "James is right. I was just saying I wouldn't mind doing some traveling again, if there was just some place to go. Reckon this is my chance."

"I'll ride with you," Sly said, turning awkwardly toward the wagon Annie had driven over. "Just let me go get my saddle horse . . ."

"Sly Shipman!" Annie cried as she emerged from the cabin. Obviously the women had been waiting just inside the doorway and listening to everything that was going on, because Marie, Hope, and Angeline followed her out. "You'll do no such thing, Sly. Your leg's in no shape for you to ride to San Antonio."

"I got to," Sly said stubbornly. "Who knows how far that army'll come if we don't stop 'em now?"

"Other people can do the stopping," Annie insisted. "If you're not careful with that leg, you're going to lose it, and by God I want you to bounce grandchildren on that knee!"

Sly sighed heavily. "You're right, blast it," he muttered. He looked up at Harvey and Chesney. "Sorry, boys, but I reckon I won't be going after all."

"And nobody holds it agin you, Mr. Shipman," Chesney said. "You done fit more'n your share o' battles for Texas." The grizzled frontiersman turned his gaze toward James, Jonathan, and Andrew. "But if you three're comin' along, you'd best light a shuck. We got some travelin' to do."

Andrew turned to his sister-in-law and asked, "Marie, can Ben and Rose stay here with you and Angeline while I'm gone?"

Before she could answer, Ben said angrily, "I ain't stayin' with Aunt Marie. I'm near a growed man, Pa, and I'm goin' along to fight the Mexicans, too!"

"No, you're not," Andrew said flatly, his tone making it clear he wasn't going to stand for any argument. "You just turned seventeen, Ben. You're not old enough—"

"Uncle Michael came to Texas when he was younger'n that," Ben protested.

Marie spoke up. "Yes, and Michael almost died here at a younger age than that, too. Please, Ben . . . I'd like for you and Rose to stay. If there's trouble abroad in the land again, Angeline and I can use the company. It would be a great favor to us."

Ben shuffled his feet and looked down at the ground and muttered for a few seconds under his breath before saying, "Oh, hell . . . I mean heck . . . I reckon I can stay if it means so all-fired much to everybody."

Andrew clapped his son on the shoulder. "Thanks, Ben," he said. "Now you get back over to our place as fast as you can and fetch my good saddle horse, that big chestnut. Can you do it?"

"Sure," Ben replied. He hopped onto the family's wagon and turned the team toward home after David had untied the mules. Ben whipped them into a trot with the reins.

James turned to his cousin and asked, "What about you, Frank?" He suspected he already knew the answer.

Frank shook his head, surprising no one. "I'm a mite too old for such fandangos, and David's too young. I reckon the three of you'll have to represent the Lewis clan in this fight."

"We'll do the family proud," Jonathan said.

Marie crossed her arms and hugged herself, as if she was cold despite the warmth of the September sun. "Just come back safely, all of you," she said quietly. "That would be the proudest thing of all."

"We're ridin'," Jordan Chesney said impatiently. "You-all can catch up with us. Reckon you'll be able to find us without no trouble."

James nodded, and the same thought went through more than one head.

The Lewises had always known how to find trouble, all right.

James and Andrew had taken part in campaigns like this before, both of them having fought in the revolution, but marching to San Antonio to do battle with an invading army was a new experience for Jonathan. Actually, they weren't marching, since all three of them had saddle horses, but many of the men who had gathered were on foot, and the force held its pace down to match the slower volunteers.

Jonathan had been through enough fights with Indians and outlaws so that he wasn't overly nervous about what was coming, but the prospect of facing a real army this time made a tingle of combined apprehension and anticipation run through him.

"How does that Mexican army fight?" he asked his brothers as they followed the trail to San Antonio with the thirty or forty other volunteers who had been alerted by Ben Harvey and Jordan Chesney.

"Like they want to live through their battles," James said with a shrug.

Andrew's answer was more lengthy. "A lot depends on their

officers,'' he told Jonathan. ''Back in the days of the revolution, a lot of the Mexican soldiers were convicts who didn't have any choice about coming up here to fight. The officers tried to keep the troops more afraid of them than they were of the enemy. It worked pretty well as long as things were going Santa Anna's way. But when the army got taken by surprise, like they were at San Jacinto, they were too spooked and confused to put up much of a fight. They broke and ran.''

''You think they'll do the same thing at San Antonio?''

''Hard to say,'' Andrew replied with a shrug. ''Depends on how well they're dug in and how big a force we're able to throw against them.'' He wiped some sweat from the heat of late summer off his face. ''I tell you one thing. If we have to go in there and root 'em out house by house, it's going to be one hell of a fight. And a lot of good men are going to die.''

Andrew's sober demeanor was the exception among the volunteers, however. Most of the men were excited, laughing and swapping ribald threats about what they were going to do to the Mexican army once they reached San Antonio. Word had arrived that when the troops under General Woll had taken over the town, the district court had been in session. Everyone in the courthouse—judges, lawyers, defendants, plaintiffs, and spectators—had been taken prisoner by the Mexicans and were being held as hostages. That news was enough to make most Texans' blood run hot.

Andrew had something else on his mind, and it was a concern he had shared with Marie before leaving the Lewis Fort. Mordecai, Edward, and Manuel were still not back from their mustanging trip, and he was worried that they might have encountered Woll's invading army. There were conflicting rumors about which route the Mexicans might have taken across southern Texas, but it was entirely likely they had marched through the Nueces country.

There was nothing Andrew could do about that now, however, so he tried to put it out of his thoughts as much as possible. Maybe by the time they got back home, Mordecai and the others would be there too, he told himself.

It took three days to reach San Antonio, and when the Lewises and their companions arrived at the Texan camp north of the city, they found they were not the first ones there, by any means. Over two hundred men had flocked to the coming conflict, the biggest delegation being led by Matthew Caldwell, who had been elected by the entire force as its leader. Captain Jack Hays would still function as the field commander, however; the Ranger captain, a seasoned fighter despite his youth, had the respect of everyone there.

Hays shook hands with James and Jonathan, who had served with him in the Rangers, and they introduced him to Andrew. "Glad to have you with us, Mr. Lewis," the handsome twenty-five-year-old said as he clasped Andrew's hand. "We're going to need every good fighting man we can get."

"What's the situation, Cap'n?" asked James. The four of them hunkered down next to one of the numerous small camp fires along the banks of Cibolo Creek.

Hays replied, "Woll's just sitting there at Bexar with between thirteen hundred and fourteen hundred men. Reckon you could say the whole city's his prisoner, but he's got around fifty official hostages he took at the courthouse, according to what our spies tell us. Nobody's got any idea what he plans to do next. If he heads north we'll be ready for him, though."

"Why don't we just go in there and kick his French ass all the way back to the Rio?" Jonathan suggested eagerly.

With a grin, Jack Hays said, "And they tell me *I'm* too reckless sometimes. We don't have enough men to run him out of the city, Jonathan. But there's more coming in all the time, and we've got a little edge on Woll. We know about how many men he has, but he doesn't have any idea of our numbers. That's why we've been staying back here in the hills, out of sight." The Ranger captain's features became more solemn as he went on, "I've been studying on a plan to draw Woll out. You boys want to take a ride with me tomorrow?"

James nodded quickly. "We'll be ready when you are, Cap'n."

The time came early the next morning. Hays and several other men, along with James, Jonathan, and Andrew, rode closer to San Antonio, pausing on a hilltop in plain view of the city only a few hundred yards away. Hays swung down from his horse and nodded for the other men to do likewise. He started building a camp fire. "Reckon we'll have us some breakfast," he said.

Taking some bacon, corn bread, and a coffeepot from his saddlebags, Hays busied himself with domestic chores. Andrew squatted on the other side of the fire and said, "I just saw a flash of light from down yonder. Must've been the sun hitting a spyglass. They're watching us, Captain."

"I sure hope so," Hays replied. "I want 'em to think there's only a little bunch of us."

"Reckon they've got cannon down there?" Jonathan asked rather nervously.

"Could be," Hays allowed.

Sure enough, after the men had eaten, Hays took a spyglass of his own and studied the town. A few minutes later, he said, "They're wheeling out one of the long guns to take some potshots at us. Unlimber those rifles, boys."

All of the men were carrying Tennessee long rifles, even James and Jonathan, who had borrowed the weapons and left their Colt's revolving rifles with their shorter range back in camp. They could see the artillery crew setting up the cannon to lob cannonballs at them. Hays said, "Use the horses to rest those rifles, and make your shots count. We want Woll good and mad."

The Texans laid their rifle barrels over the saddles of their mounts to steady them, and they quickly drew beads on the Mexican soldiers manning the cannon.

"Have at 'em, boys," Hays said quietly.

The rifles on the hilltop began to crack. Andrew saw two of the Mexican soldiers fall, and the others jumped for cover. Three more of them went sprawling to the ground before they could reach shelter, victims of the deadly accurate fire from the Texans. By now Andrew had caught on to what Hays had in mind, and as he reloaded, he said, "With any luck, that ought to do it."

"Woll's a proud man," commented Hays. "It's got to gall him that every time he's come up here on Santa Anna's behalf, he's wound up getting beat in the end. He's probably pretty anxious to teach us uppity Texans a lesson. Leastways I hope so."

The gun crew ventured out again a few minutes later to try to reclaim the cannon, and again they were peppered with rifle fire from the hilltop. This time none of the soldiers were killed, but they were forced to run like blazes once more. Some other officers arrived on the scene, and as Hays studied the goings-on through his spyglass, a broad grin spread over his face.

"Those Mex officers are really hot and bothered," he said. "They can't believe that a handful of Texans can make the Mexican army crawfish like that. They're yelling and waving their arms around." Hays snapped the spyglass closed. "It's a pretty comical sight, boys. But Woll won't think it's funny when he hears about it."

Hays stood up, walked a few yards farther down the hill, and fired his pistol into the air a couple of times. Then he took off his hat and waved cheerfully to the officers and soldiers below, no doubt adding to their anger and frustration—which was exactly what he intended.

"Let's go," he said as he returned to the others. "If that doesn't do it, we'll try something else."

There was no need to bait and enrage the Mexicans any further, though. A little later, scouts rode into the Texans' main camp with the news that General Woll was marching north out of Bexar with two hundred cavalry and six hundred infantry, for a total of around eight hundred men. That wasn't his entire force, but it was more than half of it.

Hays conferred quickly with Matthew Caldwell, then announced, "We'll hit 'em at Salado Creek. Check your powder, boys. We'll be burnin' plenty of it before the day's over."

Salado Creek was a shallow, meandering, cottonwood-lined stream like so many others in this part of Texas. The Rangers under Jack Hays moved faster than the more ponderous maneuverings of the Mexican army, and they were already in position, using the trees along the creek bank for cover, when the soldiers appeared.

"We'll get a free volley before they know we're here," Hays told the men nearest him, including the three Lewis brothers. "After that they'll come a-chargin'."

"You're saying we'd better make our first shots count," Andrew said dryly.

"That's exactly what I'm saying, Andrew." Hays grinned as he checked the powder in his rifle.

He was every bit the daredevil he'd been made out to be, Andrew thought as he looked at Hays. A glance over at Jonathan told him that the youngest brother was watching Hays with undisguised hero worship. That was all right, Andrew thought. It would keep Jonathan's mind off the fight.

James had his eyes on the approaching Mexicans, and his face was a grim, hard mask. So much of the time since Libby's death, James had seemed to live only to do battle, first with Indians and outlaws, now with the Mexican army. Andrew could understand that. He had thrown himself into the work on his farm with the same blind devotion that James had shown to more violent pursuits. But in recent days, James had shown signs of realizing that he couldn't live the rest of his days that way, and Andrew had come to a similar understanding of his own life.

The loss of Petra still hurt, hurt bad, but as Andrew knelt beside a cottonwood and watched the Mexican soldiers in their dirty white jackets and pants coming toward him, he knew that he wanted to live. The world could be as bitter as wormwood most of the time, but it had its sweet moments, too, and Andrew wasn't ready to give them up. He took a hand off the stock of his rifle and wiped it on his pants, drying the sweat. He nestled his cheek against the smooth wood and peered over the long barrel, settling the sights on one of those advancing troopers. Likely that fellow didn't much want to die, either, Andrew thought.

"Now!" Jack Hays called, his voice carrying up and down the line of Texans.

Rifle fire crackled along the creek, and a haze of powder smoke drifted up into the clear blue sky. A score or more of the Mexican soldiers went down, and others tried to turn and run, only to be driven ahead again by the slashing sabers of their officers. The troops charged toward Salado Creek, yelling and shouting, their front lines ragged. More rifle fire ripped into their ranks, spilling one man out of three. But there were hundreds more coming along behind to take the place of those who fell, and the cavalry came thundering past both flanks of the infantry, sweeping toward the creek in a classic pincers move.

"Get those horsebackers!" Matthew Caldwell bellowed.

James fired and saw a horse go head over heels as his bullet struck it. The animal rolled over its fallen rider, crushing him. At James's side, Jonathan squeezed off a round from his Colt's revolving rifle, and another cavalryman sagged in his saddle but somehow managed to stay aboard the horse. With the first volley over, some of Hays's Rangers, mounted on speedy Texas ponies, raced out of the safety of the trees in an effort to outflank the Mexican cavalry charge, while the Mexican foot soldiers stumbled on toward the stream.

The air was full of clouds of powder smoke that stung the nose and eyes. The constant booming of gunfire was deafening. Yet somehow over the din, the screams of dying men and horses could always be heard. Just before the Mexicans reached the trees, the Texans charged out from their cover to meet the assault in the open. Just as in the battles with the Comanches, the Mexicans armed with single-shot rifles were outgunned despite the overwhelming odds in their favor. James emptied both of his Paterson Colts and downed seven men with the ten shots. He rammed the empty, smoking revolvers back in their holsters and jerked his Bowie knife from its sheath in time to plunge the blade into the chest of a soldier who was trying to club him with the butt of an empty rifle. Nearby, Jonathan used his rifle to parry the thrust of a bayonet, then crushed the unbalanced

Mexican's skull with a quick stroke of his own weapon. There was chaos all around, and all a man could do was try to sort out friend from foe and act accordingly.

Andrew fought like a man possessed, whipping up a rifle that some Mexican trooper had dropped and using the bayonet still attached to the weapon to cut a bloody circle around him. An officer on horseback swooped toward him, saber upraised to slash at him, but Andrew acted first, thrusting up with the bayonet and letting the force of the officer's charge drive the blade all the way through the man's body. The officer tumbled off his horse, taking the rifle with him as the impact tore it from Andrew's hands. Andrew bent, scooped up the dead officer's saber, and began swinging the razor-sharp blade around.

James and Jonathan reached the relative safety of the trees, reloaded their pistols, and plunged into the fight again. James spotted one of the soldiers aiming at Andrew from behind and threw a fast shot at him, sending the Mexican spinning away with blood spurting from his bullet-torn throat. Andrew was caught up in the battle and had no idea how close he had come to death. James caught Jonathan's eye and jerked his head, indicating that his younger brother should follow him. Together they fought their way to Andrew's side, and James pressed his second pistol into his older brother's hand. ''Side by side!'' he shouted over the roar of battle, a savage grin on his face.

Andrew nodded, and shoulder to shoulder the three of them waded into the onslaught of Mexicans, firing until their guns were empty. Then they began clubbing the enemy with the long barrels of the rifles. Only gradually did they become aware that the Mexicans were falling back as fast as their legs would carry them. The officers had fled, and the soldiers weren't going to continue to fight without the threat of the officers behind them

The battle of Salado Creek, for all intents and purposes, was over.

By nightfall, it was obvious that the Texans had won a victory. The Mexicans had tried to take their dead with them, but some sixty bodies still littered the battlefield. Probably at least that many had been carried off by the fleeing soldiers. On the other side, many of the Texans had suffered wounds, some fairly severe, but amazingly, only one man was dead.

The Texans pulled back into the hills again. A single battle had been won, but the Mexicans still controlled San Antonio.

The war—if it could be called that—was a long way from finished . . .

☆ Chapter ☆

8

Marie paced back and forth in the dogtrot, looking at the gray October sky. The heavy clouds threatened to burst into a cold drizzle at any moment. It had looked like that all day. The weather matched her mood, Marie thought.

She had every right to be depressed, she told herself. Her husband was dead and her only son had been gone for months with no word from him. She had expected Mordecai, Edward, and Manuel to return sometime during the summer, but here it was fall and there had been no sign of them. Nor had there been any word of the mustangers from a third party. She and Michael had raised Mordecai better than that, Marie told herself. If he had run into any passing strangers heading up toward Colorado, Mordecai would have asked them to pass along to his family the news that he and his companions were all right.

Marie took a deep breath and tried not to think about the things she and Andrew had discussed before he left for San Antonio with James and Jonathan. The possibility that Mordecai, Edward, and Manuel had encountered the Mexican army under General Woll as it made its way through South Texas was all too real.

"Mama?"

The voice from the door of the bedroom cabin made Marie turn quickly. She saw Angeline standing there, frowning worriedly. "Is there any sign of them?" Angeline went on.

Marie shook her head. "No," she told her daughter. "But I would not expect them to be coming in weather like this. Look there, off to the south."

Angeline stepped out of the cabin and into the dogtrot, coming to Marie's side. Marie pointed to the south, the direction from which the three young men would probably return home. There was a shower moving across there in the distance, dropping some heavy rain from the looks of it.

"They would not drive horses in such weather, not even mustangs," Marie said. "They are holed up somewhere, as your brother would say, to wait out the storm."

Angeline nodded, accepting Marie's logic, and the older woman was grateful for that. Angeline rested her head on Marie's shoulder, just as if she were still a child instead of a young woman about to give birth to her own baby. As Angeline put her arm around her mother's waist, Marie sternly commanded herself to stop brooding so. When Angeline saw her pacing around the dogtrot and staring out into the distance, it only made her worry that much more. Marie knew she had just as much responsibility to her daughter as she did to her son, and Angeline was going through a difficult time, with the birth approaching and her husband nowhere around. Thank God the pregnancy had been a relatively easy one with no complications, Marie thought.

From now on she would just have to summon up more strength and remain calm, for Angeline's sake. Mordecai and the others would be in her prayers, but for now that was all she could do for them.

"Come," she said, taking Angeline's hand. "I think it is high time that the two of us baked a cake."

Angeline giggled, sounding for all the world like the little girl she had once been not that long ago, or so it seemed to Marie. Surely it had only been a month or so since Angeline had been scampering around the dogtrot, dragging a cornhusk doll Michael had made for her in one of his gentle moments. . . .

The two women worked in the kitchen for the rest of the morning and into the afternoon, using some of the family's precious sugar to make a sweet cake, the kind that Angeline had liked ever since she was the little girl Marie had been thinking of earlier. They concentrated on what they were doing and so were a little surprised when they stepped out into the dogtrot and saw that the clouds had broken up and partially cleared off. Bright beams of sunlight slanted down through the openings in the overcast sky. A soft breeze that was warm for October swept over the cabin. Marie smiled and nodded slightly to herself. The weather still seemed to be mirroring her emotions, and she had to believe that was a good omen.

Frank rode by later in the afternoon on one of his mules. "Just thought I'd see if you ladies need anything," he said as he swung down from the back of the mule.

"We could use some wood chopped for the stove," Marie said. "I was planning on doing it myself—"

"No need," Frank told her with a grin. He didn't have to ask where the ax was. He fetched it from the shed behind the cabin and got to work splitting some of the thicker lengths of logs stacked against the side of the cabin.

The afternoon wore on, and as it did, the rest of the clouds blew away on the breeze, leaving a gorgeous blue sky arching over the Texas countryside. When Frank was finished with the wood, Marie invited him to sit down, drink a cup of buttermilk, and share in the cake she and Angeline had baked earlier. Frank accepted the offer gratefully and sat down in one of the chairs in the shade of the dogtrot. As he was eating, his eyes followed Angeline around with approval. The young woman was glowing with health, and Frank looked on her more as a niece than a second cousin, since Michael Lewis had always been like one of his own brothers.

"How are Ben and Rose?" Marie asked while Frank was eating. Andrew's children were staying with Frank and Hope at the moment, while Ben and his cousin David tended to the fields on Andrew's place, which was closer to Frank's cabin than Marie's.

"Doing just fine," replied Frank. "They miss their pa, I reckon, but we all do. How are you and Angeline making out here by yourselves?"

Marie shook her head. "Do not worry about us, Frank. We will be fine."

When Frank was finished with his cake, he stood up and stretched. "Better be going," he said. "That was mighty—"

The suddenness with which he stopped talking made Marie glance up, a slight frown of concern forming on her face. She saw Frank gazing toward the river, looking somewhat puzzled and surprised. "What is it?" Marie asked sharply. "Did you see something?"

Frank gave a little shake of his head, then turned a sheepish smile toward Marie and Angeline, who had also visibly tensed at Frank's abrupt reaction of a moment earlier. "No, it's nothing," he assured them. "I thought for a second I spotted something off yonder in the distance, but there's nothing there now.'' He looked around. ''Where're your rifles, Marie?''

''Just inside the door,'' she replied. ''You don't think you saw some Comanches, do you, Frank?'' There had been no more reports of Indians in the area since the men had left to liberate San Antonio from the invading Mexican army, although such a possibility was a definite concern among those settlers left behind. With most of the menfolk gone, the Comanches might get it into their heads that this was a good time to come raiding. They would have been right, too.

''There's nothing over there, Marie,'' Frank said. ''I'm sure of that now. But you might want to keep those guns a mite more handy.''

Marie stepped over to the doorway, reached inside, and brought out one of the rifles. With it tucked under her arm, she said, ''I'll remember, and so will Angeline. Won't you, darling?''

Angeline nodded a little shakily, and Marie knew she must be recalling her ordeal as a captive of the Comanches. She had come through it amazingly well, but those days of terror would never again be far from her mind.

''Well, I'll be ridin','' Frank said, untying the reins of his mule, which he had hitched to an iron ring set in the wall. He threw his leg over the animal's back and kicked it into motion. He lifted a hand as he rode away and called back to the women, ''I'll ride by later, just to make sure everything's all right.''

Somehow, that didn't reassure Marie a great deal, and judging from her daughter's worried expression, it hadn't done much for Angeline, either.

For several minutes, Marie stood there in front of the cabin and looked up and down the river, studying each grassy hill that rolled along beside the stream, each grove of trees. Seeing nothing moving except a few birds that had not yet flown south for the winter and a community of squirrels that were capering around some tall cottonwoods, she finally nodded to herself and said, ''We have more work to do. There's dried corn to grind for meal, so we had better get started on it.''

She and Angeline went back into the cabin and got the corn from a bin. As they began to grind the dried-up little grains using a mortar and pestle as Marie's mother had before her, they chatted idly, but it was obvious that both of them had their thoughts elsewhere. The sweet smell of the baking cake, which had filled the cabin earlier, still hung faintly in the air.

One of the dogs began to bark outside.

Marie's head jerked up, and her hand went to the rifle beside her chair. As she picked it up, she heard the sound of hoofbeats outside the cabin, the hoofbeats of many horses. She came to her feet, and as she did, she heard Angeline say softly, "Oh no, not again. Not again . . ."

Then the door opened before Marie could even reach the window, and a tall shape stood silhouetted against the late afternoon light. Marie's heart seemed to stop.

Until she heard her son's voice saying, "I smell cake, Mama. Got any left to share with some tired travelers?"

Mordecai had expected a big welcome when he and Edward and Manuel returned home, but what he actually got was a little different than he had foreseen.

His mother stood there in the cabin staring at him, a rifle in her hands. Mordecai was glad she was being cautious, but she looked like she actually wanted to shoot him. He said tentatively, "Mama?"

Angeline cried, "Mordecai!" and jumped out of her chair as quickly as she could considering the fact that her belly was a lot bigger than the last time he had seen her. She flung herself into his arms and hugged him tightly, then pulled back slightly and looked up at him. In a voice that was little more than a whisper, she asked, "Manuel?"

"Outside tending the horses," Mordecai told her.

"No more, *amigo!*" Manuel said as he stepped into the cabin behind Mordecai. Angeline let out a cry of joy and threw her arms around him. Manuel's mouth came down on hers in a kiss that packed all the loneliness both of them had suffered during the past six months.

Marie still hadn't said anything, and she was frowning as she came closer to Mordecai. He swallowed nervously and said, "I sure am glad to see you, Mama. There were times when I didn't know if we were going to make it back or not."

"I have not known that myself for many long months," Marie said grimly. "Mordecai Lewis, if we were both younger I would take you over my knee and give you the whipping of your life! How dare you go off for so long and never send word, never let us know that you were all right? We thought the Mexican army must have gotten you!"

"Nope," Mordecai said with a sheepish smile and a shake of his head. "Those soldiers raised a lot of dust when they marched and rode up through South Texas, so the four of us just steered well clear of 'em once we figured out what was going on.'' He lowered his eyes a little. ''I'm sorry we didn't get word to you, Mama. But we were kind of busy most of the time.''

''If your father was still here . . .'' Marie began sternly, but then her relief and her motherly love visibly overcame her anger. She reached up and put her arms around Mordecai's neck, holding him tightly for a long moment. ''Welcome home,'' she whispered.

Mordecai stood there a little awkwardly while his mother hugged him. After a moment, he said, ''I reckon I ought to go back out and give them a hand with those mustangs. They're tamed down some, but they're still going to be a handful gettin' 'em into the corrals.''

''Wait a moment,'' Marie said. ''Them? You said *four* people?''

''Don't worry, Mama,'' Mordecai replied quickly. ''You'll like Felipa. She's mighty fine.'' Then before his mother could do anything except stand there with a perplexed expression on her face, he ducked back out the door.

Edward was prodding the mustangs into the corral while Felipa held the herd, moving back and forth easily on her horse to block the way every time one of the mustangs made a tentative move for freedom. There were sixty-eight horses in the bunch they had driven up from the Nueces country—the mustangs Mordecai, Edward, and Manuel had captured by themselves; the herd that the Sigala family had gathered before the Mexican horse thieves had murdered all of them except Felipa; and the other mustangs Mordecai and his companions had caught after Felipa had thrown in with them.

Somehow there had never been much question that she would join them after the battle with the horse thieves and the recovery of the stolen mustangs. She had relatives back in Mexico, of course; quite a few of them, in fact. But there were none of them with whom she would have wanted to live. None of them would have understood the life she led as a mustanger, and they would have wanted to dress her in fancy gowns and smother her with foolishness and frippery. She didn't know if she could have stood such a thing.

Mordecai agreed with her decision. As far as he was concerned, she looked just fine in *chaparejos*.

So she had helped them catch some more mustangs and had actually taught them quite a bit over the past few months, passing along the horse-hunting wisdom she had learned from her father, old Ernesto. And Mordecai had to admit that she really had a way about her when it came to gentling the wild horses. The mount she was riding was one of the mustangs that had taken to her especially well. Many of the others in the herd were well on the way to being ready for riding, and even the rest of the bunch, the stubborn ones, had some of their rough edges taken off. Once all the mustangs were at least controllable enough to drive, they had left the Nueces country behind and headed north for the Colorado.

Mordecai glanced over at the dogtrot, where his mother stood with her arms crossed over her bosom. She had expected them to return home with a herd of horses, but the pretty young Mexican girl was quite a surprise.

"Who is that, Mordecai?" Marie asked softly.

"That's Felipa, Mama, just like I told you. Her name's Felipa Sigala. She ran into a lot of bad luck down south, and we gave her a hand." Quickly, he explained about Felipa's family and how Ernesto, Isabel, Amadeo, and little Anita had been killed by the horse thieves. He glossed over the part about how he and Edward and Manuel had helped Felipa retrieve the stolen horses and avenge the deaths of her family, but he could tell from the expression in Marie's eyes that she understood.

No Lewis could allow such a wrong to go unpunished, not if there was anything they could do about it.

"So, this girl Felipa . . . what is she to you, Mordecai?"

"She's a good friend, Mama," Mordecai answered without hesitation. He didn't add that it would have been just fine with him if Felipa had decided to be something more than that. But with everything she had gone through, he hadn't wanted to push the issue, and even though the four of them had been alone out there on the South Texas plains, everything had gone along just as proper as if there had been a *dueña* lurking behind every mesquite tree.

After a moment, Marie nodded her head. "You did the right thing," she said. A smile touched her lips, and Mordecai relaxed. Everything was going to be all right now. Marie added, "As soon as those horses are in the corral, you will introduce me to your friend, and she will be welcome here for as long as she wants to stay."

Maybe, just maybe, Mordecai thought with a grin, sooner or later that would be forever.

• • •

It didn't take long for news of the mustangers' return to spread. Frank came by later in the afternoon, as he had promised, and after a round of handshaking and backslapping with Mordecai and Manuel and a bone-crushing hug for his son—and an introduction to Felipa, who seemed to impress him greatly—he got back on his mule to carry the word to the rest of the family. Edward rode along with him, anxious to get home and see his mother and brother.

"Everyone should come to dinner tomorrow," Marie called after him, and Frank turned in the saddle enough to wave and indicate that he would deliver the invitation to the others.

Mordecai hoped that someone who came to the dinner would know how the fight against the Mexicans was going. It made him a little uncomfortable to think that some of the other male Lewises were trying to drive that invading army out of Texas, and here he was, sitting safely at home. A part of him wanted to get on his horse and head down there to take part in the scrap. And yet, he knew that his mother would never stand for it. He and the others had just returned home, and Marie would be terribly upset if they turned around and left again so soon.

But if the fighting went on long enough, Mordecai would have to go. He knew that, and his mother would just have to accept it.

In the meantime, there were Felipa and those wild horses to hold his attention . . .

Felipa accepted Marie's offer of hospitality with the same cool grace she did everything else. She offered to sleep in the barn, but Marie wouldn't hear of it. Instead she fixed up a bed in the cabin for the visitor, using a curtain to partition off a part of the room where Marie herself slept. Angeline and Manuel had the other private bedroom to themselves, and Mordecai would sleep in his usual spot in the loft over the dogtrot.

That night, Mordecai lay on his pallet for a long time before he went to sleep. His mind was full of happiness at being home, but that feeling was tempered by worry about James, Jonathan, and Andrew, as well as the sorrow he felt about Petra's death, which his mother had told him about earlier. And his thoughts kept straying to Felipa too, as they had nearly every night over the past few months.

She was friendly enough, and he had never seen anyone better with horses. But did she know how he was really coming to feel about her? After all the tragedy she had been through, romance was probably the last thing on her mind, but Mordecai couldn't help thinking of her that way. He was a young man, she was a very attractive young woman, and, he told himself, there was nothing wrong with feeling the way he did about her.

With a sigh, he rolled over and clutched the blanket tighter around him. The afternoon had been warm following the brief storm, but tonight there was a chill in the air, and it crept in through the tiny cracks in the loft.

In the morning, Marie started getting ready early for the relatives who would be arriving later in the day. There was cooking to be done, and even Angeline pitched in, looking more cheerful than she had in weeks. Mordecai and Manuel saw to the stock, not only the mustangs they had brought in the day before but also the cattle and horses that had been on the farm all along.

As for Felipa, she waited until after the mustangs had been grained and watered, then moved to the corral fence where her saddle was sitting on the top rail. As she reached for it, Mordecai came out of the barn and saw her. "What are you fixing to do?" he asked.

Felipa barely gave him a glance. "I am going to work some more of the kinks out of those horses," she replied. "There is much to do before we can sell them."

Mordecai came over to her quickly and put a hand on her saddle so that she would leave it where it was. "That can wait," he said. "My mama's putting together a party for all my relatives who'll be coming over here, and I think we should just enjoy it."

"That party is to welcome home you and Manuel and Edward. It has nothing to do with me."

"Of course it does! You're our guest. You're just as important as anybody else."

"But I am not a member of your family," Felipa pointed out, and Mordecai was unsure whether he heard a slight catch in her voice or not.

He started to say that they could do something about that situation, but he stopped himself in time. Felipa seemed to be in no mood for a marriage proposal. She had watched the day before as Mordecai, Manuel, and Edward were welcomed back with open arms, and it must have reminded her that she no longer had any close family to hug her and make her feel wanted. Her mother, father, brother, and sister were all buried down by the Nueces River. She was the only survivor, and maybe she was feeling a little guilty about that, Mordecai realized, whether she had any real reason to or not.

He put a hand on her arm, ready for her to pull away. For some reason, she did not. She stood there as he said. "Trust me, Felipa. Working with those mustangs can wait another day. Otherwise my mother's liable to be offended if anybody ignores this little fandango she's throwing."

A faint, bittersweet smile touched Felipa's lips. "All right," she agreed. "The mustangs can wait." Her expression became more solemn, and she lifted a finger admonishingly. "But tomorrow, we get started gentling those horses again. I want them ready to sell by next spring."

"They will be," Mordecai promised. "And they'll bring a mighty fine price. Just you wait and see."

Felipa let him lead her back to the cabin, where she insisted on helping Marie and Angeline with the preparations while Mordecai and Manuel sat in the dogtrot and watched with smiles on their faces. Not long after, Frank and Hope arrived along with their sons Edward and David, as well as Ben and Rose. Mordecai greeted his cousins, shaking hands with David and Ben and giving Rose a hug before telling her how sorry he had been to hear about her mother's passing. Rose was becoming a beauty, Mordecai thought, and in a few years, Andrew would be stumbling over the suitors who showed up to try to win her hand. In a few more years, Andrew would probably be a grandfather.

That thought made Mordecai look over at his mother. Marie was still so slim and attractive, with only a little gray in that thick black hair, that it was hard to believe in another few weeks she would be a grandmother herself. And he'd be an uncle, Mordecai thought.

A little later, Annie and Sly and their two little girls arrived in their wagon, and when Sly got down from the vehicle and came across the yard, Mordecai saw that he was limping heavily. "What happened to you?" he greeted Sly.

Before the former smuggler could answer, Frank said with a grin, "Ol' Sly got hurt in a fight."

"A fight?" echoed Mordecai. Somehow that didn't surprise him.

"Yeah, a fight between him and the ground when he fell out of his wagon over in Bastrop. The ground won," Frank said dryly.

Sly glared. "It was an accident, pure and simple, and nothing to make a big fuss over. The doctor said my leg'd heal up just fine, but that just goes to show you what a sawbones knows about it."

"You never gave it a proper chance to heal," Annie put in as she lifted a pot of beans from the back of the wagon.

Sly waved off her comment and went over to one of the chairs in the dogtrot. As he sat down, he stretched out the injured leg in front of him and sighed in relief. "Anyway," he said, "a bum leg don't keep the more important things from working, now does it, Annie?"

Annie blushed furiously and prettily and snapped, "Go on with you, Sly Shipman. I didn't come over here for that kind of talk. I came to see Mordecai and Manuel and Edward." She smiled at Mordecai. "We were all mighty worried about the three of you."

"Well, I'm sorry, Aunt Annie," Mordecai told her as he took the beans to carry them to the kitchen. "We never meant to worry anybody. We just sort of had our hands full."

Sly called after them, "Well, woman, are you going to make the announcement or do you want me to?"

Annie stopped, and Mordecai paused as well. His aunt was flushed again. She said sharply, "You hush now, Sly Shipman, or you'll embarrass us all." Looking at the others, she went on, "What this husband of mine is trying to say is that we're expecting again."

Marie exclaimed in French and rushed over to put her arms around her sister-in-law. The other women clustered around Annie, and the men all shook hands with Sly. "We're hoping maybe it'll be a boy this time," Sly said as he accepted their congratulations.

"I wouldn't question the way the Lord works in those areas," Frank advised him. "As long as the baby's healthy, I reckon the two of you'll have a lot to be thankful for."

"That is how I feel, too," Manuel said, glancing at Angeline. "Sometimes, when the night is dark, I wonder what I would do if something happened to our baby. But such thoughts will drive a man mad if he lingers on them."

"I know, son," Sly told him. "I've already got two young'uns, so you're not telling me anything I don't already know. I'll let you in on a little secret, though."

Mordecai leaned forward in his chair, wondering what Sly was going to say next.

Sly crossed his arms over his chest and continued, "It never gets any better. From the time the little varmints are born—shoot, before that, even—you worry about 'em. And you'll keep on worrying about 'em as long as you live, no matter where they are or what they're doing. It's just the natural order of things.''

Mordecai frowned. If that was true, it was a wonder folks ever had children. Who'd want to have something you had to worry about all the time?

Then he looked over at Felipa, who was slowly being drawn into the conversation with the other women. He worried about her all the time, and he certainly couldn't deny that he wanted her. Maybe the loving and the worrying just went hand in hand, and you couldn't have one without the other.

If that was the case, it was one hell of a setup, but there was nothing a man could do about it except make the best of things, Mordecai told himself.

Marie would not allow any talk about the troubles until after dinner was over. Then, while the men sat in the dogtrot again, Sly said, "I've heard that our boys and the Mexicans had quite a set-to at Salado Creek, down there north of San Antone."

"Were there very many killed?" Mordecai asked.

"Not on our side," Sly answered with a shake of his head. "If you ask me, Woll's liable to turn tail and run when he finally figures out what he's got himself into. He may have San Antonio under his control, all right, but what's he going to do with it once we cut all of his supply lines? If he's not careful, he's going to find himself under siege. It'll be like '36 all over again, only with the tables turned this time. The Mexicans will be the ones who're trapped."

Mordecai glanced at Felipa, who was helping clear the big tables in the yard. He hoped she wasn't offended by this talk. After all, she and her family had been Mexican citizens. However, when they had spotted Woll's column of troops moving up through South Texas, Felipa had been just as anxious to avoid them as any of the others. Living out in the open most of the year, spending their time trapping wild mustangs, the Sigala family had of necessity not been very politically minded. Ernesto had never been a supporter of Santa Anna, and evidently he had passed that feeling along to his eldest daughter.

"I'm worried about Andrew and James and Jonathan," Edward said. "You reckon they're all right down there?"

"They'll be with Jack Hays and the Rangers," Frank said. "You know what that means. They'll be right in the thick of the trouble, wherever it is. But at the same time, they'll be surrounded by the best fighting men to be found anywhere. I reckon they'll have as good a chance as any to come through this safely, and better'n most.''

There were solemn nods of agreement from the other men. Despite what Frank had said, they were all worried about Andrew, James, and Jonathan, and that concern tempered the festive mood that Marie had planned to welcome home the other travelers.

Still, there was plenty of talk and laughter, and Mordecai had a good feeling inside him that evening after everyone had gone home. After supper, he strolled out to the corral and leaned on the pole fence, watching the mustangs milling around inside the enclosure. Behind him, Manuel and Angeline were sitting in the dogtrot, holding hands, and Marie had brought a bit of needlework outside to catch the last of the light as she wielded her needle and thread.

Mordecai sighed, and then there was a soft step beside him. He looked over, a little more startled then he wanted to let on. He wasn't used to anyone getting that close to him without knowing they were there. He wasn't surprised to see that it was Felipa. She had a light step, and catching mustangs required the ability to move without making a lot of noise.

She must have seen him jump, because she said, ''I am sorry if I startled you.''

''Didn't bother me,'' Mordecai said, rather gruffly. He jerked his head toward the barn. ''I heard you coming a good twenty yards ago, as soon as you left the barn.''

A slight smile curved Felipa's lips. ''That is strange, since I came from the other direction.''

Damn. One more educated guess shot down, Mordecai thought. But he ignored that and said, ''What're you doing out here?''

''The same thing as you—looking at the horses. They are beautiful, aren't they?''

He nodded. ''They sure are.'' *But not half as beautiful as you.*

''We will work with them this winter, and when spring comes, we will have no trouble selling them.''

''You're probably right.'' Mordecai hesitated, not really wanting to ask the next question but knowing that he had to have an answer to it sooner or later. He took a deep breath and plunged ahead. ''Then what? What'll you do after we sell the mustangs and you've got your share of the money? Go back to Mexico?''

''I . . . I do not know.'' For the first time there was a definite note of uncertainty in Felipa's voice. ''There is little to hold me there. I feel like . . . my home is in Texas now.''

Mordecai's heart bounced a little in his chest. Telling himself to stay calm, he shrugged and said, "I'm sure my mother would be glad to let you stay here as long as you want."

Felipa shook her head. "I could not do that. I could not impose on her indefinitely."

"You wouldn't be imposing," Mordecai said quickly. "And if you were—"

He stopped short, and after a few seconds, Felipa asked, "If I were what?"

"I don't know," Mordecai muttered, the brief surge of courage he had felt a moment earlier completely gone now. He had no idea where it had vanished, but it was sure as hell gone. Awkwardly, he went on, "I just think it'd be all right for you to stay."

"We will see," Felipa said coolly, and although they stood there together for at least ten more minutes, leaning on the fence and watching the mustangs in the fading light, not another word was spoken between them.

☆ Chapter ☆
9

General Woll had evidently learned his lesson. Even when several Texan scouting parties ventured almost within spitting distance of San Antonio over the next couple of days after the battle of Salado Creek, the Mexican troops didn't budge. Instead they stayed safely within the confines of the city.

The Mexicans weren't completely spooked, however, as the men under Hays and Caldwell learned on the evening of the second day following the battle. Hays himself brought the news to the camp fire where Andrew, James, Jonathan, Ben Harvey, and Jordan Chesney were sharing a supper of beans and salt pork.

Hays hunkered on his heels next to the fire and accepted the offer of a cup of coffee. He cuffed his hat back on his thick black hair, sipped some of the steaming coffee, and said, "I've got some bad new, boys."

When Hays hesitated and looked a little shaken, Andrew knew what he had to tell them had to be pretty bad, all right. Jack Hays generally seemed to have ice water in his veins, but even he was upset by this new development, whatever it was.

"Might as well spit it out, Cap'n," James said.

Hays took a deep breath. "All right. A relief column of fifty-five men under the command of Captain Nicholas Dawson was on its way over here from La Grange to give us a hand. Woll must've got wind of them coming, because he sent out enough men to intercept them and surround them east of here." Hays shook his head and went on, "Woll's got more sand than I gave him credit for. I figured after that licking we gave him the other day, he wouldn't show his face outside of Bexar for a while.''

"What happened to Dawson and his men?" Andrew asked anxiously. He seemed to recall meeting Nicholas Dawson in Austin at one time, back when he'd still been a member of Congress.

"There were too many Mexicans for them to fight," Hays replied, "so Dawson sent up a white flag." The coffee was cold and forgotten in Hays's cup now. The Ranger's voice hardened as he went on, "The Mexicans fired on them anyway."

Jonathan exclaimed, "They ignored the white flag?"

Hays nodded, his features bleak. "Dawson and about thirty of his men were killed in the fight. The others finally managed to surrender." His voice trembled with emotion. "The sons of bitches shot most of our boys anyway, even though they'd thrown down their guns. They dragged the rest back onto Bexar with them, except for a couple of men who got away and carried the story of what had happened." Hays drained the rest of the coffee abruptly, then tossed the empty cup down. The clatter as it landed on some rocks seemed even louder than normal in the stunned silence around the camp fire. "Don't ever run up a white flag when you're fighting Mexicans," Hays added grimly. "You're better off going down fighting."

He turned and strode toward another camp fire to pass along the tragic news of the Dawson massacre.

Hays's visit had cast a considerable pall over the group. Andrew sighed and shook his head. "Those gents they took prisoner will be doing good to ever see the light of day again," he said.

"You reckon they'll be executed, too?" asked Jonathan.

"Either that or taken back to Mexico and shut up in a prison for the rest of their days," James said. "We'd all do well to remember what Cap'n Jack said—never surrender."

The men nodded solemnly. It was a lesson that had been taught in blood.

Less than a week later, General Adrian Woll withdrew his forces from San Antonio de Bexar, heading back toward the Rio Grande and taking fifty-three prisoners with him. Ranger scouts under Jack Hays and Ben McCulloch confirmed the fact of the retreat. In fact, James and Jonathan were in one of McCulloch's scouting parties, along with Harvey, Chesney, and a gangling, lantern-jawed Ranger named Wallace, and they saw the retreating

Mexicans with their own eyes. When the news got back to the camp north of San Antonio, which by now held close to six hundred men, the reaction was immediate and nearly unanimous.

Everybody wanted to go after Woll and chase him clear back to the Rio Grande if they had to in order to free those prisoners.

For the first time in this conflict, however, politics reared its ugly head, and while Woll retreated, the Texans sat and waited for orders as the politicians in Austin debated endlessly what to do next. Some of the men, growing frustrated and impatient with the delay, simply gave up and went home, returning to their farms and families.

The Lewis brothers stayed. Andrew wasn't surprised that things had gotten bogged down. It was a near miracle, he told the others, that the early days of the fighting had proceeded without any political interference.

September turned into October, and the fall rains came, making life even more miserable for the volunteers waiting to see what was going to happen. All across the Republic, people were demanding that the Mexicans be punished for their invasion and that the prisoners Woll had taken be freed. Finally, General Alexander Somervell rode into camp bearing a letter from President Sam Houston instructing him to put together a force that would follow Woll all the way into Mexico if necessary to retrieve the Texan hostages. A cheer went up from the assembled men as Somervell, a tall, distinguished, middle-aged man, announced his intentions.

James, Jonathan, and Andrew looked at each other. "What about it?" James asked after a moment. "Are we goin' with him?"

Andrew frowned, his forehead creasing in thought. "I've been away from home a long time already," he said slowly. "I reckon everything's all right there, but it'd be nice to be sure. I'd like to know if Mordecai and Edward and Manuel ever made it back safely or not, too."

"Well, I'm sure goin'," Jonathan said without hesitation. "I don't have any old farm to go back to."

"Don't scoff at putting down roots in the land," Andrew told him. "In the long run, that means as much or more than all this helling around we've been doing." He sighed. "I'm afraid you boys will have to go on without me. I'm too old to be going off and invading Mexico."

"They invaded us first," Jonathan pointed out with some heat in his voice.

"I'm not disputing that. I'm just saying that I'm not up to a long campaign like the one General Somervell's talking about. Sorry."

Jonathan was about to say something else when James pulled his hat down over his eyes with a sharp tug. Then James turned to Andrew and put a hand on his brother's shoulder. "Don't pay any attention to this excitable little peckerwood. I reckon we both understand, Andrew. And to tell you the truth, I'm glad you're going back. Frank's a good man, but I'd like for you to be home, too, keeping an eye on things while we're gone."

"Thanks, James. I appreciate it."

"You'll stay until we're ready to pull out, though, won't you?" James grinned. "Chesney's got a jug stashed away somewhere, and I reckon we could persuade him to part with it so's we could say a proper good-bye to you."

Andrew nodded and returned the grin. "I suppose I can stay that long," he said.

Just as James had indicated, the farewell party that night was a little uproarious, with Jordan Chesney sharing the jug of *pulque* he had gotten from somewhere. James's head was pounding early the next morning as the troops now under the command of General Somervell pulled out. He looked back, saw Andrew standing there and leaning on his rifle, and James lifted a hand to wave good-bye to his brother. Nudging Jonathan in the side with his elbow, James said, "Wave to Andrew."

Jonathan turned and gave a grudging wave. "I still feel like he's running out on us," Jonathan complained. "All that talk about being too old . . . Hell, he's not that much older'n you!"

"Andrew's had more in his life to settle him down." James shot a sharp glance at his younger brother. "Don't you go thinkin' he's lost his nerve. Andrew's fought for Texas more times than you and me, on the battlefield and up there in Austin both. There's no better Texan alive, not even old Sam Houston himself."

"Well, maybe," Jonathan allowed. He summoned up a grin and urged his horse into a little faster gait. "Besides, without Andrew along, there'll be that many more Mexicans for us to shoot at."

James just looked at his brother and gave a little shake of his head. Jonathan still had some growing up to do.

There was nothing like an army for stopping and starting, James learned over the next few weeks. If they had gone straight after

Woll, even leaving in October like they had, they might have caught up to the French mercenary before he crossed the Rio Grande. But orders arrived from Austin commanding Somervell to stop and gather a larger force before continuing on toward Mexico. It was the middle of November before the march toward the Rio Grande really got underway. By that time, the Texan force had grown to well over seven hundred men. But the prisoners taken from San Antonio by Woll were probably in some Mexico City dungeon by that time, being gloated over by Santa Anna, who was still smarting from his defeat at San Jacinto over six years earlier.

This was one hell of a way to fight a war, James thought, an opinion shared by most of the men. Of course, there had been so few battles that it couldn't really be called a war yet.

James and Jonathan spent most of their time riding scout with Ben McCulloch and Bigfoot Wallace. The lanky, tobacco-chewing Wallace was full of stories about fighting Indians and taking part in the revolution against Mexico. The yarns kept Jonathan entertained, and even James had to admit that Wallace was quite a character. His eccentric personality didn't mean that he wasn't a salty, capable old fighter, though.

The weather was unusually wet for South Texas, and the mud slowed down the Texans that much more. But finally the storms cleared away and the sun came out again, still warm despite the fact that November had turned to December and winter was fast approaching. The army picked up speed after that, and it wasn't long before they were nearing Laredo, on the Rio Grande. Woll had long since crossed the Rio, of course, but Laredo was still in the hands of the Mexican army. Every Texan in the bunch was determined that was a situation that wouldn't last much longer.

In the Texan camp the night before the battle, James looked around and frowned at the hilarity he saw and heard. Most of the force was still treating the expedition as a lark, a chance to go chase Mexicans and maybe plunder a town or two in the process. Somewhere along the way, James thought, too many of the men had lost sight of why they had come down here to the Rio Grande in the first place. There were murdered Texans to avenge and prisoners to rescue. Likely though, the prisoners were beyond the reach of Somervell's force, and the desire for a just vengeance had turned into something uglier.

"I don't much like this, fellas," James said in a low voice to Jonathan, Harvey, and Chesney, who were gathered around the camp fire with him. "We don't know how many troops the Mexicans have in Laredo, and some of these boys are taking them too lightly. Could be we'll get ourselves whipped when we hit the town tomorrow."

"Hell, James, you shouldn't ought to talk like that," Jonathan admonished him. "It don't matter how many of them pepperbellies are sittin' over there. In a fight, one Texan's worth ten or twenty Mexicans, ain't he?"

Jonathan's voice was a little slurred, and James knew he had been into Chesney's *pulque* again. The man seemed to have an endless supply of the fiery liquor, although James couldn't for the life of him figure out where Chesney was getting the stuff. With a frown, James told his half brother, "You'd better drink some coffee and stay away from everything else tonight. You go into battle tomorrow seeing three Mexicans where there's really only one, you're liable to shoot the wrong one."

"I'll be all right," Jonathan insisted. "Don't you worry your head 'bout me, big brother."

James sighed and gave up. Jonathan had the Lewis stubbornness, all right, even if he sometimes didn't have the sense God gave a toad.

Early the next morning, while mist still hung over the river just beyond the town, the Texans moved into Laredo. For a change, the Mexicans were outmanned, and the battle was short, hardly deserving the name. Most of the Mexican soldiers threw down their *escopetas* at the first sight of the Texans and splashed across the shallow river to head for the hills as fast as their legs would carry them. James and Jonathan and their friends didn't have occasion to fire even a single shot. By midmorning, the Texans were firmly in control of Laredo.

That was when the real trouble started.

James watched in disgust as the looting and the harassing of the town's citizens spread. Shops were plundered, and Mexican women who happened to live on the wrong side of the river were chased down and raped by the unruly Texans. Jonathan's enthusiasm for battle vanished when he saw the ugliness of what was going on. He caught James's arm and said, "This isn't why we came down here. These folks didn't do anything wrong."

James shrugged, not liking the feeling of helplessness that had spread through him. "Not much we can do about it," he said. "Something like this has to burn itself out."

That took the rest of the day and most of the night, but by the next day, the Texans who had gone on a rampage were too tired and hung over to keep on wreaking havoc. General Somervell and some of his officers gradually restored order. James could tell that the general was furious as he called his troops together. Some of the men were shamefaced, as if the realization of what they had done had finally caught up to them, but others looked like they would be rarin' for more once their heads quit hurting so bad, James thought.

"What now?" Jonathan asked as he and the others assembled in the town square.

James nodded toward Somervell, who sat on his horse at the head of the group. "I reckon the general's goin' to tell us."

A moment later, Somervell said, "I won't address the abominable behavior of many of you men these past twenty-four hours, other than to say it was disgraceful and not worthy of men defending the honor of the Republic of Texas! However, that is in the past, and we must look to the future. I have conferred with the *alcalde* of Laredo, and he tells me that General Woll and his troops passed through here weeks ago, just as we suspected. Their destination was the interior of Mexico, and as long as they hold good Texans prisoner, so shall ours be!"

A ragged cheer went up from the volunteers at the indication that the pursuit would continue on across the border. When it died down, Somervell went on, "We shall ford the Rio Grande and advance to the town of Guerrero, where I am told there are considerable numbers of horses. We shall requisition what we need so that every man in our force is mounted. Then we shall chase down that devil Woll and show him that when he makes war on one Texan, he makes war on us all!"

That brought another cheer, although like the first one it was halfhearted. James heard a lot of grumbling in the ranks as the Texans got ready to move out. More than one man was saying that they ought to burn Laredo to the ground as they left, so that the place couldn't harbor any more "damned Meskins."

As they moved out, Jack Hays rode up alongside James and Jonathan. James hadn't seen much of the Ranger captain since leaving San Antonio, although he knew that Hays, McCulloch, and others were continuing their work as scouts. There was a dissatisfied expression on Hays's face as the volunteers began to cross the river.

"You look like you don't much care for this, Cap'n," James commented.

"I don't," Hays replied bluntly. "Crossing the Rio with this bunch is a mistake. They've calmed down now, but they could turn into a rabble again at any time."

Jonathan pointed out, "But you're going with us."

Hays shrugged. "I'm a Texan. I'll go along for a while, even with a damn fool. But this could turn really ugly, boys, and I'm not sure I want any part of it. I'll wait and see how things go in Guerrero before I make up my mind."

"There's some good men who want to press on," Jonathan argued. "I've heard Ewen Cameron, Bigfoot Wallace, and Sam Walker all say we should keep up the chase for however long it takes."

"Good men can make mistakes," Hays said. "But maybe they're right and I'm wrong." He chuckled humorlessly. "Only one way to find out."

The village of Guerrero was about seventy miles downstream from Laredo and took a couple of days to reach. By the time the Texans arrived, their scouts had told them it appeared there were no Mexican troops in the town. General Somervell advanced with a small force of some thirty men, James and Jonathan among them. They were met on the edge of town by a delegation of Guerrero's *alcalde* and several other important members of the community.

James leaned forward in his saddle and tried to keep up with the rapid flow of English, Spanish, and border lingo as Somervell informed the *alcalde* that he would require enough horses to mount all his men. The official was clearly nervous, wiping constantly at a sweat-covered face despite the relatively cool December weather, and James wondered if word had reached Guerrero about what had happened in Laredo. It must have, to provoke such a reaction. The *alcalde* nodded jerkily and promised that the horses would be provided. Through a translator, Somervell thanked the man, then motioned for those accompanying him to turn their horses and go back to the main body of troops.

There was no need for that, James saw in dismay as he swung his horse around. The Texans were already on their way, surging toward the village with a series of bloodcurdling yells. The *alcalde* and his companions spun around and ran for their lives.

"Damn it, no!" Somervell bellowed, motioning for the men to halt. They ignored him, sweeping on toward the town. Somervell put his hand on the butt of his pistol, as if he was going to draw it and start shooting his own men, and James knew if that happened the general would be cut down in a matter of seconds. Scenting fresh blood like a pack of wolves, the volunteers were not going to be denied now.

The men raced past Somervell, who watched them with stony features. James and Jonathan, along with a few other men, stayed with him until the main body of the troops had reached the village. Gunshots boomed, and they were counterpointed by terrified screams.

"It's over," Somervell finally said, his voice as bleak and cold as the grave. "I can't control them any longer—if I ever could. I'm officially ending this expedition and ordering the men to return to Texas and their homes."

"They won't do it," James said, not caring that he was speaking so boldly to a general.

Somervell looked over at him with narrowed eyes. "And who might you be, sir?"

"James Lewis, General. And beggin' your pardon, but I reckon it's too late to tell that bunch what to do."

"I'd say you're right, James Lewis," Somervell replied with a curt nod. He looked at his other officers, the few who had stayed with him rather than join the chaos in Guerrero. "But pass the word anyway, gentlemen. Anyone who does not return to Texas immediately does so in defiance of my orders and runs the risk of being branded a deserter."

Jack Hays had come up in time to hear Somervell's words. He shook his head and said, "That won't do any good, General. Those boys aren't military men, they're volunteers. And they're good honest Texans most of the time, but they've had a bellyful of Santa Anna and his tricks, and now they're taking it out on these poor folks. It's not right, but there's not a hell of a lot we can do about it."

"Except refuse to have any part of it," Somervell snapped. He pulled his horse around. "I'm riding north, gentlemen. Who'll accompany me?"

James and Jonathan looked at each other, then over at Ben Harvey and Jordan Chesney. The bearded Chesney spat on the dusty ground and said, "I come down here to fight Meskins. I ain't of a mind to go home just yet, even if I ain't one to go on a tear like them boys in town."

"I'll stick, too," Harvey added.

"Count me in," Jonathan said immediately. "I don't want any

part of that riot going on, but when the boys calm down, they'll get back to business.''

James wasn't sure of that, but he knew that Jonathan wasn't going to change his mind. And he wasn't going to ride off and leave Jonathan behind. Besides, there was still an off chance they might catch up to Woll and get a chance to rescue those prisoners who had been hauled off from San Antonio. That chance meant that James couldn't give up.

''I'll stay,'' he said quietly.

Jack Hays shook his head and extended his hand to James and Jonathan in turn. ''I've got to go back, boys,'' he said. ''This just isn't what I bargained for. If I run into any of your relatives, I'll let 'em know the two of you were all right when I left you.''

''Thanks, Cap'n,'' James said sincerely. ''That means a lot.''

He sat his horse beside his brother and their friends and watched Somervell, Hays, about half the other officers, and maybe two hundred men straggle back toward the Rio Grande and Texas beyond.

Taking into account the men who had headed home earlier, that left some three hundred men to continue the expedition. Some of them, like the Lewis brothers, took no part in the sacking of Guerrero, but most of them ran rampant through the village for the rest of the day and most of the night, just as in Laredo. They were just as hung over and tired the next day, too, but they were functioning well enough to elect a new leader now that Somervell had left the expedition. A man named William S. Fisher was selected. He had been Secretary of War during Sam Houston's first term as president, and he was obviously popular with the men. Bigfoot Wallace, always anxious for a fight, was still there, too, along with four Ranger captains—Ben McCulloch, Ewen Cameron, William Eastland, and Sam Walker, who had ridden frequently with Jack Hays. As James looked around at them, he hoped the men could command enough respect so that the whole group wouldn't fall apart. Otherwise, the excursion into Mexico was probably doomed.

''The place is called Mier,'' Ben McCulloch told Colonel Fisher as the Texans made camp on the evening of December 22, 1842, three days before Christmas. You wouldn't have known it was the yuletide season here in this land of burning deserts and sweltering skies, James thought as he listened to McCulloch's report. The Ranger captain and his scouts had been out most of the day.

McCulloch went on, "Looks like an important garrison. There's a whole passel of Mexican troops movin' around, Colonel. I figger it'd be better to go 'round the town and leave it alone."

For the past few days, the expeditionary force had been marching on the Texas side of the Rio Grande again, while McCulloch and the Rangers scouted on the Mexican side. Food and supplies were running dangerously low, and Colonel Fisher had given McCulloch orders to find some place they could stock up again.

Now, as he listened to McCulloch's advice, Fisher shook his head angrily and stubbornly. "Did you see Mexican troops in the town itself, Captain?" he demanded.

"Well, no, I don't reckon I did, Colonel. But there's aplenty of 'em right close by in that garrison."

"We must have fresh supplies," Fisher said. "There's no reason we can't cross the river, get what we need, and be back on Texas soil before those Mexicans know what's going on. Now is there, Captain?"

McCulloch's leathery features twisted in a grimace. "It'd be a near thing, a damned near thing. I wouldn't risk it."

"You're not in command of this operation, McCulloch. I am," Fisher said imperiously.

James listened to the exchange and sucked on a tooth. That wasn't a very smart way to talk to a man like Ben McCulloch, he thought.

That was confirmed by the way McCulloch frowned darkly at Fisher and said slowly, "We're all volunteers, Colonel, even if you was elected to lead a bunch o' hung over skunks. But I ain't takin' my boys under the guns of thousands o' Mex soldiers. We'll be ridin', thank you kindly."

Fisher drew himself up to his full height and glared at McCulloch. "You're deserting?" he asked in disbelief.

"Savin' our skins whilst we still got 'em to save," McCulloch said. He turned and stalked off, and most of the men from his scouting company followed him.

After a long moment, Fisher blustered, "Well, good riddance to them, if that's the way they feel. There are still plenty of loyal Texans who'll continue to show those damned Mexicans that we can't be pushed around." He turned to the other men and asked half-imploringly, "Isn't that right, boys?"

A cheer went up. Most of the men still had an appetite for plunder, and the simmering rage they felt toward the Mexicans was enough to drive them on.

Jonathan drew James aside. "I don't think I much like this," he said with a frown of concern.

"I know I don't," James replied. "Ben McCulloch's no fool. You want to light out for home while we still can?"

"Didn't say that. But it's startin' to get a little worrisome."

James nodded. "We'll see what happens in Mier. Time enough then to leave if we want to, I reckon."

The next day, December 23, Colonel Fisher and some two hundred fifty volunteers crossed the river and entered the town of Mier, which was surrounded on three sides by fierce Mexican desert. In the distance, they could see the garrison Ben McCulloch had warned them about, but there were no troops to be seen at the moment. Just as in Guerrero, a delegation made up of the town's *alcalde* and several other men met the Texans and politely inquired as to what these visitors from across the river wanted of them.

"Food, clothing, and powder," Fisher snapped. "Immediately." No translator was required, because the *alcalde* spoke excellent English.

"But that is impossible, *Señor*," the mayor said, giving the time-honored Mexican shrug and spreading his hands. "Perhaps . . . if you can allow us to have until tomorrow . . . we can provide you with what you need."

Fisher hesitated. "Tomorrow will be soon enough," he said after a moment, "but no tricks."

The *alcalde* shook his head fervently and looked as if the mere suggestion of treachery was a gross insult to his honor. "Of course not, *Señor*."

"And to insure that, you'll come with us."

The *alcalde* stiffened slightly but he nodded. "That is agreeable. I will be most happy to visit your camp."

A horse was brought up for the official, and then with him riding beside Fisher, the Texans withdrew across the river. The *alcalde* had spoken in rapid Spanish to his subordinates before going with the Texans, and as best as James could tell as he tried to follow the rapid-fire words, the man had ordered the others to comply with what the Texans wanted.

James heaved a sigh of relief as he and Jonathan followed the others back across the river. Maybe they would get out of this without a battle after all.

The *alcalde* of Mier was taken to Colonel Fisher's tent and evidently spent a pleasant enough night there, because he seemed hale and hearty the next day. However, as the day passed, the supplies Fisher had demanded were not brought down to the river, and late in the afternoon Captain Cameron, Bigfoot Wallace, and a couple of other men were sent across to see what was causing the delay. When the delegation returned, Cameron explained that the townspeople had had trouble gathering the needed supplies and had asked that they be allowed to have one more day to complete the chore. Fisher considered, then nodded.

"Tomorrow is Christmas Day," the colonel pointed out. "An appropriate time for our needs to be met, don't you think, Captain?"

Cameron nodded, then went back across the river with Wallace to convey Fisher's agreement to the terms.

Most of the men seemed unbothered by the proximity of the Mexican garrison and ignored it as they went about their business, which at this point consisted mainly of gambling and drinking. James and Jonathan and a few of the others kept a close eye on the fort, however, but there were few troops to be seen. Occasionally, they spotted a guard walking sentry duty, but other than that, the garrison seemed almost lifeless.

Christmas Eve passed quietly, and Christmas Day dawned clear and cool. Again there was no sign of the townspeople of Mier bringing the supplies down to the river, and by now Fisher was too impatient to merely send over another small delegation.

"I fear that you and your people have tried to betray us, sir," Fisher said harshly to the *alcalde*. "Very well, if that is the way you wish to conduct yourselves, we shall simply cross the river and *take* what we need."

While the *alcalde* shook his head sadly, Fisher gave the order for the men to mount up. The command met with almost universal approval, as shouts of anticipation went up from many of the Texans. Within minutes, they had saddled their horses and were splashing across the Rio, anxious to extend their reign of terror to Mier.

James and Jonathan rode along, hanging back slightly with the other men who regretted the twists of fate this expedition had taken. As far as they were concerned, they were just being loyal to

Texas, but James hoped fervently they weren't taking their loyalty too far.

The town was quiet as the two hundred fifty men rode in. Few people appeared to be stirring on this holy day. Obviously, though, the word had been passed that they were coming, because the *alcalde*'s assistant hurried out to meet them. Fisher turned to the *alcalde*, who rode beside him, and snapped, "Find out where those damned supplies are!"

There was another rapid exchange of Spanish, then the *alcalde* turned solemnly to Fisher and said, "I am told that General Ampudia has forbidden the citizens of our poor town to assist you, Colonel. General Ampudia is the commander of the garrison, and it is hoped by all that you will be reasonable about this matter."

"Reasonable, hell!" Fisher shot back. "We're not reasonable, we're Texans! And we won't be told what we can and can't do by a bunch of damned Mexicans." The colonel twisted in his saddle to look back at his men. "Take what you need!" he called loudly.

"That could be a mite hard, Colonel," drawled Bigfoot Wallace, lifting a hand to point with a long, knobby finger. "Look yonder."

Most of the men had already seen what was coming, and a nervous sound ran through their ranks. The first riders of what looked like at least a thousand Mexican cavalry troops had just entered the main street of Mier at the opposite end. They were advancing steadily, picking up speed as they came toward the Texans, stopping just short of an outright charge.

"My God," Fisher breathed. He jerked his head to the left and then the right and saw more troops closing in from that direction. Twisting even farther, he looked behind him and saw that more soldiers, this time on foot, had moved between the Texans and the river. They were pinned in, trapped as sure as blazes.

Fisher might have been a pompous ass, but James had to give him credit for what he did next. The colonel was no coward. He yanked his sword from its scabbard, waved it over his head, and shouted, "Follow me, Texas!"

Then he charged straight at the Mexican cavalry closing in from the front.

After a second or two of stunned surprise, the Texans followed after him, whooping and shooting. James unlimbered both of his Colts and galloped to the forefront of the volunteers, guiding his horse with his knees and firing both of the heavy long-barreled revolvers. Jonathan was close beside him, smoke, lead, and flame pouring from the barrel of his rifle. Ben Harvey and Jordan Chesney were close behind, and not far off, Bigfoot Wallace was roaring happily as he went into battle, the floppy brim of his shapeless felt hat pushed back by the wind of the wild charge.

The bold strategy broke the back of the Mexican attack. After a couple of largely futile volleys, the soldiers fell back hurriedly in the face of the withering fire from the Texans. The Mexicans stopped short of retreating all the way out of town, however, and through sheer force of numbers they blocked the street. The same was true in the other direction. The Texans were still trapped, despite the damage they had done in a short but bloody time.

"Find whatever cover you can!" Fisher cried over the noise of battle. "Go to ground, men!"

There was a large plaza in the center of town, surrounded by a low stone wall. That seemed to be the best cover available, so most of the men broke for it immediately. A few stragglers were caught in the open as the Mexicans resumed firing, but practically everyone made it to the dubious shelter of the plaza. As soon as James and Jonathan were inside the wall, having leaped their horses over it, they slipped down from the saddles and pulled the horses to the ground. With all the stray lead flying around, a horse made a mighty easy target. "Hang on to 'em!" James called to his brother, then pressed the reins of his horse into Jonathan's hand. He jerked his rifle from the saddleboot and leaped to the wall, sprawling behind it and lifting up enough to send a couple of shots toward the Mexicans, who were getting braver and charging the plaza again.

A moment later, Jonathan threw himself down beside James, who looked over at him and growled, "Thought I told you to hold the horses."

"Fella with a leg wound offered to do it for me," Jonathan replied. "Captain Cameron passed the word already. Men who're hurt too bad to keep fighting are to hold horses and reload for the rest of us."

James nodded curtly. That was a good idea. They were going to have one hell of a fight on their hands, and they would need every able-bodied man if they were going to have a chance of survival.

It was easy to see now that Colonel Fisher had made a mistake, a bad mistake. That Mexican general Ampudia had been smart and kept most of his men out of sight until it was time to move against the Texans. If Santa Anna had been half as wily, James thought, there might never have been a Republic of Texas.

What he and his companions didn't know yet but quickly figured out was that they were outnumbered by more than ten to one, and Ampudia's forces had them pinned down with no water except what they had in their canteens; no powder and shot other than what each man had on him; and no way to get more of anything.

They were trapped good and proper, James realized, with no way out.

One hell of a Christmas present, he thought grimly as he drew a bead on another Mexican trooper.

Gunfire and powder smoke filled the air above Mier all the rest of the day, slacking off somewhat during the night but never ceasing entirely. Then, with the rising of the sun on December 26th, the Mexicans attacked with renewed fervor. It was going to be the Alamo all over again, James thought as he lay behind the low stone wall and kept sniping at the Mexican soldiers. Sooner or later they would be overrun and slaughtered to the last man.

After the past twenty-four hours, James would have almost welcomed death. He hadn't eaten or slept, except for an occasional nap of a few minutes, snatched whenever he could find the chance. His lips were dry and cracked, the result of having only a single mouthful of water in the last day. His head pounded, and his eyes felt like a bucket of sand had been rubbed into them. Somehow, though, he kept fighting. Beside him, Jonathan wasn't much better off, although at James's insistence he had slept a little more while James kept watch. They hadn't seen Harvey or Chesney since the day before and didn't know if their friends were still alive or not.

Jonathan crawled up beside James and asked in a hoarse voice, "How's your powder holdin' out?"

James shook his head grimly. "Not much left. I reckon everybody's in about the same fix, though. It won't last much longer." Jonathan didn't ask him whether he meant the gunpowder or the battle, and James wasn't even sure he knew which one it was himself.

"Guess we should've started home a couple of nights ago, when we were talking about it."

"Yeah," James said. "I guess so. But talking like that won't change it now."

"I know. It's just—" Jonathan stopped in mid-sentence, then said, "What's going on over there?"

Colonel Fisher's command post, such as it was, was only about twenty yards from the spot where James and Jonathan were lying behind the wall. James looked over that way and saw Fisher knotting a large white rag onto the barrel of a rifle.

"What the hell's he doing?" James muttered. "He can't be—"

"Looks like he is," Jonathan said as Fisher crawled over to the wall and began to lift the rifle with the white cloth on its barrel. "He's raising the white flag!"

"No!" James cried, remembering what Jack Hays had said about the Dawson massacre and how a Texan should never surrender. They had learned that same lesson the hard way about the Comanches, and by now it was obvious the Mexicans couldn't be trusted, either.

James surged to his feet, knowing that he had to stop Fisher somehow. Better for them to all die here in this ugly little village than to turn themselves over to the mercy of the Mexicans. He started to dash toward Fisher, hoping to knock down the white flag before the enemy noticed it.

He had taken only a couple of steps when something smashed into his shoulder, spinning him to the ground. James landed hard, the breath going out of him, his entire left shoulder and arm numb. He knew he had been shot, though, and the pain would set in later—if he lived long enough.

"We surrender!" he heard Colonel Fisher shout. "We surrender, damn it! We're laying down our arms!"

"Not . . . not the . . . white flag," James muttered as darkness closed in on him. He felt too tired all of a sudden to keep his eyes open any longer, and he let them slide closed. As he did so, he heard the gunfire die away into silence, the silence of defeat.

He and the other Texans were prisoners now, James thought with his last shred of consciousness. And God would have to have mercy on their souls, because the Mexicans sure as hell wouldn't.

☆ Chapter ☆

10

James Lewis put one foot in front of the other and tried not to think about where he was going. That was what he had been doing for over a month now, and if nothing else the effort had kept him from losing his mind. At least he hoped he wasn't crazy.

On the other hand, if he had been insane, then maybe he could have drawn some comfort from the possibility that he was only *imagining* he was on his way to Mexico City to spend the rest of his days rotting in some hellhole of a dungeon.

It could have been worse. He and Jonathan and all the other Texan prisoners had come within a hen's whisker of being dead.

There was no such thing as being a prisoner of war with the normal rights of such, not where Santa Anna was concerned. James and some of the other men had known that, but Colonel Fisher had not, not until it was too late. The way the Mexicans saw it, the Texans had "surrendered at discretion," meaning that the Mexicans could execute all of them if it struck their fancy to do so. That was Santa Anna's standing order, in fact, but after a day of wavering, General Ampudia had decided to grant the prisoners some mercy. Fisher and some of the other officers were immediately taken to Mexico City by wagon, while the men left behind were forced to start marching toward the capital on foot.

The battle at Mier had ended badly, but the Texans had acquitted themselves well before the lack of gunpowder had led Fisher to surrender. They had suffered twelve deaths during the fighting, but James had heard speculation that up to six hundred Mexicans had been killed. That was an amazing total if it was true, but James didn't really doubt it too much. The Texans were good shots, and their weapons were generally far superior to the Mexican *escopetas*, many of which were ancient and misfired half the time.

Jonathan was stumbling along beside James, and he muttered, "Is that a town I see up yonder?"

James had been watching the ground as he walked, so that he wouldn't trip over any of the rocks that littered the hard, sandy surface. A man who turned an ankle would just have to suffer with it, because the Mexican guards didn't allow any lagging behind. James lifted his eyes and squinted in front of him, seeing the adobe buildings gradually taking shape in the haze.

"That's a settlement, all right," he told Jonathan. "Don't know which one, though."

Captain Cameron was walking only a few feet away, and he said, "I figure that's Saltillo. That's where we're going to make our play."

The captain's voice was firm with resolve, but James thought the big redheaded Scotsman was crazy. For the past few nights, when the group stopped to camp out in the open on the cold, windswept Mexican plains, Cameron had been talking in a low voice about how they were going to escape. It was true the prisoners outnumbered their guards; there were almost two hundred Texans and only half that many Mexicans to guard them and keep them moving south. But the Mexicans were mounted and the Texans were on foot, most of their strength already drained by the long march. As far as James could see, trying to jump the Mexicans now would just get some of the Texans killed. As difficult as it was, they needed to wait for a better time.

"We'll be ready when you give the word, Captain," Jonathan said quietly. He supported Cameron's plan, vague though it was. Jonathan had always been one to choose action over inaction, whether it was the wise thing to do or not.

The new year had come and gone while they were prisoners, and James figured it was now sometime around the first of February, 1843. He wondered if Andrew had gotten home safely and if Mordecai and the others had ever shown up. He wondered if Angeline had had her baby yet. Was it time? He had lost track. He scratched the heavy growth of beard on his face and tried to make himself think about things like that, instead of the bleak future that was facing all of them.

The Mexican village was indeed Saltillo, and although James

saw Captain Cameron talking urgently in hushed tones to Sam Walker, nobody tried to make a break for freedom. Obviously the leaders of the escape attempt had decided to wait for a more opportune moment.

For one thing, it turned out there were more Texan prisoners already being held in Saltillo; they were the survivors of the Dawson Massacre, back up near San Antonio months earlier. These men, a couple of dozen in all, were added to the group which had been brought from Mier, swelling the ranks of the prisoners that much more. Cameron and Walker seemed happy about this development, and even happier that command of the detail guarding was handed over to a young Mexican officer named Barragan.

"That boy's in for a surprise when we get to Salado," Cameron said quietly around a campfire that night. James and Jonathan sat nearby, along with Walker, Bigfoot Wallace, and several other men.

"Salado's a hacienda, ain't it?" Bigfoot asked. "Why's them Mexes takin' us there?"

"From what I've overheard, they plan to get fresh horses for themselves when we reach the hacienda," Cameron said. "And that's where we'll strike. We beat them at Salado Creek in Texas, and we'll beat them at Salado here, too."

James stared into the fire and didn't say anything. He had heard it all before.

The next day, the prisoners were started toward the Mexican ranch called Hacienda Salado. It was about a hundred miles deeper into the interior, and several days of hard marching were required to reach it. The Texans were fed only a handful of beans and a piece of stale bread each day, and they were growing weaker and weaker. By the time they reached Salado, James thought bitterly, they might all be too weak to even attempt to escape, no matter how much Cameron goaded them on.

But finally Salado came into view, a compound of buildings with a low adobe wall around them. The prisoners were prodded through the gate in the wall and into the courtyard beyond, where the Mexican guards ordered them to sit down. James and Jonathan sank down cross-legged on the hard ground, grateful for the respite.

If there were fresh horses here, James couldn't see them. He did see a squat, sturdy building with a heavy door nearby, however, and when one of the Mexican officers opened the door, James glimpsed what looked like kegs of powder and crates of ammunition. James glanced over at Cameron and saw the undisguised joy in the Scotsman's eyes. A supply of powder and shot might prove to be more important than even horses.

The night passed quietly, and Cameron and Walker spread the word that they would strike at sunrise the next morning, visiting each of the small camp fires the prisoners were allowed and alerting all of the men to what was about to happen. James had a feeling that this time, it was actually going to come about.

Maybe that was best, he thought. The way things were going, the grueling march to Mexico City was going to kill some of them anyway, and the ones who survived had nothing to look forward to except more misery. They could at least strike a blow for freedom, and if they died, well then, they did. So be it.

None of the Texans slept much, and they were all on edge when the sky in the east began to turn rosy with the approach of dawn. They waited impatiently as Cameron and Walker stood up and strolled toward the guards near the hut where the ammunition was stored. There were guards at the gate of the hacienda compound, too, as well as others scattered around the place, but none of them seemed especially alert. They must have thought that all the fight had gone out of their captives.

They were about to find out just how wrong they were.

The guards at the hut looked curiously at Cameron and Walker as the two Texans approached. James and Jonathan were sitting nearby, their knees drawn up and their heads down, but they were actually watching through slitted eyes as Cameron began trying to say something in clumsy Spanish to the guards. The Mexicans leaned closer, trying to make out the words.

Cameron moved with surprising speed for a man who had been half-starved and marched across hundreds of miles of Mexican desert. His hand shot out, closed on the barrel of a guard's rifle, and wrenched the weapon out of the man's hand before the Mexican knew what was happening. Cameron drove the butt of the rifle into the guard's stomach, doubling him over, then slapped the stock against the side of his head, sending him down to the ground unconscious. At the same time, Walker grabbed the rifle away from another guard and slammed a fist into his jaw, knocking him back against the wall of the ammunition hut.

That was the signal for the rest of the Texans to strike. With an awful cry that was torn hoarsely from hundreds of throats, the prisoners surged up off the ground and threw themselves at their warders. James clubbed his fists together and slammed them into the face of a startled young Mexican, feeling the satisfying crunch of cartilage and bone as the guard went down. Beside him, Jonathan was grappling with another guard. James scooped up the musket that had been dropped by the man he had felled and thrust the bayonet on the end of the barrel into the side of the man Jonathan was fighting. The Mexican screamed and sagged against Jonathan, and blood poured from the wound as James ripped the bayonet free.

The fight was short but brutal. When it was over, a dozen or more Mexicans had been killed, and five Texans were dead. But the Mexican cavalry had retreated from the hacienda compound, leaving the Texans in control of the ranch, the ammunition stored there, and the rifles that had been taken from the guards. The Mexican foot soldiers still inside the walls were now the prisoners of the Texans.

James figured there would be a massacre as the Texans vented their rage and resentment on the Mexicans, now that the former captors were prisoners themselves, but Cameron and Walker cannily kept things under control. Dead, the Mexicans wouldn't be any good as hostages. Exhibiting either daring or foolhardiness— or maybe a little of both—Cameron stepped up on the wall and called, "Barragan! Come out here so we can talk, damn you!"

The young officer, pale and trembling now that the tables had been turned, rode toward the wall from the knot of Mexican cavalry waiting a hundred yards or so away. His hat had been knocked from his head during the fighting. James watched him coming and couldn't tell if Barragan was furious or scared. Probably both, James thought. Santa Anna wouldn't like it when he heard about this, wouldn't like it one little bit.

Glaring across twenty yards of distance at Cameron, Barragan said tightly, "If you wish to surrender, Texan, I will accept it."

Cameron laughed. "Surrender, hell! We've got guns, and we've got enough powder and shot in here to fight for a year. Now I'm going to tell you how it is, Barragan, and what you're going to do."

James could almost see the young officer quivering with outrage, but Barragan sat on his horse and listened quietly as Cameron told him to take all his cavalry troops and withdraw from the area. Otherwise, Cameron threatened, the Mexican soldiers who had been captured would all be killed.

James didn't expect the threat to do any good. Mexican officers had never set much store by their troops. Barragan would probably tell Cameron to go ahead and kill them, James thought. But after a tense moment, the young officer called out, "It will be as you say." Barragan pulled his horse around and galloped back to join the rest of his men.

Jonathan let out a low whistle. "Never expected him to do that. I reckoned we'd have to fight the little bastard some more."

"He's young," James said with a shrug as they watched from the wall. "Maybe he's never had to deal with anything like this before. Or maybe he's just trying to pull some sort of trick."

That didn't seem to be the case, however. The Texans watched, Cameron and Walker taking turns with a captured spyglass, as Barragan and the rest of the cavalry rode off to the south. They kept going until even the dust raised by their passing had vanished in the sweltering blue sky.

"What do we do now?" muttered James. "Take those prisoners all the way back to Texas with us?"

It quickly developed that wasn't what Cameron and Walker had in mind. Cameron called Bigfoot Wallace over to him, and James and Jonathan trailed along behind the lanky frontiersman. Bigfoot spoke passable Spanish, and Cameron told him, "Tell those Mex soldiers to get the hell out of here. If we see any of them again, we'll kill them. Got that?"

Bigfoot nodded. "Sure, Cap'n. You figger that's the best thing to do?"

Cameron sighed. "We're at least a hundred miles from the border, we've little water and food, and we don't have time to herd along a bunch of prisoners. We've got to get back to the Rio Grande just as fast as we can, before Barragan brings back reinforcements."

"You reckon that's what he's gone to do?" James asked.

Cameron nodded. "That's about all he can do. He can't recapture us with the few men he has left on horseback, and this bunch . . ." He waved a hand at the Mexican prisoners. "Well, they don't have a lot of fight left in them. Most of them are convicts, and they won't be anxious to get in a battle again, especially since they're unarmed and there are no officers around."

James saw the sense of Cameron's words. The captain had put his escape plan into effect, and so far it had actually worked. Maybe he had been too pessimistic about Cameron, James thought. Maybe the man would get them out of this mess yet.

But like Cameron himself had said, they were a long way from the border, with scanty supplies, and their long ordeal had weakened them considerably. Add to that the fact that sooner or later the Mexicans would come after them again like bats out of hell.

Well, all they could do, James told himself, was make a run for the Rio Grande. And pray.

Cameron, Bigfoot Wallace, Sam Walker, and some of the other men put their heads together and decided that instead of heading north, the men would strike out east, figuring that it might be closer to the Rio Grande in that direction as the border river curved down toward the Gulf of Mexico. It was still early in the day when they set out after freeing the Mexican prisoners. As Cameron had predicted, the soldiers didn't show any inclination to stay and fight once they got it through their heads that they were free again. Instead they took off running as fast as they could, most of them heading south, deeper into the interior of the country. A few of them went north or west, however: no doubt men who had families living in villages in those directions.

There was a well inside the walls of the *rancho*, but there was little water in it. The winter had been a dry one, and unless heavy spring rains came, this well and others would probably run completely dry. But the Texans were able to fill up several canteens they had taken from the Mexican soldiers.

"This'll have to do us until we find more water," Cameron said as he capped one of the canteens. "It probably won't take us long."

The big Scotsman wasn't one to give up easily, James thought with a wry, tired smile. But he had to admit that Cameron's enthusiasm had carried them along so far. Without him prodding the rest of them to fight back, they might have still been prisoners.

All that day, the fugitives stayed on the road as they traveled east. The road was narrow and poorly maintained, but at least they could tell they were going in the right direction. That evening, before they made camp, however, Cameron led the men away from the highway.

"That's where Santa Anna's men will look for us first thing," Cameron insisted. "We'll have to cut across country if we're going to have any chance to escape."

That made sense to James, but within two days, he saw that it was a potentially fatal mistake. True, the Texans would have been more likely to encounter resistance if they had stayed on the road, but they were well armed and would have had a chance to fight their way through any trouble they ran into. As it was, they were soon helplessly, irrevocably lost. None of the men were familiar enough with these Mexican deserts to know where they were going, not even Bigfoot Wallace.

Not only that, but there was evidently no water to be had in these arid wastes. The officers kept the canteens and doled the water out in increasingly small rations, but it still ran out in only a few days. The sun, which beat down blindingly despite the season, only added to their misery. There were cactuses, snakes, and scorpions the size of a man's palm. James had never been in such a fix in his life.

"We're not . . . going to make it . . . are we?" Jonathan asked him one day as they stumbled along with the other men, some one hundred seventy-five in all.

James shook his head wearily. "Not unless we're damned lucky," he replied.

"Some of the men have thrown away their guns. They're too tired to carry 'em anymore."

James's hands tightened on the musket he had brought from Salado. It might be just a Mexican *escopeta*, but there was no way he was giving it up, nor the powder and shot he was carrying for it, either. If the soldiers found them, he wanted at least to be able to put up a fight.

Several times, the Texans had been forced to hide behind scrub brush or in gullies as Mexican patrols passed far in the distance, no doubt searching for them. So far they had been able to dodge the riders, but like James had said, it was going to take a lot of luck to see them through to the Rio Grande without being discovered.

A couple more days passed, and still there was no sign of the border. The food they had brought from the hacienda was gone now, along with the water, so the men began catching grasshoppers and even small snakes to eat. The vile carcasses also provided a little moisture, but not enough to make up for what the sun and the heat leached out of the desperate Texans. And at night, as the warmth of the day disappeared and a bone-numbing chill settled down on the land, the Texans scratched out holes in the ground, praying that the earth would turn muddy as they dug deeper. Sometimes it did, and then they pressed their cracked lips and swollen tongues to the mud, trying to suck out any last vestiges of dampness.

They were all going to die. James knew that now, and it was

almost a relief when, a week after the escape from Salado, a troop of Mexican cavalry boiled over a ridge and charged toward them. A bullet through the brain was a hell of a lot better than the torture they had been enduring.

James jerked his musket to his shoulder, pulled back the hammer, and aimed as best he could at the onrushing Mexicans. He was so weak that the barrel wavered back and forth ludicrously. He took a deep breath, firmed his grip on the weapon, and pulled the trigger. The *escopeta* boomed, and its recoil against his shoulder was almost enough to knock him down in his weakened condition. Beside him, Jonathan's musket also blasted.

Unable to tell if he had hit anything or not, James began reloading as quickly as he could, but his movements were slow and awkward. All around him was chaos. The men who had thrown away their weapons were running frantically in all directions, some of them so crazed by fear and exhaustion that they fled directly toward the charging Mexicans. Sabers rose and fell, and men screamed. James got one more shot off, then had to dodge aside as he was almost ridden down by one of the cavalrymen. As it was, the horse's shoulder banged against him hard enough to send him spinning to the ground.

He looked up in time to see Jonathan jerk and stiffen. Blood came down in a sheet over the young man's face, and he crumpled loosely to the ground.

"Jonathan!" James shouted as he scrambled to his hands and knees and crawled over to his brother. He grabbed Jonathan's shoulders and shook him, but Jonathan's head lolled loosely on his neck. James bent over him and began to cry. One of the stray bullets flying around wildly had hit Jonathan in the head, and James knew it was too late to do anything for him.

But at least Jonathan was out of his misery now. That thought burned through James's brain, and he surged to his feet, snatching up the musket Jonathan had dropped. He gripped it by the barrel and swung it like a club as one of the Mexicans galloped by. The stock caught the cavalryman in the stomach and shattered, but the impact was enough to knock the rider out of the saddle. He landed hard on the ground, gasping for breath. James didn't give him a chance to regain it. He stepped over to the man and crushed his skull with two blows of the musket's barrel.

James leaned over and jerked the dead man's pistol from its holster. The Mexican must have been an officer, James realized belatedly, otherwise he would not have been carrying a handgun.

Swinging around, James spotted the man's horse not far away. It had come to a stop and was now dancing around skittishly, its nerves stretched taut by the continuing gunfire, shouting, and screaming.

James had the same knack with horses as all the Lewises, and he called out softly, reassuringly, to the animal as he approached it, his free hand outstretched. The horse shied away a little, gave him a walleyed look, then paused long enough for James to grab the dangling reins and swing into the uncomfortable Mexican saddle before the horse knew what was going on. He settled his feet in the ornamented stirrups, checked the loads in the pistol, and then kicked it into a gallop. He pointed its nose straight at the heaviest concentration of Mexican soldiers.

If he was going to die, then by God, he was going to do some damage first!

With a high-pitched shout, James rode into the thick of the fighting. The pistol bucked in his hand as he triggered off shot after shot. He saw men fall, saw horses jerk away from him, then suddenly he was through them and there was nothing but open prairie in front of him. The mount beneath him sensed freedom and stretched its legs into an even more ground-consuming gait.

James was so tired all he could do was hang on for dear life. The horse, desperate to be out of the fighting, was doing it all. A couple of times James thought he heard something whip past his ear and figured that some of the Mexicans were shooting at him, but their bullets missed.

Jonathan was still back there, and it tore at James's guts that he would not be able to give his brother a decent burial. But somehow he had been given an unexpected chance at life, and he could not turn it down. He rode for all he was worth, leaning far forward over the neck of the Mexican cavalry mount.

The patrol had its hands full just rounding up the escaped prisoners, and James supposed later that they didn't have time to bother sending anyone after just one man. Because as he rode on, there was no sign of pursuit behind him. Gradually he became aware that the horse was heading north, and he didn't try to change its course. Heading east hadn't worked out anyway, and he knew that as long as he kept going northward, he would come to the Rio Grande sooner or later.

James threw back his head and laughed hysterically at that thought. Sure, he would reach the Rio Grande eventually—if he didn't get caught first, or die of thirst or starvation. That was all he had to worry about.

Still laughing, he rode on into the late afternoon, the horse galloping madly beneath him.

Hacienda Salado was even uglier coming back than it had seemed the first time he saw it, Jonathan Lewis thought as he staggered into the *rancho*'s compound several days after all but a handful of the escaped prisoners from Texas had been recaptured.

Jonathan's head throbbed horribly. The only treatment his wound had received was having a strip of dirty cloth bound around it by Bigfoot Wallace. Bigfoot had assured him, however, that the bullet which had struck his skull had glanced off, causing a messy wound but doing little real damage. The big frontiersman had also told him he would probably recover from the injury. "Less'n you get brain fever, or it goes to festerin'," he added.

As he sank down on the hot ground with the other exhausted prisoners, Jonathan managed a grim smile. He wasn't sure how he was supposed to know if he developed "brain fever." He didn't see how he could possibly feel any worse than he did now.

At least there was some slight consolation in the knowledge that James had gotten away, along with a few other men. Bigfoot had told Jonathan about seeing James huddled over his body.

"Reckon he thought you was dead, son, 'cause he come up off that ground like a man gone crazy with sufferin'. Knocked one o' them Mexes off a horse, he did, then got on that cayuse and rode right into the big middle of 'em, firin' off a pistol as he went. He probably killed two or three of 'em bustin' through there, and I seen him ridin' off north like a bat out o' hell. Didn't notice much after that, 'cause I sort of had my own hands full tryin' to stay alive."

Most of the prisoners had been taken alive, in fact. It seemed that Santa Anna had already heard about the escape from Salado, and he had given orders that the Texans were to be recaptured if possible so that they could be properly executed. The story was already going through the ranks of the ragged men from north of the border. All of them were going to be shot by a firing squad.

Jonathan hated to give Santa Anna that much satisfaction, but there wasn't a damn thing he or anybody else could do about it. The Texans had shot their bolt in the first escape attempt, and there would not be another. Even Captain Cameron seemed to sense that.

Still, at least until the execution came, they had food and water, even if it was just moldy tortillas and a cup or two of brackish liquid each day. That was better than nothing, and as several more days passed after their return to Hacienda Salado and there was still no move to put the prisoners in front of a firing squad, Jonathan felt some of his strength returning to him.

He prayed that James had gotten safely back to the border. At first he had felt some irrational resentment over the fact that James had left him behind, but he soon put that behind him. James had been convinced he was dead, or else his older brother never would have left his side. Jonathan was sure of that. And *somebody* needed to come out of this fiasco alive. Jonathan shook his head ruefully as he recalled how he had regarded this whole thing as an adventure, a chance to pay back the Mexicans for past wrongs. Now it had turned into a disaster, and the Texans had no one to blame but themselves.

It was impossible to keep rumors from circulating, and those rumors were fueled by the Mexican guards, some of whom had become rather friendly toward their captives. The way Jonathan heard it, Santa Anna's execution order was being resisted by the governer of the province of Coahuila, one Francisco Mexia. If that was true—and it had to be, otherwise they'd all be dead by now, Jonathan reasoned—then the help was coming from an unexpected source. He never would have thought a Mexican politician could be capable of mercy toward a bunch of raggedy-ass Texans.

After a few more days went by, the prisoners were prodded to their feet one morning and marched into the center of the courtyard. Even though they were all in irons now, their feet shackled together, they were ringed tightly by serape-wrapped guards, all of whom were heavily armed. A passage was formed for the officer now in charge of the prisoners, young Barragan having been replaced by a colonel named Canales. The colonel's aide, who marched just behind him, carried a small earthen mug.

For some reason, when Jonathan saw that mug, a shiver went through him.

Canales spoke loudly in English. ''By the order of his merciful highness, General Antonio Lopez de Santa Anna, all of you criminals will be spared—''

A brief, ragged cheer went up, an expression of gratitude that was silenced quickly and replaced by stunned horror as Canales went on.

''All of you will be spared except for one in ten, and those men will be selected by the luck of the draw," Canales said. He motioned his aide forward with the mug. "In this mug there are one hundred and fifty-nine white beans." He reached into the pocket of his uniform jacket and brought out a handful of small black objects. As he dribbled them one by one into the mug, he continued, "To them are added seventeen black beans. The white beans signify exemption from the sentence, and the black beans signify death." Once all black beans were in the mug, the colonel nodded to the aide, who gave it a slight shake, hardly enough to even begin to mix the beans. Then, with an ugly smile, Canales turned to Ewen Cameron, who stood at the forefront of the men. "You will choose first, Captain."

Cameron didn't flinch. With a slight smile on his battered face, he said, "Well, boys, we have to draw, so let's be at it." He reached up without hesitation, plunged his hand into the out-stretched mug, and withdrew a white bean.

A sigh of relief came from the Texans, and Colonel Canale's face tightened with anger. Obviously, he had been expecting Cameron to draw one of the black beans. With a curt gesture, he ordered Cameron to step back so that the grim lottery could continue.

One by one, the men filed forward to draw a bean from the mug. A major named Cocke was the first one to draw a black bean, and although he paled at the sight of it, he said jauntily, "Boys, I told you so. I never failed in my life to draw a prize."

Another man, when he pulled a black bean from the mug, announced loudly, "Well, they murdered my brother with Colonel Fannin, and now they're about to murder me."

Jonathan's heart was slugging wildly in his chest as his turn approached. Bigfoot Wallace was right in front of him, and he gave Jonathan a crooked smile. "Don't worry, son," Bigfoot told him. "I reckon the Lord's got His own reasons for lettin' this go on, and I ain't about to argue with Him."

With that, Bigfoot reached into the mug and pulled out a white bean.

Jonathan took a deep breath. As he hesitated, he glanced around at the Mexican officers and guards and saw that many of them had sickened expressions on their faces. They didn't like this any better than the Texans did. Santa Anna couldn't have come up with a more cruel punishment, Jonathan thought. But there was nothing anyone here at Salado could do about it. Jonathan plunged his hand into the mug, felt his fingertips close on the smooth surface of a bean. He started to push it aside and pick another one instead, then realized the futility of the gesture. He plucked the bean out of the mug.

It was white.

Jonathan stumbled aside to let the next man take his turn. He heard groans go up from the assembled prisoners and knew that the man had selected a black bean. Jonathan's pulse hammered with relief at his own good fortune, but the feeling warred with guilt. He was going to live, and seventeen of his comrades were going to die. But he had taken his chance just like all the others, and fate had smiled on him for some reason. Like Bigfoot had said, there was no point in arguing with Providence.

When the grisly drawing was over, the unlucky seventeen were tied together and marched over to a long log which had been placed next to the wall. They were forced to sit down on the log, their backs to their executioners.

"For God's sake," one of the men cried out, "at least shoot us from the front!"

Colonel Canales ignored the plea. He spoke sharply to the men he had selected to carry out the sentence of death. Rifles were raised and readied. Some of the other Texans turned their eyes away while others watched in horrified fascination, knowing that it could have just as easily been them perched awkwardly on that log.

"Fire!" Canales ordered.

A volley rang out, and several of the men on the log were knocked forward by the bullets, pulling with them the men they were tied to. Jonathan hoped that would be the end of it, but Canales callously ordered his men to reload and fire again, then again, and again. For almost a quarter hour, rifles crashed and bullets tore into the sprawled bodies of the Texans, mutilating some of them almost beyond recognition as something that was once human. A few of the men did not die immediately but suffered through the whole dreadful time before death claimed them. One of them, who was somehow still alive and uttering taunts in a feeble voice when Canales finally gave the command to cease fire, was silenced only when Canales strode forward and fired a pistol round through his skull.

At last, silence hung again over Hacienda Salado, silence broken only by the faint, impatient cries of buzzards circling far overhead in the clear blue sky.

Canales turned to face the surviving Texans and said, "You will dig a grave for these men, and when that is done, you will be taken to Mexico City to serve there in prison for the rest of your natural lives. Such is the order of General Antonio Lopez de Santa Anna!'' With that, he turned and strode back to the quarters he had appropriated, the aide trailing after him and carrying the now empty mug.

Jonathan lifted the white bean that had saved his life and stared at it. Beside him, Bigfoot Wallace said quietly, ''Better hang on to that bean, Jonathan. I figger to keep mine.''

''For good luck, you mean?'' Jonathan asked.

''Good luck, hell!'' snorted Bigfoot. ''May come a time when you're stuck in some Mexico City dungeon and that bean'll be all you've got to eat. And let me tell you, son, you may be glad to get it.'' The lanky frontiersman hitched up his pants. ''Now come on. We got some buryin' to do.''

☆ **Chapter** ☆

11

Andrew Lewis sipped from the cup of apple cider in his hand and watched the young people dancing under the lanterns that hung from the trees and cast a warm yellow glow over the yard. There had been a time when perhaps Andrew had been a mite too fond of whiskey, but now a little cider suited him just fine.

This was a happy occasion, he told himself. Marriages always were. And he had to admit that Mordecai and Felipa made one fine, handsome couple. But still there was a feeling of melancholy inside him that he couldn't seem to shake. It had been there ever since he had gotten back from San Antonio.

"Can I liven that up for you a mite, friend?"

Andrew looked up to see the man who had asked the question standing there with a silver flask in his hand, his bushy eyebrows lifted enquiringly. Andrew shook his head. "No, thanks. This'll do me just fine."

Jud Bramson sighed and sank down on a three-legged stool beside the chair where Andrew sat. He was a heavy man, and he had evidently been hitting that flask pretty frequently. His normally florid face was even redder than usual.

"That nephew of yours sure got himself a pretty little wife," Bramson said. "He's a lucky man."

"I reckon so," Andrew nodded. "I don't know Felipa that well yet, but she seems like a nice girl."

Bramson nudged him with an elbow. "Hell, when a gal looks like that, it don't matter how nice she is, does it? Might even be better if she ain't so nice, if you get my drift—and I think you do."

142

"Yeah," Andrew said curtly, lifting his cup of cider to hide the grimace that passed over his face. Jud Bramson was a crude, arrogant, unlikable man, but Andrew didn't want to offend him. After all, Bramson was going to pay damned good money for that herd of mustangs Mordecai, Felipa, Manuel, and Edward had brought back from South Texas.

Bramson was a rancher with a place northwest of Austin, in country that was plenty rugged but ripe with potential. Those mustangs would be the basis for a horse herd that would soon put all the other horse-raising operations in Texas to shame, to hear Bramson tell it. And there was every possibility that he was right, Andrew reflected. Texas was a horse-hungry land, and there would always be a strong market for good mounts, especially as settlement expanded farther west and north. Bramson's spread was on the edge of that country.

The rancher had come to Austin specifically to buy horses a few weeks earlier, and luck had taken Mordecai and Felipa to the capital city on the same day with a small string of their animals. Bramson had seen them, been impressed by their quality, and quickly come to terms for the entire herd. The price he was paying was more than fair, in Andrew's opinion, and it had made a fine wedding present for Mordecai and Felipa.

The two of them were as well matched a pair as he and Petra had been, Andrew thought, or Michael and Marie before them. When he'd gotten back from San Antonio, he'd been introduced to Felipa and had heard the story of the tragedy that had befallen her family. Right from the first, Andrew had seen the way Mordecai looked at the girl, and he wasn't surprised when the engagement was announced. It had been a fairly short engagement, as such things go, but out here in Texas there wasn't a lot of time for drawing things out. Spring was just around the corner now, and if Mordecai was going to get a cabin built and some crops in before summer, he was going to have to get started soon. Already the days were starting to warm up, and within a couple of weeks, the fields of blue flowers that covered so much of this part of Texas would begin to bloom.

Andrew became aware that Jud Bramson was still talking to him, and he said, "Sorry, I didn't catch that. Bad ear sometimes. What were you saying?"

"Just that that sister-in-law of yours is a damned fine-looking woman, too," Bramson said. "Look at her. Whooee, I could eat her right up!"

Taking a deep breath, Andrew bit back an angry response. Bramson was a boor, but Marie wouldn't like it if anyone caused trouble at this party in honor of the wedding that had taken place that afternoon, not even if Andrew was just defending her honor.

Besides, Bramson wasn't saying much of anything that Andrew hadn't thought himself in unguarded moments. His eyes went to Marie as she danced with Frank, and at that moment Andrew had to envy his cousin. Marie looked slim and elegant and beautiful in a dark blue dress. This was Felipa's evening, of course, and Andrew had to admit she looked spectacular in a white gown made by Marie and Angeline that set off her dark beauty, but to Andrew's way of thinking, Marie was just as lovely.

"Now, don't get me wrong," Bramson went on. "I don't mean no offense. But I do appreciate a good-lookin' woman, and there's plenty of them around here."

Andrew couldn't argue with that. The Lewis family seemed to be blessed with an abundance of feminine beauty. There was Annie, her belly slightly swollen now with the third child growing within her. And Angeline, with whom motherhood was agreeing. Her long dark hair shone in the light of the lantern as she danced and laughed with her husband. And Andrew's own daughter Rose, who at the moment was holding little Michael Elizandro Zaragosa while Angeline and Manuel were dancing; although it pained him a little as a father to do so, Andrew had to admit Rose was growing up and turning into an attractive young woman. Yes, like Bramson said, there were plenty of beautiful women in the Lewis family.

There were a half dozen musicians playing fiddles, guitars, and in one case a mouth organ, and as they came to the end of the current song, the dancers stopped and applauded. Probably fifty people in addition to members of the family were attending this celebration. They had come from all over the countryside earlier, arriving in wagons and on horseback and in a few cases on foot. Life was too often a rugged, solitary business out here on the frontier, and folks were always eager for an excuse to get together and kick up their heels a mite. A wedding was one of the best reasons of all. The priest had come up all the way from San Antonio to perform the ceremony, and now he was sitting nearby, enjoying the festivities along with a glass of wine made from mustang grapes.

Bramson corked his flask, stowed it away, and stood up.

"Reckon I'll see if I can find me a partner for the next dance," he said as he moved away with a casual wave for Andrew.

The man had been invited to the wedding and the party afterward primarily as a business move, Andrew figured, but in truth, no one had been turned away, and no one would be. The rule of hospitality was inviolate in these parts unless a would-be guest was wearing feathers and war paint. To guard against that, an alternating series of guards had been set up, and all the men were armed. Andrew himself wore a Colt on his hip under the long tails of the coat he had worn when he was a politician up in Austin, and a rifle leaned against the cabin wall beside his chair where he could reach it in a hurry if he needed to. The priest was just about the only grown man in attendance who wasn't packing iron.

Andrew sat up straighter as he saw Jud Bramson stop beside Marie and speak to her. He was probably asking her to dance with him, Andrew thought, and for some reason that made him angry. Marie smiled politely enough at Bramson—she would never insult a guest at her home—but she shook her head rather firmly, and that made Andrew lean back and relax again. Bramson grinned, shrugged his shoulders, and moved on. Marie had turned aside his request in such a way so as not to offend him.

A moment later, Marie came up to Andrew, who immediately stood and offered her his chair. "Sit down," she told him with a laugh as she sank onto the same stool where Bramson had been sitting. She laced her fingers together around her knees and smiled up at him. "You are having a good time?"

"Of course," Andrew told her. "How could I not? Good food, good company, plenty of reason to celebrate."

"Yes, there is," nodded Marie. "I am so happy to know that Mordecai has found himself a good woman."

"Moved sort of fast, didn't he?"

"He knew Felipa for several months before they came back here. And besides, how long does it take when a man and a woman both know that it is right between them?"

"Can't argue with that," Andrew said with a chuckle.

"I worried only that Felipa was so caught up in her grief over the loss of her family that she would never see what was so plain to the rest of us. But as she and Mordecai worked with the horses all winter, they grew closer together. And when little Michael was born, she was there to help, and that brought her closer to the rest of the family, too." Marie smiled. "It was only a matter of time."

"Michael Elizandro Zaragosa," Andrew said. "That's a mighty

fine name, and I reckon both of his granddaddies would be right proud.''

"I know they would. He carries a proud heritage: American, Spanish, French . . .''

"Texan," Andrew said firmly. "That's all you really need to say.''

"Yes," Marie agreed. "Texan says it all.''

Andrew leaned back against the wall and enjoyed the warm sensation of companionship he felt as both he and Marie grew silent. Without really thinking about it, he slipped an arm around her shoulders, and she moved a little closer against him while they watched the dancers. The musicians had launched into another number, a slower one this time. Mordecai in his Sunday suit and Felipa in the fancy white gown swayed in each other's arms in the center of the yard, and the other couples orbited around them. Andrew saw Angeline and Manuel dancing, and his son Ben was frowning in utter concentration as he moved through some steps with Emily Harris, the daughter of a neighboring settler. Edward and David were dancing with the Steagall sisters, Melody and Janie Ruth; might be a double wedding there one of these days, Andrew reflected. Even Frank and Hope were out there with the younger people, along with Annie and Sly, whose leg was finally getting better.

Romance really seemed to be in the air tonight, Andrew thought, and who could blame folks for feeling that way at a wedding?

Andrew cleared his throat rather self-consciously and said quietly, "There's something I've been meaning to ask you, Marie.''

She turned her head and looked up at him. "What is it, Andrew?''

"Well . . . maybe it wouldn't be so good to talk about it out here. Maybe we could go back in the dogtrot.''

He saw a slight frown of concern appear on her face, and he wished he could set her mind at rest. He needed privacy for what he was about to say, though; some things a man just couldn't get into right in the middle of a big party.

"Of course," Marie said as she stood up. She led him back into the shadows at the rear of the dogtrot and then asked, "What is on your mind, Andrew? I can tell something is troubling you.''

"Well, not troubling me, exactly.'' He hesitated, unsure how to go about this, then took a deep breath and did the only thing he knew how to do. He plunged ahead, but as he did so, he sure wished he still had some of that gift for silver-tongued oration he seemed to have left behind in Austin.

"Marie," he said, "I reckon you know I think you're just about the finest woman to ever set foot on this earth. I always figured brother Michael was one lucky man to've married you."

In the faint light, he saw her smile. "I was the lucky one," she said.

"I don't know about that. Michael was always out wanderin' . . . But I didn't come back here to talk about him. I was talking about you. I didn't think I'd ever find anybody half as good as you to marry."

"Petra was a good woman, a wonderful friend. I still miss her very badly."

"So do I," Andrew said, "but I didn't really want to talk about Petra, either."

"Then what *do* you want to talk about, Andrew?"

"Us." There, he'd said it!

"Us?" repeated Marie, sounding puzzled. "You mean you and me?"

"That's exactly what I mean," Andrew said hurriedly. "I've been thinking about it a lot since I got back from San Antone. We've both been alone for a long time . . . well, you longer than me, but still . . . and I just thought . . . Like I said I think you're just about the finest . . . Oh, hell . . . !"

And with that, he put his hands on her shoulders, drew her firmly toward him, and brought his mouth down on hers.

Marie didn't resist, didn't do much of anything, in fact. She stood there as Andrew wrapped his arms around her and kissed her with all the passion and fire he could muster. Her lips were warm and soft and sweet under his, but they were also utterly still. Her arms hung loosely at her sides, rather than coming up to twine around his neck the way he had hoped they would. After a moment, Andrew realized that he wasn't getting a thing back from Marie.

He let go of her and stepped back quickly, searching her features in the dim light for any clue as to what she was thinking and feeling. He saw her lips curve in a sad smile, and finally she reached out to touch him, but there was infinite sorrow in the way her fingertips brushed his cheek.

"Oh, Andrew, I am so, so sorry . . ." she whispered.

"There's nothing there, is there?" he asked in a choked voice. "When Michael died . . ."

"Yes. That part of me died with Michael. There are times I . . . I wish it was not so, but I cannot deny it. You are my good friend, Andrew, and I love you in that way, but . . . that is all it can ever be."

His hands tightened into fists, and bitterness flooded through him. In a hoarse voice, he said, "I reckon I made a damned fool of myself, didn't I?"

"Not at all. I—"

"Hell, next thing you know you'll be telling me how flattered you are that I feel that way about you." He shook his head ruefully. "When Petra died, I wanted to die, too. But eventually I got to feeling that maybe I could go on after all, and when I knew I could, I started to get lonely. I just thought . . ." He gave another shake of his head and started to turn away.

Marie caught his arm and stopped him. "Please, do not be angry with me, Andrew."

"I could never be angry with you," he said.

"And do not be angry with yourself, either. I . . . I cannot tell you how much, how very much, I wish at this moment that things could be different between us, could be the way you want them to be. If it was only possible, I would . . ."

Andrew forced the bitterness to the back of his mind. He would have to deal with that himself, and he didn't want this sweet woman hurting because of him. He managed to smile, and he said, "Come on, we've got a party to get back to." He slipped his arm around her shoulders again, in the same comradely fashion as before, and started to lead her out of the dogtrot.

They had gone just a couple of steps when somebody screamed.

Andrew's hand went to the Colt on his hip, and he snapped at Marie, "Stay here." As he ran out of the dogtrot, though, he sensed that she was right behind him. Whatever the trouble was, as the mistress of the house she would feel obligated to help deal with it.

Spotting a knot of people on the far side of the yard, Andrew swung in that direction in time to see a man on horseback who had evidently just ridden into the circle of light. The horse on which the man rode was sweating and exhausted, its mane and tail matted with burrs, its head drooping. The rider looked even worse. He was thin to the point of gauntness, and his deep-set eyes seemed to shine with fever or madness or both in the haggard, bearded face. His clothes were nothing but rags.

There was nothing ragged about the pistol he carried, though. The barrel gleamed in the lantern light as the man brandished the weapon. "Get back!" he howled in a cracked voice. "Get back, you goddamned Mexes, or I'll kill the lot of you!"

The voice was somehow horribly familiar, and Andrew felt his guts knot as he stepped forward, motioning for the others to say back. Several men had their guns drawn, and it was obvious this gaunt spectre wouldn't be able to stay in the saddle for more than a few seconds if trouble started; he would be riddled with bullets almost immediately. But Andrew didn't want it to come to that, especially not before he discovered if his suspicions were true.

He kept his hands well away from his gun as he looked up at the man on the horse and said, "James? Is that you, James?"

"Who the hell are you?" the bearded apparition demanded.

"I'm Andrew Lewis. I'm your brother. You're James Lewis, and you've come home."

Andrew heard the shocked cries behind him as some of the other people at the party realized the truth of what he was saying. Now that he was closer, he recognized the newcomer. The man was definitely his brother James. But James had been through some experience so terrible that it had stretched his mind almost to the breaking point. James's eyes glittered with near-lunacy.

Slowly, Andrew held out his hand. "Give me the gun, James, and step down. We're having a party. Mordecai just got married this afternoon. You remember your nephew Mordecai, don't you?"

"M—Mordecai . . . ?" James closed his eyes for a moment and shook his head. There was a visible struggle going on inside him as he tried to regain his senses. When he opened his eyes again, he peered around and asked, "This is Michael's place, isn't it?"

Marie stepped up beside Andrew. "Yes, it is, James," she told him. "You're home, you're really home."

James's grip on the butt of the pistol relaxed, and the gun slipped from his fingers to fall to the ground. His eyes rolled up in his head as he swayed in the saddle.

"Somebody catch him!" Andrew cried, leaping forward.

Mordecai was even quicker. As James slumped out of the saddle and pitched toward the ground, Mordecai lunged ahead and grabbed him. Manuel was there an instant later, helping support James and keep him from falling.

"Bring him in the house," Marie said quickly and urgently.

James was so thin he seemed to weigh little or nothing as Mordecai and Manuel half-carried, half-dragged him into the cabin and placed him on Marie's bed, following her instructions. Andrew stood by the doorway and let the relatives in, but he politely asked everyone else to stay outside for the moment. "Go back to playing," he told the musicians. "Nobody said the party was over yet. We've just got us another guest, that's all."

He wished he could believe that. But James's condition was appalling, and the fact that Jonathan was not with him didn't bode well. Andrew shut the door and joined the other Lewises around the bed where James was lying.

Sly had come up with a jug of whiskey from somewhere—no great surprise, that, Andrew reflected with grim humor—and he was forcing some of the fiery liquid between James's lips. James sputtered and choked, but enough of the whiskey went down his throat to have a revitalizing effect on him. He opened his eyes, blinked a few times in confusion, and finally focused on the circle of anxious faces around him. His mouth opened and closed a time or two as he tried to force words out, finally managing, "I . . . I really did get . . . home . . . didn't I?"

"Yes, you did," Marie told him gently as she knelt beside the bed and took his thin hand between both of hers. "Just rest, James. We will take care of you."

James closed his eyes again and let his head sag back against the pillow, and for a moment Andrew thought he had fallen asleep. But then without opening his eyes he uttered the words all of them had dreaded hearing.

"Jonathan's dead."

Andrew knew he ought to let his brother rest, but he had to know what had taken place down there along the border. Judging from the expressions on the faces of the others, they shared his feeling. He moved up next to the bed, put a hand on James's shoulder, and grimaced at how wasted James's body felt. "What happened, James?" Andrew asked in a low voice. "We've heard nothing except that General Somervell turned back after his forces took Laredo. What happened to Jonathan?"

"Mexicans caught us . . . at a place called Mier . . . took us all prisoner . . . We got away after a while, but . . . they caught up to us again . . . Jonathan got hit . . . by a stray bullet."

Annie's hands went to her mouth, and she stifled a horrified cry. Angeline sobbed, and beside her Manuel tightened his arm around her shoulders. The younger ones, Edward, David, and Ben all looked solemn, while Rose fought back tears. Mordecai's head dropped forward on his shoulders, and a shudder went through him. He and Jonathan had been close, more like brothers than uncle and nephew. Felipa laid a hand on his arm, trying to comfort him. As for the others, all of them had seen more than their share of death in the past, but at the same time they were all shaken. Unlike most of them, Jonathan had come out from Tennessee only in fairly recent years, and he had not been in Texas as long as most of his relatives. But he had been a member of the family, well-loved, and his loss now hurt each and every one of them in their own way.

Andrew pulled a deep breath into his lungs. "What happened after that?"

James's tongue came out and licked over dry lips. "I knocked some Mex officer off his horse," he said, his tone a bit more coherent now. "I grabbed the horse and charged into the thick of them, figuring I'd be killed. Somehow I got through 'em, and I headed north. I . . . I don't know if any of the others got away or not. I headed north. Hid out a lot during the day, rode at night. Patrols almost caught me . . . a time or two. Reckon I crossed the Rio sometime, but I never noticed it. Didn't know if I was still in Mexico or not. Been hiding out . . . stealing a little food when I could . . . figured they'd kill me if they caught up to me."

Andrew repressed a shiver. It must have been a horrible time for James, wandering up from Mexico, half-crazed, always thinking there was danger right behind him, even after he had crossed the Rio Grande and was safe.

"Something must've led me here," James went on. "Instinct, I reckon. Whatever it was, it got me home."

A sigh gusted between his lips, and his eyes closed again.

"Enough," Marie said quietly but firmly. "He needs rest, and he is going to get it. And when he has rested, he will have plenty of good food. His strength will come back."

Andrew didn't doubt that for a moment. Under Marie's excellent care, James's health would return if at all possible. She wouldn't allow anything else.

But would his mind ever be the same after all he had been

through? That was an entirely different question, and Andrew had no idea what the answer was.

Still, Marie was right about James needing plenty of rest at the moment. He shepherded everyone else out, leaving her sitting beside the bed and its frail occupant. As they emerged into the yard, Andrew said to Mordecai and Felipa, "Sorry your wedding celebration got ruined, you two."

Mordecai shook his head. "It's hard to worry about that when Uncle James is lying in there in such bad shape, and after what he told us about Jonathan . . ."

"I am so sorry," Felipa said quietly. "I never met Jonathan Lewis, but I'm sure he must have been a fine man."

"He was," Andrew said, smiling a little as he remembered Jonathan's recklessness and exuberance. "A mite headstrong, maybe, but a good man. A good Texan, even if he hadn't been here long. He'll be missed."

As the head of the family, Andrew told the assembled guests what had happened, passing along the news of the tragedy south of the Rio Grande that had taken Jonathan's life, as well as the lives and freedom of scores of other men from Texas. Not surprisingly, the news cast a pall over the celebration, and folks said their good-byes quickly and headed home.

Well, there was one thing that could be said about all this, Andrew mused as he watched the last of the guests drive away in a wagon. It had forced him to forget all about the bitterness and shame that had gripped him after his disastrous romantic approach to Marie. There was a lot more important things to think about now—like the fact that he had lost one brother and had another who might never be the same.

A tear trickled down Andrew's leathery cheek, and he wiped it away, unnoticed in the night.

PART III

THE JOURNEY TEXAS, SPRING 1843

☆ Chapter ☆

12

A fine sheen of sweat covered Mordecai's shirtless torso as he swung the ax again and again at the trunk of the oak tree. The sharp blade bit deeply into the wood with each stroke. There were few chores in this world that Mordecai despised more than cutting down trees, but they had to be felled in order to build a cabin. And he wanted a cabin of his own, wanted it as soon as possible. A young man only two weeks married oughtn't to be spending his nights under his mother's roof.

He and Felipa had the cabin to themselves now. At least he had that much to be thankful for. The original plan had called for Marie to go and stay with Frank and Hope after the wedding, so that Mordecai and Felipa could be alone at the cabin. James's arrival had changed all that. For the first few days after the wedding, Marie had deemed James too weak to be moved and she'd had to stay there and take care of him. Once some of James's strength had returned, Frank had brought his wagon over and taken both James and Marie home with him.

But even without anyone else at the cabin with them, Mordecai seemed to sense other presences. There were too many reminders of his father, too many familiar things bringing home the fact that this was where he had grown up. A newly married man needed a place of his own, a fresh start, something that he and his wife could build together.

Like this spot here, half a mile upriver from the cabin his father had built. There were plenty of trees and grass and water, and it would be a fine place to live once he was through with it. There would be a snug double cabin and maybe a barn—folks would come from miles around for a barn-raising and the festivities that went with it. And he would need some fields planted with corn, beans, and wheat . . .

The sound of hoofbeats made Mordecai look up. He shifted the ax into his left hand so that his right would be free if he needed to reach for the Colt on his hip. He lifted his right arm and used his forearm to wipe sweat from his brow. He didn't want his palm getting slippery.

A moment later he saw that there was nothing to be alarmed about. A man was riding toward him at a gentle lope, and Mordecai recognized the horsebacker's burly shape: Jud Bramson. Mordecai wondered what the rancher wanted. Bramson had gone back to Austin after the wedding celebration, saying that he would be in touch concerning the mustangs he had promised to buy. Since then Mordecai hadn't seen hide nor hair of him, and he had begun to worry that maybe Bramson had backed out of the deal.

Bramson drew rein and brought his horse, a big bay gelding, to a halt. He was wearing store-bought pants, a buckskin shirt, and a broad-brimmed brown hat with a rounded crown. There was no belt gun at his waist, but a pair of rifle butts stuck up from beaded sheaths, one on each side of the saddle.

With a friendly grin, Bramson cuffed back his hat and nodded to Mordecai. "Mornin', young man," he said. "Looks like you're working mighty hard."

"Good morning, sir," Mordecai replied. He shrugged his shoulders slightly and added, "I was taught a man's got to work hard if he's going to get anything worth having."

"Well, that's a fine philosophy, but it don't always take into account the heat of the sun. Spring ain't much around here, is it? Sort of goes from winter to summer with nothin' in between."

Mordecai knew from talking to Bramson that the man was originally from Georgia. He shrugged again and said, "For Texas, this isn't bad spring weather. You come to take delivery of those horses, Mr. Bramson?"

The rancher's grin widened, and he swung down from the saddle, obviously in no hurry to get around to whatever had brought him out here. He said, "You cut right to it, don't you, son? Something else your daddy taught you?"

"You could say that."

"Well, since you're in a hurry . . ."

Belatedly, Mordecai remembered that he was talking to a man

who might well hold the key to his future. Without the money that Bramson had promised to pay for the horses, Mordecai might not have enough funds to buy everything he and Felipa needed to set up housekeeping in their own place.

"I didn't mean to rush you, Mr. Bramson," Mordecai said quickly. "And I sure didn't mean any offense."

"Oh, hell, I'm not offended. I was just joshin' you a little. What I came here for was to ask you a question."

"I'll try to answer it," Mordecai said.

"I've been thinking about those horses I'm going to buy from you and your little lady . . ."

Here it comes, Mordecai thought. He's decided not to buy the mustangs after all. The whole deal is going to fall through.

"I was just wondering how much extra it'd cost me for you to deliver those horses personally to my ranch up north of Austin."

Mordecai blinked in surprise. That was not at all what he had expected to hear from Bramson. Slowly, he said, "You mean you want us to deliver those mustangs up to your ranch?"

This time it was Bramson who looked slightly impatient. "That's what I said, isn't it?" he asked. "I got to thinking about it. I don't have a very big crew, just three men, and I left them up yonder on my spread to watch the place for me. Never figured on running into such a big, fine bunch of horses as what you've got for sale. I sure can't drive them all by myself, so I'm going to have to hire some men to do the job for me." He lifted his broad shoulders, then let them drop. "Finally occurred to me that what better men to get than the ones who already know those animals so well."

Mordecai's brain was whirling. He had just assumed that Bramson would be responsible for driving the mustangs on up to his ranch. Besides, Mordecai had responsibilities of his own right now.

"I don't rightly see how we can do it," he finally said. He gestured at the tree he was cutting down. I've got timber to fell, and then a cabin to build. You'll recollect I just got married."

"'Deed I do. Fact is, it was that pretty little wife of yours who told me I could find you up here when I stopped by your mama's cabin. You probably figured on putting up a place of your own and then gettin' a crop in, didn't you?"

Mordecai nodded. "Yes, sir. That's just what I'm going to do."

"But I'm talkin' about cash money, son. Enough money so that you won't have to worry about a crop this year. And when you get back in the fall, you'll have plenty of time then to build yourself a cabin before winter comes. You'll have enough money to furnish it right nice, too. Hell, you could afford to put glass in the windows.''

Mordecai's eyes widened. Glass had to be brought by ship from New Orleans to the Texas coast, then freighted overland by wagons, and so it was expensive, too expensive for normal folks to buy.

Despite the temptation of Bramson's offer, though, there was something else that was going to keep Mordecai from accepting it. ''I've only been married a couple of weeks, Mr. Bramson,'' he said. ''I'm not of a mind to go off and leave my wife this soon.''

''I thought you might say that,'' the rancher replied. ''And I can understand the way you feel, Mordecai. That's why I'm willin' to pay you an extra twenty-five percent for delivering those horses to me. I knew your services would come high.''

Mordecai couldn't help but let out a low whistle of surprise. That much extra money would put him and Felipa in fine shape for a couple of years, so that they wouldn't have to worry about drought, flood, locusts, or any of the other things that could drive a new farmer right under. By the time that money ran out, he could have his farm well-established and earning good money. He would be well on his way to being a rich man.

And there wasn't just himself to consider, either. Edward and Manuel ought to have some say in this, since the herd of mustangs belonged to them, too.

''I'll talk it over with my wife and my brother-in-law and my cousin, Mr. Bramson. That's all I can promise right now.''

''You want to hash it out with them, that's fine. But don't wait too long, Mordecai. I want to get those mustangs up to my ranch 'fore the middle of summer, when the really hot weather sets in.''

''We'll give you our answer as quick as we can, sir.''

Bramson nodded. ''All right. I'll ride back out here day after tomorrow. How'd that be?''

''Reckon that'll be long enough to make up our minds. And don't think I don't appreciate the offer, Mr. Bramson. I surely do. It's hard to know what to do, though.''

Bramson laughed and said, ''Don't worry 'bout it, son. I've been caught 'tween a rock and a hard place a time or two myself. You study on it, and there won't be no hard feelings no matter what your answer is.''

Mordecai grinned. ''Couldn't ask for no fairer than that.''

The rancher stepped back up into his saddle and swung the bay gelding around. With a wave, he rode off toward Austin.

Mordecai looked down at the ax in his hand, then slung it over his shoulder. No point in trying to do any more work today, he decided. His mind was too full for that.

He had some thinking to do.

With a start, Jonathan came awake. His eyes stretched open painfully, and his heart thudded madly in his chest. A throbbing like a blacksmith striking an anvil filled his skull. With a noise that was half moan and half sob, he fell back against the stone floor of the cell.

A big, rough hand touched his shoulder, and Bigfoot Wallace said, "Take it easy there, son. You're safe. We're all right here with you."

Jonathan recognized Bigfoot's voice and drew some scant comfort from it. More sobs wracked him, but finally he was able to draw a couple of deep, ragged breaths and bring his wildly racing pulse under control. "How . . . how long was I out this time?" he asked.

"Couple hours, that's all," replied Bigfoot. "And it weren't so bad this time. You just did some yellin' and thrashin' around."

"Did I say anything?"

"Nothin' I could understand."

Jonathan forced himself into a sitting position and put his face in his hands for a moment. Even living in such hellish conditions, these blackouts he suffered from time to time were the worst. They came on with no warning, lasting sometimes only a few hours, sometimes all day or night. When he was in their grip he had no idea what was going on around him. The first few times it had happened while he was on the road gang and the Mexican guards had whipped him unmercifully, thinking that he was feigning in order to get out of work. In fact, they had beaten him within an inch of his life, and he still bore the scars of their whips and clubs. Bigfoot had finally convinced them that his condition was no sham, that he actually was out of his head, but that realization had come almost too late.

It had to have something to do with that head wound, Jonathan thought. That was the only thing that made any sense. The bullet bouncing off his skull had done something to his brain, scrambled it all up somehow, so that every now and then it just quit working right for a while.

One of these days . . . one of these days it was going to stop working altogether, Jonathan told himself. Then he'd be dead, or as good as. And the frightening part was that he'd probably be better off when that happened.

He looked around the cell in the basement of Castle Perote, a huge, ugly rock structure east of Mexico City, on the road to Vera Cruz. The cell was fairly large as such things go, Jonathan supposed, almost sixteen feet square, but there were close to twenty-five men packed into it. High on one wall was a tiny window with a grate of iron bars covering it. The window was just above ground level, so a little air came through it. Not enough, though, for so many men. The only other opening in the cell was a small, similarly barred aperture in the thick wooden door. Everywhere else were stone walls that dripped with moisture and slime. Jonathan constantly felt short of breath here, and he wished they were back out on the road, even though the work there was brutal and backbreaking.

They had been confined to the dungeon for a week now as punishment for the latest escape attempt, which had failed just as all the others before it. Jonathan couldn't blame the men for wanting their freedom, but each time they tried to make a break and failed, the vengeance of their Mexican jailers grew worse. Some of the men had been whipped this time and dragged off to a hole even deeper in the bowels of the castle, and Jonathan doubted seriously if he would ever see those men again.

At least Captain Cameron had been spared this, Jonathan thought. Such a horrible existence would have driven the big Scotsman mad in no time.

The group of Texan prisoners being escorted by Colonel Canales and his men had almost reached Mexico City when a special messenger sent out by Santa Anna had intercepted them. Santa Anna had heard of Cameron's good fortune in drawing a white bean back at Salado, and it had infuriated the dictator that the ringleader of the defiant Texans was still alive. His messenger carried explicit orders: Captain Cameron was to be shot immediately. Those were orders Colonel Canales was more than happy to carry out.

Jonathan would never forget the captain's reaction. Cameron had shown no interest in either the priest or the blindfold Canales had offered him. He strode off to the side of the road, under some trees, and turned to glower at the Mexicans. "For the liberty of Texas, Ewen Cameron can look death in the face!" he declared, then he ripped his own shirt open to bare his chest. "Fire, damn you!" he bellowed. "Fire!"

Canales repeated the order, and the executioners fired.

Jonathan shuddered as he remembered the awful scene. Cameron had been arrogant to the last, but there was no denying his courage. Jonathan knew he could not have faced death with such bravery.

But at least Cameron's end had been a quick one. The other men faced a slow, lingering death as prisoners.

For a time after their arrival, the Texans had been imprisoned in a jail in Mexico City. Conditions there had been bad, but not nearly as much so as here at Castle Perote. In between, they had been forced to work on the road between Mexico City and Vera Cruz, widening it and improving its surface. That had been the best of all, because they were outside and could breathe fresh air and feel the sun on their faces. Unfortunately, their captors were quick to throw them back into the castle's dungeon every time there was even a minor infraction of the rules.

Sooner or later, they would all die here. Jonathan was sure of that. In his case, the question was what would kill him first—the brutal treatment by the Mexicans or the lingering effects of his head wound?

The influence of Bigfoot Wallace was the only thing that had kept him sane so far. Bigfoot never seemed to lose his head and, like Jonathan, most of the men seemed to draw strength from his calm demeanor. He was always quick with a joke or a tall tale, and in his more serious moments he urged the men not to give up. He was certain that somehow, sooner or later, they would all be free again. Jonathan wanted to believe that and, in his more optimistic moments, he could. But those moments were becoming more and more rare.

Now, as Jonathan tried to shake off the effects of his latest blackout, Bigfoot said, "Come on over here, son. Got somethin' to show you that might make you feel a little better."

Jonathan didn't feel much like looking at anything, but he didn't want to disappoint Bigfoot either. With a groan, he started to get to his feet. Bigfoot uncoiled his lanky frame first and put out a hand to help Jonathan. With that steadying influence, Jonathan managed to stay upright and after a few seconds, his head quit spinning. "All right," he said. "What is it you want to show me?"

"Come on," Bigfoot urged as he led Jonathan over to the far wall of the cell, the wall in which the tiny window was placed. At a gesture from Bigfoot, several men stepped aside.

Jonathan blinked in surprise at what was revealed by their movement. Somehow, they had managed to prize a couple of the flat stones free from the wall, uncovering dirt on the other side.

Some of the dirt had been scratched away. A small hollow had been formed, no more than a few inches deep.

"It'll take a while," Bigfoot said in a low voice, "but that's our way out of here."

Jonathan looked up at him. "You mean we're going to dig an escape tunnel?"

"Damn right. It ain't more'n twenty yards to the outer wall. Once we get past it, there won't be nothin' stoppin' us from takin' off for the tall and uncut."

With a frown, Jonathan considered the plan. It was surprising to see how easily the men had gotten past the wall of the dungeon, but at the same time, it was typical of the slipshod way their captors did most things. On the other hand, they had no tools, and digging a tunnel by hand through solid earth for a distance of more than twenty yards was not going to be an easy task.

"What'll you do with the dirt?" Jonathan asked, as one of the obstacles occurred to him.

"We've got to work it down 'tween the stones on the floor," Bigfoot told him. "That'll slow us down some, but maybe not too much. And any time we hear somebody comin', we'll put those wall stones back in place. Won't nobody be able to tell what we're doin'."

For the sake of all of them, Jonathan hoped the big frontiersman was right. If what they were doing was discovered, the Mexicans might lose the last of their patience and just shoot the whole lot of them.

But if they were successful . . . if the tunnel could be extended past the outer wall of the castle . . . then there would be at least a chance for freedom. Castle Perote was rather isolated, with Mexico City itself several miles away. If the Texans could slip out of the castle during the night and get a head start of several hours, some of them might make it back to Texas—with a lot of luck along the way.

"Well, Jonathan, what do you think?" asked Bigfoot. "This's the best chance yet, ain't it?"

Jonathan let himself smile wearily. "You may be right, Bigfoot. You just may be right."

And saying that, he went to his knees, crouching in front of the rudimentary tunnel. He lifted his hands and began scratching at the dirt. There was a lot of work to be done, and he intended to do his share.

From the grim expressions of the people in the room, this looked like a council of war, Mordecai thought. The only one who appeared to be happy about the situation was Edward.

"I say we take him up on it," Edward declared as soon as Mordecai was through putting forward the proposition made by Jud Bramson.

"You don't have a whole lot of responsibilities, son," Frank reminded him. "Mordecai and Manuel are married men."

This meeting was taking place in the big kitchen of Frank's cabin. Everyone had gathered there at Mordecai's request. He was sitting at the long table along with Manuel, Angeline, Felipa, Edward and Frank. Marie sat in a rocking chair to one side, holding little Michael Elizandro. Next to her in another rocker was James, who was looking much better after two weeks of Marie's care. He had shaved off his long beard, which at first had revealed just how gaunt he really was, but he was filling out again as Marie, Hope, Angeline, and Annie kept him full of good food. For the first few days, he had suffered spells of not knowing where he was, but now he was lucid again, and Mordecai could almost see him growing stronger by the moment.

"I don't see what being married's got to do with it," Edward said to his father. "That's a lot of money Bramson's talking about."

"That's true," Mordecai agreed. "Enough money to make things easier for all of us involved."

Manuel shook his head. "There is more to life than money, *amigo*." He looked at his wife and then over at his child, and a smile lit his face. "No amount of money can truly pay for the time spent away from our families. And I have been apart from mine enough."

"You're saying you don't want to take Bramson's offer?"

"I am saying that Angeline and I have been away from our own ranch for too long. She is strong enough now to travel, and the baby is doing fine. I think it is time we went home."

Quietly, Angeline said, "I agree with Manuel. We appreciate Mr. Bramson's offer, but we have to get on with our own lives."

Edward made a frustrated sound and leaned back in his chair. "You mean you'd turn down all that money?"

"My share in the actual purchase price for the mustangs is enough for us," Manuel said firmly. "I am not interested in anything more."

Mordecai sighed. He had been leaning toward accepting Bramson's offer, but he had to respect Manuel's decision. Manuel had a right to make up his own mind. But there was no way Mordecai and Edward could drive that many mustangs by themselves. It was a three-man job at the very least, and four or five would have been better.

"Well, I guess that settles it," said Mordecai. "I'll tell Mr. Bramson he'll just have to hire a crew in Austin to take those horses up to his ranch. He shouldn't have too much trouble—"

"I'll go."

The quiet voice made everyone look around in surprise. For a moment, no one said anything, then Mordecai asked, "What did you say, Uncle James?"

"I said I'll go with you," James replied, sitting up straighter in his rocking chair. "If you and Edward want to go, Mordecai, I'll be your third man."

Mordecai glanced over at Felipa, trying to read her expression, but he could not. Ever since he had told her about Bramson's proposal, he had been trying to find out what she thought about it, but she was being stubbornly noncommittal, telling him that he would have to make the decision for himself. Her lovely features were still set in that carefully neutral mask.

"James, you can't be serious," Marie said to him. "You were in such bad shape when you came back to us, and you are still weak."

"Getting stronger all the time," James insisted, "and I need something to do again. I've never been as far north as where Bramson says his ranch is. High time I saw that part of the country."

"That's a fine idea!" Edward exclaimed. He stood up and went over to James to clap a hand on his shoulder. "We'll show 'em how to drive horses, won't we, James?"

"Sit down, son!" Frank said sharply. "This isn't your decision to make."

Edward wheeled toward his father, his face flushing angrily. "Why the hell not, I'd like to know! I'm not a kid anymore, Pa. I was old enough to go down yonder to the Nueces country and help catch those mustangs, so I'm old enough now to decide whether or not I want to deliver them to Bramson!"

Frank's jaw tightened, but he couldn't refute Edward's argument. Besides, Edward was twenty years old, nearly twenty-one, and anywhere out here on the frontier that was a full-grown man. Most youngsters past the age of fifteen or sixteen considered themselves grown up, in fact. It was hard to admit that, though, when you were talking about your own son.

"All right, it's your choice," Frank admitted. "And nobody's ever been able to tell ol' James there what to do. But what about

Mordecai?'' He turned to face the tall young man on the other side of the table. ''What do you want to do?''

Mordecai took a deep breath, glanced one more time at Felipa, and then said, ''I think we ought to do it.''

''It's settled then,'' Edward said quickly. ''You and me and James'll take those mustangs up to Bramson's place.''

Felipa spoke for the first time since the meeting had begun. ''No,'' she said simply.

Mordecai looked at her in surprise and a little bit of anger. She'd had plenty of chances to speak up, he thought. Hell, he'd almost begged her to offer an opinion. Now, after everything had been decided, she was going to try to dictate what he could do.

''You mean you don't want me to go?'' he asked.

Coolly, she regarded him, and he was reminded again that even though he loved her, even though he was married to her, half the time or more he didn't know what was going on behind those deep brown eyes. It was damned frustrating, and he had a feeling that no matter how long they were together, he would still never fully understand her.

''I told you to make your own decision,'' she answered quietly. ''But I will make mine. And I'm going with the mustangs too.''

Mordecai came halfway out of his chair. ''What?''

''I said I'm going,'' Felipa replied in a calm voice. ''I think it is a good idea to accept *Señor* Bramson's offer.''

''But you can't—''

''And why not?'' Felipa demanded. ''I know what you are going to say, Mordecai Lewis. I cannot go along on this trip because I am a woman, because I am your wife. But many of those mustangs were caught by my hand, and even more of them were gentled by me. I was capable of that, so I should be more than capable of helping to drive them to *Señor* Bramson's ranch.''

''Damn it, it's different now,'' Mordecai insisted. ''You were a woman when we were catching those mustangs, sure, but you *weren't* my wife then. You are now.''

''That does not render me incapable of making my own decisions!'' she shot back at him.

Mordecai was angry and humiliated at the same time. He had known Felipa was strong-willed and had a mind of her own; that was part of the reason he had been so attracted to her right from the first. But a wife had no business arguing with her husband in front of the family like this. The place to settle this was in private.

Felipa leaned back and crossed her arms on her chest, giving him a defiant look. Mordecai glanced around, hoping that one of the others would jump in here and give him a hand convincing Felipa she was crazy to have such an idea. None of them seemed to want to get involved, though. Frank had already lost an argument with his own son, so he was in no hurry to get mixed up in another controversy. Edward was grinning broadly, obviously seeing nothing wrong with Felipa joining them on the drive. And Manuel and Angeline both seemed to think the whole thing was rather amusing; they weren't smiling, but Mordecai could see grins lurking in their eyes.

"What about you, Mama?" he finally asked. "What do you think about this idea of Felipa's?"

For a moment, Marie did not reply, then she said solemnly, "Many times I watched your father ride away, Mordecai, and wished that I could have gone with him, no matter what he would have thought of such a thing. I cannot condemn Felipa for feeling the same way and having the courage to act on those feelings where I did not."

Mordecai bit back a curse. When his own mama wouldn't back him up . . . ! He looked at James and asked, "How about it, Uncle James? If you're going along, I reckon you ought to have a say."

James grinned broadly, looking more like his old self than he had in a long while. "I don't know that woman of yours too well yet, Mordecai," he said, "but I'm told she was with you during most of that mustanging trip. I've seen her work with those animals, too, and she's got a touch like nobody else I've ever seen. I'd be right happy to have her come along, since she'll probably be able to handle those mustangs better'n the three of us put together. And I reckon you and me and Edward can look after her if there's any trouble."

Mordecai threw his hands up in the air. "I give up," he said. He turned to Felipa. "You can come along. There, is that what you wanted?"

She smiled sweetly, maddeningly, at him. "Try to contain your enthusiasm, my husband," she said.

And as the others in the room burst out laughing, Mordecai realized that was probably the first joke, however slight, he had ever heard her make.

He had to grin. Felipa still had some bad things to put behind her, and maybe this trip would help her do that. Maybe everything would be all right after all. He put out a hand and took hold of hers, twining their fingers together.

"All right. Let's take those mustangs north," he said.

☆ Chapter ☆

13

Jud Bramson seemed very pleased to hear their decision when he rode out to the Lewis Fort the next day. He had brought with him the purchase price for the mustangs, which he handed over to Mordecai. "I'll have that extra twenty-five percent for delivery when we get to the ranch," Bramson said.

"Fair enough," Mordecai replied, hefting the small leather sack containing the coins Bramson had given him. It was mighty heavy for such a small bundle. Mordecai made an effort to keep from grinning at the feel of it.

He made arrangements with Bramson to meet the rancher just east of Austin a couple of days later. Bramson would be accompanying them, which made sense considering that he was the only one in the group who knew exactly where his ranch was. After Bramson was gone, Mordecai divided the money up into four equal shares, giving one each to Manuel and Edward and keeping two for himself and Felipa.

Turning to Felipa, he said, "Maybe you'd rather hang on to your part of the money yourself. Bein' as you're so independent-minded, you might not want your husband looking after your money."

"I trust you, Mordecai," she replied with a smile. "You may be stubborn, but you are an honest man."

"Thanks, I reckon." To Edward and James, who had both come over from Frank's place, Mordecai said, "We'll leave here at sunup, day after tomorrow. That all right with the two of you?"

167

Edward nodded eagerly, and James said, "I'm looking forward to it. Thanks for letting me go along, Mordecai."

"Glad to have you, Uncle James."

As a matter of fact, Mordecai was a little worried about James's health. James was still rather thin, but he looked like he felt well enough. Marie was convinced, however, that he was too weak to undertake a journey like this. The trip to Bramson's ranch might well prove to be uneventful, but there was the potential for plenty of trouble along the way. They could run into Indians or horse thieves or spring storms or any number of other problems.

All they could do was hope for the best, Mordecai told himself. After all, they were Texans and Lewises. They could handle just about anything fate chose to throw at them.

The mustangs seemed to sense what was going on, because on the morning they were to leave, the horses were a little more nervous and high-strung than usual. In the gray, predawn light, Mordecai, Felipa, Edward, and James moved them out of the big corral and onto the trail leading toward Austin. Most of the family had turned out to bid them farewell. Annie wasn't feeling well due to her pregnancy, so she had stayed home, but Sly was there, a big grin on his lean face. "Wish I was going with you," he told Mordecai as he reached up to shake hands while Mordecai was still in the saddle. "Folks say that's rough, hilly country up where Bramson's ranch is, and I wouldn't have minded seeing it. You be careful now, you hear?"

"We will, Uncle Sly," Mordecai promised.

Nearby, Andrew and Marie came up to James, and Andrew asked, "Are you sure you're up to this, James? It's going to be a long trip."

James grinned at them as he swung down from the saddle. "Nothing like fresh air and hard work to set a man straight," he told them. He looked like a different person from the crazed scarecrow who had ridden in during the party to celebrate the marriage of Mordecai and Felipa. He wore a new brown hat with a wide brim and a low, flat crown and a band studded with silver conchos. His fringed buckskin shirt was new, too, as were the whipcord pants and the high black boots. He was as well armed as ever, wearing two of the long-barreled Texas Patersons as well as carrying two more of the heavy revolvers fastened to his saddle. Other than a slight hollowness around his eyes, he looked just about like the dashing Texas Ranger he had once been.

Marie put her arms around his neck and hugged him tightly. "I put some food in your saddlebags—" she began.

"I know," James said. "Enough for a troop of Rangers, from the feel of it. I appreciate it, Marie." He shook hands with Andrew, then remounted the sturdy chestnut with a blazed face he had selected out of the herd as his saddle horse.

Frank and Hope were saying good-bye to Edward, and once again David was feeling somewhat resentful at being left behind. He got over it long enough to pump his brother's hand and slap him on the back to wish him well.

Mordecai hugged Angeline and chucked little Michael under his fat chin as Angeline held him. Manuel extended a hand to Mordecai and said, "I hope you understand why I cannot come with you."

"I sure do," Mordecai told him. "I'm not that fond of the idea myself, but it was just too much money to turn down. Hope you'll come see us when we get back."

"Of course we will," Angeline said. She smiled and added, "Maybe next time when we come to visit, you and Felipa will have one of these yourselves." She lifted Michael slightly.

Mordecai grinned sheepishly. "I wouldn't count on it. Felipa doesn't seem to be in too much of a hurry to start a family. I reckon those horses are her babies. I hope she doesn't mind leaving them once we get to Bramson's place."

"I am sure she'll be fine," Manuel said.

Marie came over then to say good-bye, and Mordecai was just as glad to drop the subject of having children. To tell the truth, he found the prospect rather scary. He remembered what Sly had said about how once you had kids, you always worried about them. Mordecai wasn't sure he was ready for anything like that.

The farewells took a while, what with all the hugging and handshaking, and it was hard to keep the mustangs bunched up and under control at the same time, so Mordecai felt a sense of relief when they finally got underway. Turning in the saddles for a few last waves, they got the horses moving up the trail toward Austin. Edward took one flank and James the other, and Mordecai and Felipa rode along behind the mustangs.

"I'm glad we finally got started," Mordecai said to her. "Sooner we get there, the sooner we can come back home."

"Yes. I will miss your family, Mordecai."

"They're your family now, too. You know that."

She nodded. "I know. All the Lewises have been wonderful to

me.'' She looked over at him with one of the few genuine smiles he had seen from her lately, and she put her hand on his arm, a brief touch that said a great deal. ''Especially one of the Lewises.''

Mordecai rode on into the morning, knowing that he had a silly grin on his face and not caring one little bit.

Jonathan's fingernails were long since worn down to the nub by all the digging he had done over the past month. The Texans worked at the escape tunnel every chance they got, and for a change Jonathan found himself hoping that the Mexicans would not take them back outside and put them to work on the road gang.

That hope was answered. Their captors seemed to have forgotten about them except for bringing a small pitcher of scummy water and a bowl of insect-infested beans down to the dungeon every day. The food would have been barely enough for a dozen men; given the fact that there were twenty-five prisoners crammed into this one cell, all the Texans stayed weak from hunger and malnutrition.

No matter how bad they felt, however, they somehow mustered up the strength to keep scratching away at the tunnel hidden behind the stones. Their progress went faster when one of the bowls of beans was ''accidentally'' broken. One of the shards of pottery was hidden and later used to scrape away at the dirt at the end of the tunnel. The broken piece of bowl lasted only a day before it crumbled and became useless, but in that day's time the prisoners dug farther than they ever had before.

It was hard to measure the tunnel, harder still to be sure it was heading in a straight line toward the outer wall of the castle. Some of the men wore shoes that laced up, and Bigfoot Wallace tied together three of the laces to make a line approximately a yard long. That was used for judging distance, and it was decided that for safety's sake the tunnel would have to be at least twenty-five of those measures before the diggers would angle upward toward the surface.

Jonathan would never forget moving through that dark, narrow space. There was no light, and the walls of the tunnel pressed in against his shoulders. He couldn't lift his head more than a few inches without hitting the top of the crude passage. His nose was filled with the dank smell of rich, wet earth. The diggers crawled straight to the end, then had to wriggle backwards to get out when their turn was over. Jonathan never failed to heave a huge sigh of relief when he slid back out into the cell. Its stone walls might be cramped and confining, but they seemed like the wide open spaces of the Texas prairie compared to the tunnel.

If he hadn't been crazy to start with, he had told himself more than once, working in the tunnel would have made him that way.

But with each day that went by, the tunnel crept a little closer to freedom. The men worked around the clock, except for the short period of time when the guards brought that day's rations. Finally, they were sure the passage was long enough, that it had penetrated beyond the castle's outer wall. It was time to start digging toward the top.

In some ways, that was the worst job of all, Jonathan discovered, because the dirt that he dislodged as he dug fell down into his face, clogging his nose and mouth and getting painful grit in his eyes. Still he and the others struggled on, each man taking his turn except for Bigfoot whose shoulders were too broad for him to make the sharp angle upward. The tunnel would have to be widened a little at that spot when the time came for the actual escape.

And that time was fast approaching, Jonathan realized. The men could not dig too close to the surface until they were ready to actually make their bid for freedom, for fear of weakening the ground so that some unwary Mexican might fall through and uncover their scheme. Once it was decided that the tunnel was as far along as it could safely go, the men stopped and rested for a day, waiting for nightfall to put the final phase of the plan into operation.

Jonathan sat with his back against the damp stone wall next to Bigfoot Wallace. Scratching at the long beard he had grown during his confinement, the young man said, "We been workin' at this so long, it seems hard to believe we're so close to being out of this hellhole."

"Ain't out yet, son," warned Bigfoot. "Still lots of things that could go wrong."

Jonathan glanced over at him in surprise. "Hell, Bigfoot, I thought you were the one who always believed things were going to work out."

"Just sayin' you got to be ready for whatever tricks fate decides to pull on you." The frontiersman grinned in the faint light filtering down from the tiny window. "But what the hell, I'm just as hopeful as anybody."

Leaning his head against the wall, Jonathan closed his eyes and let the weariness flood through him. He didn't want to admit it, but he was scared. If the escape attempt failed, the vengeance of the Mexicans might be terrible to behold. And if it succeeded, then he'd be out there on his own in the middle of a foreign, hostile land, hundreds of miles from his home. Either way there were risks.

But the alternative was sitting here and rotting, and Jonathan wasn't going to do that. He was still a Texan, by God, he told himself, and Texans didn't give up.

He was still clinging to that thought as night fell. The waiting got even harder after darkness had closed in, and it seemed like the time to go would never arrive. A few of the men dozed, their snores filling the air of the cell, but most of the prisoners were too nervous to sleep.

Finally, when it seemed to Jonathan like at least half the night had passed, Bigfoot said in a low voice, "Reckon it's just about that time, boys."

The sleepers were awakened, and everyone gathered around the mouth of the tunnel. "One at a time," Bigfoot told them, "and keep about a dozen feet 'tween you and the men in front of and behind you. Anythin' happens, we don't want it wipin' out all of us." Bigfoot's hamlike hand fell on Jonathan's shoulder. "You go first, son."

Jonathan swallowed hard. Bigfoot was handing him a lot of responsibility. He had to finish out the tunnel and break through to the surface. If everything went well, he would be the first one to breathe the air of freedom. But if anything went wrong, he would probably be the first to die.

"Thanks," Jonathan said dryly, and that brought a chuckle from Bigfoot.

"I'll bring up the rear," the frontiersman said. "You boys scratch out that turn a little wider when you go through, you hear?"

There was a mutter of agreement. Even though they were all equal here, there was no doubt Bigfoot Wallace was their spiritual leader, and they would do everything they could for him.

Jonathan crouched and reached out in the darkness, finding the opening of the tunnel with his hands. He bent low and thrust his head and shoulders into the opening. Again he felt that all too familiar sensation of the walls of the tunnel closing in around him, but he fought it off. They had all come too far for him to let them down now. He went to his belly and began slithering into the darkness like a snake.

The crawl was only twenty or thirty yards, but it seemed like a mile or more to Jonathan. He panted for air, and his heart hammered crazily in his chest. A scream welled up in his throat, but he forced it down. His toes and elbows dug into the dirt floor of the tunnel and pushed him steadily forward.

Finally, reaching out in front of him, he touched the end of the passage and twisted himself upward. He paused and clawed at the sides for a moment, widening it slightly as Bigfoot had requested. Then he levered himself up and got busy on the most important task: breaking through to the surface.

Once again the dirt showered down on his face. Jonathan turned his head and spat out grit as he continued clawing at the ground over his head. Long minutes passed, and he knew the men in the tunnel behind him—as well as those still back in the cell—must be getting anxious. Maybe they hadn't been as close to the top as they had thought.

Suddenly, his fingers were thrusting up into open air. Jonathan pawed desperately at the edges of the tiny hole and pushed his face up next to the opening, ignoring the dirt that cascaded down faster than ever. He gulped down a lungful of air, air that was infinitely fresher in comparison with the stale atmosphere inside the tunnel. Choking back a sob, Jonathan rapidly widened the hole. More and more of the dirt fell away until he could get both hands through the opening, then his arms, then his head and shoulders . . .

Fighting to stay calm, Jonathan pulled himself out of the tunnel and rolled over onto his back. Gasping, his chest heaving, he looked up at the stars, seeing them for the first time in long weeks. No stars had been visible through the window in the cell, only a section of the castle's outer wall. Now, as Jonathan stared up at them, pinpricks of light against a deep blue background, he realized how truly beautiful they were.

He lay there only a couple of moments, then rolled back over and stuck his head in the hole where he had emerged. It was hard to do even that much, but he forced himself. He gave a low whistle that would carry back down the tunnel and let the others know they could come ahead. Then he scrambled to his feet and looked around.

There was no moon tonight, another reason for picking this particular time to attempt the escape. The starlight seemed unnaturally bright, however, and Jonathan could plainly see the wall of the castle some fifteen feet away from him. If he could see the wall that well, it meant any of the guards who strolled around the parapet could see him, too. The castle appeared to be dark and quiet, and he knew it was likely the sentries would be dozing at their posts, but the chance of discovery still made his skin crawl. He wished the others would hurry up.

As if in answer to his silent plea, the head and shoulders of the second man through the tunnel appeared. Jonathan reached down, grasped the man's hand, and helped him through the opening. The man was named Phillpot, and Jonathan didn't know him very well. At the moment, that didn't matter.

"Are the others coming?" Jonathan hissed.

Phillpot nodded jerkily. "Cass was right behind me," he whispered.

Jonathan crouched by the hole and waited. A couple of minutes later, the man called Cass stuck his head up and wriggled out of the tunnel with Jonathan's help. He gave a little giggle that told Jonathan he was half out of his head from nerves. "They're comin'," Cass said. "Comin' right along."

"Good," Jonathan said. His legs ached to be away from here. The muscles quivered with the need to run, to run away into the night, far from the prison. He forced himself to stand still.

The harsh yell forced him to spin around, terror spurting through his veins.

"Look out!" Jonathan cried, launching himself toward Phillpot even as he spotted the Mexican guard on the wall, aiming a musket toward the escaping prisoners. The musket boomed, the sound of it almost deafening in the still night, and as Jonathan knocked Phillpot aside, he heard the whistle of the lead ball through the air next to his head. Phillpot went to one knee from the impact, but Jonathan kept his feet and jerked the other man upright again.

"Come on!" Jonathan grabbed Cass's arm as well and forced both of them into a run away from the wall. More shouts floated through the night. Their luck had run out just as things were getting underway. Now there would be more guards converging on the parapet above the tunnel's exit, and they could pick off anyone who stuck his head up through the opening. The only ones with a real chance to get away were Jonathan, Cass, and Phillpot.

Guilt clutched at him like a giant hand as he raced through the darkness. There were still nearly twenty-five men back there in the tunnel and the cell, among them Bigfoot Wallace, who had become his best friend. Jonathan hated to leave them behind, but he knew Bigfoot would have wanted him to get away if it was at all possible. James had escaped out there in the Mexican desert, thinking that Jonathan was dead, and Jonathan had not been able to bring himself to hate his brother for that act of self-preservation. This was just about the same thing. There was nothing he could do for Bigfoot and the others by staying and remaining a prisoner.

Besides, it was questionable whether or not he would even live to enjoy his newfound freedom. Muskets crashed from the walls of the castle, and he heard bullets whining through the night around him. None of them came very close, however, and as he put more distance between himself and the castle, the firing died away. He could still hear shouting, though, along with the harsh, rasping breaths of Cass and Phillpot and the pounding of their feet as they ran alongside him. Fear had given all three men more speed and stamina than they would have dreamed they still possessed.

Jonathan kept running. He had no idea where he was going, but it didn't matter. The dungeon was far behind him now, and as he ran he made a vow to himself.

He would die before he would go back.

Bramson met the four of them at the agreed-on spot on the plains east of Austin. They would skirt the capital city itself, swinging to the north and then turning west. According to the rancher, there were places where the escarpment known as the Balcones was gentle enough so that the mustangs could be driven to the top of it. Once they had negotiated that obstacle, there would be another stretch of prairie before the landscape became more hilly and rugged.

Bramson rode behind the herd with Mordecai and Felipa. "It's good country up yonder," he told them, "but most men'd think twice 'fore settin' off into it. Lots of hidey-holes where Injuns can ambush you. We'll have to keep our eyes open."

Mordecai nodded. "I intend to."

"You must have been nervous the first time you rode up there," Felipa commented to Bramson.

The rancher laughed. "I said *most* men would think twice, missy. When Jud Bramson sees something he wants, he goes after it."

Mordecai frowned a little, not caring for the way Bramson had spoken to his wife. It probably didn't mean anything, though, Mordecai told himself. Bramson was a blunt, plainspoken man, the kind who sometimes talked without thinking first.

Bramson still carried the two rifles on his saddle, and he had buckled on a Colt as well. There were five people in the party, counting Felipa, and Mordecai knew she could use a gun. In fact, she was damn near as fast and accurate as he was, although he figured his uncle James could shade any of them without much trouble, even recuperating like he was. With this many folks, and as well armed as they were, Mordecai thought just about anybody they might run into would leave them alone, even the Comanches.

They camped the first night on the prairie. Mordecai and Edward close-hobbled all the mustangs, allowing them just enough freedom to move around and graze a little. New grass was popping up everywhere, and it was already pretty lush in places.

A couple of days passed without incident. The riders kept the mustangs moving at a steady pace, but not so fast that it would wear out the animals. They stopped several times a day to let the horses rest and crop some grass; they weren't getting there in a hurry, but when they finally got to Bramson's ranch, the mustangs would be in almost as good shape as they had been when they left the Lewis place.

Everyone switched around during the drive, so that each person got to ride in all the positions at one time or another. Nobody got stale that way, and they stayed more alert. Felipa found that she liked riding the flank, but as they got farther away from Austin and left the established trails far behind, it was necessary for someone to ride point, too. That proved to be Felipa's favorite spot. It was nice to be out in front, to be seeing such a land with fresh eyes. She had grown up in the deserts of northern Mexico and southern Texas, and mesquite trees were the biggest vegetation she had seen until coming up to the Colorado with Mordecai and the others. Now she saw cottonwoods, oaks, cedars, junipers, and fields of wildflowers that looked like waves of blue and red and yellow and white. The land grew rougher, with rocky bluffs shouldering into the sky, but even those rugged features were dotted here and there with flowers and grass. Through it all twisted creeks that were shallow but that ran swift and cold. Felipa could understand the good things Bramson had said about this country.

She didn't even mind riding behind the herd. The horses didn't raise a great deal of dust, so the air was not bad. The view was not that appealing, she supposed . . . but she would rather see the back end of a horse than more desert. If she never went back to that hot, dry southern country, it would be all right with her.

One day when they were a week northwest of Austin, Felipa found herself riding drag with Jud Bramson. The mustangs had entered a wide valley between two ranges of hills, and they had spread out a good deal, glad to have some room to scamper again. Felipa could tell that by the way they held their tails. Mordecai had the point, while James and Edward were out on the flanks. She and Bramson brought up the rear, keeping an eye out for any stragglers, but there weren't liable to be any today, Felipa thought. The mustangs felt too good to hang back. They were ready to get to where they were going, which in this case was the far side of the valley where a cottonwood-lined creek ran.

"Beautiful day, ain't it?" Bramson asked as he rode beside her.

"Yes, it is," Felipa agreed. "By now in Mexico, the days would be so hot as to make a lizard hunt for shade."

Bramson threw back his head and laughed. "Reckon I know what you mean, little lady. I been in some places that hot myself. One thing you can say for that land down there though—it warms the blood, don't it?"

With a frown, Felipa said, "I do not know what you mean."

"Sure you do. That Mexican sun makes all you little *señoritas* ready for some lovin', don't it?"

Felipa stiffened in the saddle and glanced over at him. Bramson was grinning broadly as he jogged along on his big horse. She felt a surge of anger, then controlled it. "I said I do not know what you mean, Mr. Bramson," she replied tightly. "And I do not wish to discuss this subject any further."

"Sure, sure." Bramson waved a big hand negligently. "Didn't mean no offense. Say, look at that field o' Indian paintbrush over there. Ain't that something to take your breath away?"

Felipa had to agree that the brilliant wildflowers were lovely, and Bramson kept talking about the land as they rode along together. He did not say anything else that she could even remotely consider improper, and she began to wonder if she had reacted too strongly to his earlier comments. She had thought Bramson might be leading up to making advances toward her, but now she decided he was just an earthy man who said whatever was on his mind, regardless of the company or what might be considered proper.

Still, it would be all right with her if she didn't have to ride behind the herd with him again, and if he said anything else that stretched the bounds of propriety, she would speak to Mordecai about it.

They made good time that day. They didn't have to push the mustangs toward the far range of hills; the prancing animals went on their own, and it was all the riders could do to keep up with them properly. They camped that night on the far side of the creek, under cottonwoods and willows that whispered as the evening breeze moved their branches back and forth.

So far they had seen no Indians and damn few people of any kind, in fact. A couple of times they had spotted riders in the distance, but in each case the other travelers had been white, a fact confirmed by Bramson after studying them through his spyglass. White or not, they'd steered clear of the riders, because as Bramson put it, "Out here a lone rider's likely to be up to no good, no matter what color he is."

The Comanches came through this part of the country from time to time, the rancher explained, but they were only passing through, hunting game. They had no villages in the area. All the Comanche towns were far to the north and west, in the land known as Comancheria. Felipa knew from things her husband had said that Mordecai had been out there himself, and so had James, but neither of them mentioned it when Bramson brought up the subject, so neither did she. Felipa knew the story had something to do with her sister-in-law Angeline, but she had never been given the details, nor had she pressed for them. Mordecai would tell her about it if and when he was ready.

The upshot was that Bramson considered it safe enough for them to do a little hunting of their own, so he and Edward rode out and came back an hour later with a good-sized buck. The three left behind in camp had heard only one shot, and they assumed that Bramson had probably brought down the deer.

"Nope," the burly man said when Mordecai congratulated him on the kill. "Wasn't me. Was this young fella here." He clapped a grinning Edward on the shoulder, then cut the cords that held the carcass of the deer on the front of the horse. It slid bloodily to the ground, and Mordecai and James got busy skinning it and dressing it out. They'd roast some of the meat tonight, smoke some of it, and cut the rest in strips to dry for jerky.

Felipa went to check on the mustangs while Mordecai and James were busy with the deer. Now that they were around trees again, most nights they strung ropes from trunk to trunk to make a crude corral. Such an arrangement wouldn't have held these mustangs when they were newly caught, but now that the rough edges had been worked off them, they were mostly content to abide by the rules. There was always a night guard, though, just in case something spooked the animals.

This evening they were peaceful, already settling down for the night. The sun had dropped behind the hills to the west, but there was still a rosy glow in the sky that lit Felipa's way as she circled the herd. She was on the far side from the camp when a figure loomed out of the dusk in front of her.

Instinctively, her hand went to the butt of the revolver on her hip. All her muscles tensed. Then she recognized the shape of the hat on the man's head, and a second later Bramson chuckled.

"Sorry, *señorita*," he said. "Didn't mean to give you a start."

"*Señora*, Felipa corrected rather curtly, letting her hand fall away from the gun. "I am a married woman, Mr. Bramson, as you well know."

"Yeah, it's kind of hard to forget about that, what with ol' Mordecai hangin' around all the time, ain't it?" He came a step closer to her. "But I'm willin' to try if you are."

She could see him better now in the twilight, could see the dried blood from the deer on the front of his shirt and his pants. She felt revulsion rising up in her throat and tried to move past him, saying, "I do not know what you mean."

He caught her arm, a smile stretching his lips under the prominent nose and the bushy moustache. "Oh, I reckon you do," he said coolly. "You recollect when we were talkin' about hot-blooded little *señoritas*. Well, I figure your blood's startin' to boil just about now, and I'm just the gent to heat it up some more."

He leaned closer to her, close enough for her to smell the whiskey on his breath as he tried to kiss her.

Felipa acted without stopping to think. One of her booted feet thrust itself between Bramson's legs, hooked behind one of his knees. At the same time as she jerked on the knee, she slammed her left hand into his broad chest as hard as she could. As big as he was, the maneuver probably would not have worked if he had been braced and expecting it, but taken by surprise, he found himself falling hard, slamming to the ground on his back. The impact knocked the air out of his lungs and left him gasping for breath.

Moving quickly to utilize her momentary advantage, Felipa slid the Colt from her holster and hooked her thumb over the hammer, letting the weight of the gun cock it as she brought it up. She dropped into a crouch and put the barrel of the revolver against Bramson's temple. He became very still.

"I know you will owe us money when we deliver these horses

to your ranch," Felipa said quietly, "but despite that, if you touch me again I will kill you. Do you understand, Mr. Bramson?"

"Hey there," Bramson gulped. "Be careful with that thing, girl! Shit, that gun could go off—"

"It will unless you promise me that this will never happen again."

"Hell, yes! I promise. I was just havin' a little fun with you—"

Again she interrupted his protest. "I am a married woman. You will not touch me, and you will not say anything to me that you would not say to your own mother. Agreed?"

Bramson swallowed hard. "Agreed. But you drive one hell of a . . . I mean, you drive a hard bargain, Mrs. Lewis. A fella like me, he sometimes says things he don't mean."

"Then I would advise you to start thinking before you speak." Felipa straightened, stepped back, carefully let the hammer down, and slipped the Colt back into its holster.

From the other side of the herd, Mordecai called anxiously, "Any trouble over there?"

Felipa turned and called, "No trouble. Mr. Bramson and I were just chasing away a coyote." She looked at Bramson and added under her breath, "A small, troublesome creature."

Bramson sat up, touched the spot on his head where she had held the gun, and started to laugh. Felipa gave him an arch look. If he wanted to think the whole thing was humorous, then let him. She didn't care, as long as he left her alone in the future. She stalked away, heading back around the herd toward the campsite.

For a moment after she left, Bramson kept chuckling at her audacity, but as he climbed to his feet, the last of the fading light showed something else in his eyes. It was a mixture of anger, lust, and injured pride. As he clapped his hat back on his head, Bramson thought that while he might admire Felipa, before this trip was over he would damn sure show her who was really running things.

☆ Chapter ☆

14

Jonathan was stumbling along, his eyes fixed on the sandy ground so that he wouldn't trip over a rock or a clump of bunchgrass, when Phillpot suddenly clutched his arm. The other man's fingers closed so tightly that Jonathan let out a surprised yelp of pain. "Hey! What the hell—"

"Up there," Phillpot said in a cracked, shaking voice. "Look up there. It's the Rio Grande!"

"It's another damn mirage," Jonathan said without lifting his gaze from the ground in front of him. "You been seein' the Rio Grande every day for a week now, Phillpot."

"No, I mean it!" Phillpot jerked urgently on Jonathan's arm. "It really is the river this time!"

Jonathan jerked loose and turned to face Phillpot, his hands clenching into fists as he did so. Anger flared in him as bright as the sun overhead. If it hadn't been so hot, and if he hadn't been so tired, he would have clouted Phillpot a good one. The first few times the man had started pointing and yelling about seeing the Rio Grande, Jonathan had gotten just as excited as Phillpot and Cass, only to have his hopes blasted apart by the realization that the brush-lined river was nothing but a mirage, a trick of the light and eyes desperate to see something hopeful.

"Just shut up, Phillpot," he said, his voice quivering with anger and exhaustion. "We don't want to hear any more about the Rio, do we, Cass?" There was no answer, and after a moment Jonathan said, "Cass?"

"Jonathan," Cass replied, his tone hushed, almost reverent, "I think ol' Phillpot's right this time. I think that there's the Rio Grande, all right.''

Jonathan swung around to glare at Cass, but he saw that the third man wasn't even looking at him. Cass was staring off to the north, transfixed by whatever he saw there. There was a light in his eyes like the one Jonathan had seen in paintings of folks looking at Jesus Christ, the kind of pictures they had in the missions in San Antonio. Slowly, Jonathan turned and looked in the same direction as Cass and Phillpot.

He blinked once, then a couple of more times. He wanted to rub his eyes, but he was afraid to. He was scared that if he did, the thing he saw out there about three hundred yards ahead of them would disappear. It was a low line of green growth snaking along the horizon. Jonathan saw some scrubby little bushes and some mesquites and even a few cottonwoods.

''It . . . it's just a mirage,'' he whispered.

''Nope.'' Phillpot gave a cackling laugh. ''It's the real thing, Jonathan. It's the Rio Grande!''

''And that on the other side,'' added Cass, ''that's *Texas*!''

He broke into a shambling run.

Phillpot followed him, letting out a couple of weary whoops as he went. Jonathan still stood there, knowing that he was staring stupidly after them but unable to do anything about it.

If that line of vegetation up there was only an illusion, just like those other times, at least for once it had lasted longer. In fact, as Jonathan finally lurched forward in an awkward run, it was being downright stubborn about not going away.

It was real this time, Jonathan realized. By God if it wasn't.

He started laughing, laughing with sheer relief. For close to a month now—it was hard to keep track of time when you were a fugitive—he and Cass and Phillpot had been working their way northward from Mexico City, hiding during the day and moving at night while they were passing through the more populated areas, stumbling along during the day across isolated stretches like this. Stealing food. Sucking stagnant water out of streambeds that had almost dried up. Living in fear that somebody would see them and report them to the authorities. The only good thing Jonathan could say about it was that the blackouts he had suffered earlier in his captivity seemed to have stopped. It had been a month of sheer hell, and all three of them were even more gaunt and filthy and bushy-bearded than they had been when they escaped from Castle

Perote. Jonathan figured by now they looked like things that weren't hardly even human.

But it was all going to be worthwhile now, because that was the Rio Grande up ahead, and on the other side was Texas.

He had run perhaps fifty feet after Phillpot and Cass when he heard the pounding of hoofbeats behind him.

Jonathan's head jerked around, and his eyes widened in horror and disbelief as he saw the Mexican cavalry patrol galloping toward him. They were a good five or six hundred yards away, but the river was still almost half that distance beyond Jonathan and his two companions. There were a dozen or so men in the patrol, and they could cover ground a lot faster even on tired horses than Jonathan and the others could run.

It would be a race with life and death as the stakes.

"Mexicans!" Jonathan howled as he spurted forward. That dash brought him almost even with Cass and Phillpot. Both of them looked back, and Phillpot stumbled. Jonathan slowed long enough to put out a hand and steady him, then said urgently, "Come on! We can beat them to the river!"

He didn't believe that even as he said it, but damned if he wasn't going to try, he thought. Muscles that had been starved and overworked and stretched until they were like rawhide jerked back and forth and sent his legs flying over the dusty, arid ground. His arms pumped back and forth frantically as he ran. He knew he probably looked ridiculous but he didn't care. All that mattered was reaching the river.

Of course, they was every chance in the world that even if they made it to the river before the patrol caught up with them, the Mexicans would just cross over the Rio and kill them on the Texas side. Out here in the middle of nowhere like this, with no witnesses around to bother them, a little thing like an international boundary might not be enough to stop a bunch of bloodthirsty soldiers.

Jonathan kept running, afraid to look back again because he knew he would see how much the Mexicans had gained on them. Beside him, Cass and Phillpot panted and gasped but continued running just as fast as he was. The soles of their boots, which had gaping holes worn in them, slapped the ground in an irregular rhythm that sounded like the music of fear, counterpointed by the steadily louder beat of hooves as the patrol cut the gap between them.

But maybe they had been closer to the river than he had thought at first, Jonathan realized, because the line of green making the stream's course was drawing nearer and nearer. He could make out individual trees and bushes now. Maybe there was a chance after all. He risked a glance over his shoulder and saw that the patrol was still at least two hundred yards back, maybe more. And the Rio Grande was only seventy or eighty yards away now. Hope gave Jonathan a fresh burst of speed.

He looked back again when the river was no more than fifty yards ahead, and his heart pounded as much from excitement as exertion. They were going to make it to the border before the Mexican soldiers caught up to them, so there was at least a chance they would be safe. Some of the members of the patrol already seemed to be giving up the chase, in fact. At least they were pulling their horses to a stop.

Jonathan glanced over his shoulder, saw smoke bloom from the muzzle of a musket. "They're shooting at us!" he cried.

More guns boomed behind them, and Cass suddenly grunted and stumbled at Jonathan's side. Jonathan looked over at him as Cass's momentum carried him on for several steps before he collapsed. A lucky Mexican shot had taken him in the back of the head, and as Cass pitched forward, Jonathan saw the bloody ruin of his friend's skull. Cass had already been dead while he was still running, Jonathan realized in horror.

Phillpot let out a scream. "We'll never get away!" he babbled hysterically. "They're going to kill us!"

"Come on, damn it!" Jonathan urged him as they left Cass's body behind. "We can still beat 'em!"

It sounded like the whole patrol was firing at them now, and while the range was pretty far even for rifles, the Mexicans were unusually good shots. Lead kicked up dust around Jonathan's feet.

A bullet ripped through the meat of Phillpot's right thigh, spinning him to the ground. He screeched in pain. Jonathan came to a stop a few feet further on and turned to look back at him as Phillpot pushed himself to his knees. "Oh, God!" Phillpot reached out imploringly toward Jonathan. "Don't leave me, Jonathan! Don't let them get me!"

Jonathan hesitated. Some of the soldiers were mounting up again, and they would be galloping after him in a matter of seconds. Phillpot would slow him down at best, maybe fatally . . .

But Jonathan couldn't just abandon him. He took a step toward his fellow fugitive.

More smoke and flame belched from the muskets of the

Mexican cavalrymen still on foot, and Phillpot swayed forward on his knees as a double thud sounded. Jonathan realized the grisly noise had been the sound of two more rounds striking Phillpot in the back. Phillpot opened his mouth and a thick gout of blood welled from it as his eyes widened and bulged. Then he fell forward onto the ground and didn't move again.

Jonathan didn't wait. There was no time to mourn. That could come later if he lived through the next few minutes. He ran as hard as he could toward the river, the elusive river that might mean safety . . . or might mean nothing.

Something plucked at his right side, and a split second later he felt the pain like wet fire splashing against him. It was just a bullet crease, he told himself as he gasped against the fresh agony. But the furrow was bleeding; he could feel the wetness spreading on his tattered shirt. Despite all his effort, his steps slowed. The river was right there in front of him, maddeningly close, but he didn't know if he would ever reach it.

Then his feet were wet, and it wasn't from blood. Silvery droplets of water flew in the air as he splashed into the stream. He was so light-headed now that he hadn't even noticed coming down the gentle slope of the riverbank. A noise came out of his throat that was a half sob, half shout of triumph. He had reached the Rio Grande, and if he had to die, then by God he'd at least do it on Texas soil! Jonathan stumbled on into the river, the water reaching his knees and then the middle of his thighs. Then he was past the center of the stream and heading on to the other side. His feet churned up the sandy bottom and fouled the sluggish water even more. His muscles almost totally out of his control, he careened out of the river into Texas as the Mexican cavalrymen reached the other side. He heard their shouts of anger and frustration.

Then something tripped him—probably a mesquite root, although he never knew for sure what it was—and sent him sprawling to the ground. Dust billowed up around him, coating his wet clothes and skin. He tasted it in his mouth and wanted to spit it out, but his throat was too dry. He rolled over and lay there, pain spreading through him from the wound in his side. Blinking his eyes, he squinted up at the bright blue sky above him.

They could come kill him now, finish him off. None of it mattered anymore. None of it. He was back home in Texas, and that was all that counted.

But no one came to kill him, and as Jonathan drifted in and out of consciousness, unable to tell how much time had passed, he realized that the Mexican cavalrymen weren't going to come across the river after all. For some reason, they had stopped on the other side of the Rio Grande. Maybe they were satisfied to have killed two out of the three escaping prisoners.

And maybe it was going to soon be three out of three, Jonathan thought, because he was sure as hell going to die if he just lay here in the dirt and let himself bleed to death. But there was nothing he could do about it because all his strength was gone. He could no more have gotten to his feet than he could have picked up Castle Perote with his bare hands.

Suddenly, something blotted out the sun above him, some dark shape that Jonathan couldn't seem to focus on. The figure seemed vaguely human. Maybe one of the Mexicans had come across the river after all.

Or maybe he'd died and this was an angel coming down from heaven to get him, because the dark, blurred shape abruptly resolved itself into the face of a pretty woman. Jonathan gaped, and his mouth and throat worked as he tried futilely to get some words out. All he managed was a croaking sound.

The woman said something, and Jonathan let his head drop back and closed his eyes. The long ordeal, the weakness, the pain of his wound . . . all of it finally overwhelmed him, and he felt consciousness slipping away from him. But even as the darkness closed in around him, he wondered what kind of heaven it was where the angels spoke some sort of foreign language that folks couldn't even understand.

He would ponder some on that question later, he decided, if and when he ever woke up again.

Felipa kept a close eye on Jud Bramson, suspecting that the man might try something again, but over the next couple of weeks she realized that the rancher was avoiding her without being overly obvious about it. Their earlier encounter must have taught him a lesson, she decided.

Beyond the most rugged stretch of hill country, the landscape became more open and rolling again, although there were still ranges of good-sized hills here and there. The mustangs and their drovers reached the Colorado River again, after having been away from its course for a considerable distance. Now, though, they followed the river as it slanted northwestward. After a couple of days on that route, a smaller river flowed into the Colorado from the west, and as they camped beside the juncture of the two rivers,

Bramson explained that the smaller stream was called the San Saba.

"I hear tell there was an old Spanish mission out there somewhere on the headwaters of the San Saba," Bramson said as he sat cross-legged by the camp fire that night. "Those old *padres* tried to bring religion to the Indians and wound up gettin' scalped for their trouble."

"I've heard that story, too," James put in. He sipped from his cup of coffee and went on, "Heard tell that Jim Bowie found himself an old Spanish silver mine out yonder somewhere. Silver was the real reason the Spaniards went up the San Saba, I reckon."

Bramson shrugged his broad shoulders. "I never knew Bowie, but I don't put much stock in stories about lost treasures. Riches don't fall in a man's lap. He's got to work for 'em."

"Can't argue with that," James said.

They turned in and slept well, with the exception of the night guards, which tonight were Felipa and Edward. Felipa took the first shift and Edward the second, but as dawn approached, Felipa was awake early, despite the fact that she'd been up half the night standing watch. Mordecai, James, and Bramson were still snoring in their bedrolls when Felipa slipped out of hers, stretched tired muscles, and looked toward the river. It had been a while since she'd had the chance to wash up properly, and she decided to take advantage of the opportunity.

She didn't bother fetching her rifle, but she did pause long enough to buckle on the Colt. A glance at the other side of the camp showed Edward walking slowly back and forth beyond the makeshift corral that held the mustangs. She slipped out of camp quietly and walked down to the river in the gray light, confident that no one had noticed her leaving.

Mist hung thickly over the slowly flowing surface of the Colorado and over the San Saba as well. The heat of the day would burn off those tendrils of fog quickly enough once the sun was high in the sky, but that time was still a few hours off. For now the air was cool and pleasant, and Felipa looked forward to a peaceful few minutes alone.

She unbuckled the gunbelt around her waist and hung it over a nearby bush where she could reach it in a hurry if she needed to. Then she took off the black, beaded vest she wore, hung it on the same bush, and pushed up the sleeves of her black shirt so that they were above the elbows. She unbuttoned the top three buttons of the shirt and knelt on the bank of the river, reaching out to cup a handful of cool water and let it drip over the hollow of her throat and into the valley between her breasts. The water felt good . . .

There was a footstep behind her, and she turned quickly, straightening as she did so. Her left hand shot out toward the butt of the pistol in the nearby holster.

"Wait a minute!" Bramson exclaimed, taking a sudden step backward. He held up his right hand, palm toward her. In his left hand, he carried a canteen. "Hold on, Mrs. Lewis," the rancher went on. "I just came down here to fill up this canteen."

Felipa stopped reaching for the gun and let her hand fall back to her side. She realized that with her shirt open like this, Bramson could see just about all of her breasts, although he seemed to be making a point of not looking at them. Flushed with anger and embarrassment, Felipa quickly buttoned her shirt and then said, "You should not sneak up on me like an Indian, Mr. Bramson. That is a good way to get shot."

"Reckon I know that, ma'am. And I didn't mean to sneak up on nobody. Fact is, the way I was stumbling along with sleep still in my eyes, I figured I was making enough noise to wake the dead."

Felipa's brow furrowed in a frown. If Bramson had really been making that much noise, she ought to have heard him. But perhaps she had been distracted by the pleasantness of the early morning. He seemed genuinely flustered by the whole situation.

With a sigh, Felipa abandoned the idea of taking her shirt completely off so that she could bathe her upper body. In fact, Bramson's blundering in on her had ruined her good mood, and now all she wanted to do was go back to camp and heat up the coffee left over from the night before. She reached for her holster and gunbelt again.

Somehow, though, Bramson had gotten between her and the Colt. He grunted, "Just let me fill up this canteen," as he started to brush past her.

Then, without warning, he whipped around, dropping the canteen and reaching out to clap one hand over her mouth as he looped the other arm around her and jerked her roughly to him. "Just keep quiet, *señorita*," he hissed, "and you won't get hurt."

Felipa's mind exploded with anger. She tried to bring her knee up into Bramson's groin, but the rancher twisted so that the blow landed harmlessly on his muscular thigh. He gave a low laugh and tightened his grip on her.

"Settle down, damn it," he told her. "Fightin's not goin' to do you a damn bit of good. It's time you and me had us a little fun, *señorita*. And you won't say anything about this to that husband of yours, unless you want me to have to kill him.''

He had her arms pinned, and he was holding her too close to him for her to struggle effectively. The fingers of the hand over her mouth dug painfully into her cheeks. She tried to bite him, but his grip was too tight even for that. Inside, she was screaming, but his callused palm muffled the cries until they were almost inaudible.

"Now don't you try nothin'," Bramson warned her with a growl. He shifted his hold on her a little, and she felt the fingers of his other hand pawing at her breast, sinking into the softness of that fleshy globe. She winced in pain at the roughness of his unwanted caress. There had to be *something* she could do . . .

"You son of a bitch!"

The hoarse, furious cry came from just above them, where the riverbank climbed slightly to the plains beyond. In the dawn light, Felipa saw a flicker of movement up there. An instant later, Mordecai crashed into both of them, having thrown himself at them from the top of the bank. The impact knocked Felipa out of Bramson's grip.

She staggered backward and tried to catch her balance. Her foot slipped in the mud at the edge of the river, and she fell, sending up a shower of water as she landed. Spluttering and dripping, she emerged from the stream in time to see Bramson slam a fist into Mordecai's face and knock the younger man backward.

That slowed Mordecai down only for a second. Then he was boring in again, driving punch after punch at Bramson's face and midsection. The rancher blocked most of the wild, flailing blows, but some of them got through and rocked him. Mordecai was wearing his revolver, but he made no move to reach for it. The kind of rage that filled him at this moment had to be expressed with bare hands.

Felipa looked past the battling men and saw James and Edward hurrying toward them. James skirted Mordecai and Bramson and ran to her side. As he reached down to grasp her arm and help her to her feet, he asked anxiously, "What happened? Are you all right, Felipa?"

"I . . . I'm not hurt," she told him as she pushed some wet strands of hair out of her eyes. "But you have to stop them before something happens to Mordecai!"

Edward let out a whoop as Mordecai landed a right cross to Bramson's jaw, staggering the rancher. Bramson caught his balance in time to hook a wicked punch into Mordecai's belly. Mordecai doubled over, and Bramson swung both hands high, leering triumphantly as he clubbed them together and set himself to bring them down with crashing force on the back of Mordecai's neck.

He never got the chance to do so. Mordecai flung himself forward, butting his head into Bramson's wide open stomach. Mordecai's arms went around Bramson's thighs in a tackle, and he drove hard with his legs, forcing Bramson back and down. Bramson landed with a crash that seemed to shake the very earth, and Mordecai was on top of him, jabbing punches at his face.

"Looks like Mordecai's doing all right for himself," James said, sounding concerned and amused at the same time. "Only time I've seen a man fight like that was when somebody was messin' with his woman. Bramson get fresh with you, Felipa?"

There was no point in denying it, since Mordecai had obviously seen what was going on just before he jumped them. She nodded shakily and said, "It was not the first time, either."

James's hand went instinctively to the butt of his own Colt, and he growled, "That son of a . . . Well, never mind. I reckon you know what he is as well as the rest of us. But if Mordecai don't teach him a good enough lesson, I'll be more'n happy to help out!"

Mordecai was not going to need any help. That was becoming more evident by the second. Bramson might have been taller and heavier than him, but he had finally controlled his rage and was turning it to his advantage now, using it to channel his strength into blow after blow that slammed into the bigger man's face. For a few moments, Bramson twisted and heaved, trying to get Mordecai off of him, but Mordecai wasn't going to be dislodged. He stayed where he was, gradually beating Bramson into the soft ground alongside the river.

Finally, when it seemed like the blows had risen and fallen forever, James stepped forward and said sharply, "That's enough, Mordecai! If you keep that up, you're going to kill him."

From the looks of it, that was exactly what Mordecai had in mind, and as he smashed a couple more blows into Bramson's bloody face, Felipa thought that James might have to bodily pull him away from the rancher. But then Mordecai paused and drew a deep breath into his body. A shudder ran through him. He slipped off of Bramson, pushed himself to his feet, and took a couple of stumbling steps backward, away from the semiconscious man. Mordecai lifted a shaking hand and wiped sweat and blood out of his eyes. There was an ugly cut above his right eyebrow from one of the few blows Bramson had been able to land.

Felipa ran to him, came into his arms, and they stood there for a long moment, holding each other. Finally Mordecai said breathlessly, "I . . . I woke up and you were gone. Figured you . . . had come down here to the river. God, Felipa, I'm sorry! I should have been here sooner—"

"No," she said. "It is not your fault, Mordecai. I am just glad you came and that you are all right." She glared at Bramson, who was shifting around and moaning a little. "He did not hurt you too badly, did he? You are bleeding."

Mordecai summoned up a faint grin. "It's nothing to worry about. He didn't land but one or two good punches."

Edward slapped him on the back, making him wince. Edward didn't appear to notice that as he enthused, "You never gave him a chance to hit you, cousin! Boy, I never saw anything like that. You were on him like a cyclone!"

James said dryly, "You'd better get back up there and keep an eye on those mustangs, Edward. We don't want anything happening to them after we've come this far with them."

"Yeah, I reckon you're right." Edward clapped a hand on Mordecai's shoulder again. "Heck of a fight!" Then he turned and hurried up the bank to the camp.

James hooked his thumbs in his gunbelt, ambled over to Bramson, and prodded the rancher roughly in the side with a booted toe. "Can you get up?" he asked.

Bramson groaned again, but he rolled onto his side and then over on his stomach, so that he could get his hands and knees underneath him and push himself up off the ground. He climbed slowly and painfully to his feet and turned a blood-streaked glower toward the other three.

"You bastard," he grated at Mordecai. "You had no right—"

Mordecai cut in, "You're the one who had no right, Bramson. Felipa's my wife, and you're lucky I didn't kill you for what you were doing to her." His eyes still blazed with anger that the violence had not dissipated.

"I gave a little thought to shooting you myself," James added, "when Felipa told me this wasn't the first time you'd bothered her. Maybe you can get away with that in Georgia, mister, but not in Texas."

Mordecai looked sharply at Felipa. "Not the first time?" he repeated.

She shook her head. "Please, don't get more upset. The first time was just words, and I thought he was truly sorry he offended me." She looked at Bramson, and her mouth twisted like she wanted to spit out a bad taste. "Obviously he has just been waiting for a better chance, and this morning he thought he had found it."

Bramson pointed a shaking finger at Mordecai. "I'll see you in jail, boy," he threatened. "You attacked me for no good reason—"

"Shut up," James snapped. "You try spreading that story and we'll tell the truth about you, Bramson. You'll be lucky if you don't get strung up from a tree branch." He looked thoughtful, then went on, "But what *are* we going to do with you?"

"Leave him out here," Mordecai said without hesitation. "Leave him and those mustangs and let him drive 'em on to his ranch by himself . . . if the Comanches let him get there."

Felipa saw a faint flicker of fear appear in Bramson's eyes at the thought of being left alone out here in the middle of the wilderness by himself. They were still at least a week away from his ranch, judging by what he had said about it, and it was unlikely he would ever reach the place alive without their help.

"No," she said.

Mordecai and James looked at her in surprise. She went on, "We should finish our job and deliver the horses to Mr. Bramson's ranch. Then he will owe us the rest of the money he promised us."

Bramson laughed harshly. "If you think I'm going to pay any of you another penny after what happened, you're crazy!"

"Nope," James said coolly, a grin of admiration appearing on his face. "Felipa's right. We have a deal, Bramson, and if you don't honor it, there wouldn't be a court in Texas that'd find against us for fillin' you with lead. In fact, I reckon most judges would award us what you'd owe us . . . out of your estate."

Bramson blinked a couple of times, muttered, "You're bluffing. It's nothing but a goddamned bluff."

James shrugged. "Reckon we can find out easy enough. What do you say, Mordecai?"

After a moment of hesitation, Mordecai replied, "I say we deliver the mustangs, just like we said we would. And you'll pay up or else, Bramson."

Bramson started to turn away, but Mordecai's voice lashed at him and stopped him.

"One more thing. You keep your distance from my wife. You even go near her again and I'll kill you, you understand?"

"Sure, sure," Bramson answered in a surly tone. He was pale underneath his tan, and evidently he was starting to realize just how close indeed he had come to death on this warm morning. He trudged away up the riverbank.

"I meant it, you know," Mordecai said after a moment, giving a rather defiant look to his wife and his uncle. "If he causes any more trouble, I'll kill him, money or no money."

James laughed. "If he causes any more trouble, nephew, you may have to stand in line to kill him."

☆ Chapter ☆

15

Jonathan struggled up out of the blackness that sought to hold him down. It would have been easier, not to mention less painful, just to stay where he was, wrapped in a comforting cloak of nothingness. But the Lewis stubbornness wouldn't let him do that. Once his wits returned enough for him to realize that he wasn't dead after all, then nothing would do but that he fight his way back to consciousness.

His eyelids lifted, and even though he was lying in the shade, he winced from the brightness of the day. After the peaceful darkness, the light stabbed his eyes like knives. He shifted slightly, blinked several times, and finally forced his eyes to stay open.

"You are awake, yah?"

The woman's voice came from beside him, and he thought he had never heard a sweeter sound in all the world. Despite a faint guttural undertone, to Jonathan it was like honey and molasses. He turned his head slowly so that he could see who it belonged to.

She made it easier by leaning over to study him, an anxious frown on her face. Jonathan liked that face as much as he did her voice; it had slightly rounded cheeks that blushed with color under his frank scrutiny, light blue eyes that seemed bigger and brighter than any eyes had a right to be, a full-lipped mouth maybe a little too wide for classic beauty but possessing an undeniable sensuousness, and the whole arrangement was crowned by thick, pale blond hair that was pulled back in a sensible bun at the moment. Jonathan wondered what she would look like if he took her hair loose and let it fall around her face.

She had to be one hell of a beautiful woman, he realized, to have this effect on a man who was just waking up from a brush with death. Or maybe it was the close shave he'd had that made him appreciate the wonders of life that much more. He pushed the thought out of his head. He could worry about such things later. Right now he wanted to sit up and find out just how badly he was hurt.

He started to, and pain laced through him, centered around his right side. That was where the bullet crease was, he remembered as he gasped with the agony of it.

Gentle hands on his shoulders pressed him back down. "No, you must not get up," the woman told him, her tone even more concerned now. "You are hurt, a lot of the blood you lost. You must rest now."

"Wh . . . where am I?" The hoarse voice issuing from cracked lips didn't sound like his, Jonathan thought, but he must have been the one who spoke. There didn't seem to be anybody else around.

"You are lying under a tree not far from where we found you," the blond woman said. "Now please be quiet. You must rest."

Jonathan let his head sag back against the pillow underneath it. It wasn't really a pillow, he decided; more than likely a rolled-up blanket. But it felt just fine at the moment. He closed his eyes and took several deep breaths.

As he did so, his mind insisted on starting to work again. The woman had said "we." That meant she wasn't traveling alone, which didn't really come as a surprise. It would have been much more unusual for a young woman to be out here in the wild Texas border country by herself. Taking the thought a little further, Jonathan reasoned that the presence of the woman and her companions, whoever and however many of them there were, was probably the reason the Mexican cavalry patrol hadn't crossed the Rio Grande to finish him off. They had been too leery of venturing across the border with witnesses around. Which told Jonathan there was likely a good-sized group with the blonde, otherwise the soldiers would have considered wiping them out too, just to tidy things up.

Jonathan didn't mean to, but he fell asleep anyway, and when he woke up again it was a more natural thing, not like when he had regained consciousness earlier. The ache in his head was less, and there was a hollow feeling in his gut that reminded him how long it had been since he'd eaten anything, let alone any decent food.

A savory aroma drifted to his nostrils and made the hunger ache even worse. He tried to sit up again.

This time the blond woman was not there to stop him, and he made it after a moment of struggle. The world seemed to spin crazily around him for a few seconds, but it gradually settled down into its proper position. Jonathan felt something around his midsection and explored enough to discover that he was wrapped with strips of cloth that had been pulled tight to serve as a bandage for the bullet wound. His touch made a throb of pain go through him, so after that he left the bindings and the injury alone.

He heard voices and looked around. He was sitting under a cottonwood, and he had been lying on a bedroll. A few feet away, a wagon with a canvas cover over its bed was parked. There were other wagons nearby, a whole line of them, in fact. He could see them against the light thrown by a camp fire on the far side of the vehicles. Night had fallen, which was not surprising because he figured he had slept for quite a while. His rumbling stomach had told him that.

He had heard of wagon trains moving west up in the States, but he hadn't expected to run into one here in South Texas. Lucky for him he had, though, otherwise he would no doubt be dead now. Even if the Mexicans hadn't crossed the river, he probably would have bled to death lying there on its banks. He had these pilgrims, whoever they were, to thank for saving his life.

"Oh! You are awake again." The blond woman stepped between two of the parked wagons and hurried over to kneel beside him. "But should you be sitting up? You are badly hurt—"

"I reckon I'll be all right, ma'am," Jonathan told her. His voice was still hoarse but stronger than he had thought it might be. "You took good care of me, bandaged me up real good."

"Gerhard did that," she said. "The closest thing to a doctor we have with us he is." She smiled, and in the firelight coming through the gaps between the wagons, he saw her flush a little in embarrassment. "The way I talk you must pardon. Your language, it still troubles me sometimes."

Jonathan summoned up a smile, which wasn't hard to do considering how pretty the young woman was. Now that he had gotten a better look at her, he was sure of a couple of things: she was around his own age, and her face was the one he had mistaken for an angel looking down at him earlier, when he had thought he was already dead.

"You talk just fine," he said. "Who's this Gerhard gent?"

"Gerhard Roche. My husband he is. I am Evalinde, Evalinde Roche. We come to this Texas place from our homeland. We are German."

Jonathan had already figured out that much from her accent; there were quite a few German immigrants coming to Texas these days, and some of them were establishing their own colonies on land grants they got from the Republic. But the news that Evalinde Roche was married came as a surprise. He wouldn't have thought that a girl as young and pretty as she was would already be tied down with a husband. He recognized the sigh that came from him as a sound of disappointment.

Evalinde leaned toward him anxiously. "You are all right?" she asked. Her breath was warm and sweet.

"Yeah, I'm fine for a fella who's been chased by Mexicans, shot in the side, and seen a couple of his friends killed right in front of him."

"So sorry I am. We saw what happened, and we would have gone across the river to bury your friends, but our leaders said we could not. They were afraid those soldiers would kill us."

"Likely would have," Jonathan told her, a grim look on his bearded face. "You did the right thing, hard as it is. The Mexicans are out to kill every *gringo* they can get their hands on, even German ones."

"*Gringo*," repeated Evalinde. She shook her head. "I do not know this word."

"You will, happen you stay around the border country very long. Listen, Miz Roche—"

"Oh, call me Evalinde you must," she interrupted with a smile.

"Well, all right, Evalinde. I don't mean to be rude, but I've been on mighty short rations for the past month or so, and right now my belly thinks my throat's been cut. Reckon you could rustle me up some food?"

"Yah, of course." She stood up with a rustle of her long calico skirts. "You stay here and rest. Stew I bring you."

She hurried off between the wagons.

Jonathan scooted over a little so that he could place his back against the trunk of the cottonwood. He leaned against it and sighed again, feeling the weariness still strong in him. But the hunger was stronger, and he was determined he wasn't going to sleep until he had some of that stew in his belly.

From the sounds he heard and the wagons he could see, he figured this group of immigrants was a good-sized one. There were fifteen or twenty wagons, which meant around a hundred folks in the bunch. They were being smart, traveling together like this. Smaller groups could have easily run into trouble from bandits or Mexican patrols venturing across the Rio Grande.

He was safe now. That realization hit Jonathan with enough force that he went numb for a moment. After his long ordeal, after the months of captivity and the weeks of being a fugitive, he had reached a haven. It felt so good that he couldn't quite comprehend it.

Evalinde reappeared, carrying a bowl of stew. Jonathan sat up straighter and started to reach for it, but she said, "No, I will feed. You just eat."

"I never argue with a beautiful woman."

She blushed again as she spooned some of the stew into his mouth. It was good, filled with beans and chunks of meat and wild onions. Jonathan's stomach gave a little lurch right at first, unaccustomed as it was to such substantial food, but then it settled down and he was able to eat without any trouble. He could almost feel the strength flowing back into him as he finished off the stew. Evalinde gave him a smile, let the spoon rattle against the empty bowl, and stood up. "Coffee I will bring—" she began, then stopped herself, took a deep breath, and made herself say slowly, with great concentration, "I will bring you coffee now. That is correct, yah?"

"I reckon so," Jonathan told her. "I'm not really the right fella to ask about such things as talking proper, though. My mama gave me some schoolin' back in Tennessee, but that's all the education I ever had, and that was a while back."

She smiled at him again. "You sit. I will bring coffee." Then she went between the wagons, into the main part of the camp that the immigrants had established.

Jonathan had seen quite a few people moving around over there, and it looked like in addition to the big main camp fire, they had several smaller blazes going, too. Jonathan frowned a little. You'd be able to see this place from a long way off tonight, he thought. The Comanches seldom came down this way, but sometimes Apaches still wandered over from Mexico. He recalled hearing men talking about the Apaches and how the Comanches had driven them out of Texas for the most part and how they still raised hell over in Mexico.

If there were any Indians within fifty miles tonight, likely they had already spotted the camp. But with the immigrant group being so large, Jonathan could at least hope that no Indian in his right mind would want to attack them.

When Evalinde came back, there was a man with her. He wore a white shirt and a dark vest, along with whipcord pants and high black boots. He sported a short, sandy-colored beard, but most of his skull was bald. He looked to be in his late thirties or early forties, Jonathan judged. As the man looked down at Jonathan, he said, "You are feeling better, yah?"

"That's right," Jonathan told him. "Some fella named Gerhard patched me up real good, and this little lady here has been taking fine care of me."

The man knelt beside Jonathan and started poking around the bandages. "I am Gerhard Roche," he said. "I tended your wound."

Jonathan blinked in surprise. He had expected Evalinde's husband to be older than her, but this man had to be at least twice her age.

Gerhard grunted, evidently satisfied that Jonathan hadn't torn the bandages loose or damaged his handiwork in any other way. He hunkered back on his heels and said, "We heard the shots and saw the Mexicans chasing you and your comrades. What did you do to arouse their anger so?"

"Not a blessed thing except be born *gringos*," Jonathan said. He reached up and took the cup of coffee Evalinde held out to him. He breathed in the steam that rose from it, reveling in the aroma of the first coffee he had smelled in months. After he had taken a couple of sips, he realized Gerhard was looking at him impatiently, and he went on, "Me and those two gents with me were Texans. That was enough for that Mex patrol. But I reckon they must've been looking for us, too. We escaped from prison in Mexico City a while back, and we'd been dodging the cavalry ever since."

"Prison?" Gerhard repeated with a frown. "You and your friends were criminals?"

"Not hardly," Jonathan said vehemently. "Prisoners of war is more like it, although the Mexicans don't much believe in anything that honorable. Leastways their leader, a dictator named Santa Anna, doesn't."

Gerhard nodded in understanding. "I have heard of this Santa Anna. At Indianola, where our ship came ashore, men talked of him and said that he was very bad."

"That ain't the half of it."

"You were a political prisoner, then."

"Guess you could call it that."

Gerhard stood up and said, "Then I am glad we were able to help you. What is your name?"

"Jonathan Lewis. And I thank you, Mr. Roche, for taking care of me."

"You are a Texan, you say?"

Jonathan shrugged his shoulders. "Well, an adopted one, anyway. I was born and raised in Tennessee, back in the States, but I've been out here on the frontier for a while. And I've shed blood for the Republic, which I guess makes me just as much a Texan as anybody."

"Excellent. And you know this land?"

"Some. Although right now I don't even know where we are, except beside the Rio Grande somewhere."

"We are headed for a place called El Paso del Aguila. Do you know it?"

"The Pass of the Eagle," Jonathan mused. "I've heard of it. It's a crossing on the Rio, upstream a good ways from here, I reckon. Unless we're farther west than I figure. How long out of Indianola are you?"

Evalinde said, "We left the Gulf two weeks ago."

"Then you haven't had time to reach Eagle Pass yet. It's bound to still be upstream." Jonathan noticed the sharp look Gerhard gave his wife when she spoke up, as if he disapproved of her taking part in this conversation. He didn't say anything about it, though. Things like that were strictly between a man and his wife, the way Jonathan saw it, and he didn't have any business interfering. Instead, he continued, "If you keep following the river, you can't miss the place when you get there."

"We could use a guide," Gerhard said stubbornly, confirming Jonathan's suspicions that was what the man had been leading up to with all his questions. "This Texas land is so large . . . It is intimidating, to say the least."

"I reckon so, but I'm not in much shape to travel."

Gerhard shrugged. "We can wait a few days if necessary. There is water here, of course, and graze for our oxen and horses and cattle. But I think you will be much better tomorrow. I cleaned your wound. It did not require stitches, and I believe it will heal nicely. Tonight you are weak from loss of blood, but your strength will return quickly." He shot another glance at Evalinde. "My wife will see to that. She is an excellent cook."

"Yes, sir, I reckon I already know that." Jonathan took a deep breath, wincing a little as the bandages pulled at his side. "I can't make you no promises, but I'll give it some thought."

"Good," Gerhard said with a curt nod. "Sleep on it, as you Texans say. I bid you good night."

"Good night. And thanks again for . . . well, for everything."

Gerhard smiled thinly, turned, and went back to join the other immigrants. Evalinde stayed behind, and she said to Jonathan, "Do not be angry with Gerhard. He is accustomed to having people do as he says."

"What was he over yonder in Europe, some sort of prince or something?" Jonathan asked, half-jokingly.

"Yes," Evalinde said simply. When she saw Jonathan's upraised eyebrows, she went on, "Not a prince, but a baron. His land and his title were taken from him in a . . . a shift of power, I suppose you could say. For a time it looked as if he would be executed. So that is why he understands about political prisoners."

Jonathan let out a low whistle. "I never would have figured . . . Is that why you folks are this far south, instead of up north of San Antone with the other German immigrants?"

Evalinde nodded. "That is one reason. It would not be safe for Gerhard if certain parties knew where he could be found."

Something else occurred to Jonathan, and he said, "If he was a baron, I reckon that makes you a baroness."

She blushed and shook her head. "Oh, no. I was not Gerhard's wife when he still held his title. We were married on the ship, coming over to this country. The baroness, she died several years ago."

Since she seemed to be in a talkative mood, Jonathan asked, "What about this guide business? You think you folks really need my help to find where you're going?"

"It would be good if you went with us," Evalinde answered without hesitation. "Gerhard is a good man, a good leader, but this land is strange to him. I . . . I would feel better if you would come. As soon as you are well enough, of course."

"Well, like I told your husband, I'll think about it." Jonathan sighed tiredly. "Right now I just want to finish this coffee and get some more sleep."

"I can have your bedroll moved over under one of the wagons," Evalinde offered.

"Nope, right here under this ol' cottonwood tree's just fine.

There's a little more fresh air that way, and the night feels like it's going to be a warm one.''

"Yes," she said. "I fear you are right." She looked between the wagons at the camp fire for a moment, then back at Jonathan. "I will say good night."

"Good night, ma'am. And thanks."

"You are very welcome." She smiled at him, then turned and left just like Gerhard had done.

Jonathan leaned against the tree and sighed again. He had promised to consider Gerhard's suggestion, but he didn't really have to. The folks in this wagon train had saved his life, and he owed them. A Lewis always paid his debts.

As soon as he felt up to it—maybe even in the morning—the immigrants could start on their way to Eagle Pass again. And when they went, Jonathan would go with them.

Jonathan's face felt funny. He rubbed the back of his hand over the smooth cheeks and chin. He'd had a beard for so long that being clean-shaven was a strange sensation.

Wearing clean clothes was the same way. Gerhard had found some pants and a shirt to fit him, as well as a black felt hat. Jonathan even had new boots . . . well, not new, exactly, but they didn't have huge holes in them, so that was practically the same thing as far as he was concerned.

He sat on the seat of one of the wagons with a heavyset, florid-faced German who had bushy red hair sticking up a couple of inches all over his head. The man's name was Albert, but Jonathan had already started calling him Bert. The German seemed to like that, nodding his head and babbling in a mixture of English and German. Jonathan didn't understand even half of what he said, but Bert obviously didn't care. He just liked the sound of his own voice.

The wagon was the second one in line, right behind the vehicle belonging to Gerhard and Evalinde Roche. Jonathan would rather have been on horseback, but it was too soon after his injury to risk that. For a few days, he would ride on the wagon with Bert, then pick one of the extra horses for a saddle mount and take his place at the head of the wagon train. If he was going to serve as scout for this bunch, he wanted to do the job right.

Jonathan's headache was just about gone now, and when Gerhard had changed the bandages and checked his wound before the group broke camp that morning, the former baron had pronounced that the bullet crease was healing well. Jonathan agreed. The pain from the wound was less, although he still had to be careful how he moved around. A sharp, sudden jolt could send a fresh stab of pain through him.

The wagons followed a trail about an eighth of a mile from the Rio Grande that paralleled the river's course. From time to time, Jonathan glanced in the direction of the slow-moving stream and the flatlands beyond it. He couldn't get it out of his head that that was Mexico over there, the place where he had been forced to endure so much torment. He would have liked to put more distance between himself and the border, but under the circumstances he would just have to put up with the mental discomfort. Once the immigrants reached their destination, however, he intended to head north as fast as a horse could carry him.

The day went smoothly and the wagon train covered some eight or nine miles before nightfall. Evalinde insisted that Jonathan have supper with her and Gerhard, and although he felt a little awkward about doing so, Jonathan accepted. Gerhard was a stiff, humorless gent, at least on the surface, and Jonathan found himself wondering what a pretty young girl like Evalinde had ever seen in him. Of course, he had been a nobleman back in Europe, and he was the leader of this bunch of pilgrims. Jonathan figured that Gerhard's political rivals hadn't gotten their hands on *all* of his money, either. The Roches' wagon was an expensive one and well furnished. Power and wealth could be mighty attractive, Jonathan supposed. He'd never had much of either one of those things, so he couldn't judge from experience what effect they had on women.

There were no cottonwoods where the wagons camped that night, so Jonathan pitched his bedroll under Bert's wagon. They were up and moving early the next morning, heading north and west along the river again.

By the time a week had passed, Jonathan was feeling much better. He was able to wear a smaller bandage over the wound in his side, and Gerhard said it was still healing quite cleanly. He was a lucky man, Jonathan knew. Without Gerhard's medical help, the bullet crease would have likely festered and maybe even killed him. Instead, his head was clear and most, if not all, of his strength had come back. Evalinde's good cooking helped, too, just as Gerhard had predicted it would.

Jonathan spent his days on horseback, sometimes riding as far as a mile ahead of the wagons to make sure the path was clear and there was no trouble lurking up ahead. He carried some sort of European pistol that was not nearly as graceful—or as powerful— as his old Paterson Colt. It was the only extra handgun Gerhard had been able to come up with, though. Jonathan was just grateful to be armed again after being defenseless for so long.

After another day of riding ahead of the train and seeing no one—white, Mexican, or Indian—Jonathan returned to the wagon and unsaddled his horse, turning it into the rope corral that held some of the stock. The oxen and the cattle were hobbled and staked out, but the horses were usually kept in the corral. Jonathan had given the travelers some tips on how to make the arrangement stronger. He carried his borrowed saddle toward Bert's wagon. There was no sign of the jovial German, and Jonathan supposed he was off visiting at some other wagon.

He stowed the saddle away just inside the back of the wagon and was about to turn away when a voice said, "Hello, Jonathan." He recognized the voice immediately as Evalinde's and turned toward her with a smile.

She was standing on the far side of the wagon, with the canvas-covered body of the vehicle between her and the rest of the camp. Jonathan nodded pleasantly to her and said, "Howdy, Evalinde. Where's Gerhard?"

"Talking to some of the others, I suppose," she answered. "I do not really care. Since he is the leader, he has to do many things that do not interest me."

"Well, he's got a lot of responsibility, I reckon." Jonathan frowned a little. Something about this situation didn't strike him as quite right. Maybe it was the way Evalinde was looking at him, or the way she stood there by the wagon, one hand resting easily on the sideboards. Somehow she made even that pose pensive and appealing.

"I do not want to talk about Gerhard," she said firmly. "I see him enough during the day. I want to talk about you."

"Me?" Jonathan said.

She came a step closer to him. "Yes. Is your wound healing?" She put out a hand and touched his side where the bullet had gouged out its shallow furrow.

Jonathan caught his breath, but not from any pain her touch caused him. Just the opposite, in fact. Her hand was warm and soft, and it felt good lying against his skin. Still, he knew they shouldn't be standing here together like this.

"I'm fine," he said curtly. He tried to step back, to put some distance between the two of them, but her hand caught at his shirt.

"Evalinde, you shouldn't oughta be doin' that—"

She came into his arms then, moving so smoothly and quickly that he didn't know what she had in mind until it was too late. His own arms went around her instinctively, and when she tilted her head back and opened her lips just slightly, his mouth came down on hers seemingly of its own volition. It was as if he had no control over what was happening here, but was just an interested, somewhat shocked bystander. The thought that he was kissing a married woman slammed through his brain. He was kissing her right out in the open where anybody might see them, in fact. But she was so soft in his embrace, and her lips were so wet and hot and sweet that he couldn't bring himself to stop.

Finally reason asserted itself, and Jonathan pushed away from her. "This is crazy, Evalinde!" he said, his voice little more than a whisper. "We can't be doin' this—"

"Why?" she moaned. "Gerhard is not good for me, not the way you could be."

"Then why'd you marry him?" Jonathan demanded.

"He . . . he swept away my senses. He had been a baron. In my eyes, he still was. I . . . I did not know that a nobleman is first just a man."

Jonathan sighed heavily. It had been just like he figured between Gerhard and Evalinde, but that knowledge didn't make him feel any better. He said, "I like kissing a beautiful woman just as much as any gent would, but not when she's hitched up to somebody else. You've been mighty good to me, Evalinde, and I'm beholden to you, but that doesn't mean we can be anything else to each other."

"You are lying," she insisted. "You want me as much as I want you."

"Maybe so, but—"

She came up on her toes, leaned toward him, and kissed him again. Jonathan wanted to pull away but couldn't bring himself to do it. Finally, after what seemed like an eternity, Evalinde took her lips from his and whispered, "There. You think about that, Jonathan Lewis. I will come to see you again."

Then she slipped out of his arms, turned, and sauntered away with a maddening sway of her hips. Jonathan watched her go and said softly to himself in awe, "Son of a bitch."

Looked like he had gotten away from the Mexicans only to land smack-dab in the middle of more trouble.

☆ Chapter ☆

16

Mordecai kept a close eye on Jud Bramson, as did the others in the group, but the beating the rancher had suffered at the hands of the younger man seemed to have demoralized him almost completely. He rode apart from the group, leaving Mordecai, Felipa, James and Edward to handle the mustangs without any help from him. That was fine with Mordecai. Every time he looked too long at Bramson, he remembered seeing Felipa struggling in his arms, and that old familiar hot rage welled up in him.

Times like that, he had to force himself to think about other things, or his hand started creeping toward the butt of his Colt.

Felipa seemed to have recovered from the incident without any aftereffects. She rode point most of the time, preferring to be out in front. Mordecai couldn't blame her for that. This was pretty country, full of wooded hills and broad valleys. If Bramson could survive the isolation, this was indeed good ranch country. There was grass and water in abundance.

Bramson sat by himself in the evenings when they camped, too, and he never spoke unless somebody asked him a direct question. Mordecai was forced to do that from time to time, just to make sure they were still on the right trail. Bramson usually answered with just a surly nod, but sometimes he volunteered a little more information, like the fact that they ought to reach his ranch in another two or three days.

Whenever it was, it couldn't be soon enough to suit Mordecai. He wanted to deliver the horses, get their money, and head home, never to see Jud Bramson again, with any luck.

Finally, after the hills had pinched in again on both sides of the river for a ways, then opened up once more into a wide, green valley, they spotted Bramson's spread. James noticed the first evidence, a thin curl of smoke that lifted into the clear blue sky. A little while later, they were all able to see the stone chimney the smoke came from. It was attached to a good-sized log house. The building had two stories and a long, covered gallery in front of it. On the other side of the house were two barns, several corrals, a smokehouse, and a couple of other outbuildings. The ranch was situated on a long shelf that sloped down to the river, close enough for water to be handy but far enough away from the stream that in times of flood the rising waters would not reach the house. A couple of hundred yards behind the house, a steep, rocky bluff rose sharply for fifty or sixty feet before leveling out into plains again. There were plenty of trees around the house, mostly post oak from the looks of them.

Mordecai nudged his horse over closer to where Bramson rode and said grudgingly, "Nice place. Looks like you put a lot of work in it."

"Man's got to be willin' to work if he's goin' to build something," Bramson replied. He glared straight ahead, never looking over at Mordecai.

Mordecai reined his horse back to the herd's flank without saying anything else to the rancher. Bramson was a damned frustrating *hombre*, he thought. There was much about the man that was admirable; nobody built a place like this so far from civilization without plenty of determination and grit. And there was no doubt it took a sizeable amount of courage to settle out here, either, what with the nearest settlement over two hundred miles away. Bramson's spread was just about as far out on the edge of the frontier as a man could get without falling off. But at the same time, he was a crude, arrogant son of a bitch who believed in taking whatever he wanted, whether it belonged to another man or not. Maybe he had moved out so far from civilized folks because he just couldn't get along with them, Mordecai mused.

They drove the mustangs on toward the ranch, and as they drew closer, Mordecai frowned in puzzlement. The hands Bramson had left behind must have seen them coming, but no one was venturing out from the ranch to meet them. Maybe the three men weren't at the house or the barns. Could be they were off on some other part of the spread. Still, if they were anywhere close by, they should have heard the thunder from scores of hooves by now or at least seen the haze of dust that rose in the air from the passage of the herd. An uneasy feeling crept through Mordecai, but he shook it off. They had come this far with no problems except among themselves; no use borrowing trouble now, he told himself.

Felipa galloped ahead and leaned over from her saddle to open the gate of the largest corral. She pulled her horse to the side, out of the way, as Mordecai, James, and Edward pushed the mustangs into the enclosure. The horses balked a little at first, but they were used to being driven by now and they went on into the corral without too much trouble. James caught the gate when the last mustang was inside, swung it closed, and dropped the latch. Mordecai rode over next to Felipa, brought his mount to a stop, and leaned forward in the saddle, resting his hands on the horn as he looked in satisfaction at the herd milling around inside the sturdy fence made of peeled poles.

He glanced over at Bramson, who sat his horse on the other side of the corral gate. "Well, they're here," Mordecai said. "Didn't lose a one. So I reckon you owe us some money."

"It's in the house," grunted Bramson. "I'll go get it."

Evidently James shared some of the same worries that had gnawed at Mordecai, because he asked, "Where are those hands of yours? I figured we'd find them here."

"So did I," Bramson replied, a worried frown on his craggy face. "Could be they're out doing some chores elsewhere on the spread."

"You don't reckon they left for good, do you, and took your money when they went?"

That same thought had occurred to Mordecai, and it was a worrisome possibility. Bramson waved it off, however. "Those boys come all the way from Georgia with me," he said. "I'd trust 'em with my life."

"Yes, but what about our money?" Felipa asked.

Bramson jerked his head toward the ranch house. "Come on. You'll see. I'll pay you what I owe you."

He jogged his horse easily toward the house, followed by Mordecai, Felipa, James and Edward. They were about twenty yards from the building when several men stepped out of the house onto the gallery. They had rifles in their hands, and Bramson let out a startled curse and yanked his horse to a stop as the strangers leveled the weapons at them. Mordecai and the others followed suit. "What the hell?" Mordecai heard James mutter. Obviously, these weren't the ranch hands Bramson had left behind to keep an eye on the place.

More men stepped onto the gallery from the house, all of them heavily armed. Bramson glared at them and demanded, "Who in blazes are you men? This is my ranch, and you got no right to be here!"

Mordecai's mouth had gone dry as he looked at the men arrayed on the gallery. They were roughly dressed in a mixture of buckskins and range clothes. There were a few Mexicans in the bunch, complete with tall sombreros and brightly colored serapes. The guns in their hands didn't waver, and Mordecai knew that he and his companions were well and truly caught. The strangers had the drop on them, and any move toward a gun would just get them blown out of the saddle. He gave James and Edward a warning glance, hoping they would understand not to try anything.

Bramson was trembling with anger as he repeated, "This is my ranch. You'd better get the hell off it, right now!"

"We ain't goin' anywhere, mister, and neither are you," said one of the men. He gestured with the barrel of the pistol he held and went on, "You just sit still now." He turned his head and addressed someone in the house. "We got 'em covered, Luke, just like you said. What you want us to do with 'em now?"

Another man emerged from the house and stepped onto the gallery, and Mordecai felt his backbone go cold as his whole body stiffened. He recognized the tall, burly man with the bushy black beard.

So did James. "Luke Blackwood," he murmured in disbelief.

Luke had a shotgun tucked under his arm and a smug look on his face as he regarded the prisoners. His dark eyes widened in surprise as he saw Mordecai, James and Edward. Bramson and Felipa would be strangers to him, but he would know a Lewis anywhere. All the Lewis men had the same stamp on them, and it was a stamp that was truly despised by the Blackwood family, had been ever since the two families had had trouble back in Tennessee.

"Step out here, Finis," Luke called back into the house, an ugly grin splitting his face under the tangle of whiskers. "Got a little surprise for you."

Another bearded man, a little shorter and more thick-bodied, shuffled out onto the gallery. He blinked rheumy eyes as he stared at the captives. After a moment, he tugged at his beard and rasped uncertainly, "Them ain't Lewises, are they?"

"Sure as hell are," Luke replied.

Finis Blackwood, Luke's older brother, leveled a filthy finger at Mordecai. "I know that 'un! That's Michael, the sumbitch who shot me in the arm all them years ago! Oughta kill him right now!" And he reached for the big pistol holstered on his hip.

Luke stopped him. "Hell, no! We don't want to shoot 'em just yet. That wouldn't be no fun. Anyway, that ain't Michael. That's his git, little Mordecai."

Bramson glanced over at Mordecai and asked under his breath, "You know these gents?"

"We know 'em," Mordecai replied quietly. "They've been a thorn in my family's side for years. We thought we'd seen the last of 'em. Hoped so, anyway."

One more figure came out of the house and stood behind Luke and Finis. He was younger, not much more than a kid, and more rawboned than either of the brothers. His hair was thick and dark, but he didn't have a beard yet. Still the resemblance was unmistakable. "Cyrus?" Mordecai asked in surprise.

"Hello, Mordecai," Cyrus Blackwood said with a nod that might have been friendly under other circumstances, like if there hadn't been six men pointing rifles and pistols at Mordecai and his companions.

"Howdy, Cyrus," Mordecai said. His mind went back to one of the last times he had seen Cyrus. The boy had brought a message over to the Lewis compound, and Annie had insisted on giving him something to eat, even though he was a Blackwood. Cyrus had hesitated at first, sort of like a starving wild animal who wants to trust somebody but doesn't know how to. Then he had eaten a little and taken some more food back to his younger brothers and sisters. None of the Blackwood brood had gotten enough to eat in those days. Finis and Luke were supposedly farming some land along the Colorado River, but most of the time they spent drinking and fooling around with one of the succession of slatterns Finis had brought out to their place. All of the Blackwood youngsters had different mothers, because no woman could stand to stay with Finis for very long at a time. And since the brothers generally took turns with the women, it was hard to say for sure who the fathers were, too. Young Cyrus had been named for his grandfather, who had originally come to Texas with the first Mordecai Lewis, only to desert him when trouble cropped up. That had been the beginning of the deadly feud between the two families, although there had already been some bad blood. Annie had always suspected that Isaac Blackwood, the third member of the trio of brothers that had come out from Tennessee, had fathered young Cyrus, Mordecai recalled, and looking at Cyrus now, he was almost sure of it. The resemblance was strong. Isaac had been the only halfway decent member of the Blackwood family, and he had died at the Alamo with Crockett, Bowie, Travis, and the others. It was a damned shame too, Annie had said, because she had seen the good in Isaac Blackwood, but at least he had a son to live on after him, even if Finis did claim the boy as his own.

Those thoughts raced through Mordecai's head, but none of them did a damned bit of good right now, he realized. He and his companions were in a bad way, a mighty bad way. From the looks of them, the men who had taken over Bramson's ranch were Comancheros, white and Mexican renegades who traded with the Comanches, and a more vicious bunch didn't exist on the face of the earth.

"Where are my men?" Bramson demanded. "What the hell have you done with them?"

Finis let out a crackling laugh, and Luke said, "They didn't give us a friendly enough welcome when we rode up and said we needed to use this place for a meetin' with some friends of our'n. Tried to run us off, they did." He jerked a dirty thumb toward the rear of the house. "We threw their bodies out back for the coyotes. Too damned hot to dig graves in this weather."

Mordecai's pulse was hammering in his head, and it raced even faster when he looked over at his wife. Felipa was pale, but her face bore the usual defiant expression it took on whenever he ran into trouble. It was bad enough that he and James and Edward had blundered into such a mess, but Felipa's presence made things a lot worse. He wished they had left her back home, like he had wanted to do.

Bramson glowered at the Blackwoods and their men and snapped, "You still haven't told me who you are."

"They're Comancheros," James said coldly, having come to the same conclusion as Mordecai. "I reckon they've got a rendezvous set up here with a bunch of redskins."

"That's right, ol' hoss," Luke confirmed. "Black Feather and his band are comin' down here all the way from up in the badlands to do a little tradin' with us. We got our mules and our goods in the barn, just waitin'. We didn't figure on somebody bringin' us a whole herd of mustangs, to boot." Luke used the barrel of his revolver to push his battered hat farther back on his tangle of hair.

"Question now is, what're we goin' to do with all of you?" He grinned widely, his eyes fixed on Felipa's pale but angry features. "Reckon we all know the answer to that, don't we? 'Specially you, little lady. Just who are you, anyway? I never seen you before."

"She's just some gal we picked up down the trail," Mordecai said quickly before Felipa could answer Luke's insolent question. If the Blackwoods knew that she was his wife, it could make things even worse. He went on, "She doesn't have anything to do with this, Luke, and I don't think she even speaks English. You could let her ride out and she couldn't do you any harm."

"Ride out? Hell, no!" Finis rumbled. "She stays. I want me some o' that."

Suddenly, Felipa whirled her horse, the mustang responding immediately to her touch. The long rowels on her Spanish spurs raked the horse's sides and it lunged into a gallop. Mordecai jumped his own horse to the side, putting himself between her and the house as he grabbed the butt of his gun. "Ride, Felipa!" he shouted to her. "Don't look back!"

Now that the bottle had been unstoppered, there was no putting the lightning back. James's hands flashed to the guns on his hips, and the Colts were booming as he brought them up. Rifles cracked from the gallery of the house. Lead whined past Mordecai's head as he drew his gun, drew back the hammer, and sent a shot toward Luke and Finis, who were scurrying for cover. Mordecai saw the ball smash splinters from the log jamb of the front door.

Bramson and Edward had their guns out and firing, too, but in the chaos, most of the shots on both sides went wild. James dropped a couple of the Comancheros as they scattered, and Mordecai winged another one in the leg, sending the man spinning to the ground. Mordecai's horse was dancing around wildly, and it was hard to keep the animal under control and shoot at the same time. He hauled back on the reins, making the horse rear up.

There was a thud as a bullet slammed into the horse's chest while it was pawing frantically at the air with its front hooves. The horse screamed and went over backward, and Mordecai kicked his feet out of the stirrups and desperately flung himself clear to avoid being crushed. He hit the ground hard and felt the Colt being jarred out of his hand by the impact. He rolled over and groped through the dust for the gun, unable to find it.

As the guns kept booming, there was a harsh cry somewhere nearby, and an instant later, Jud Bramson crashed to the ground only a few feet away from Mordecai. The rancher's chest was a bloody ruin, but his eyes were still open. He fixed his gaze on Mordecai, and his mouth moved as he tried to say something. What it was, Mordecai never knew. Bramson's eyes glazed over in death.

Mordecai was still trying to find his gun when the shooting ended abruptly. He froze as a hard ring of metal was pressed to his head. He recognized the touch of a gun barrel and knew he was damned close to having his brains scattered all over the ground.

"You just keep still," Luke Blackwood rasped. "That mouthy fella's dead, and your uncle and your cousin are both shot up some. I don't want to kill you just yet, Mordecai, but I will if I have to. Now get up, slow and easy."

Mordecai climbed to his feet as Luke had ordered, and he looked around the yard in front of the ranch house. Bramson was dead, of course, but James and Edward were both still alive. James was clutching a bloody left arm, and Edward was sitting down, blood pooling on the ground around his foot where it was leaking out of his boot. He was already pale and shaking from loss of blood.

"You've got to help Edward," Mordecai said desperately, "or he'll bleed to death." Appealing to the Blackwoods for mercy was probably futile, he knew, but he had to try anyway.

Cyrus stepped forward. Mordecai noticed now that the youngster wasn't wearing a gun or carrying a rifle, so he probably hadn't participated in the battle. Cyrus bent, slipped an arm around Edward's waist, and helped him to his feet. "I'll take him inside and patch him up," he told Luke, who hesitated for a second and then nodded in agreement. Luke gestured for one of the other Comancheros to give Cyrus a hand.

Mordecai looked around, searching the nearby hills for any sign of Felipa. She seemed to have vanished completely, and he was grateful for that. The rest of them would die at the hands of these renegades, he had no doubt of that, but at least Felipa would have a chance to survive. A slim chance, considering where they were, but a chance nonetheless.

"I know what you're thinkin', Mordecai," Luke said with a laugh. "But we'll hunt her down and bring her back. You got my word on that. And I know she ain't just no Mex gal you picked up on the trail. Not the way you looked at her. She's your woman, ain't she?"

"Go to hell, Luke," Mordecai said coldly.

Luke cackled again, and Finis joined in. "I reckon that's where we'll end up," Luke said, "but we'll have us some fun 'fore we get there. 'Specially when we get that gal back. We'll all have us a good time with her." He prodded Mordecai in the chest with the barrel of a rifle. "Tell you what—you can even watch." He turned to the other men. "Lock these two up in the smokehouse."

Mordecai and James were prodded at gunpoint toward the sturdy little building. "She'll get away," James said in a low voice as they went. "You know how she can ride. None of these bastards can keep up with her."

"I hope so," Mordecai muttered. "I'm praying you're right."

And that was all they could do now, he realized as bleak despair flooded over him. They could pray for a while.

And then die.

The smokehouse had no windows, and only a few chinks between the logs where precious little light filtered in. It was blistering hot inside the small building. Sweat coated both men as Mordecai ripped some strips from the tail of James's shirt and used the cloth to bind up the wound in his uncle's arm.

"I've been hit worse," James said as he rolled his shoulder and flexed the arm. He winced. "It's still a mite uncomfortable, though."

"What about Edward?" Mordecai asked. "You think he'll be all right?"

"If Cyrus gets the bleedin' stopped, he should be." James chuckled grimly. "For a little while, anyway."

Mordecai leaned back against the thick wall and closed his eyes. "Damn the luck," he said softly. "Who would have figured we'd run into a bunch of Comancheros led by the Blackwood brothers?"

James eased himself into a more comfortable position and stretched his legs out in front of him. "I've been thinking about that. Something seem a little different to you about those two bastards?"

"Well, now that I think about it," Mordecai said with a frown, "Finis wasn't tossing around orders like he used to. Looked more like Luke was running things."

James snorted in contempt. "Luke Blackwood never bossed anything in his life. He never was smart enough to be anything but lapdog to Finis. So what changed things?"

"Don't know," Mordecai said, shaking his head. "I don't

reckon it matters overmuch, though. We'll be just as dead no matter who gives the order to kill us.''

That gloomy statement made both of them fall silent for a while. The heat grew even more oppressive. Mordecai wondered how long Luke and Finis intended to leave them in here.

After what seemed like several hours, they heard footsteps approaching outside. A moment later the footsteps stopped, and a voice called, ''You boys stay away from that door now, you hear? I got a scatter-gun out here, and Luke says that if you try anything, I got leave to blow you clean in two.''

The latch on the outside of the door rattled, and a moment later the massive panel swung open, letting in the brilliant late afternoon sunlight that was blinding to the eyes of Mordecai and James, who had been shut up in near darkness for so long. They winced from the light, barely able to make out shapes. Someone was shoved into the smokehouse, and whoever it was fell heavily to the ground at their feet. The door slammed shut and was fastened again.

''Edward!'' Mordecai cried as he scrambled over to the newcomer. ''Is that you, Edward?''

''M—Mordecai . . . ?'' Edward's voice was weak, and as Mordecai's eyes adjusted to the dimness again, he could see that his cousin was only semiconscious at best. But the material of Edward's pants had been cut away around his calf, and the wound there that had bled so badly had been bound up. Mordecai hoped Cyrus had cleaned the bullet hole first, even if it was just to pour some rotgut whiskey over it.

Gently, Mordecai lifted Edward's head into his lap. ''You'll be all right,'' he said quietly. ''You just hang on, Edward, because we'll all be fine. You'll see.''

James gave him a look that let him know that neither of them believed that. But neither of them believed in giving up, either.

The inside of the smokehouse gradually grew darker as night settled down outside. The darkness was a small blessing, because with it came a slight lessening of the heat. Edward slept restlessly, muttering incoherently from time to time, and Mordecai and James talked quietly. They could hear faint laughter drifting from the house. Mordecai believed that Felipa hadn't been recaptured yet, because if she had there would have been more noise coming from the house.

He thought about Jud Bramson. As close as he himself had come to killing Bramson at one point, he still felt that the rancher had deserved a better end than to be shot down by a bunch of bloody-handed Comancheros. But that was how things sometimes happened out here on the frontier. Death jumped out at you like a snake hidden in tall grass, and there was no time to get ready for it. Anyway, most folks were never really ready for death, Mordecai thought. They hung on to each little bit of precious life that they could, even when the time left to them could be measured in mere moments. He intended to be the same way, fighting right to the last.

A little later, footsteps approached the smokehouse again, and another harsh voice ordered them away from the door. Mordecai and James were already on the far side of the chamber from the door, and Edward was still asleep. The door was opened, and Cyrus Blackwood stepped through, carrying a lantern in one hand and a small black iron pot in the other. He set the pot on the ground and said, "Here's some beans for you. Sorry, but you'll have to eat 'em with your hands." He stepped back but didn't leave the smokehouse. After a glance over his shoulder at the men who stood outside holding rifles, he asked, "How's Edward?"

"We're hoping he'll be all right," Mordecai answered. "Looks like you got the bleeding stopped in time. Although what difference it'll make in the long run, I don't know. You intend to kill all of us anyway."

"Not me," Cyrus said. "That's up to Finis and Luke."

Mordecai searched the youngster's face. Cyrus was a few years younger than Edward, maybe seventeen or eighteen. He wasn't a bad-looking boy; some of the brutal appearance of the other Blackwoods had missed him somehow. Mordecai said, "Why don't you leave us that lamp to eat by?"

Cyrus shook his head. "Can't do that. But I'll wait while you finish off them beans." He set the lamp on the ground just inside the door and hunkered beside it. To the guards outside, he said, "Don't worry, I'll be through here in a few minutes."

"Don't know why you're bein' so nice to those jaspers, Cyrus," one of the Comancheros said with a laugh. "They'll all be dead in a day or two anyway."

"What I do's my business," Cyrus said sharply.

The renegades just laughed again and moved off a few paces, began rolling quirlies. One of them said, "They give you any trouble, boy you just holler."

Mordecai scooped some beans out of the pot with his hand and passed it on to James. They would have to try to wake Edward up so that he could eat. After a long day without food, even half-cooked beans tasted good, and Edward was roused long enough to swallow some of them before he went back to sleep. As Mordecai and James were wiping the last of the grease and bean juice out of the pot with their fingers, Mordecai took a chance and asked Cyrus, "What's really going on here? Finis and Luke don't seem like themselves anymore."

Cyrus shook his head, and for a moment Mordecai thought he wasn't going to answer. Then the youngster said quietly, "Finis ain't right in the head these days. Too much bad whiskey muddled his brain, I guess. And then he took up with some tavern woman who wasn't too healthy. He caught some sort of sickness from her. He's getting worse all the time, and I don't reckon he'll live too much longer."

"Wish I could say I was sorry, him bein' your pa and all," James said.

"I don't believe that about him being my pa, not anymore. My pa died at the Alamo. Only decent thing a Blackwood ever did."

"So Luke started running things when Finis got sick?" Mordecai asked.

Cyrus shrugged. "Luke gives the orders. I try to help out a little bit when I can."

The simple statement told Mordecai a great deal. Luke Blackwood hadn't gotten suddenly smarter when his brother became ill and feeble-minded. Cyrus was the one pulling Luke's strings now, just as Finis had for years. This band of renegades would never have taken orders from a boy, so Cyrus let Luke and everybody else think that Luke was in charge. In truth, though, Luke would have been lost in a minute without Cyrus's help.

That meant there was a chance for him and James and Edward. A small chance, to be sure, but anything was better than nothing.

"Look, Cyrus," Mordecai said earnestly, "I don't know how you and Luke and Finis came to be running with a band of Comancheros, but you know the Lewises never were as black as your bunch painted them. There was bad blood between my grandfather and yours, sure enough, and my pa did shoot Finis in the arm back there in Tennessee, but only because Finis was trying to ambush him."

"I know," Cyrus said, so softly that they almost couldn't hear him.

"And my Aunt Annie and your pa—your *real* pa—got to be friends there for a while, before Annie married Sly Shipman. She was good to you, remember? Remember the time she fed you and gave you food for your little brothers and sisters?"

"I remember . . ."

Mordecai leaned closer to him. "You've got to help us, Cyrus. Maybe you can talk Luke and Finis out of killing us. We can't do them any harm. There's no law for a couple of hundred miles, at least. They can leave us locked up in here until after they've done their trading with the Comanch', then let us go. They can even take those mustangs. Those horses are a fair trade for our lives, aren't they?"

In the flickering light of the lamp, Cyrus grimaced. "I already told them all of those things, Mordecai," he said. "They don't take orders from me, you know. All I can do is sort of steer them in the right direction sometimes. But Finis don't know what's going on most of the time, and Luke can get stubborn now and then. He ain't forgot how your family ran us off from our land down on the Colorado." Cyrus shook his head. "I'm sorry, Mordecai, but they've got their hearts set on killing the three of you, and I don't reckon there's anything I can do about it."

Mordecai sighed and sat back in defeat. Well, he had tried anyway, he told himself. After a moment, he asked, "What about the girl?"

"Your wife?" Mordecai's sharply indrawn breath told Cyrus that his guess was right, and he went on, "I figured that was who she was. She looked like a right nice young woman, Mordecai, real pretty and full of spunk. I hope she gets away. But I wouldn't count on it. Luke's got a couple of trackers out looking for her. They're half-breeds and they can follow a trail no matter where it goes. I reckon in a day or two they'll bring her in."

Mordecai cursed in a low, miserable voice.

"Don't worry, though," Cyrus went on quickly. "They won't kill her. I ain't sayin' they won't abuse her, because we all know they will. But we've got some women and kids with us, camp followers and the like, and the girl'll end up with them most likely. It's not much of a life, I reckon, but it's better'n being dead."

"Cyrus . . . I got no right to ask, but if there's anything you can do for her . . ."

"I'll try to look out for her, Mordecai. You've got my word on that." Cyrus picked up the empty bean pot and the lamp. "I got to be going now, before the others get too suspicious. Sorry I can't do any more for you."

Mordecai nodded, and James said, "You've still got some

decency in you, son. No matter what happens to us, you'd better give some thought to getting away from this bunch before you wind up as bad as they are.''

"I'll do that, Mr. Lewis," Cyrus promised. Then he ducked out of the smokehouse and shut the door behind him.

In the darkness that followed, Mordecai said, "I still think Felipa will get away. She's got to."

"I hope you're right. But we've got to start thinking about us, Mordecai."

"What do you mean?"

"I mean," James said, "that the first time they take us out of here, I'm going to jump one of those guards and try to get my hands on his gun."

"They'll shoot you full of holes!" Mordecai protested.

"That's right. But at least I'll die quick and cheat Luke and Finis out of any satisfaction they might get in torturing me to death. And besides, I figure to take one or two of the bastards with me."

"Well . . . maybe you're right."

"You give it some thought," James advised. "Right now I'm going to get a little shut-eye."

Within minutes, James's deep, regular breathing told Mordecai that his uncle was asleep. James's time as a Ranger—as well as his service in the Texas militia—had taught him to snatch sleep whenever he could, even with death waiting for him when he woke up. Mordecai wished the blood in his own veins flowed that cool.

But he couldn't stop thinking about Felipa, and the Blackwoods, and Jud Bramson, and all the family back home, far down the Colorado. Maybe there were times when dying well was the only thing a man could do, but he wanted to live.

God help him, he wanted to live.

☆ Chapter ☆
17

Jonathan went out of his way to avoid Evalinde Roche for the next few days after the kisses they had shared. He couldn't help but see her occasionally, though, and whenever he did, she wore the same smug smile on her lovely face. Obviously, she was completely confident in her appeal and figured he would come back to her sooner or later.

The bad thing was that Jonathan was considering it.

He knew it would be wrong, that she was a married woman, but her face haunted him both night and day, and the memory of how her body had felt in his arms, the sweetness of her lips, stayed with him as well. Hell, he was only human, he told himself. How much temptation could a man stand, anyway?

Several nights later, he found out.

The wagon train was still following the Rio Grande. In a lot of places, the semi-arid plains ran right up to the bank of the river, with little vegetation to mark its course except for stubby mesquite trees and scrub brush. But in other spots, there were islands of green along the riverbank where cottonwoods, willows, live oaks, and soapberry trees grew. Whenever possible, the immigrants camped under the trees, which were something of a reminder of their homeland. Bert had told Jonathan quite a bit about the thickly wooded Bavarian mountains, and Jonathan knew the travelers had to be at least a little homesick when they looked out over the Texas plains and saw miles and miles of nothing. He didn't begrudge their choice of campsites. Besides, he like the trees himself.

The wagons were parked under the trees and the usual rope

corral was set up for the horses. The oxen and cattle were hobbled, also as usual. After everyone had eaten, Jonathan carried his bedroll to the far side of the little grove and spread it under a live oak. He generally slept a little apart from the wagons, so that if anybody was moving around in the night who shouldn't be, he would stand a better chance of hearing any telltale noises. Gerhard posted guards every night, but Jonathan was exempt from that duty since he rode ahead as scout every day. Still, he usually kept one ear open as he slept, just out of habit.

Tonight, tired after a long day, he dozed off more quickly than usual, and he slept unusually soundly. So much so, in fact, that when something touched him lightly on the arm, it took a moment for his senses to come alive. When they did, though, he twisted sharply in his bedroll, and his arms shot up instinctively, his hands closing around the throat of the figure looming over him in the darkness. He rolled over, putting the lurker on the bottom, and he was ready to drive his thumbs into the person's larynx and crush it before he realized that the soft, slender neck he held was undoubtedly female.

"Son of a bitch!" Jonathan exclaimed, jerking his hands away from the woman's neck. "Who—?"

He figured out the answer even before she spoke in a hoarse, startled whisper. "It is me, Jonathan—Evalinde!"

He realized he was sitting on her chest, and he was suddenly all too aware of how the soft mounds of her breasts were being flattened by his inner thighs. He slid off of her but stayed crouched beside her as she gulped down several lungfuls of air.

"Sneakin' up on a man's a good way to get yourself killed!" he hissed at her. "What in blazes were you doing?"

"I . . . I came to see you," she said. "You have been so unfriendly to me the past few days, and after all I did for you."

He could hear the pout in her voice. He took hold of her upper arm and helped her sit up. "Look, I wasn't trying to be unfriendly," he said sincerely. "And I know better'n anybody how much you've done for me, Evalinde. You and Gerhard saved my life."

"Oh, do not talk about Gerhard!" she said, frustration plain to hear in her tone. "He would have let you die if not for me."

Somehow, Jonathan doubted that. Gerhard had been interested in his services as a guide and scout right from the first. But he didn't feel much like arguing the point with Evalinde. The main thing he wanted was for her to go on back to her wagon before she got both of them in trouble.

The camp seemed to be asleep, and a glance at the stars through the overhanging limbs of the live oak told Jonathan the hour was after midnight. He said firmly, "You go on back to where you belong now. You coming out here won't do either one of us any good."

"How can you be so cruel?" Evalinde demanded in a hurt voice. "Here I have risked everything to be with you."

"You don't understand. You *won't* understand. I don't want—"

"Yes, you do," she interrupted calmly. "You want me. A woman knows these things." She leaned closer to him. "And whether you like it or not, Jonathan, I am your woman."

He sighed heavily. The last thing he needed right now was a damned stubborn female pestering him.

Especially when what he wanted more than anything else in the world was to take her into his arms and plunge his face into that thick, sweet-smelling blond hair.

"You see." He knew she was smiling without even being able to see her face that clearly. "I knew you wanted me. We both know it."

"Damn it," Jonathan said softly.

Then there was no time to say anything else, because he was pulling her toward him, his hands tight on her shoulders, and kissing her with all the hunger he had been trying to deny for days now. His arms went around her and his hands slid down her back to the gentle swell of her hips. She wore a dressing gown of some sort, but from the feel of her body there was nothing beneath the gown but firm, warm flesh. She moaned deep in her throat as Jonathan's hands closed over her hips and pressed her belly against him. Her fingers worked frantically at the buttons of his shirt and then stole under the fabric to caress his chest. He brought one hand back around, slid it up her body to her left breast. He felt the urgent prod of the nipple through the gown as he closed his hand over the mound.

There was no turning back now, and both of them knew it.

Gerhard was either blind or stupid or both, Jonathan thought more than once during the next week, because he didn't seem to notice that his wife was slipping out of their wagon in the wee hours just about every night. Of course, it was possible that he slept like a log and didn't give Evalinde the attention a pretty young woman like her deserved. That would be one more reason explaining why she had chosen to abandon her marital vows.

Jonathan felt guilty about it, too, damned if he didn't . . . but he didn't turn her away or tell her to stop coming to him. He couldn't.

One night, when they were finished for the moment, she let herself sag down atop him, resting her head on his chest as they both tried to catch their breath. His fingers strayed along the soft golden curves of her body, and he thought about the luck that had brought him to this place in his life. By all rights, he should have been either dead or still wasting away in that dungeon back at Castle Perote, not snuggling in a bedroll with a beautiful young woman who happened to be buck naked at the moment. Yep, he decided, he was a damned lucky *hombre*.

Evalinde lifted her head a little so that she could look into his face in the starlight. "Jonathan?" she said quietly.

"What is it, darlin'?"

"How far are we from Eagle Pass?"

It seemed like a strange question to ask under the circumstances, but he frowned and tried to answer it as best he could. "I can't be sure, but I reckon we ought to get there in another two days, maybe three at the most. If we don't run into any trouble. Why do you ask?"

"Is it not obvious?" There was a hint of snappishness in her voice. "We must decide what to *do*."

"Do about what?"

That was the wrong thing to say, he realized an instant later. She rolled off him and sat up, pulling the blanket around her. "I am talking about us," she said coldly. "What will we do once the wagon train reaches Eagle Pass?"

"Well, to tell you the truth, I haven't given it much thought. After all that's happened to me in the last year, I sort of just try to get through one day at a time."

That only made things worse. There was a sliver of moon tonight, and in the light that it cast, he saw her frown. She said, "We must think about these things. We have to decide what to do about Gerhard."

Jonathan sat up, enjoying the way the night breeze cooled the sweat on his lean body. He would have enjoyed it even more if he hadn't been having this particular discussion, he thought.

"I don't see that there's anything we can do about Gerhard," he said after a moment. "He's your husband. Nothing's going to change that fact."

"Then when we get to Eagle Pass . . . ?"

"I'm afraid you'll have to go your way, and I'll go mine. I've got family back up north that likely thinks I'm dead. I'd like to go disabuse 'em of that notion."

Evalinde did not say anything for a minute, but her breathing got harder. Sometimes that was a good sign, but somehow Jonathan didn't think this was one of those occasions.

"You would abandon me," she finally said. "You have had your pleasure, and now you would condemn me to a life with Gerhard. There is more passion in a stone on the bottom of the river than there is in that man!"

"Maybe you just haven't given him a chance. He seems like a decent sort of fella—"

"Oh! You do not understand!"

She was angry and upset, and Jonathan wished this conversation had never gotten started. He sat there in miserable silence for a few minutes, then said, "I'm sorry, Evalinde. I just don't see what we can do. You're married to Gerhard and, like I said, nothing's going to change that."

"One thing would."

Jonathan frowned. "But you folks are Catholics, aren't you? I didn't think you were allowed to divorce anybody."

"A widow can remarry," Evalinde said simply.

It took a few seconds for Jonathan to understand what she meant, but when he did he felt a chill go through him that had nothing to do with the night wind. Slowly, he asked, "Has ol' Gerhard got some sort of illness I don't know about?"

"He is as healthy as a horse—and about as imaginative."

"Then you're talkin' about . . ." He couldn't bring himself to say it.

That same reluctance didn't apply to Evalinde. "If Gerhard were to die in some sort of . . . accident," she said, "then everything he possesses—including me—could be yours, Jonathan."

He rubbed a hand over his face and gave his head a little shake, wishing that his ears were playing tricks on him but knowing that they weren't. He said in a stunned voice, "You mean for me to . . . to . . ."

"To kill him, yah. You have killed men before, haven't you?"

Jonathan came to his feet and paced a short distance away from her, heedless of his nudity. He felt a shiver go through him. She had asked him if he had killed anyone before, and the answer to that was yes. He had killed outlaws and Indians who were trying to kill him, and he had killed Mexican soldiers in battle. All of those cases had been life or death, and he had killed to save his own hide. But never in his life had he killed anyone in cold blood, and he had sure as hell never been asked to murder somebody by a sweet-faced naked blonde. He took a deep breath. It was enough to twist a man's guts into knots, all right.

Keeping a tight rein on the emotions raging through him, he turned to face her again. She was watching him with such an innocent look that it was hard to believe she had just made the suggestion she had. But Jonathan knew he hadn't imagined it. Sounding a lot calmer than he felt, he said, "I can't do that, Evalinde. I'm sorry. I'm sorry you ever asked me to do such a thing."

She uncoiled, came to her feet in a little movement of taut muscles under bare skin. She padded toward him and said, "Please, Jonathan. We could be so happy together. Gerhard is nothing compared to what we could have."

Jonathan's jaw tightened. When a man saw a rattlesnake, heard its deadly buzzing, he just naturally wanted to shoot the thing. Some of that same instinct had his nerves jumping right now. He said, "You'd better put your clothes on and go back to your wagon. And don't come to see me again, Evalinde. Please don't."

She stared at him, her lovely mouth open slightly in amazement. "You cannot mean that," she said after a moment.

"Damn straight I mean it. We would've been splittin' up in a couple more days anyway. I reckon we can go ahead and do it now. Better all around that way."

She shook her head and whispered, "No. No, you can't—"

"Just get away from me," Jonathan said, and there was infinite weariness in his voice now.

For a long moment, she glared at him, and he thought she might come at him and try to claw his eyes out. But then she turned, gathered up her clothes, and pulled them on quickly without looking at him again. She slid off into the shadows under the trees where the wagons were camped.

Jonathan let out his breath in a long sigh. That just went to show how quick things could turn sour, he thought. Still, despite everything, there was a pang of regret deep inside him. He was going to miss Evalinde, miss her more than he would have thought possible under the circumstances. He was glad the wagon train would be reaching its destination in only a few more days, and then he could be on his way. He needed to get back home and put everything that had happened behind him.

He got dressed except for his boots, and then as he was about to slide back into his bedroll, a noise from somewhere in the night caught his attention. It was the cry of a coyote, a sound that seemed to pack all the loneliness of the human soul into it despite its animal origins. But something wasn't quite right about it.

Jonathan listened intently for several more minutes, but the howl was not repeated. He told himself he was being overly suspicious just because he was upset about Evalinde, and he stretched out to get some rest. A man couldn't get his hackles up about every noise in the night, else he'd never get any sleep.

But as he dozed off, Jonathan slid his fingers around the butt of the revolver he had been given, and he felt a little better after that.

Jonathan's sleep was restless, and he finally gave up about an hour before dawn. He rolled his blankets and headed back to the wagons, hoping that someone else was already up and would have a coffeepot on the coals. After the night he'd had, he needed something to brace him.

At least there had been no more cries in the night other than those he could positively identify as night birds or other creatures that normally roamed the darkness. He decided he had been wrong about that coyote howl. Indians used noises like that for signalling, but sometimes a coyote was just a coyote, Jonathan told himself.

Several people were indeed already awake, and a few of the cook fires had been stirred up and were blazing brightly. Jonathan nodded pleasantly to a bearded man called Rudy Wolff and accepted with thanks a cup of coffee offered to him by a woman named Anna Ulmer. He hunkered next to one of the fires as he sipped the hot, strong coffee. Even this far south, there was a slight chill in the morning air, but it wouldn't last long once the sun was up. Jonathan hoped they covered plenty of ground today; the sooner they reached Eagle Pass, the better as far as he was concerned. He couldn't shake the image of sweet, innocent Evalinde pleading with him to murder her husband. He wanted to put the whole sorry business far behind him.

As the eastern sky lightened with the approach of dawn and more people began moving around the camp, Jonathan finished his coffee, accepted a chunk of hard black bread from *Frau* Ulmer, and wandered over to the corral to check the horses. The corral was one of the places where Gerhard posted a guard every night, just to make sure that no Indians tried to sneak up and make off with some of the mounts under cover of darkness.

Jonathan nodded to the man who was still standing near the corral with a rifle cradled in the crook of his arm. "Any trouble last night?" Jonathan asked.

The man shook his head and said, "*Nein*. Everything, it was quiet, *nicht wahr*?"

"I reckon," Jonathan muttered, not completely sure what the gent had said. He had picked up some of that German lingo during the past couple of weeks, but when they talked amongst themselves he could barely understand any of it.

As he looked over the horses and ate his bread, Jonathan thought about Mordecai, Edward, and Manuel and their mustanging expedition to South Texas. If nothing had happened to them, they would have long since been back home. Shoot, they might even be getting ready to head down to the Nueces country for a second trip. He wished he was back on the Colorado so that he could go with them. He missed his family, especially James and Mordecai. The three of them would have made quite a team, he thought. He wished he knew whether or not James had made it out of Mexico safely. If anybody could have, he reckoned it was James . . .

"There!" the voice said shrilly. "There he is! The one who attacked me!"

Jonathan winced, realizing that the angry words had come from Evalinde. He turned, saw her standing about ten yards away. She was pointing a shaking finger at him. Beside her stood Gerhard, and his normally fair-skinned features were mottled red with rage.

"Wait just a damned minute!" Jonathan said. "I don't know what she's been tellin' you, Gerhard, but it's not true—"

"So, you molest my wife and then call her a liar, eh?" Gerhard shot back. "You are not the man I thought you to be, Jonathan Lewis. But even the best of men can be a poor judge of character at times."

That was the truth, Jonathan thought grimly. Look at the way he had misjudged Evalinde.

"Just hold on, Gerhard." It was doubtful that he could talk his way out of her lying trap, but he had to at least try. "I never hurt Evalinde. I never would, not after everything she's done for me."

"You deny that you attacked her?" Gerhard demanded haughtily.

"Damn right I deny it."

"You are the liar, Jonathan Lewis," Evalinde said. Her accusations were drawing a lot of attention now, as quite a few people from the camp began to gather around.

And who were they going to believe, Jonathan asked himself. The innocent-looking young woman married to their leader, a former baron? Or some Texan who didn't even speak their language, a man they'd pulled out of a bad hole when he was nothing but a bloody, vermin-infested fugitive?

It didn't take long for Jonathan to get the answer to that question. Several of the men muttered and took a step toward him, and he saw callused fingers clench into fists.

"Wait!" Gerhard said to them. "It is I and my wife whose honor this man has offended. It is my privilege to settle this matter with him."

"There's nothing to be settled," Jonathan insisted, "because nothing happened."

"Have you ever touched my wife?" Gerhard's eyes bored into Jonathan's as he asked the question.

Damn! Jonathan had been hoping that Gerhard wouldn't be quite so specific about that question. He'd been raised to tell the truth, and he didn't want to lie now. But if he revealed what had really been going on, nobody would believe him anyway. They would all think he was just trying to deflect trouble by throwing the blame back on Evalinde.

"There's not point in talking about this," he snapped. "You're not going to believe me anyway." Disgusted and frustrated, he started to turn away.

Gerhard closed the gap between them in a hurry, his hand coming down roughly on Jonathan's shoulder. Gerhard jerked him back around and said, "How dare you!"

Jonathan pulled free and warned, "Back off, Gerhard. You'd better let this go right now, or you're liable to hear some things you don't really want to."

"More lies, you mean," Gerhard snapped. "In my homeland, we know how to deal with matters of honor. I extend you that courtesy, even though you do not deserve it."

With that, his hand flashed up, and he slapped Jonathan right across the face.

Jonathan blinked in surprise. The slap hadn't been that hard, but it had stung. What shocked him was that one man would slap another like that. He looked past Gerhard and saw the satisfied little smile on Evalinde's face. He hated to add to her satisfaction, but things had gone too far to stop now. "What the hell was that?" he asked Gerhard.

"I have challenged you to a duel," Gerhard said, his chin lifting imperiously.

"Well, you're in Texas now, mister, and we don't believe in anything as fancy as duels. And we don't turn the other cheek when somebody wallops us one, either!"

Jonathan's fist came whistling up and caught Gerhard right on the point of that bearded chin the former nobleman was sticking out in the air.

A shout of outrage and offended honor went up from the circle of immigrants as Gerhard sailed backward and slammed down onto his back. Some of them had started for Jonathan when Gerhard got up, shook his head, and called, "No!" Gerhard climbed shakily to his feet, took a couple of deep breaths, and went on, "If this man wants to be a barbarian, we will let him. Out of the way!"

And with that, he charged toward Jonathan, head lowered like a mad bull.

Jonathan just had time to see the delighted expression dancing in Evalinde's eyes, even though she had clapped her hands to her mouth in mock horror as the fight began. Then he darted aside to let Gerhard's momentum carry him on past. Gerhard was quicker than Jonathan expected, however, and he managed to lash out with an arm and snag Jonathan as he went by. Both men crashed to the ground.

Gerhard slammed a couple of blows into Jonathan's chest before Jonathan rolled away and landed a kick on the immigrant leader's shoulder. That gave Jonathan enough breathing room to scramble to his feet. He waited until Gerhard was up again, then stepped in and threw a right and left that rocked Gerhard's head back and forth. Gerhard was tough, though; Jonathan had to give him that much. He shook off the blows and plowed ahead, swinging long looping punches that Jonathan avoided most of the time. The ones that landed rocked Jonathan. He was starting to think maybe he had made a mistake by getting into this fight. After everything he had been through in the past months, he didn't know how much stamina he had built back up. Gerhard might just be able to wear him down and emerge victorious, unless Jonathan could come up with something to end the fight quickly.

Gerhard left his feet in another dive, and Jonathan wasn't able to avoid this one at all. Gerhard's shoulder slammed into his midsection, sending pain from his recently healed wound shooting through him. Jonathan gasped and tried to twist out of Gerhard's grip, but he felt himself being bulled backward, felt his feet come off the ground. He landed hard, all the breath knocked out of him as Gerhard's weight came crashing down on him.

The blood was roaring so loud in Jonathan's ears that he didn't hear the screaming at first. Evidently neither did Gerhard, because he kept pummeling Jonathan even after someone began shrieking in pain. Suddenly, Jonathan realized that the noise wasn't coming from him, and then the crash of gunfire told him something else was wrong. He grabbed Gerhard's ears, twisted hard, and rolled over to throw the man off.

"Stop it!" Jonathan bellowed as more shots rang out nearby. "Stop it, you damn fool!"

He let go of Gerhard and scrambled to his feet in time to see one of the women fall, her chest pierced by an arrow. Men, women, and children were running everywhere. The camp was in total chaos. Jonathan dodged aside as a screaming woman dashed past him, and his hand went to the butt of his gun as he spotted a short, thick-bodied Indian in leggings, high moccasins, and a brightly colored headband around long raven hair. *Apache*! Jonathan realized, and he knew in that instant that he'd been right to be suspicious of that coyote howl the night before. Old instincts took over as Jonathan palmed out the revolver, thankful it had not been knocked out of its holster during the fracas with Gerhard. He pulled back the hammer and squeezed the trigger as the Apache dashed at him, knife upraised for a killing stroke.

The bullet blew the Indian straight back, a bloody hole appearing on his bare chest. Almost before the Apache had hit the ground, Jonathan was swiveling, searching for another target. There was no shortage of them, he saw to his dismay. The Apaches were all around the camp. They had slipped up while everyone was distracted by the fight, and Jonathan cursed bitterly, feeling guilty for his part in it. He squeezed off another shot and saw another Apache stumble and fall.

"Get to your wagons!" he shouted to the immigrants. "Stay low and fight back!"

The immigrants were putting up little if any defense, too terrified to do anything except let the Apaches overrun them. There were quite a few Indians in this war party, but Jonathan realized the immigrants would have had them outnumbered and outgunned if only they would settle down and put up a fight. One man who carried a new Colt on his hip broke and ran, and an Apache leaped on his back from the brush and plunged a knife into him. Jonathan shot the Indian off, but it was too late to save the man. Maybe his gun could still do some good, Jonathan thought grimly as he wrested it free of the holster. With a revolver in each hand now, he faced the charge of the Apaches.

For a long, hellish moment, it was cock and fire, cock and fire as arrows whipped past Jonathan's head and bullets tugged at his clothes. But the Apaches were falling before his rolling onslaught of gunfire, and he suddenly realized there was someone beside him. He glanced over and saw big ginger-haired Bert standing there with a scatter-gun clutched in his sausagelike fingers. The shotgun boomed and cut another swath through the attackers. Bert grinned over at Jonathan, blood streaking his freckled face from a cut just below his eye.

A rifle cracked on Jonathan's other side. Gerhard was there, and as one of the Apaches dropped from the rifle shot, the former baron tossed aside the empty weapon and jerked a revolver from his belt. He and Jonathan strode forward, firing as they went, and beside them Bert reloaded his shotgun and sent two more loads of buckshot slamming into the Apaches.

The sight of the three men defiantly facing up to the savages rallied the rest of the immigrants. More guns began to join in the battle, and although the war party was a large one, their numbers were cut down quickly. Many of the men from the wagon train had been hunting all their lives, relying on their skill with a gun to put meat on the family's table. Now that they had gotten over their initial panic, their accurate fire took a deadly toll.

Jonathan fired his last shot and started looking for cover so that he could reload. As he turned toward Gerhard, he heard the sound of an arrow striking flesh and saw Gerhard double over, a feathered shaft protruding from his midsection. "Gerhard!" Jonathan yelled, grabbing him so that he wouldn't fall. "Give me a hand, Bert!"

Bert took hold of Gerhard's other arm, and together they hustled him into the shelter of a wagon. As they laid him gently on the ground, Jonathan wondered where Evalinde was. He hadn't seen her since the Apache attack had started, and despite all the trouble she had caused, he prayed she wasn't lying somewhere with an arrow in her or having that thick mane of blond hair lifted by an Indian with a scalping knife.

The German pistol was a cap-and-ball job, and loading it was awkward for him. He managed the task as quickly as possible, then ducked around the end of the wagon and threw more shots at the Apaches. Some of them were breaking and running now, heading back to wherever they had left their horses. Once the retreat began, it spread quickly. Jonathan downed a couple of them, but then there was no more left to shoot at. The firing gradually died away.

Blowing to catch his breath, Jonathan turned back to where he had left Gerhard and Bert. There was a huge crimson stain on Gerhard's shirt around the shaft of the arrow, and his eyes stared glassily upward, seeing nothing. Bert sat beside him, tears rolling unashamedly down his beefy cheeks.

"The baron was good man," he said, looking up at Jonathan. "I know you fight with him, but he was still good man, yah?"

Jonathan knelt beside Gerhard and closed the dead man's eyes with his free hand. "Yes," he told Bert honestly. "Gerhard was a good man."

He had just made the mistake of marrying the wrong woman.

"Jonathan!"

He heard her shouting his name, stood and turned as she came running up to him. She threw herself into his arms, paying no attention to the body of her husband at her feet. As far as Jonathan could tell, she was unhurt. Luck had carried her through the attack.

"Oh, Jonathan, I was so afraid! I thought you would be killed!"

"Gerhard was," Jonathan said coldly.

"Don't tell me that," she said, burying her face against his chest. "Just hold me, hold me."

His free hand came up, patted her back once, then dropped to his side. He shrugged out of her grasp and stepped away from her. Cries of both pain and mourning filled the camp, and he saw bodies scattered along the line of wagons. Men, women, children . . . it was all a horrible waste, he thought.

But there were things to be done. Evalinde clutched at his arm, but he shook her off and strode around the camp, setting out guards just in case the Apaches came back, sending men to check on the stock, organizing a group of men to bury the dead. Life, with all of its harsh details, had to go on.

Evalinde followed him, tugging at his arm, until finally he couldn't stand it anymore. He whirled to face her, using all his self-control not to strike her. "Get the hell away from me!" he grated.

"But . . . but Jonathan!" she wailed. "I do not understand.

Gerhard is dead, yah? We can be together now, just as we wanted.''

Jonathan stared at her for a second, then said, "No, you don't understand, do you? Your husband was a brave man, and he died fighting at my side. I reckon he thought I didn't know a damned thing about honor, but I can tell you this much: I won't dishonor his memory by having anything to do with the likes of you!''

For a moment she was too stunned by his angry words to speak, then a torrent of her own language poured from her. Jonathan figured she was giving him a good cussing in German, but he didn't care. He only moved when she tried to slap him, and then he just grabbed her wrist and held it in the air for a second before shoving her away.

Most of the others had seen, and now they knew her for what she was. A small part of him felt sorry about that, just as he felt bad about having given in to her in the first place. Not that it would have changed anything, he reminded himself. What had happened between him and Evalinde had nothing to do with the Indian attack. Gerhard and all the other victims would be just as dead no matter what. But he sure wished things had happened differently all around.

By the middle of the day, the wounded were patched up as well as could be expected; the dead had been buried and words said over them, words that Jonathan couldn't understand for the most part, but the language of sorrow was pretty much worldwide, he supposed.

And by the middle of the day, he was ready to go.

"You are sure about this, Jonathan?" Bert asked him. "I am no baron, no leader of men."

"You'll do fine, Bert," Jonathan assured him. "Just follow the river, and you'll be in Eagle Pass in a couple of days' time. There's a little settlement there, I've heard, and I know you'll be welcome."

"But what about the Indians?"

"After the licking we gave those 'Paches, I don't think they'll come back. I reckon they're over in Mexico now, lickin' their wounds in some village back in the mountains." He clapped a hand on Bert's shoulder. "Keep your eyes open, post plenty of sentries at night, and don't let yourself get distracted. You'll make it through, Bert. I know you will."

"Yah," Bert said, nodding slowly. "I think we will, too. But if you came with us—"

Jonathan shot a glance toward the wagon where Evalinde was sitting on the seat, a huddled, lonely figure. "Can't do that," he said. "Part of me wishes I could. You folks are going to make fine Texans. But I've got to be riding." He turned to the horse he had been using, swung up into the saddle, and patted the animal's flank. "Thanks for giving me this old boy, too, and the rig. Mighty generous of you."

Bert waved off the thanks. "It is little enough, after all you do for us, *mein* . . . my friend."

Jonathan grinned, touched the brim of his hat with a finger, and turned the horse. He heeled it into a trot that carried him past the wagons and away from the river. Some of the immigrants called farewells after him, but he didn't turn to wave. He didn't figure looking back was a very good idea. There were too many bad memories behind him—the disaster at Mier, the frenzy of battle at Hacienda Salado, the failed escape attempt, the episode of the black beans, the long ordeal of his imprisonment and ultimate escape, and finally Evalinde and the bittersweet time he had spent with the wagon train. Someday, maybe, he'd be able to look back on all of it, sort out the good from the bad, and make some sense out of it all.

But that day, if it ever came, was in the future. For now, Jonathan Lewis pointed his horse toward home, and he kept his gaze fixed in that direction, too.

☆ **Chapter** ☆

18

Mordecai spent a restless night in the smokehouse, not knowing what the morning would bring. James, on the other hand, seemed to sleep well, and when he awoke as the dawn light began to filter through the cracks in the walls, he asked, "Anything going on out there?"

A few minutes earlier, Mordecai had noticed the sound of a baby crying, as well as the laughter of children. He had his eye pressed to one of the chinks between the logs and was watching as several women built a large fire in the yard in front of the ranch house.

"Looks like those camp followers Cyrus told us about," Mordecai replied. "Looks like Mexican and Indian women, from what I can see. They've got their kids with them, too. I reckon those Comancheros stashed them somewhere yesterday when they realized somebody was coming."

James grunted as he got to his feet and came over to join Mordecai. He looked through another crack for a few minutes, then said, "I've heard about this. Some of the Comanchero bands carry their families around with them, just like the Indian tribes do."

Mordecai watched half a dozen mostly naked children running around, and he asked, "You reckon some of those little 'uns are Blackwoods?"

"I'd bet on it."

From behind them, Edward asked, "Mordecai? James? What's going on?"

Mordecai turned around quickly and went to his cousin, kneeling at Edward's side. "We're right here, Edward," he said, trying to make his tone reassuring. "You're doing just fine."

Edward pushed himself into a sitting position and shook his head as he rubbed at his eyes. "Damn, my leg aches," he said.

"That's because you got shot in it," James pointed out dryly. "Cyrus Blackwood patched you up, though, and I reckon you'll be all right—for a while, anyway."

"Cyrus Blackwood?" echoed Edward. "Why would a Blackwood do anything to help a Lewis?"

"Finis and Luke want to keep us alive for the time being," James replied. "More'n likely, they intend to have a little fun with us. Might even save us for that bunch of Comanches that're supposed to meet 'em here."

Edward swallowed hard. "You're talkin' about torture, aren't you?"

Mordecai nodded and said, "I'm afraid so. Can't think of any other reason the Blackwoods wouldn't kill us outright, like they did Bramson."

"Mordecai . . ." Edward clutched at his arm. "What about Felipa?"

"As far as we know, she got away."

"Thank the Lord for that. I hope she doesn't slow down until she gets all the way back to Austin."

Felipa would have to stop before she reached Austin, of course, but in general Mordecai shared his counsin's sentiments. The fact that Felipa had escaped was the only good thing to come out of this catastrophe so far.

"I'm sure as hell thirsty," Edward went on. "Don't they believe in givin' a fella something to drink?"

"I reckon we'll get some water and something to eat soon," James said. "Looks like those women are cookin' up a little breakfast over that fire."

The smell of bacon frying drifted into the smokehouse a few minutes later and confirmed what James had said. The smokehouse itself was empty of meat at the moment; it would be autumn before anyone did much smoking. And of course, Jud Bramson would never put the sturdy little building to the use for which it was intended. Mordecai hoped the Comancheros had at least had the decency to bury the rancher, but somehow he doubted it.

Edward stood up and tested the strength in his wounded leg. It almost buckled under him as he walked around the close confines of the smokehouse, but he nodded and said, "It's a lot better. I reckon I'll be all right."

"Don't try to do too much," Mordecai cautioned him. "You lost a lot of blood."

"It won't matter much, I reckon. Not after the Blackwoods get through with us." Edward's voice was calm, but Mordecai could hear the undercurrent of fear in it. All three of them were feeling the same thing, he supposed.

But he wasn't ready to give up yet. He had thought long and hard about what James had said the night before about jumping one of the guards and grabbing a gun. If they did that, they would go down fighting, all right, but they would still die. And that notion didn't suit Mordecai even a little bit.

"Cyrus could still give us a hand," he said, ignoring the look of disbelief that James gave him. "There's still some good in that boy, even if he is a Blackwood."

"Maybe so," Edward replied dubiously, "but I'm not goin' to hold my breath waitin' for anybody named Blackwood to do something decent."

A few minutes later, while Mordecai was watching through the cracks in the wall again, he saw Cyrus approaching, along with a couple of the women. They were trailed by a pair of guards carrying rifles. Cyrus held a bucket in his hand, and the women were bringing bacon and some corn bread. Cyrus called for the prisoners to stand back, and the door of the smokehouse was unbarred again.

Cyrus carried in the bucket, which was sloshing with water. As he set it on the ground, he motioned for the women to give the food to the three captives. As soon as they had, they withdrew from the smokehouse, but not before giving Mordecai, James, and Edward hate-filled glances that sent shivers up and down their spines. The women looked to be a cross between Indians and Mexicans, with the Indian blood being dominant. The Texans knew there were no more vicious torturers in the world than Indian women, and they were glad when they were left alone in the smokehouse with Cyrus. The guards stood just outside the door, however, with their rifles cocked and ready in case of trouble.

"Mornin', fellas," Cyrus said. "Hope you slept well last night."

"Middlin'," James said. "Sort of hard to sleep when you know that each dream might be your last."

"Well, I'm sorry about that. You know I am." Cyrus took a

deep breath. "Luke and Finis figure that band of Comanch' we've been waitin' on will be here late this afternoon. They're countin' on you boys bein' the entertainment tonight."

James said grimly, "That's the way we figured it, too."

"So I thought you might as well have a good breakfast." Cyrus gestured at the bucket. "And drink deep. That river water's mighty good."

"Hey, Cyrus," one of the guards called to him. "Why're you bein' so nice to them bastards? Thought your family hated theirs."

Cyrus's face twisted in a grimace as he looked at Mordecai, James, and Edward. "Yeah, I reckon you're right, Johnny," he said after a moment. He leaned over and spat into the water bucket.

James clenched his fists and started to take a step toward Cyrus, but Mordecai caught his arm and held him back. "You can jump him, all right, but those guards'll just come in here and wallop you with a gunstock," Mordecai told his uncle. "Let it go, James."

With a curt nod, James relaxed and shrugged out of Mordecai's grip. To Cyrus, he said, "Why don't you get the hell out of here and let us eat our breakfast in peace?"

"I'm goin'," Cyrus said. "But you mind what I told you." With an arrogant laugh, he stepped out of the smokehouse and swung the door shut. A second later, the latch was thrown and the bar lowered.

"Little son of a bitch," James said quietly. "I guess his true colors are finally comin' out."

Mordecai knelt beside the bucket and scooped out a handful of water where Cyrus's spittle was still floating. As he cast it aside, he frowned and said, "I don't know why he told us how good this water was. Looks mighty muddy and murky to me."

"I don't care," Edward said. "I'm parched. Let me see that bucket."

He started to tip the bucket up to his mouth, but Mordecai stopped him. "That's got to last us a while. You drink out of it that way, you'll slosh too much of it out. Cup it with your hands."

Edward frowned, but he did as Mordecai suggested. The three of them drank some, then ate the food the women had left. As he chewed slowly, Mordecai kept staring at the water bucket. Finally, when he was finished with his food, he reached over, took hold of the bucket, and pulled it to him. He plunged his hand into it.

"Hey!" exclaimed Edward as some of the water splashed onto the ground. "You were the one who said to be careful!"

James looked surprised, too. "That's probably the last water we'll get," he said.

"Maybe not," Mordecai replied as a grin began to form on his face. He felt around in the water for a moment longer, then pulled his hand out.

He was holding three small, short-bladed knives.

James and Edward stared at the blades in the dim light. "What the hell . . . ?" muttered James.

"Cyrus kept trying to draw our attention to the water bucket," Mordecai said. "I finally figured out there must have been reason for it. That water's muddy enough to hide anything on the bottom. I reckon when Cyrus filled the bucket from the river, he slipped these knives into it." Mordecai kept his voice low, just in case there were any of the Comancheros standing near enough to the smokehouse to hear normal conversation. As he spoke, he dried the water and mud from the knives with the tail of his shirt, handed one to James and one to Edward, kept one for himself.

"I don't see what good this is going to do us," James said. "We can't fight a whole band of Comanches and Comancheros with three little knives."

"No, we can't," Mordecai agreed. "But maybe Cyrus has got something else in mind."

"Maybe." James still sounded skeptical. But having a weapon in his hand again felt good, and he clutched the handle of the knife tightly.

The morning passed slowly. The prisoners would have made plans for a potential escape, but there was no way of knowing what was going to happen, no way to guess how the hand would play out. Was Cyrus really going to try to help them get away? That seemed likely, or else he would not have smuggled the knives into the smokehouse. But what did he have in mind?

In the meantime, James experimented with using his blade to try to dig out of their makeshift prison. Given enough time, he probably could have done it, but not in less than a day. He gave up the effort, not wanting to risk breaking the blade on the hard-packed ground. The same was true of cutting a way out through the back wall. If they'd had a month, or even a couple of weeks, that might have been a possibility, but considering the fact that they likely had less than twelve hours to live, it was a futile hope. Finally James just shook his head and sat down cross-legged on the ground to conserve his energy.

They were all likely to need their strength, Mordecai thought.

No lunch was brought to them, but hunger pangs were minor compared to the nervous tension that gripped them. Mordecai had to exert his will to keep from getting up and pacing back and forth in the smokehouse. As it was, he almost jumped out of his skin when the latch was abruptly unfastened and the door unbarred. The three of them blinked rapidly as the afternoon light struck eyes accustomed to the gloom.

The knives were hidden under their shirts, easy to grab but not so easy to spot. Cyrus wouldn't be able to tell right away if they had found the blades in the water bucket or not. He would be taking quite a gamble, too, if he had something planned, because he had no way of knowing if they were armed.

A figure loomed in the doorway, silhouetted against the bright light, and Cyrus's voice said, "All right, you three. On your feet. You've got some visitin' to do."

Mordecai climbed slowly to his feet, followed by Edward and James. James took hold of Edward's arm to steady him a little as he swayed. "Sorry," Edward grunted. "I reckon I'm still a mite tired."

Cyrus stepped back and motioned for them to come out of the smokehouse. "Come on," he snapped. "Luke and Finis want to see you."

One of the guards spoke up. "You sure about this, Cyrus? Your daddy and your uncle usually take a *siesta* 'long about this time of day, like the rest of us."

"I don't know anything about it, Mort," Cyrus answered with a shrug. "All I know is they told me to fetch these boys. You want to go check with 'em 'fore we do it, that's all right with me."

"No, no," the guard said quickly. "I ain't doubtin' you, boy. Just a little surprised is all."

Mordecai exchanged a quick glance with James and Edward. This was something out of the ordinary, but was it the time when Cyrus meant for them to make their break?

Still squinting as their eyes tried to adjust to the light, the three prisoners stepped out of the smokehouse. Cyrus motioned them toward the main building. As he faced them for a moment, the guards couldn't see his features, and from the look in Cyrus's eyes and the miniscule nod he gave them, Mordecai knew it was going to be now or never.

With Cyrus leading them, they started toward the ranch house. Mordecai's gaze darted around the place. The only Comancheros in evidence were the ones following them with rifles. The others were no doubt dozing inside the house. A couple of the women had set up a washtub and were heating water in it, and a few of the children played lazily in the midday heat. The herd of mustangs was still in the corral, and the route to the ranch house would take the prisoners fairly close to the animals. Mordecai looked over at James and knew his uncle's mind was working along the same lines. Edward was grimacing with each step he took on his injured leg, but Mordecai knew he would follow their lead. He wouldn't have any choice.

Mordecai lifted a hand as if he was going to scratch his belly, but instead he slipped his fingers inside his shirt and closed them around the handle of the knife. James did the same thing next to him. They exchanged one more look, then James said softly, "Now!"

Both men spun around, whipping out the hidden knives. If the guards had been fully alert, Mordecai and James wouldn't have had a chance. But the two Comancheros were sleepy and upset about missing their *siesta*, not to mention being forced to move around in the hot early afternoon sun. They were still trying to bring their rifles into position when Mordecai and James struck.

James knocked a rifle barrel aside with one hand and with the other slashed the knife across the throat of the man holding it. The blade was short but razor-sharp, and it sliced easily through the guard's neck. The man tried to scream, but it was too late for him to make any sound except a ghastly gurgle as blood fountained from his throat. James ripped the rifle from the man's nerveless fingers, barreled into him, and knocked him to the ground, where he twitched and poured out the rest of his life onto the dirt.

Mordecai tried to duplicate his uncle's move, but the Comanchero on his side moved too fast. The man got the barrel of his rifle up in time to deflect the knife, although Mordecai managed to hold on to it. Off balance, Mordecai tried to buy some time by kicking his opponent in the groin. That blow landed on its target, and the man started to double over as he bellowed in pain. Swinging his arm back from the missed thrust, Mordecai drove the blade into the side of the guard's neck and felt it grate on bone as it hit the man's spinal column. The Comanchero collapsed, jerking the handle of the knife out of Mordecai's fingers as he fell.

Both guards were dead, or so close to it that it didn't matter anymore. But the yell let out by the second one had already done its damage. More of the Comancheros would be emerging from the house at any second. James held the rifle he had taken from the first dead man and bent quickly to pull the guard's Colt from its holster. Mordecai did the same with his man, then turned in time to see Edward holding Cyrus on the ground. Edward had his knife in his hand, and his arm was raised over his head.

"No!" Mordecai cried as he sprang forward to grab Edward's wrist. "Let him up, Edward! He's on our side now!"

Edward gave a little shake of his head, as if he was coming back to his senses, and scrambled off of Cyrus. Cyrus rolled over, pushed himself to his feet, and said urgently, "The mustangs! They're our only chance!"

James was already heading in the direction of the corral. Mordecai, Edward, and Cyrus ran along behind him. Mordecai didn't take the time to wonder about what Cyrus was doing. It was obvious the youngster intended to go with them when they made their escape, and after what he had done for them, that was all right with Mordecai.

James had tucked the pistol behind his belt, and he used his free hand to knock the top corral pole down. He vaulted over the others and plunged into the now-milling herd of horses. The fight nearby had made the animals nervous, but James was able to catch one of them, grab hold of its mane, and swing himself lithely onto its back.

Mordecai held up to let Edward and Cyrus climb over the fence in front of him. He heard someone shout a curse from the house and turned to see one of the Comancheros standing on the gallery and tugging a pistol from its holster. Mordecai brought the rifle to his shoulder and sighted in one smooth motion, and a split second later pressed the trigger. Smoke and flame belched from the muzzle, and the man on the gallery was thrown backward by the ball punching into his chest.

Inside the corral, Cyrus helped Edward onto one of the horses, then caught one for himself. Mordecai tossed the empty rifle aside and joined them, picking out the buckskin he had been riding most of the time during the journey. It happened to be close enough for him to catch, and he swung up quickly onto its back.

James lifted his voice in an ear-shattering whoop as more men began to run out of the house. The others yelled, too, and the mustangs inside the corral began to surge against its sides as panic gripped them. The section where James had knocked the pole down was already weakened, and it gave way first. The unruly mustangs kicked the poles out of the way and surged through the opening. Yelling, "Hyah! Hyah!" the four men prodded them into a stampede.

Bullets whined over Mordecai's head as he leaned over and slapped the rump of a mustang beside him. The horse leaped into a gallop, just like the others were doing. Once they started running, they didn't need any more urging. The herd poured out of the corral and went thundering away, their path taking them right past the house. Mordecai, James, Edward, and Cyrus rode among them, using the racing animals and the billowing dust as cover for their escape.

Most of the Comancheros had leaped from the safety of the house as the stampede began, but Mordecai suddenly saw Finis Blackwood stumbling around up ahead, his bearded features twisted by confusion and fear. His weakened mind couldn't make sense of the chaos surrounding him, and he cried, "Luke! Cyrus! Cyrus, where are you, boy?"

Then Finis turned just as the first of the mustangs reached him. The panic-stricken horse didn't slow down but slammed directly into Finis, knocking him off his feet. The burly Comanchero's scream of agony rose over the pounding of hooves, but it was cut short. A few moments later, after the herd had swept past Finis, Mordecai risked a glance back.

The bloody, tattered thing that had been driven into the ground by the hooves of the mustangs didn't even look human anymore. This time, Finis Blackwood would never again return to plague the Lewis Family.

But Luke was a different story. He ran out of the house and sent a rifle round screaming after the former captives. Mordecai ducked instinctively as he saw Luke fire, but the bullet didn't come anywhere close to him. Luke was still a threat, though, because in a matter of moments, he would have the pursuit organized and would be coming after them.

Mordecai looked over at Cyrus, who rode nearby. Cyrus had to have seen what happened to Finis, but his young face was set in steely lines. Cyrus had made his choice, severed his ties with the Comancheros, as well as what was left of his family. He would have to live—or die—with that decision, just like the rest of them.

The stampeding mustangs ran all out, but gradually Mordecai, James, Edward, and Cyrus dropped back, slowing their mounts until the horses were moving along in an easy lope that would cover a lot of ground but still not wear them out. Just because they were momentarily free didn't mean this was over, not by a long shot. Luke and the others would be coming after them, to avenge Finis's death if nothing else. Mordecai called over to Cyrus, "How many of them are back there?"

"There were sixteen, but at least four of them are dead now," Cyrus replied, not pointing out that one of those four was Finis. "That leaves twelve at most."

"More'n enough," grunted James. He handed the rifle he still held to Edward. "We're outgunned. All we can do is try to stay ahead of 'em until they give up the chase."

"They won't do that," Cyrus predicted. "Luke's a crazy man when he's been crossed."

The youngster wasn't telling them anything they didn't already know. But Mordecai held out some hope anyway. Luke would take it personal, of course, but the other Comancheros had to be more interested in making a profit than they were in settling up a score. They might not be willing to keep up an indefinite pursuit if it meant missing out on some lucrative trading with the Indians. And there was the horse herd to consider, too.

But the mustangs were already scattering to hell and gone, and Mordecai knew they would spend their days roaming free on the West Texas plains unless they were captured by the Comanches. He hated to lose the mustangs after all he and the others had gone through to capture them and then bring them out here, but a few dozen horses was a small price to pay for their lives. He and Felipa could always go back to South Texas and catch some more horses.

Felipa! Mordecai's heart leaped. Maybe they would catch up to her before they got back to Austin. She had only a day's start. But maybe the Comancheros would catch up to her, too, and that thought made Mordecai's belly turn cold. By escaping, maybe he and James and Edward had endangered Felipa that much more.

He pushed the thought out of his mind. There was no point in torturing himself with useless speculation. All they could do now was to keep riding and hope they stayed ahead of the renegades behind them.

James and Edward pushed ahead a little, but Mordecai hung back beside Cyrus. "Finis and Luke didn't really want to see us, did they?" asked Mordecai. "That was just an excuse to get us out of the smokehouse."

"Seemed like the easiest way," Cyrus admitted. "I knew those ol' boys wouldn't ask too many questions when I told 'em it was orders from Luke and Finis to bring you out. Nobody liked to argue with those two."

"Reckon I can understand that." Mordecai hesitated, then said, "Cyrus . . . about Finis . . . I'm . . . well . . ."

"No need to say you're sorry," Cyrus cut in. "I know you really ain't. How could you be, after all the misery he gave your family over the years?" Cyrus shook his head. "Like I said yesterday, I know good and well Finis wasn't my true daddy, and I'm not goin' to waste any time feelin' sorry 'cause he's gone."

"Must've been hard, though, leaving your brothers and sisters behind."

Cyrus shrugged. "Most of 'em might as well be either Mex or Comanch', considerin' how they was raised. Shoot, some of 'em the Indians already took to raise. I've been lookin' out for 'em all my life, Mordecai. I finally realized they can look after themselves. They're all mean as skunks and cunning as coyotes. They'll be fine."

It sounded to Mordecai like the younger Blackwoods would be as dangerous as the older ones when they grew up, but he kept that thought to himself.

The mustangs were well rested, and they kept up the ground-eating lope without much difficulty until late in the afternoon. By that time, James had spotted the dust cloud behind them, and all four of the fugitives knew that the Comancheros were back there, coming after them. Luke was pushing his men hard, too, because the dust kept coming steadily closer.

"We'd better make a run for it," Mordecai suggested.

"We'll wait," James responded patiently. "They're a long way from being in rifle range yet. Let's save these mounts as long as we can."

His uncle's decision made sense, but impatience still ate at Mordecai's guts. He wanted to be long gone, to leave the Comancheros far behind. But James said they would wait until the right moment to make their move, and Mordecai couldn't argue with that.

The pursuit drew nearer and nearer until Mordecai could look back and see individual shapes of horse and rider at the base of the dust cloud. He and the others were kicking up considerable dust themselves. Anyone watching from a distance could follow the progress of the chase just by watching the plumes of dust, but out here in the wilds of the Texas frontier, there wasn't likely to be anyone watching except maybe a stray band or two of Comanches.

"Now!" called James, and the four of them urged their mounts to a higher speed. Mordecai leaned far forward on the neck of his

horse, holding tightly to its mane and guiding it as best he coul
with his knees. Riding bareback like this, the fugitives had to trus
their mounts to pick their own route through this rugged land
scape.

The Colorado River was off to their right somewhere as the
headed generally southeast. Mordecai knew the river was probabl
within a few miles, but they couldn't see it over the wooded fold
of the hills. If they could stay in front of the Comancheros unt
nightfall, they could angle toward the river, cross it, and mayb
shake the pursuit that way. Staying alive until nightfall, that wa
going to be the hard part.

Far behind them, they heard a few faint pops that had to be th
sound of rifles being fired. They were still well out of range
though, Mordecai knew. Some of the Comancheros were jus
letting their anger get the best of them and blowing off some stean
by taking a few shots.

The mustangs were running full out now, and they were fairl
flying across the landscape. Mordecai looked back again. It migh
have been wishful thinking, but he was convinced the pursuers ha
fallen back a little. It looked like James had been right to advis
caution and that their attempt to outrun the Comancheros wa
going to work.

At least it might have, if Cyrus's horse hadn't stepped in
gopher hole.

With a shrill scream, the mustang went tumbling, flinging Cyru
off its back as it fell. The youngster landed hard on the ground, bu
he was lucky; if he had not been thrown clear, the horse migh
have rolled on him, crushing him. As it was, Cyrus was able t
scramble to his feet and hurry over to the fallen mustang as th
other riders hauled their mounts to a stop and turned to ride back

Cyrus's horse was dead, its neck broken. As soon as he saw
that, he turned and waved to the others. "Keep going!" he
shouted. "You can't let them catch you!"

Mordecai rode up to him. "What about you?" he asked. "We
can't leave you here!"

"The hell you can't. Give me a gun, and I'll slow 'em down for
you!"

"No, you can ride double with one of us."

James said, "That'll slow us down, Mordecai. They'll catch us
that way."

Mordecai's jaw tightened, and he extended a hand toward

Cyrus. "Come on, damn it! We're wasting time. Climb up here behind me."

Cyrus stared at him. "Why . . . ?"

"You gave us a chance to save our lives," Mordecai said. "I'm not going to throw yours away in return. Now come on!"

Cyrus hesitated only an instant longer. Then he reached up and took Mordecai's hand to swing aboard the mustang. At that moment, a friendship was born that both young men knew would stand the test of time and last the rest of their lives.

Which didn't figure to be very long under the circumstances.

Mordecai kicked the horse back into a gallop almost before Cyrus's backside had landed. On three horses now, the four fugitives raced on.

The Comancheros narrowed the gap steadily. James and Edward could have ridden ahead, but both of them were as stubborn as Mordecai had been. They would be free together, or die together. It was that simple.

Suddenly James waved toward a brushy knoll in front of them. "We'll fort up on that hill!" he called over the rolling hoofbeats. "Maybe we can make 'em pay such a high price they'll turn back!"

It was a hope—probably a futile one—but Mordecai knew it was the best chance they had. He and Cyrus followed James and Edward toward the knoll and then up its slope. There was a cluster of rocks at the top of the rise that would give them some cover.

When they reached the crest, they pulled the horses to a stop and dropped off the sweaty backs of the animals. The mustangs stood, heads drooping and sides heaving from their long run, while the four young men ran over to the rocks and crouched behind them.

The two revolvers each held five shots, and the rifle Edward carried was loaded and ready to fire. Eleven shots, Mordecai thought, and as the Comanchero pursuit strung out across the open ground in front of the knoll, he counted twelve of them, just like Cyrus had said.

A wry grin creased Mordecai's face. "Twelve of them, and eleven shots," he said. "Simple enough. We kill one of them with each shot, then finish off the last one with that knife of yours, James."

"Yep, that's what we'll do, all right," James replied, grinning back at his nephew.

Cyrus shook his head. "Finis and Luke were right about one thing," he said. "You Lewises are crazy."

"Reckon you've got to be a little crazy to settle in Texas." James raised his head and peered over the rock behind which he crouched. "Here they come!"

The Comancheros were pounding up the slope toward the rocks. Mordecai, James, and Edward waited a second, then nodded to each other and stood up. The two pistols and the rifle spoke as one, giving off a thunderous roar, and two of the attackers pitched out of their saddles. The remaining ten men hauled back on their reins, veered off, and pounded down the slope again.

As they dropped into their crouches again, James said, "One of us missed. There goes your plan, Mordecai."

"I reckon so. But they'll think twice about charging us again like that."

"Yep. Now they'll settle down and throw lead up here for about an hour, try to cut down the odds some before they come again."

As a matter of fact, the renegades had regrouped at the bottom of the hill, out of pistol range. A bearded figure pushed his way to the forefront of the group and bellowed up the slope, "You goddamn Lewises might as well come on down here! We're goin' to get you one way or the other. And then we're goin' to peel you alive, you bastards!"

"Give it up, Uncle Luke!" Cyrus called back to him. "You'll never take any of us alive, and you'll die gettin' us down from here."

"Cyrus? That you, boy? You no-good, back-stabbin' little runt! Your pa's dead 'cause o' you!"

Cyrus lifted himself a little and shouted, "Finis wasn't my pa! I don't want nothin' more to do with any of you!"

"Well, you're goin' to get it, boy, whether you want it or not!" Luke replied, and he lifted his rifle. The weapon blasted and sent a ball whining off the rocks as Cyrus ducked back down.

"See what you went and did," Mordecai said. "You got him mad."

Cyrus just shook his head. "Well, if I've got to die today, I'm glad I'm here with you fellas and not down there with that bunch. Thanks." He looked around at James and Edward and Mordecai. "Thanks to all of you."

Mordecai nodded and clapped a hand on Cyrus's shoulder, then lifted himself cautiously for another look down the hill. He frowned suddenly and said, "Who in blazes is that?"

James peered over the rocks and said, "Where?"

Mordecai pointed. "Over there."

He was indicating a lone man who had ridden out from a stand of trees about two hundred yards away. There was something familiar about him, but Mordecai couldn't place him. He rode steadily toward the group of renegades, not getting in any hurry but not wasting any time, either. The Comancheros noticed him, too, and spread out to present a united front as the stranger approached.

"My God!" James exclaimed abruptly. "That's Cap'n Jack!"

Mordecai recognized him now, too. The newcomer was indeed Captain John Coffee Hays of the Texas Rangers, and as he brought his horse to a stop about a hundred yards from the Comancheros, he lifted his voice and shouted plainly, "Is that you and your boys, Luke Blackwood?"

Mordecai saw the confusion among the Comancheros, and then Luke edged his horse out a little apart from the others. He called angrily, "I'm Luke Blackwood. Who the hell're you?"

"Captain Hays of the Texas Rangers! You're under arrest, Blackwood!"

Mordecai heard the laughter of the Comancheros at that bold statement. The idea of one lone man putting them under arrest was ludicrous, even if that man was a Texas Ranger.

Then the laughter died away as four more men rode out of the trees where Hays had emerged. They brought their horses to a stop and then sat there waiting.

Mordecai could almost see Luke's confusion, even at this distance. He needed Cyrus there to tell him what to do, but Cyrus would never be by his side again. He was going to have to make up his own mind.

"It's still two to one!" Luke suddenly shouted. "Kill the sons o' bitches!"

The Comancheros surged toward the Rangers, who heeled their horses into motion and loped forward to join Hays. Guns began to crash, and powder smoke floated in the late afternoon air.

"I'm going to give them a hand," Mordecai said as he tucked his pistol behind his belt and ran for his horse.

James followed, saying over his shoulder, "Edward, you and Cyrus stay up here!"

Edward looked like he wanted to go with them, but the long chase had stolen most of his strength. He nodded weakly and propped himself up so that he could watch the battle below. Cyrus joined him.

Mordecai and James vaulted onto their mustangs and sent the horses sliding and bounding down the knoll. The field between the hill and the trees was full of noise and smoke as guns boomed and hooves pounded and men cried out in anger or pain. As Mordecai and James drove into the middle of the fracas, Mordecai saw that a couple of the Rangers were down. At least four of the Comancheros had been hit and knocked out of their saddles, though, and as James opened fire another of the renegades threw up his arms and pitched to the ground.

"Lewis! Mordecai Lewis!"

Mordecai heard his name being screamed and twisted around to see Luke Blackwood galloping at him from the side. Luke fired his rifle one-handed. Mordecai felt the tug of the bullet as it whipped the sleeve of his shirt. He jerked his pistol from his belt and brought it up as Luke cast aside the empty rifle and drew his own Colt. Mordecai stood his ground, the mustang trembling beneath him, as Luke kept charging toward him, the gun in his hand spitting flame as he fired wildly.

There was an icy ball of fear in Mordecai's belly as the lead sang around him. He ignored it as best he could and settled the sights of the Colt on Luke's chest. He pulled back the hammer, steadied the gun again, and pressed the trigger. It roared and bucked against his palm.

Luke screamed and went flying backward out of the saddle. He bounced once when he landed on the ground, then lay still except for a couple of spasmodic breaths. Blood welled from his chest where Mordecai's shot had struck him. A tremor ran through him, and he was dead.

Another measure of revenge for the Lewis family, Mordecai thought. Funny how he still felt too scared and sick to take any real pleasure in it.

There were a couple of more shots, then silence settled down. Mordecai looked around. All of the Comancheros were dead. The Rangers who had been wounded were being tended to by their comrades, and James and Captain Hays were riding side by side toward him. Mordecai grinned tiredly and greeted them by saying, "I don't know where you came from, Cap'n, but we sure were glad to see you."

"Been tracking your dust and that of those Comancheros," Hays replied as he brought his horse to a stop and began to calmly reload his revolver. "We knew you were out there somewhere."

"How'd you know that?" James asked.

Hays nodded toward the trees. "She told us."

Mordecai turned his head and looked, saw the slender figure on horseback emerging from the shelter of the trees. She carried a rifle in her hands, and knowing Felipa the way he did, Mordecai was sure it had been difficult for her not to ride out and jump right into the middle of the battle.

"Ran into her downriver a ways while we were on patrol," Hays went on to James. "She filled us in on the trouble you boys had run into and led us back up here. Quite a gal. When we met her, she was making plans to go back, sneak onto that ranch, and rescue the lot of you. Yessir, quite a gal."

Mordecai shared that opinion, of course, but he didn't hear Hays voice it because he had whirled his horse and ridden out to meet Felipa. They had thrown themselves into each other's arms, and Mordecai was kissing her for all he was worth. Felipa tried to say something, but Mordecai just kissed her again.

They could talk all they wanted to . . . later.

☆ **Chapter** ☆

19

Jonathan dropped the reins of his horse and swung down from the saddle, weariness pulling at his muscles as he did so. He had been riding for a long time, a damned long time. But it didn't matter. None of the things that had happened to him in the past mattered.

He was home.

He hesitated, looking at the yellow light in the window of the cabin. He had been following that light for nearly a mile now, letting it give him strength and draw him on. It represented everything he had nearly lost, everything he had fought to return to for so long. Now . . . now he was almost scared to go in there. He had been gone for what seemed like decades, instead of less than a year. What if they didn't recognize him? What if they had given him up for dead and didn't even want him to be part of the family anymore?

He told himself he was thinking crazy. He stepped into the dogtrot.

And then the thought struck him. Where were the dogs? Those hounds should have been baying his return by now.

Once again he paused, but then he heard a burst of laughter from inside, and it drew him on just as the lamplight had done. He reached out, turned the latch on the door, opened it and stepped inside.

His question about the dogs was answered. They were inside, along with everybody else. There was some sort of celebration going on, because the entire Lewis family—at least the Texas branch—was packed into the cabin. There was a table full of food and drink, and the warm sounds of laughter and talk washed over Jonathan for a long moment, renewing him, making his long journey worthwhile. Finally they began to notice him and a hush gradually fell over the room.

He swallowed hard and made the words come out. "Howdy, everybody. It's me . . . Jonathan. I'm home."

And then the sound came back, stronger than ever, a tidal wave of shocked, happy cries, shouts of welcome, sobs of thanksgiving. One by one they threw their arms around him: Frank and Hope, Marie, Annie, James, Mordecai, Angeline, Rose, Annie and Sly's two little girls, Edward and David, Ben, even some beautiful Mexican girl Jonathan had never seen before. From the way Mordecai put his arm around her shoulders, Jonathan guessed the two of them were a couple, though. Yep, that was a wedding ring on the girl's finger, he decided. Sly Shipman and Manuel Zaragosa grabbed his hand and pumped it, and then the other male Lewises had to do that, too. Jonathan was just about worn out from all the greetings when he noticed a slender youth standing back a little, one of the group yet somehow apart from it. Jonathan frowned and asked, "Who's that?"

"Cyrus Blackwood," Mordecai told him.

Jonathan blinked in surprise and said, "One of the Black-woods?"

"That's right," Cyrus said, reaching out to shake Jonathan's hand with a friendly smile. "Welcome back. I've heard a lot about you. Glad to have the chance to meet you."

"We all thought you were dead, Jonathan," Marie said. She hugged him again, just for good measure. "Come. You must sit and eat. Later you can tell us how you came back to us."

In a daze, Jonathan let his sister-in-law lead him over to the table. Marie sat him down in front of a heaping plate of food, and he looked up at her to ask, "What are we celebrating, anyway?"

"I am going to be a grandmother—again," Marie replied. "Mordecai and Felipa are going to have a baby."

"See I'm goin' to have a lot of catching up to do," Jonathan muttered. Felipa . . . that'd be the pretty Mexican gal.

But there was one thing that was still an almighty puzzle to him, and as everyone settled down a little and went back to their eating and drinking and talking, Jonathan motioned Mordecai over to him. As his nephew straddled the bench next to him, Jonathan leaned over and asked in a low voice, "Mordecai . . . what the hell is a Blackwood doing at a Lewis family get-together?"

"Well, it's a long story, Uncle Jonathan," Mordecai said with a chuckle. "Has to do with some mustangs and a bunch of Comancheros and damn near getting killed. I'll tell you about it sometime."

"You do that," Jonathan said, more confused than ever.

"For now, let's just say that Blackwood or not, Cyrus is a friend of the family. There's something else he is that's even more important."

Jonathan looked at Mordecai. "What's that?"

"A Texan," Mordecai said simply.

Jonathan took a bite of fried chicken and nodded in understanding. That was the bond that tied them all together. He had felt it beyond a shadow of doubt, there in the prison in Mexico. The Lewises were part of a bigger family that stretched all the way across the Republic, and whenever trouble cropped up again in the future—as it no doubt would—the proud sons and daughters of Texas would face it together.

In the meantime, he had this fried chicken to eat, and down at the other end of the table, he had spied some deep-dish apple pie . . .

☆ **SPECIAL PREVIEW!** ☆

*If you like Westerns, here's a special
look at an exciting new novel by America's new
star of the classic Western*

Will a son pay for his
father's past—in blood?

CHEROKEE

A stunning novel of family pride
and frontier justice by acclaimed
Western storyteller Giles Tippette

*The following is an excerpt from this
new, action-packed Western novel,
available from Jove Books . . .*

Howard said, "Son, I want you to get twenty-five thousand dollars in gold, get on your horse, and carry it up to a man in Oklahoma. I want you to give it to him and tell him who it's from, and tell him it's in repayment of the long-time debt I've had of him."

I didn't say anything for a moment. Instead I got up from the big double desk we were sitting at facing each other, and walked over to a little side table and poured us both out a little whiskey. I put water in Howard's. Out of the corner of my eye I could see him wince when I did it, but that was doctor's orders. I took the whiskey back over to the desk and handed Howard his tumbler. It was a little early in the afternoon for the drink but there wasn't much work to be done, it being the fall of the year.

Howard was father to me and my two brothers. Sometimes we called him Dad and sometimes Howard, and in years past quite a few other things. He liked for us to call him Howard because I think it made him feel younger and still a part of matters as pertained to our ranch and other businesses. Howard was in his mid-sixties, but it was a poor mid-sixties on account of a rifle bullet that had nicked his lungs some few years back and caused him breathing difficulties as well as some heart trouble. But even before that, some fifteen years previous, he had begun to go down after the death of our mother. It was not long after that that he'd begun to train me to take his place and to run the ranch.

I was Justa Williams and, at the age of thirty-two, I was the boss of the Half-Moon ranch, the biggest along the Gulf Coast of

Texas, and all its possessions. For all practical purposes I had been boss when Howard called me in one day and told me that he was turning the reins over to me, and that though he'd be on hand for advice should I want it, I was then and there the boss.

And now here he was asking me to take a large sum of money, company money, up to some party in Oklahoma. He could no more ask that of me than any of my two brothers or anybody else for that matter. Oh, he could ask, but he couldn't order. I held my whiskey glass out to his and we clinked rims, said "Luck," and then knocked them back as befits the toast. I wiped off my mouth and said, "Howard, I think you better tell me a little more about this. Twenty-five thousand dollars is a lot of money."

He looked down at his old gnarled hands for a moment and didn't say anything. I could tell it was one of his bad days and he was having trouble breathing. The whiskey helped a little, but he still looked like he ought to be in bed. He had a little bedroom right off the big office and sitting room we were in. There were plenty of big bedrooms in the big old rambling house that was the headquarters for the ranch, but he liked the little day room next to the office. He could lie in there when he did feel well enough to sit up and listen to me and my brothers talking about the ranch and such other business as came under discussion. It hurt me to see him slumped down in his chair looking so old and frail and sunk into himself. I could remember him clearly when he was strong and hard-muscled and tall and straight. At six-foot I was a little taller than he'd been, but my 190 pounds were about the equal of his size when he'd been in health. It was from him that I'd inherited my big hands and arms and shoulders. My younger brother Ben, who was twenty-eight, was just about a copy of me except that he was a size smaller. Our middle brother, Norris, was the man out in the family. He was two years younger than me, but he was years and miles different from me and Ben and Howard in looks and build and general disposition toward life. Where we were dark he was fair; where we were hard he had a kind of soft look about him. Not that he was; to the contrary. Wasn't anything weak about Norris. He'd fight you at the tick of a clock. But he just didn't look that way. We all figured he'd taken after our mother, who was fair and yellow-haired and sort of delicate. And Norris was bookish like she had been. He'd gone through all the school that was available in our neck of the woods, and then he'd been sent up to the University at Austin. He handled all of our affairs outside of the ranch itself—with my okay.

I said, "Dad, you are going to have to tell me what this money is to be used for. I've been running this ranch for a good many years and this is the first I've heard about any such debt. It seems to me you'd of mentioned a sum of that size before today."

He straightened up in his chair, and then heaved himself to his feet and walked the few steps to where his rocking chair was set near to the door of his bedroom. When he was settled he breathed heavy for a moment or two and then said, "Son, ain't there some way you can do this without me explaining? Just take my word for it that it needs doing and get it tended to?"

I got out a cigarillo, lit it, and studied Howard for a moment. He was dressed in an old shirt and a vest and a pair of jeans, but he had on his house slippers. That he'd gotten dressed up to talk to me was a sign that what he was talking about was important. When he was feeling fairly good he put on his boots, even though he wasn't going to take a step outside. Besides, he'd called me in in the middle of a workday, sent one of the hired hands out to fetch me in off the range. Usually, if he had something he wanted to talk about, he brought it up at the nightly meetings we always had after supper. I said, "Yes, Dad, if you want me to handle this matter without asking you any questions I can do that. But Ben and Norris are going to want to know why, especially Norris."

He put up a quick hand. "Oh, no, no. No. You can't tell them a thing about this. Don't even mention it to either one of them! God forbid."

I had to give a little laugh at that. Dad knew how our operation was run. I said, "Well, that might not be so easy, seeing as how Norris keeps the books. He might notice a sum like twenty-five thousand dollars just gone without any explanation."

He looked uncomfortable and fidgeted around in his rocking chair for a moment. "Son, you'll have to make up some story. I don't care what you do, but I don't want Ben or Norris knowing aught about this matter."

Well, he was starting to get my curiosity up. "Hell, Howard, what are you trying to hide? What's the big mystery here? How come *I* can know about the money and not my brothers?"

He looked down at his hands again, and I could see he felt miserable. "If I was up to it *you* wouldn't even know." He kind of swept a hand over himself. "But you can see the shape I've come to. Pretty soon won't be enough left to bury the way I'm wasting away." He hesitated and looked away. It was clear he didn't want to talk about it. But finally he said, "Son, this is just something I got to get off my conscience before it comes my time. And I been feeling here lately that that time ain't far off. I done something pretty awful back a good number of years ago, and I just got to set it straight while I still got the time." He looked at me. "And you're my oldest son. You're the strong one in the family, the best of the litter. I ain't got nobody else I can trust to do this for me."

Well, there wasn't an awful lot I could say to that. Hell, if you came right down to it, it was still all Howard's money. Some years back he'd willed the three of us the ranch and all the Half-Moon holdings in a life will that gave us the property and its income even while he was still alive. But it was Howard who, forty years before, had come to the country as a young man and fought weather and bad luck and *bandidos* and Comanches and scalawags and carpetbaggers, and built this cattle and business empire that me and my brothers had been the beneficiaries of. True, we had each contributed our part to making the business better but it had been Howard who had made it possible. So, it was still his money and he could do anything he wanted with it. I told him as much.

He nodded. "I'm grateful to you, Justa. I know I'm asking considerable of you to ask you to undertake this errand for me without telling you the why and the whereofs of the matter, but it just ain't something I want you or yore brothers to know about."

I shrugged. I got a pencil and a piece of paper off my desk. "Who is this party you want the money to go to? And what's his address?"

"Stevens. Charlie Stevens. And Justa, it ain't money, it's got to be gold."

I put down my pencil and stared at him. "What's the difference? Money is gold, gold is money. What the hell does it matter?"

"It matters," he said. He looked at the empty glass in his hand and then across at the whiskey. But he knew it was wishful thinking. Medically speaking, he was supposed to have but one watered whiskey a day. Of course we all knew he snuck more than that when there was nobody around, but drinking alone gave him no pleasure. He said, "This is a matter that's got to be done a certain way. It's just the way and the rightness of the matter in my mind. I got to give the man back the money the same way I took it."

"But hell, Howard, gold is heavy. I bet twenty-five thousand dollars' worth would weigh over fifty pounds. We'll have to ship it on the railroad, have it insured. Hell, we can just wire a bank draft.''

He shook his head slowly. ''Justa, you still don't understand the bones of the matter. You got to take the gold to Charlie on horseback. Just like I would if I could. You understand? I'm askin' you to stand in for me on this matter.''

I threw my pencil down and stared at him. I nodded at the empty glass in his hand. ''How many of them you snuck before you sent for me? You expect me to get on a horse and ride clear to Oklahoma carrying twenty-five thousand dollars in gold? And that without telling Norris or Ben a thing about it? Howard, are you getting senile? It's either that or you're drunk, and I'd rather you was drunk.''

He nodded. ''I don't blame you. It's just you don't understand the bones of this business. Justa, this is a weight I been carrying a good many years. I done this man wrong some time back, but it took a while for me to realize just how wrong I done him. When I could of set matters straight I was too young and too smug to think they needed setting aright. Now that I can look back and be properly ashamed of what I done it's too late for all of it. But I got to make what amends I can. If you knew the total of the whole business you'd agree with me that the matter has to be handled in just such a way.''

I got up, got the whiskey bottle, and went over and poured him out about half a tumblerful. It was dead against doctor's orders, but I could see he was in such misery, both in his heart and his body, that I figured the hell with what the doctor has to say. I went back over to my desk, poured myself out a pretty good slug, and then said, ''All right, Howard, you want me to do something I find unreasonable. I think the least you can do is tell me something about what you call the 'bones' of the business.''

''Justa, you done said you'd do it without asking me no questions.''

''Well, goddam, Howard, that was when I thought you were just talking about the money. Now you're talking about me riding all the way clear up to goddam Oklahoma hauling a tow sack full of gold. Hell, Oklahoma is a pretty good little piece from here. Where in Oklahoma, by the way? What town?''

He shook his head. ''I don't know,'' he said. ''I've lost track of Charlie Stevens for better than twenty years.''

''Aw, hell!'' I said in disgust. I took a sip of my whiskey and got out another cigarillo and lit it, having let the first one go out unsmoked in the ashtray on my desk. We sat there in silence looking at each other. It was quiet in the house. The room we were sitting in had once been practically the whole house. It had been built of big sawn timbers that Howard had had hauled in by ox teams after he'd started making some money. The rest of the house had just kind of grown as the need arose. Far off in the kitchen I could hear the sound of the two Mexican women going about the business of starting supper for the fourteen or fifteen hired hands and cowhands we kept about the place. A man named Tom Butterfield cooked for the family. Us boys had always called him Buttercup just to get him riled up. As near as I could figure he was as old as Howard and should have been in worse shape, judging by the amount of whiskey he could put away on a daily basis. Outside, in that year of 1896, it was a mild October and the rolling prairies of two-foot-high grass were curing off and turning a yellowish brown. We'd hay some of it, but the biggest part of it would be left standing to be grazed down by our cattle and horses. The Half-Moon was right on the Gulf Coast of Texas about ninety miles south of Houston. Our easternmost pastures led right up to the bay, where soft little waves came lapping in to water the salt grass and lay up a little beach of sand. All told we held better than sixty thousand deeded acres, but we grazed well over a quarter of a million. At any one time we ran from five thousand to ten thousand cattle, depending on the marketing season. A more gentle, healthy, temperate place to raise cattle could not be imagined. There was plenty of grass, plenty of water, and except for the heat of the summers, a climate that was kind to the development of beef.

The nearest town to us was Blessing. It was nearly seven miles away and we owned about half of it, including the bank, the hotel, the auction barn, and any number of town lots. Blessing had once been a railhead for the MKT railroad, but now it was a switching point between Laredo and San Antonio. It would have been no trouble at all to have shipped $25,000 to a bank or a business or some party in Oklahoma. But it sure as hell was a different proposition to ride a horse all that way and try to protect such a sum in gold. Hell, you'd need a packhorse just for the gold, let alone your own supplies. And such a ride would take at least three weeks, going hard, to get there, not counting coming back. And even if it was all right with Howard to come back on the train, that was another three days.

Of course that didn't count the time that would have to be spent looking for this Charlie Stevens. That is, if he wasn't dead. Hell, the whole idea was plain outlandish. But I didn't want to tell Howard that, not as serious as he seemed about it. But I said, "Howard, you know this is a busy time for us. We got to get the cattle in shape for winter, and then there's the haying. And there's also this business with the Jordans."

The Jordans were our nearest neighbors to the southwest. They were new to the country. They'd bought out the heirs of one of the earliest settlers in our part of the country. And now they were disputing our boundary line that was common with theirs. They'd brought in a surveyor who'd sent in a report that supported the Jordan's claim, so Norris had hired us a surveyor and he'd sent in a report that backed up *our* position. So now it looked like it was going to be work for the lawyers. And it was no small dispute. The Jordans were claiming almost nine thousand acres of our deeded land, and that was a considerable amount of grazing. But what was more worrisome, once that sort of action got started in an area it could spread like wildfire, and we'd spend half our time in court and hell only knows how much on lawyers just trying to hold on to what was ours. And the fact was that there was plenty of room for argument. Most land holdings in Matagorda County and other parts of the old Nueces Strip went back to Spanish land grants and grants from the Republic of Texas, and even some from when it first became a state. Such disputes were becoming common, and I wanted to put out our own little prairie fire before it got a good start and spread. Norris was mainly handling the matter, but it was important that I be on hand if some necessary decision had to be made.

I finished my whiskey and got up. "Howard, I don't want to talk about this no more right now. You think on it overnight and we'll have a talk again tomorrow."

He said in a strong voice, "Justa, I know you think this is just the whim of a sick ol' man. That ain't the case. This is something that is mighty important to me. It's important to you and your brothers too. Ain't nobody in this family ever failed to pay off a debt. I ain't going to be the first one."

"Something I don't quite understand, Howard. You appear to be talking about some money you borrowed some twenty-five or thirty years ago. Is that right?"

"Maybe even a little longer than that."

"Howard, who the hell did you know had that kind of money

that many years ago? Hell, you could have bought nearly all of Texas for that sum in them days.''

He fiddled with his glass and then drank the last of the whiskey. He said, clearing his throat first, ''Wasn't exactly twenty-five thousand. Was less. I'm kind of roughed in the interest.''

''How much less was it? Still must have been a power of money. Interest is four percent right now, and I don't reckon it was anywhere near that high back then.''

He looked uncomfortable. ''Damnit, Justa, if I'd been lookin' for an argument I'd of sent for Norris! Now why don't you go on and do like I tell you and not jaw me to death about it!''

I gave him a long look. ''Who you trying to bully, old man? Now exactly how much was this original loan that you've 'roughed' in interest to bring it up to twenty-five thousand dollars?''

He looked at me defiantly for a moment, and then he said, ''Five hunnert dollars.''

I laughed a little. ''Now that *is* roughing in a little interest,'' I said. ''Five hundred to twenty-five *thousand*. How come you didn't pay this back twenty years ago when five hundred dollars wasn't more than a night of poker to you? And you and I both know you can't turn five hundred into twenty-five thousand in thirty years no matter how hard you try. Just exactly what kind of loan was this?''

He got slowly up out of his rocking chair, and then started shuffling the few steps toward his bedroom. At his door he turned and give me a hard look. ''Wasn't no loan a'tall. I stole the money from the man. Now put an interest figure on that!''

I just stood there in amazement. Before I could speak he'd shut his door and disappeared from my view. ''Hell!'' I said. The idea of our daddy, Howard, stealing anything was just not a possibility I could reckon with. As far as I knew Howard had never owed anybody anything for any longer than it took to pay them back, and as for stealing, I'd known him to spend two days of his own time returning strayed cattle to his bitterest enemy. I could not conjure up a situation in which Howard would steal, and not only steal but let the crime go unredeemed for so long. Obviously he'd been a young man at the time, and he might have committed a breach of honesty as a callow youth but there'd been plenty of years in between for him to have put the matter right rather than waiting until such a late date.

The truth be told, I didn't know whether to believe him or not.

Howard's body might be failing him, but I'd never found cause to fault his mind. And yet they did say that when a man reached a certain age, his faculties seemed to go haywire and he got confused and went to making stuff up and forgetting everyday matters. But for the life of me, I just couldn't see that happening to Howard. And yet I couldn't believe he'd actually stolen $500 from a man and let it slide over all these years either.

I was about to leave the office when the bedroom door opened and Howard stood there. He said, "I charge you on your honor not to mention this to either of your brothers."

"Hell, Howard, I ain't going to mention it to nobody as far as that goes. But look here, let me ask you—"

I got no further. He had closed the door. I had seen the hurt and the helplessness in his face just before the door had closed. It did not make me feel very good. Now I was sorry I had questioned him so closely. But never in my wildest dreams would I have figured to stir up such a hornet's nest.

If you enjoyed this book, subscribe now and get...

TWO FREE

A $7.00 VALUE—

If you would like to read more of the very best, most exciting, adventurous, action-packed Westerns being published today, you'll want to subscribe to True Value's Western Home Subscription Service.

Each month the editors of True Value will select the 6 very best Westerns from America's leading publishers for special readers like you. You'll be able to preview these new titles as soon as they are published, *FREE* for ten days with no obligation!

TWO FREE BOOKS

When you subscribe, we'll send you your first month's shipment of the newest and best 6 Westerns for you to preview. With your first shipment, two of these books will be yours as our introductory gift to you absolutely *FREE* (a $7.00 value), regardless of what you decide to do. If you like them, as much as we think you will, keep all six books but pay for just 4 at the low subscriber rate of just $2.75 each. If you decide to return them, keep 2 of the titles as our gift. No obligation.

Special Subscriber Savings

When you become a True Value subscriber you'll save money several ways. First, all regular monthly selections will be billed at the low subscriber price of just $2.75 each. That's at least a savings of $4.50 each month below the publishers price. Second, there is never any shipping, handling or other hidden charges—*Free home delivery*. What's more there is no minimum number of books you must buy, you may return any selection for full credit and you can cancel your subscription at any time. A TRUE VALUE!